WEDDING DAY
SHENANIGANS

TRACY BROEMMER

Wedding Day Shenanigans

by

Tracy Broemmer

Contemporary Romance

Published by Tracy Broemmer

Edited by Lexie Broemmer

Cover Photo: Deposit Photos

Cover Design by Redbird Designs & Tracy Broemmer

All Rights Reserved

Copyright © 2017, 2nd Edition 2019

ISBN#: 978-1-7334023-2-3

CHAPTER ONE

JUNE 22, 2015

Kaki Steed eyed the teetering stack of boxes someone had dumped in the corner of the living room. She had no desire to tackle them. No desire to tackle any of the haphazard piles of boxes in the house, but someone had to do it. Wasn't like Jordy could start on it since he'd already gone back to work. And the boxes sure weren't going to take care of themselves.

From far away, she heard Billy Joel's song "Only the Good Die Young." She rested her hands on her hips and hung her head. Closed her eyes and thought back for a moment to the weekend, to the previous week. Last weekend. The wedding.

Suddenly she remembered Jordy had changed her ringtone to that Billy Joel song while they were gone, and she ran through the living room to the back of the house, pausing to listen every few seconds. She'd been all over the house this afternoon; she didn't have the slightest idea where she might have left her phone. From the kitchen doorway, she eyed the nearly empty room. No iPhone on the countertops or floor. No other surface for her to have left it lay, unless she'd put it in the fridge. Which, Kaki had to admit, was entirely possible, considering how crazy her life had been the past few weeks.

1

Billy Joel stopped singing. Kaki sighed and slumped in the doorway. Probably just Jordy anyway. Asking her to get him tortilla chips or pickles or something when she went to the store. As if she'd find the time to go to the store.

When Billy Joel started singing again, she decided it definitely wasn't Jordy calling, and she had to find the phone and answer it. By the time she found it, she wouldn't have time to practice a smile and a happy hello. Darting back down the hall, she decided it sounded like it was coming from upstairs. God, by the time she got to it, she wouldn't be able to *breathe*.

She laughed to herself as she wrapped her fingers around the handrail on the staircase and hauled her ass up the steps. Maybe that was a good thing. At least she'd probably sound like the typical happy newlywed if she answered the phone breathless.

Good thing she was barefoot, or she might have slid across the shiny wooden floor in the hall and flown past the bedroom door. She stopped in the doorway, the ringtone much louder. The big bed—the one she'd slept in last night next to her husband—looked almost as it had when they'd gone to bed last night. Certainly wasn't messy and tousled, the corners of the sheets slipped free of the mattress and pillows half hanging off the sides. Not the way it should look for a couple back the first night from their honeymoon.

No long stem red roses on her pillow. No sweet love note. Just her phone. Screen down. Purple Speck case up. She glanced at the alarm clock on her side of the bed. The digital display said 4:10. Probably Lauren.

She scooped it up and looked at the screen, sank gratefully to the side of the bed when she saw her friend's name.

"Hey."

"Hey, Mrs. Steed." Lauren's voice made her smile. "How was the honeymoon?"

Kaki fanned the fingers of her left hand out in front of her and studied the square cut diamond on her ring finger. She could lie. She'd been living a lie for a week now. Well. She'd been living this lie willingly for well over a week. She'd walked in with her eyes wide open, all in.

And already she was miserable.

No point in lying to her best friend; Lauren could read her better than anyone, not to mention she knew everything, anyway. Instead she took a deep breath and flopped backwards on the bed.

"It sucked."

CHAPTER TWO

She'd been kissed before. Good grief, even Jordy had kissed her before. But here she was over twenty-four hours after the ceremony, still thinking about it. The way he'd turned to her. Those green eyes kind of drinking her in; she wasn't used to that. The press of his soft lips against hers. Who'd have thought? A guy like Jordy had soft lips. It hadn't lasted five seconds. They'd been in a church, after all, with hundreds of people looking at them. But still, hours and miles later, that soft, sweet kiss was all she could think about.

"You hungry?" he asked around a yawn. Kaki glanced at him now as he stretched. He'd worn shorts on the plane. Khaki shorts and a soft, black t-shirt. He looked comfortable and sexy; Kaki had seen three girls on the plane eyeing him appreciatively. At least he hadn't flirted back. Or maybe he just hadn't noticed them.

She nodded. He knew she was hungry; he'd heard her stomach growling during the flight. Handed her his package of snack crackers with that grin that brought girls to their knees—he liked girls on their knees, no secret there—and they'd laughed about it.

4

"What do you want?"

They walked through the throng of people already itching to line up to board the next flight. Kaki curled her fingers around the strap of her bag on her shoulder. Decided she could go for a margarita right about now, but if she said that, he'd only tease her. Margaritas wouldn't help with the hunger, unless she planned to drink several.

She might, but she wasn't about to tell him that.

"How about Mexican?" he suggested. Kaki looked up with a grin and nodded. "You wanna find something on Yelp or just get a rental and drive around for a while?"

Kaki looked around the airport as they made their way to baggage claim. It was early evening; they had plenty of time to mosey around for a bit.

"Let's just drive around. See what we find."

He nodded. Took her hand as they stood at the carousel awaiting their luggage. Startled her. They were in Florida, for God's sake, no need to keep up pretenses here. She wasn't crazy about math, but even she knew the odds of running into someone they knew here were pretty slim.

"Have you talked to Lauren?" He tugged on her hand to pull her closer.

Kaki arched her eyebrows as she looked up at him.

"No. Not since..." She shrugged. Seemed weird to say something about the wedding. "Yesterday."

A little bit relieved, she sighed when he let go of her hand. But rather than move away from her, he draped his arm around her shoulders and leaned into her. They'd talked about this. She was used to being close to him; they'd grown up together, after all. Still. Things felt weird to her now, since he'd slipped that ring on her finger. Even though she knew Jordan Steed as well as she knew herself, things felt awkward between them now and she felt like she was standing here next to a stranger.

5

"So, how much did that wedding dress set you back, anyway?"

"What?" Her mouth dry, Kaki dropped her gaze. She watched two little girls chase each other in a circle around their mother's legs rather than look at Jordy.

"I feel bad." His mouth was close to her ear, and Kaki shivered a bit at the feel of his breath on her skin. "Asking you to do—"

"Jordy, we talked about this. Remember?" She tilted her head to the side and looked at him. "Its not a big—"

"Yeah, but that dress, Kaks." He wiggled his eyebrows. "I mean, wow."

She laughed softly.

"Imagine me standing up there in front of all those people, seeing you coming down the aisle in that dress."

Still leaning just a bit sideways to see his eyes, Kaki wondered if he'd liked what he'd seen. Mostly, Jordy hadn't ever seemed to notice she and Lauren were girls, even after they'd grown up and started high school.

"It's not a big deal," she assured him, even though it was a big deal. The dress had cost her a small fortune. She'd admitted to Lauren what she'd paid for it, and Lauren had scolded her and loved it all at the same time.

"Did your parents buy it?"

"I did," she answered simply.

"Let me give you money for it," he offered yet again. She'd argued over the several months of wedding planning that she didn't want his money. He'd countered with the fact that his family had more than enough, and she was doing him a favor, and he wanted to do something in return.

She wondered now what he would have said if she'd told him last night all she wanted from him in exchange for the wedding dress was for him to take it off her. Well. For him to get excited about helping her take it off. She wasn't sure he'd even let his fingers skim her back when he'd unzipped it.

She'd fallen in love with the dress simply because it was beautiful. White tulle. Beautiful lace and beadwork. Lauren's eyes had lit up when she'd tried it on; they'd gone straight to the plunging neckline and Lauren had laughed softly and told Kaki she couldn't get that dress, because Jordy would have a heart attack having to dance that close to her cleavage all night.

If she was doing him a favor with the whole wedding thing, she thought the least he could do was treat her to a real wedding night. Sure, they'd talked about how important it was that they not take part in that particular ritual. Not if Kaki wanted an annulment when the game was over. She'd been so caught up in the whole charade, and okay—a little bit hard up for sex—she'd decided to play with fire and get the dress with the plunging neckline and cross her fingers.

No dice. Jordy hadn't touched her. Except around four in the morning when he'd flipped over to lie on his back and his foot had nudged hers when he stretched.

"Jordy." She shook her head. "I got a beach vacation. And a new house. And a nice rock." She held up her hand to look at the ring he'd given her not quite a year ago when they'd first hatched this plan together. When it was over, she'd get to keep the ring. He'd put it in writing.

Wondered now just how much she'd had to drink to agree to this. Enough that she hadn't thought about all the ways it could backfire.

"Ah." Jordy dropped his arm from her shoulders and squeezed through a few people to grab one of their bags from the carousel. She leaned forward to take it from him and then watched him as he watched the carousel for the other one. They hadn't brought much. Kaki had packed a few swimsuits. A couple pairs of shorts. One dress, though certainly nothing fancy. She was ready to spend the week on the beach.

"Okay." He wormed his way back through the people between them, more had gathered there since the luggage had finally begun to appear on the carousel, and reached for the handle on the bag he'd already handed off to her.

"I got it."

"I'll take it," he said quietly. Kaki gave in, let him take the bag, and followed him out of the crowd and to the rental car counter.

"I think we might need a margarita," he announced. Kaki eyed the two couples in front of them in line. One couple might have been their age, the other easily her parents' age. "How about you?"

She nodded as she dragged her eyes back to his.

"I could definitely use a margarita," she agreed.

"Do you feel bad?" he asked her. "For screwing everyone out of the wedding gifts?"

She laughed softly. "Well, I assume we'll get some use out of them. And even when the jig's up, one of us will still use them."

Jordy's eyebrows shot up in surprise.

"Did you just say *when the jig's up*?"

"I did." When the line moved, Kaki nudged him just a bit.

"That's so harsh," he said with a laugh. "Calling the wedding a jig."

"You just asked if it bothered me that we scammed people for wedding gifts," she reminded him. "I mean, it's not like we're gonna play this out for a week and then split up with irreconcilable differences, right?"

He shrugged his eyebrows in response, but when he looked away, Kaki wondered what he was thinking. What kind of timeline he had in mind for his plan. She reached for him again, touched his arm as she had hundreds of times before. Felt that little jolt of electricity, amazed that he didn't.

"What?" He didn't look at her.

"What's wrong?"

Jordy huffed out a sigh and looked around. "She was there."

Kaki winced and nodded. Brianna Fleer. She'd seen her there on Jordy's side of the church. With a date.

"I saw her."

"You think she was into that guy?" Jordy turned to look at her again, and the intensity in his green eyes zapped her in the heart. She hated to see her best friends hurting. Lauren was happily married with a baby on the way, but Jordy seemed to be a long way from peace, let alone happiness.

"Doesn't she get into every guy she dates?" she asked quietly.

"Yeah, for about five minutes."

Kaki nodded, but she didn't say anything. They'd been through this. Several times. She had no idea what her friend saw in the girl; to Kaki, she was trouble wrapped in pretty paper. Apparently, Jordy liked her bows.

Then again, didn't she know that about him? Didn't *everyone* back home know that about him?

Wondering again if he hadn't noticed she was a woman— she'd had boobs since she was fourteen, for God's sake—she looked down at herself. Okay, so she couldn't rock a double D to save her life, and Brianna Fleer had more than enough in Kaki's opinion, but she *had* boobs. And they were perky. She'd never heard anyone complain about them.

"What are you doing?" Jordy reached out and tugged at her t-shirt. "Did you spill something on the plane?"

"Mm." She nodded, grateful for the excuse he'd given her for checking herself out. "I thought I did."

He studied her, maybe the first time he'd really looked closely at her chest. Actually, she'd seen him *look* a couple of times yesterday after the wedding, when they were dancing at the reception. She'd been stupid enough to think he might be interested enough to play later, but once he'd unzipped her dress, he'd turned the TV on and watched some cowboy movie instead.

"Aren't you two cute?"

Kaki covered his hand with hers as they turned to look at the woman now behind them in line. Fifty-something, maybe, she stood behind and to the side of Kaki, big gray eyes taking in the way Jordy had been ogling Kaki's t-shirt.

"Are you newlyweds?" the woman asked them. Kaki swallowed hard; since they'd left the familiar, she'd let the pretense slide, and she was at a loss as to how to respond.

"Yes, we are," Jordy answered smoothly.

"Oh, that's perfect!" she gushed. "Can't wait to get her alone to get the honeymoon started, I'm sure."

Kaki ducked her head, embarrassed heat flooding her face. She and Lauren and Jordy had talked about sex together for almost as long as they'd known each other. First they'd joked about it because they were only kids, and they were curious about the things they weren't allowed to watch in rated R movies, and then as they'd gotten older, they'd shared some of their experiences. Well. Jordy shared them all; Kaki had shared a few things. Lauren was somewhere in the middle, she supposed.

"No, ma'am." Jordy slung his arm around her shoulders again and kissed her cheek. He'd done that a time or two through the years. Once when he'd been upset because his parents had nearly called it quits. He'd climbed the tree outside Lauren's window and snuck in and told them both everything. Hadn't been a surprise; Jordy had been a bear for weeks at a time as his parents tiptoed into a separation and narrowly avoided divorce. Lauren, one of seven kids and teased ruthlessly about how badly her parents needed a television, had listened quietly. Kaki's parents fought sometimes, but nowhere near the way Jordy's did that year. She'd listened to him, nodded when she knew he'd needed her to, and even reached out once to put her arm around him.

He'd kissed them both that night. Just a kiss on the cheek and an embarrassed, mumbled thank you. Kissed her the night of graduation, too. Just a quick little peck on her cheek.

This was different, though. With this strange woman watching them, kind of like she was watching a rom-com movie, waiting for the first kiss scene.

"George and I've been married thirty years," the woman continued. Kaki kind of wanted to look behind Jordy, to see if the other couple had moved, if they could move up the line a bit. Get to the counter faster and get their car and get the hell out of there. But if she turned her head right now, her lips would be plastered to his. Wouldn't be a problem, but she already wasn't looking forward to trying to sleep again tonight. If she had to close her eyes and remember his lips touching hers again, it would be that much more difficult.

"Congratulations," Jordy told the woman. Kaki swallowed hard. Where were her manners? She should've said something like that. She was the woman, after all. The one who was supposed to engage in small talk with other women about their marriages and their husbands and their…nope. She was lost. Brain. Dead. Jordy had moved just enough to brush his lips against her neck again. That would have been bad enough. But that little flick of his tongue against her skin had rendered her breathless. Completely unnecessary, because she doubted the woman even noticed. "You ready, babe?"

Kaki nodded, though she didn't move. Jordy slid his hand back over her shoulder, but rather than drop it away, he dragged his fingers down her back and over her hip. Okay, he'd done that a few times last night when they were dancing. Not the first dance, but later, when everyone had had a little to drink. He'd played with her butt. Put on a show when he'd flipped the skirt of her dress up and removed her garter with his teeth.

Funny, Kaki had thought of Owen when Jordy'd done that, but she hadn't thought of him before or since then.

"You kids have a good time," the woman said with a big

smile. "There's nothing quite as much fun as honeymoon sex!"

"Well, we're sure gonna find that out, aren't we, Kaks?"

Kaki almost swallowed her tongue. Wide-eyed, she looked at Jordy and then nodded as she turned back to the woman.

"You bet we are!" Her laugh was a little bawdy, but as Jordy turned her around and led her to the counter, she leaned into him and giggled. Jordy kissed the top of her head and squeezed her butt (at the moment, she was glad she was wearing skinny jeans) just in case the woman was still watching them. But she heard the low rumble of laughter in his chest.

"I bet she keeps George pretty happy." He rubbed his hand up over her hip again and then dropped it away and pulled his billfold from his shorts as he stepped up to the rental car counter.

"I bet she does," Kaki agreed. She stood beside him as he signed the rental papers. Leaned in and signed her name when he poked her, but her mind was miles away.

Nothing quite as much fun as honeymoon sex.

Sadly, Jordy was probably the only one who was going to be having fun honeymoon sex. As ready as she'd been last night to offer him everything, Kaki wasn't really the kind of girl to hook up with a stranger for vacation sex. And her husband wasn't remotely interested in bedding her.

CHAPTER THREE

KAKI OFFERED to drive when they left the airport, but Jordy didn't mind climbing in behind the wheel. He tossed their luggage into the hatch of the black Subaru Outback and then shrugged her off and headed to the driver's side, keys in hand. It felt weird to look at Kaki and think of her as his wife. Sure, it was in name only, but still. He'd known her since they were, like, ten. Hell, he'd probably married her and Lauren a few times over back in those days when the girls were into playing pretend. He'd been a doctor—though not *that* kind of doctor, darn his luck—and he'd been a cop and a robber, too. Surely, he'd married one or both of them when they'd been in their wedding phase.

Still. It had been a little bit weird in there in line for the rental car when that woman had started talking to them. Jordy's mom was the friendly sort, but he couldn't imagine her striking up a conversation about honeymoon sex with a young couple. He'd jumped in to do the talking, because he wasn't sure Kaki was too impressed with their deal. She'd been all in when they'd talked about it the first time, and the engagement had been uneventful and the wedding itself had been pretty perfect. But still. This was his thing, his deal. Kaki was doing him a favor, and who the hell knew what she was really thinking.

Jordy didn't think she had anyone serious waiting in the wings for his and her marriage to hit the skids, but then Kaki had always been a little tighter-lipped about that kind of stuff. No middle ground with the two of them. Lauren spilled all the details, and Kaki rarely said much at all about her personal life. She'd dated someone pretty steady for a while when they started college, but Jordy wasn't sure how that ended, and he had no idea if she was seeing anyone now. He'd have to guess no, because he didn't think any guy would be okay with Kaki Harper marrying someone else for a while, just as part of a greater plan.

Scheme, maybe, was the better word.

He glanced at her as she reached up and tapped the stereo to change the station. Her ring caught his eye. Gave him another little zap. He'd picked it out for her as a surprise. Well. She'd known it was coming, obviously, since she'd agreed to help him out with his plan. But he'd picked the ring on his own; something he'd imagined would be pretty on her hand, and every time he got a glimpse of that sparkle, he decided he'd been right. The square cut diamond was perfect for her, the platinum band a match to the simple white gold stud earrings she'd worn since her dad had given them to her on her sixteenth birthday.

She groaned out loud when the new station blared yet another commercial and tapped a different button. When Little Richard's voice belted through the SUV, Jordy met Kaki's eyes with a grin. They'd danced to this just last night at the reception. In fact, the dance floor had been packed for this one. It had been a blast out there dancing and singing with all of their friends, knowing everyone was having a good time. But dammit all, Kaki in that dress had been enough to make him crazy. That neckline, whatever the hell the dress designers called it, Jordy called it a sneak peek and then some. He'd been hard all damned day after seeing her coming up the aisle at the church. Seeing her shaking those hips and yes, watching the way her breasts had moved in that dress had just about done him in.

He'd never been one for fast dances; he'd always liked the slow songs when he could pull a girl in to hold her tight, press up against her, and slide his hands over her hips and her butt. And he'd done the same last night with Kaki, even though he'd told himself nothing could happen. He'd made a promise to her from day one that he wouldn't expect anything like that from their marriage; that way, maybe when they divorced, she could have the marriage annulled and be completely free to marry someone else. And their friendship would still be in tact.

But damn, Kaki shaking that body with that big, happy smile on her face had just about done him in. Kaki moving that body right up against his during the slow songs. He couldn't win. He'd been surprised late in the evening when Lauren's husband Tyler had mumbled something about Brianna and her date leaving the party early. Jordy hadn't even noticed; he'd been too busy ogling his wife, a woman who was completely off-limits to him.

The dress had been hell back at the honeymoon suite, too. He'd helped her with the zipper, and his mouth had gone dry at the glimpse of her smooth, bare back. He'd been so damned careful not to touch her. Touching her skin would have been like lighting a match and dropping it in a bucket of gasoline; he'd have blown sky high. She'd given him a look then, arms plastered up over her chest, holding the halter part or whatever it was, up over her bare breasts as she'd made her way to the bathroom. He'd thought when they were dancing that she was bare under the dress, and his suspicion had been confirmed when he'd unzipped it for her. He'd wanted to look; dammit, he'd wanted just a peek at her breasts that promised at perfection, because the eyeful he'd gotten through the reception had been so tempting.

He'd turned the TV on and watched a bunch of cowboys ride horses and shoot guns, and when he'd gone to sleep beside her in that bed, his cock had been so stiff, he'd thought he had a rifle in his pants.

"What?"

"Hmm?" Jordy shook his head and blinked. Embarrassed to be caught thinking about her, about what she'd look like naked (he had no idea; he'd never seen her nude) and afraid the look on his face would give him away, he looked back at the road. Hoped he hadn't been staring at her breasts, because how embarrassing would that be? She'd probably slap him.

"Why're you looking at me like that?" she asked him. Okay, she didn't sound pissed, so he hadn't been staring at her breasts while he'd wished he'd gotten just a look at them last night.

From the corner of his eye, he saw her shake her head. She sat back in the seat and turned a bit sideways to watch him. This was familiar. They'd ridden like this hundreds of times in the years they'd been friends. Lauren in the backseat. Or Lauren driving and Jordy in the back. Whatever. When they were twelve, their teachers had started calling them the three musketeers.

"I wasn't aware I was looking at you like...that." He shrugged.

She grinned.

"So. What's next?" She crossed her arms over her chest.

"Margaritas. Dinner. And then like...an hour on the road to Fort Walton—"

"With Brianna."

"Mmm."

Funny. He'd hatched this scheme of marrying Kaki to make his ex-girlfriend jealous. Wasn't terribly original, and yet, it had always made Brianna crazy that his two closest friends were girls. Pretty girls. True, Brianna had cheated on him, but he'd hoped that by marrying one of those pretty girls, he would make her so jealous she'd come back.

Now he didn't want to talk about her. Instead, he answered Kaki with a lazy shrug. Turned to look out his window as he drove.

"I dunno," he mumbled.

"She doesn't deserve you."

Jordy had dated every pretty girl in his class. He'd bedded over half of them and walked away with no regrets. He'd been the heartbreaker who'd used women, and it had killed him when Brianna had beaten him to the punch. Kaki had asked him when Brianna first cheated and then broke up with him if that was what got his goat. If maybe he wasn't heartbroken, but just sore over the fact that a woman had beaten him at his own game.

There was enough truth to that it made him uncomfortable to think about it. Then again, he did *like* Brianna. She had tits like a porn queen, and she liked sex almost as much as he did. She had a cute little laugh, and she liked puppies. It was enough for Jordy, but neither Lauren nor Kaki liked her.

"I thought you said once that Brianna and I deserve each other," he reminded her. "What do you think of that place?" He pointed at what appeared to be a Mexican restaurant down a block on her side of the road.

"At this point, anything'll work." She nodded.

"That hungry?"

"No." She sighed and turned in her seat again, this time to face the front of the car. "I need a drink."

"I like her." He was kind of tired of defending himself. And his argument had started to lose steam. He had liked Brianna, and he had wanted her back. Now, he kind of just hoped all the wedding day shenanigans yesterday made her crazy with jealousy. He and Kaki were going to spend a week on the beach. What could be better? Hang out with one of his best friends by day and maybe tap some hot chick later when Kaki went back to the condo to read or sleep.

They might be married, but they weren't physically involved and had no plans to be. Jordy would be discreet; he wouldn't do anything to embarrass Kaki. But she knew him well enough to know he'd be window-shopping out there on the beach.

"Can you believe that woman?"

He'd grabbed at whatever came to mind to change the subject. He hated when Lauren and Kaki were upset with him. About women, especially. And nine times out of ten, when they were upset with him, it was about a woman.

Unfortunately, he'd come up with the wrong conversation changer and now the thought of honeymoon sex hung in the air between them.

"When was the last time you had sex?"

Wasn't something he'd normally plunge in and ask Kaki. Wouldn't sweat hitting Lauren with that kind of question; well, not before she was married, anyway, but he'd always tiptoed around this stuff with Kaki. She wasn't innocent; he knew that, but there was still something so reserved about her, it had always been a bit terrifying to talk about sex with her.

He chanced a quick peek at her as he changed lanes. He was afraid she would be embarrassed or maybe even angry with him, but her face was twisted in thought.

"That long?" he asked with a grin. Kaki laughed softly and shook her head. She turned away from him, though, as if she were embarrassed to admit how long.

"Um. My bachelorette party, actually," she said quietly.

"Wait." He took his right hand off the steering wheel and draped it over her leg. Made sure to keep it closer to her knee than her zipper area. He'd groped her butt a few times last night, and he'd done it back at the airport just in case that woman had been watching them. But sliding his hand too close to her crotch right now probably wasn't a good idea. As much as he might like to do it, he wouldn't.

He made a quick turn into a shopping area and then pulled the SUV into the parking lot at what appeared to be a decent Mexican restaurant, judging from the number of cars there. Jordy agreed with Kaki now, though. Just about the only thing he needed at the moment was a strong drink. Maybe he'd skip the frilly stuff and do a shot of tequila.

"You had sex? The night of your bachelorette party?"

Kaki opened her door and turned sideways to get out, but she looked back at him over her shoulder.

"Yeah. I did."

"But." He shook his head, stunned not only by her response, but the nonchalant delivery. "What the hell—Kaks. Wait."

She slid out of the SUV, closed the door, and waited for him to round the back of the vehicle to start walking.

"You didn't?"

"Didn't? I didn't—what?'" He leaned into her as they walked. Slid his arm around her waist and squeezed her. Friendly squeeze as he'd done a million other times. She smelled the same; her perfume was some rich, heady scent that could make a guy crazy.

"You didn't have sex?" She looked at him as she reached to pull the door open. Jordy hurried around her to take the door from her. "At your bachelor party?"

"No!" He shook his head, a little disappointed in himself for not enjoying himself now that he knew Kaki had had a good time. "I mean...strippers? They don't...do that stuff. They take their clothes off. And you pay 'em, and they go back home to their kids."

"Jordy." Kaki hung her head and looked at him upside down as they walked into the waiting area in the restaurant. "Really?"

"Yes, really. One of 'em had stretch marks—"

"Jordan Steed." She turned this time to give him *the look*. "That's an incredibly rude thing to say."

He shrugged and tucked his hands in his pockets. Watched as the host appeared at the counter and eyed Kaki appreciatively before asking how many they had in their party. Kaki didn't flirt with him. She simply said two and smiled at the guy, and with those blue eyes and her butter-scotch voice, Jordy figured the guy would be jacking off with her in mind later. They fell in line behind the host as he led them through the restaurant to a booth near the back. Jordy had assumed Kaki would want to sit outside, but it was still warm and sticky, and she did have jeans on. Maybe she just wanted to get dinner and a drink and get on the road. He was certainly ready to get to the condo and get settled. Odds were, she was, too.

"So." Jordy eyed the young girl who brought them a basket of chips and a bowl of salsa. Turned his gaze back to Kaki when the girl walked away. "You seriously hooked up with the stripper? Did you know him?"

"Wasn't the stripper, and yes, I knew him."

He watched her carefully, but she'd taken her phone from her purse and she was looking at something now rather than paying attention to him. She'd said all she planned to on the subject. Jordy was torn between wanting to know more—not because he was jealous about her hooking up that night—and being relieved that she hadn't just got it on with a stranger Lauren had hired to grind on her a little bit.

"Lauren and Tyler heard the baby's heartbeat today." Kaki's face was flushed with happiness when she looked up at him. Jordy was thrilled as hell for them, but he was still wondering who Kaki had done the deed with and was having a hard time switching gears to married life and babies.

"That's cool," he said quietly. He meant it, but when Kaki looked up at him and set her phone, screen down on the table, he assumed she was going to give him hell.

"Was I..." She rested her elbows on the table and licked her lips. Met his eyes. "Was I not supposed...to...do that? Like...while we're..."

"No!"

His answer was too loud and too quick to sound normal, and he winced and looked up at the waiter as he approached them to get their orders. Both of them asked for a margarita; Kaki asked for chicken nachos and Jordy asked for a steak burrito.

"So." She cleared her throat. "I know we didn't talk a lot about this part of it." She pursed her lips. "If you don't want me to be with someone else, you need to say so. I mean...it's not like...I mean...I would be discreet. And it's not like it really happens a lot—"

"Kaks." Jordy held his hands up, palms out, when she looked at him again. "It's fine. I was just surprised."

"What about you?" she asked quietly.

She looked a little sad suddenly, and while he intended to answer her, it bothered him to see the smile fade away. Kaki had the prettiest smile; and yesterday, when he'd kissed her, he'd been reminded of how soft her lips are. He'd kissed her before. A couple times in front of their families. The quick pecks on her lips or her cheeks that engaged couples did when they were in a hurry, but some longer, wetter kisses they'd pretended to sneak now and then when his or her family was in another room, but headed their way.

The memory of those kisses shot a jolt of electricity straight through him. Made his cock jump to salute her. Soft pale lips and that warm, velvety tongue. She'd kissed him back, eagerly rubbed her tongue over his and nibbled on his lips.

"Jordy?" she prompted him now.

Well. He couldn't lie. But he sure as hell couldn't tell her the truth, either. He hadn't hooked up the night of his bachelor party, but he'd had a fan-fucking-tastic twenty-two minutes two nights ago. The night before he'd taken Kaki's hand and said he'd love and respect her until death would they part.

They were playing at the love part, just another game of pretend. But he had promised to respect her, and doing one of her college friends the night before he married her wasn't a good start.

"Mmm." He shrugged. "Not too long."

She nodded slowly. Finally sat back in the booth and then turned that heart stopping smile on the waiter when he came back with their drinks. Jordy wanted to tell him to keep his pants on, the look of bliss on Kaki's face was about the tequila, not the deliveryman.

CHAPTER FOUR

KAKI LIFTED her eyes and watched Jordy over her coffee mug. Back to her, he wasn't aware she was there in the kitchenette, hands cupped around her mug, just about to lift it for a sip. Jordy had just climbed out of bed; from where she stood in the little kitchen, she could see into the bedroom where they'd slept. He rubbed his hand over his short dark hair and then stretched and yawned.

Last night had been a repeat of the wedding night. Well. No. Not quite. At least the wedding night had been exciting. They'd had a few drinks, and they'd danced. Okay, they'd had a lot to drink, and they'd danced a lot, which meant at least he'd put his hands on her. Maybe she'd been dressed, but it was something. Last night, after grabbing dinner at the Mexican restaurant, they'd driven the hour to Fort Walton and hit a grocery store. Kaki had sent Lauren a text, detailing the excitement of married life, complete with pictures of Jordy carrying a bag of Doritos, a twelve-pack of Blue Moon beer, and a twelve-pack of Mountain Dew. Lauren had responded with a picture of Tyler asleep in the recliner.

Jordy had asked what she was laughing about, but she'd

simply said *Lauren*. No explanation. He'd given her a look, but then he'd shrugged, and they'd put their groceries in the SUV and headed to the condo. They'd put the stuff away and crashed on an overstuffed sofa and watched TV. Jordy had flipped through the channels at a breakneck speed, until Kaki reached to take the remote from him.

"What—?" He'd looked at her with a frown. "What are you doing?"

"How can you possibly know what's on when you fly through the channels like that?"

"I—Kaks—what?" He'd lunged at her, but she'd twisted away from him with a laugh and aimed the remote at the big screen.

She'd settled on an eighties movie she'd seen before. He probably had, too, but he didn't seem to mind. When they'd gone to bed—one bed, a little bit smaller even than the one they'd slept in on their wedding night—Jordy had turned away from her on his side to sleep.

Then again, this morning, when she got up and went to the kitchen to make coffee, she was happy they had at least partaken in the exciting married ritual of buying groceries.

"Kaks?"

She watched him brace his forearms on the doorframe and lean out to look at her. He grinned when their eyes met. Her eyes roamed; she couldn't help it. He'd slept in shorts over his boxer briefs. His shoulders and chest were bare, though, and Kaki catalogued the muscles in his arms (not the big in your face kind she didn't like; nope, Jordy's muscles were just right) and the sparse hair on his chest and the whorl of dark hair further down on his stomach that disappeared into his shorts.

"See something you like?"

When she lifted her eyes to meet his, he wriggled his eyebrows suggestively. Kaki snorted and finally took a drink.

"Well, that was hurtful," he mumbled, but when he

ducked his head to rub the back of his neck, she saw the smirk on his lips.

"Big plans today, Mr. Steed?"

"Absolutely. I'm gonna go plant my ass in the sand and soak up some sun."

"Just don't get any sand in any of the wrong places." She nodded and turned her back to him. "Hungry?"

"I could eat." His voice suddenly louder, she looked over her shoulder and found him standing behind her in the kitchen.

"When have you ever turned down food?"

"Um." He pursed his lips as he scanned the counter for the box of Captain Crunch cereal he'd picked up last night. "That one time…"

"Oh, yeah." She didn't even try to hide her sarcasm as she reached around him and opened the cabinet in front of him.

"Seriously?" He glanced at her and grabbed the box. She watched him open it and then tug the plastic bag inside open, winced when he ripped it wide, and shook her head when he plunged his hand inside to grab some. "So. That day we went to the Baron's Post for breakfast."

"With Lauren and Tyler?" Kaki opened the bag of bagels she'd grabbed from the bakery corner of the store, but she shot Jordy an *are you kidding me?* look.

"Yeah." He nodded and leaned his hips on the counter at his back. Jammed his hand into the box of cereal again.

"You were hung over." She rolled her eyes. "That's the only time you don't eat. And that lasts all of an hour."

"I was not hung over," he argued.

"Right." She put half a bagel in the wide-slotted toaster on the counter and then wrapped the tie around the bag again. "That's right. You had the flu."

When she looked at him this time, he grinned sheepishly and ducked his head.

"How can you drink that stuff?" He turned his nose up when she sipped her coffee again.

"How can you drink Mountain Dew for breakfast?"

He shrugged and set the box of cereal on the counter. Moved around her to help himself to a bottle from the refrigerator. When her bagel popped up, she snatched it from the toaster and then dropped it quickly to the plate she'd put on the counter.

"Damn." She sucked on her finger for a second. "That's hot."

She met Jordy's eyes. He only cleared his throat and nodded. Mumbled something that she couldn't quite make out. Kaki had found the silverware drawer when she'd searched earlier for a spoon for her coffee creamer, so now she went to it easily and grabbed a knife.

His gaze was heavy on the back of her neck; it chased a chill into her hair and she had to concentrate really hard not to shiver. But when Jordy nudged her, her knees were suddenly weak, and she was breathless when she turned to look at him.

"Need this?" He held the container of cream cheese out to her. Still breathless and feeling kind of silly now, she nodded and took it. Gave him a small smile and turned her back to him again. She heard him chug from the bottle and then gasp for breath, like a little boy.

Bagel topped with just the right amount of cream cheese, Kaki dropped the knife in the sink and then carried her plate and her coffee across the living room to the sliding glass door. She glanced back to see if Jordy would follow her, but she saw him slip into the bathroom. Maybe he wouldn't, anyway. Hell, maybe he had no intention of hanging out with her on the beach. She'd assumed they'd spend *some* time together here; they were friends, after all. But then again, Jordy might intend to spend the entire week on the prowl for sex.

"He'll get it, too," she mumbled as she set her plate and

cup on the two-top table on the balcony. She lifted her eyes from the table and looked out at the gulf. The sun off the white sand on the beach was dazzling. Kaki forgot her breakfast for a moment and leaned her elbows on the railing, eyes roaming the beach and the blue water as far as she could see.

Folded navy umbrellas lined the beach near the water line. Okay. She could handle hanging out down there with a fruity drink, one with a miniature umbrella, of course, and a book. She'd brought a few. Maybe she'd even close her eyes and take a nap. She wasn't a brain surgeon, but she worked forty hours a week, and maybe the wedding she'd just spent the past eight months planning had been a hoax. But for appearances sake, it had been quite a show, and she was exhausted.

For just a moment, she wondered if this was a mistake. If she and Jordy would walk away from this the same kind of friends they'd always been. They'd talked about it. She loved him; she didn't like that chick he was after, but she loved *him*. And if he honestly thought Brianna Fleer was going to make him happy, she was all for helping him get her back. Even marrying him in a beautiful wedding, the likes of which she'd never see again. No sex. Not like she'd ever entertained the thought. Jordy was a player, and she moved much slower. She doubted he'd ever been interested in her, and she'd had a few of her own involvements and hadn't spent her time mooning over her drop-dead gorgeous best friend. Jordy had insisted on no messing around because he wanted her to be *intact* when they divorced. She'd wondered if he thought she was a virgin, if he thought she was that inexperienced. He'd argued that maybe she could get the marriage annulled if it wasn't consummated. Kaki had nearly choked on her beer when he'd used the word *consummated*. She'd agreed to it, nevertheless, because she wasn't dying to get her hands on him, and she suspected that if she did, it would end up ruining their friendship.

Except who the hell had a gorgeous wedding like that,

dropped a few paychecks on a knockout gown, and then had an epic reception with family and friends and didn't get laid when it was over? Who did that? Who went to the beach for a honeymoon and kept their clothes on?

God, Kaki. Get a grip. You're hard up for sex, *not* Jordy.

She sighed, scrubbed her hands over her face, and then let them fall again. She wasn't hard up for sex. She *had been* with Owen the night of her bachelorette. But seriously. She had to be the only bride in the western world whose husband wasn't interested in jumping her the second he got her wedding gown off her and riding her until she was saddle sore.

"Don't jump! I promise I didn't leave the seat up."

She listened to the door slide open and closed as he joined her on the balcony. Stared hard at the water, waiting for it to calm her. She was embarrassed to be caught standing here bemoaning the fact that her best friend hadn't taken advantage of the situation and her and banged her senseless on their fake wedding night. She'd been feeling a little *woe is me*, but now that he'd caught her brooding over the idea, her heart was pounding in her throat.

"It's sand. That'd be a soft landing, wouldn't it?" she joked. Her lips tugged up in a smile as he joined her at the railing. Maybe there were parts of her body wishing she'd had a real wedding night, but the rest of Kaki Harper Steed relaxed into Jordy like he was a pair of worn, faded jeans.

"Um." He tilted his head to the side as he folded his forearms over the railing, elbow to elbow with her, and studied the beach four stories below. "I don't think you would bounce."

She laughed softly and turned to meet his gaze.

"Pretty," he said quietly, and then he nodded to the view stretched out in front of them. She smiled again; she'd known he was referring to the beach and their panoramic view, rather than her. Turned around and pulled out one of the chairs at the table so she could sit down.

"So." He stood there a moment longer. "Did you see much of Brianna at the reception?"

Kaki stared at her bagel for a moment. There went her appetite. She and Lauren had warned Jordy through the years that one day he'd meet his match. One day, he'd meet some hot chick that burned through their relationship and walked away faster than he did. Brianna Fleer hadn't been the first to walk away faster than Jordy, but for whatever reason, she'd been the one to bring him to his knees.

"Tell me again what you see in her," she mumbled. She picked up the bagel and took a bite as Jordy turned to look at her.

"You don't think she's pretty?"

"Sure." She nodded. "So's black ice. But she's a viper, Jordy. She breaks hearts. It's what—"

He sighed, dragged the other chair out, and joined her at the table.

"She's me." Leaning forward, he stared at his bare feet for a moment and finally looked up at her with a shrug. "Right?"

"No."

"No?" He sat back, linked his fingers together over his stomach. Still bare, though he'd changed from the boxer briefs and red shorts to long black trunks. "You and Lauren always tell me I'm bad because of the way I go through women."

"Well." She crunched a bite of the bagel and then reached to catch a blob of cream cheese on her fingertip. She laughed when he rolled his eyes. "Did you happen to grab napkins when you came out?"

He waved his empty hands at her and shook his head. She leaned forward to get up, but Jordy leaned in at the same time. She stared at him in shock when he took her hand and sucked her fingertip, cream cheese and all, into his mouth.

"What're you—" She gasped, breathless again, when he leaned even closer and pressed his open lips to the corner of her mouth. She felt the flick of his tongue on her lip, his warm breath over her face. Afraid her heart was going to explode out of her chest, maybe the base of her throat, she lifted her hand to his face. Grazed her fingertips over his jaw as his tongue rubbed once over hers.

"—doing?" She let out a long, shaky breath when he backed away from her. "What're you doing?"

He grinned. That same damned sheepish grin that she figured had been his access to countless zippers through the years. If his body, his eyes didn't do it for women, that grin had to undo damned near every woman he looked at.

"You had…" He waved his hand at his face and nodded at her. "Some cream cheese on your lip, too."

She stared at him for a moment, stunned by the move. Her heart was still thudding painfully hard in her ears, her throat. She felt it in other places, too, but maybe it was best not to think about those places right now. He arched his eyebrows now and gave her his next best grin. This one was a mix of *sorry, not sorry.* Again, probably very successful in the bedroom.

She laughed softly and shook her head. Swallowed the bite she'd taken when he leaned in close to her.

"Damn, Jordy."

"I didn't grab any napkins," he reminded her.

She licked her lips, tasted him there again. Something unmistakably male, but even more than that, something definitely Jordy Steed. And peanut butter.

"That was peanut butter flavored Captain Crunch?" she asked quietly.

He threw his head back and laughed. "Damn, woman. I kiss you as a favor, and all you comment on is my cereal?"

Kaki set her bagel down and started to pick her coffee up.

"You know I had a mouthful, right?"

"Now you're just trying to freak me out."

She shrugged and pointed at her bagel.

"So." She cleared her throat. "I really didn't pay much attention to Brianna. At the reception." She winced apologetically. Probably, she should have paid more attention to the reason they'd gone through with this charade, rather than have a good time at her wedding reception.

"I didn't, either," he admitted. "But. Wait. You didn't… explain. About how you and Lauren—"

"You're not vicious, Jordy," she said simply.

"What?" Now he leaned forward and reached to pick up what was left of her bagel.

"What're you—?"

He took a bite and licked his lips as he chewed it. Grinned and shrugged again.

"So." He swallowed and rubbed his hand over his lips. Reached it out to her as a joke, but she grabbed his hand and licked each of his fingers. "Jesus, Kaki." He groaned and sat up straighter. "Warn a guy."

"Payback." She winked at him. "Yeah, so, anyway. You like women. You like sex. Brianna uses men for status. And for revenge. And for…God, I don't even know. I'm sure she liked your money, too."

She took another drink of her coffee, but it was lukewarm, and she was ready to hit the beach.

"You don't think she liked sex? With me?"

"Um." Kaki shrugged and raised her eyebrows at him as she stood up. "I dunno. I guess you'd have to make that call. I just don't think she's good enough for you, Jordy. I don't wanna see you get hurt."

"Where're you going?" he asked as she slipped around him. When she stood beside his chair, she took a moment to be glad she was still wearing her sleep shorts and tee, rather than one of the bikinis she'd thrown in her bag. His eyes were right in line with her waistline, and she wasn't a big fan of that part of her body. No need to draw Jordy Steed's attention to it, not when he was most likely reminiscing about sex with Brianna Fleer.

"To change."

CHAPTER FIVE

"TO CHANGE?" he repeated.

"Yep."

He heard the door open and slide closed. Sat for a moment longer. He needed a second or two for his dick to relax. Wondered if the gulf was cold. If not, he could go jump in the swimming pool to make everything shrivel. *Dammit*. So he'd been teasing her, but he'd wanted to kiss her. Hell, he'd wanted his mouth on hers since he unzipped the damned wedding dress and feasted his eyes on her smooth bare back. But this morning, when he'd caught her looking at his chest, at the line of his shorts, good grief, he'd wanted to kick the shorts off and get her back in the bedroom and show her that the whole thing—the wedding and honeymoon—didn't all have to be a hoax.

When he'd licked the cream cheese from her lip, he'd thought he would surprise her. But she'd moved. She'd moved her mouth under his. Stroked her tongue against his. *Kissed him*. Holy son-of-a-beach, she'd kissed him back. He lifted his hand now and touched his face where her fingertips had skimmed it when she'd kissed him.

And what the hell was up with her licking his fingers?

She'd flicked the tip of her tongue over each of his damned fingers and brought to mind what it would feel like to have her tongue in other places, and fuck it all, if he wasn't harder than a frigging rock all over again just thinking about it.

Change. She'd said she was going to change.

He jumped up from his chair and nearly tripped over it trying to get to the door.

"Change into what?" he called. The bathroom door was closed. He crossed the beige tile floor and stood at the closed door. "What're you changing into?"

"A swimsuit," she answered through the door.

"A swim—a…like…"

Jesus. He hadn't considered this. He hadn't thought about having to see her in a bathing suit out there on the beach all week. Sure, they'd hung out at the pool together. They'd spent days on end in the pool in his backyard when they were younger, but this was different. She was wearing that ring, the one he put on her finger, and he could still taste the coffee on her lips, and he'd looked down her dress at their reception.

"Yep. Hang on."

He leaned on the doorframe and folded his arms over his chest. Lifted a hand to rub over his messy hair. He should've grabbed a cap. He'd do it before they went down to the beach. Huffed out a breath in frustration.

Well, okay, this was Kaki he was with. Not Lauren. He wouldn't be surprised if it was Lauren and she waltzed out wearing a string bikini a size too small. Kaki wasn't bold like that. Hell, she might even walk out wearing a tank suit or something that would have her mistaken as a lifeguard at the local swim club back home.

He jumped and scooted back when he heard the doorknob turn. Kaki pulled the door back and eyed him curiously as she stepped out of the room. In the tiniest two scraps of white material he'd ever seen.

A string bikini. A *white* string bikini.

Fuck me.

"What?" she asked as she leaned into the bedroom and tossed her pajamas on the foot of the bed.

"Um." He shrugged and rubbed his eyes. "Nothing."

"You don't like it?" she asked as she looked down at herself.

What the hell was there *not* to like? He wondered. God, he'd never understand women. He loved them; Kaki was right about that. He loved everything about women from their hair (short and spiky or long and curly or somewhere in between) to their eyes to their soft skin and their tits—

He gave himself a mental shake.

Kaki. Kaki is your best friend. Kaki does not have tits.

Why would she think he didn't like the bikini?

"Um." He winced and chewed on his lip for a second. "Do you have another one?"

She'd left the bedroom, but now she stopped walking and looked back at him.

"What?"

"Well." He shrugged. Already doomed, he could tell from the look on her face, he plunged ahead. Maybe she'd packed another suit. One that wouldn't have him slipping away once they hit the beach to sneak back up here and jack off.

"Seriously?" She opened her arms and spread them as if to ask him what was wrong with the bikini. As far as he could tell, not a damned thing. Her tits—*breasts*—more than a handful, if he had to guess, were perfectly round behind the small triangles, and Jordy's cock twitched at the thought of that material getting wet. He might break. If he got a glimpse of her nipples through a wet bikini, his cock might just break.

"Kaks." He sighed.

"I know I need some color," she said quietly. "But I thought that's what we—"

35

He cleared his throat and shook his head. "There's nothing wrong with the suit."

She lifted her chin to look up at him as he approached her. "Really."

"Really." He nodded.

"Great." She sighed and moved to sidestep him.

"What're you doing?"

"I guess I'll change."

"Why?"

"You don't like the suit—"

"I like the suit, Kaki!" He tossed his hands up in frustration.

"If you did, you've have said so. Immediately. You'd have said, *wow, Kaks, you're packin'* or something Jordy Steed like. Instead you said *there's nothing wrong with the suit.*"

He stared after her when she disappeared into the bedroom. Seriously? He'd hurt her feelings? She made his dick hurt. Even? Could they just *please* call it even?

"Kaki." He followed her back to the bedroom, caught her with her hands behind her neck, fingers on the strings of the bikini top tied in a bow. "Don't."

"I brought other—"

"The suit is smokin' hot, and you look delicious, and that's the problem."

He'd pulled the heavy drapes open when he got up but left the sheer, filmy curtain things closed. Sunlight was filtered out, but there was enough daylight that he saw her fingers still. Saw them move from the strings to rub her neck.

"Why is that a problem?" Her husky butterscotch voice traced chills over his sweat-slicked skin. Good grief. He was sweating. Because they were already arguing? Or because his best friend was a sex kitten in disguise?

Dammit. He hadn't meant to hurt her feelings. The last thing he ever wanted to do was hurt Kaki or Lauren. Now that he was Kaki's husband, the potential for hurting her had multiplied by about a zillion.

He moved closer to her and reached for her hand. Pulled it down from her neck. He met her eyes for a moment and then rubbed his thumb over the diamond he'd put on her finger. The one that meant nothing, really, and yet, it did mark her as his. Stupid of him. Wasn't fair for him to impose rules on her, if he had no intention of keeping his own vows.

"Because you're my wife," he said quietly. "And every damned guy on the beach is gonna be falling over to get an eyeful."

She stared up at him silently. She was still hurt; he knew her well enough to see that in her eyes. But she was confused now, too, and he didn't blame her. Standing so close in the bedroom with her, he thought again of whisking her off her feet and untying the strings at her neck and exposing her breasts so he could look his fill.

Look. Touch. Suck.

What would she do if he kissed her now?

Before he could decide if he wanted to gamble, she swallowed hard and stepped around him again.

"I'm going down looking for sun," she said quietly. "Not looking to get laid like you are."

He stood for a moment when she disappeared. Heard her moving around in the living area. Probably grabbing the beach bag she'd packed. Making sure she had towels and sunscreen. Her visor and shades. A book to read. Kaki carried books with her everywhere she went.

Sunscreen.

He moved quickly, heard the heavy door close as she left. Someone would have to put sunscreen on her. Damned if he was going to let just anyone touch her, even if it was solely to rub sunscreen all over her delicious-looking body.

His cock throbbed again, and he hung his head as he hurried out the front door of the condo and down the runway to the elevator. It was going to be a hell of a week if he had to deal with a seven day hard on and no release.

———

HE FOUND HER AT ONE OF THE BEACH UMBRELLAS. SHE'D PUT THE visor and her shades on. The yellow and white striped canvas bag was in the sand at her feet. She was talking to a guy. Looking up at him like she was waiting with baited breath for every word out of his mouth. Jordy decided he'd like to yank the guy's blond ponytail off his head and maybe shove it somewhere the sunlight wasn't likely to touch. Like maybe down his throat.

He heard her laughter as he crossed the beach and neared them. Now that he was closer, he realized the guy was holding a clipboard. Decided he was a cabana boy or something. Umbrella rentals, maybe. Jordy wondered how the hell he was going to keep Kaki out of the water. Damned if he was going to let her get that damned white bikini wet and show her nipples to the world.

Maybe it wouldn't be a problem out here. Kaki wasn't big on ocean life. Gulf waters. She'd wade in, sure, but he didn't think she'd go so far as waist deep. But if she decided to go back up closer to the condo and get in the pool, he was going to have a problem.

"Oh." Kaki turned to him with such a sweet smile, he wondered if she'd forgiven him for the little scene up in the bedroom. Or if she was just playing the part of the happy bride for the umbrella guy. "This is my husband, Jordy."

Jordy gave himself another mental shake. Wondered if he might return to Prior with brain damage. If he had to shake himself out of sexual fantasies about his bride every day they were here, he might indeed do some damage. Then again, maybe he could fix it. Find someone warm and willing later tonight.

Kaki reached for his hand as he stopped to stand beside her. He didn't know if she even noticed, but his legs rubbed against hers. Her skin was already warm from the sun.

She'd pulled her hair into a messy little bun on her neck. Too damned cute for her own good. Did she have plans to hook up and enjoy vacation sex while she was here? He was surprised when the thought socked him in the gut and stole his breath away. He didn't want her to. No way in hell he'd ever hurt a girl, but that didn't mean all guys who wanted a quick piece from girls like Kaki were nice.

Okay, so what the hell was he going to do if hooking up with some chick at a bar later didn't do it for him? At the moment, he couldn't imagine anyone relieving him of his current problem except his wife. And she was completely off limits.

Jacking off in the shower wasn't a tempting option, either. For one thing, she might hear him. For another, he'd spent several nights of his life with only his hands. They had nothing on Kaki Harper Steed.

"Enjoy your day," the umbrella guy said to both of them as he ambled away from them to the next open umbrella, three or four down the beach. Jordy looked down at her and held his breath.

"I'm sorry—"

She shook her head and shrugged. "It's fine."

He watched her lean over and snag the handles of her bag. Scoot it closer to the lounge chair.

"It's not fine. I didn't mean for you to think that."

She pulled a lime green beach towel from the bag and draped it over the chair, all without looking at him.

"Jordy." She finally stilled and stood up straight. Propped her hands on her hips and looked at him. "Women are insecure about their bodies." She shrugged. "You gotta handle us a little better than that. That's all."

"Women."

"Yeah." She nodded. Turned and looked out at the water again. She stood mesmerized for so long, that he looked to see what had grabbed her attention. Nothing other than the gorgeous, rolling blue water meeting the lighter blue on the horizon. Jordy'd rather look at her, so he did. Finally, she looked back at him. "Maybe not women like Brianna, but pretty much the rest of us. Even fake wives."

"Kaks."

"Even Lauren," she mumbled, and Jordy felt a jolt of panic rip down through his chest and his middle—by God that had killed the painful hard on instantly—to his toes. He watched her sit down on the chair. Felt a flash of regret. She wasn't going to ask him to put sunscreen on her after all.

He stared at her for a moment. Couldn't see her face because of the visor. His eyes roamed over her breasts, over the small triangle of material that covered little at the apex of her thighs, and down over her legs. Her toenails were painted some dark shade of blue. The color of the dresses their brides-maids had worn.

Jordy had a flash of memory. He and Lauren and Kaki racing their bikes down Shenandoah Drive when they were ten or eleven. Hauling ass home to get away from a dog that had pulled his chain taut enough for it to break. They'd been scared shitless and laughing like hyenas all the way to safety.

He didn't deserve a woman like Kaki Harper. He shouldn't have involved her in this hare-brained scheme. Should've just let Brianna walk and found someone else. Now instead of nursing his ego and flipping Brianna the bird, he was going to end up hurting someone he really cared about.

"I'm gonna..." He cleared his throat. Looked out at the water. Refused to look when he felt her eyes on him. "Gonna go...down by the water."

Finally, he did look. Still couldn't see her eyes with those damned shades on. Which reminded him. He'd left his shades and his cap inside.

"Dammit."

"What's wrong?"

He dragged his eyes away from her lips. Pushed the thought of the cream cheese and that kiss from his mind and lifted his hands to cup the back of his neck.

"Forgot my hat and shades."

She moved quickly. Sat up and reached for the bag. Pulled out his old Prior College Pirates ball cap and handed it to him without looking. He swallowed hard and put it on. Pulled the bill down low over his forehead and then gave it one more tug for good measure. Watched her take his shades from the soft drawstring bag she'd insisted on packing for him. Took them when she held them out.

Such a nice thing that she'd thought of him. A wifely thing? Or just his friend looking out for him? Really nice, considering all he'd thought about since getting here was getting laid. More specifically, getting laid by Kaki.

CHAPTER SIX

MORNINGS, they had breakfast on the balcony. Jordy's breakfast never varied. A few handfuls of Captain Crunch and a 16 oz. bottle of Mountain Dew. Mostly, Kaki toasted half a bagel and spread cream cheese on it and sipped a cup of coffee with it. Though one morning, she'd swiped the box of cereal from him and helped herself to a handful. She'd been sorry she had, though, because then her teeth had that sugary, waxy coating from eating artificially sweetened stuff. After the first day, she was careful to grab a couple of napkins, but she needn't have bothered. Jordy hadn't touched her since then. No kisses, but he'd hardly bumped up against her in his sleep or walking on the beach, either. Except to rub sunscreen on her back, and he did that the way he changed TV channels on a remote. Like he wasn't interested in what he was doing, simply going through the motions.

They went down to the beach together every day after the first morning. Kaki hadn't worn the white bikini since the first day. She'd been a little nervous about it anyway, and then the way Jordy had reacted hadn't helped at all. She had no idea, even four days later, what he really thought. Seemed like the bikini had been an epic fail. Sure, he'd handed her the line of bullshit about not wanting other guys to look at her, but she didn't believe it. She'd worked her butt off before the wedding. Literally worked her butt off. She'd gone from a size eight to a six, and she'd bought the string bikini on a whim, uncertain as to whether or not she'd actually wear it. She hadn't thought it was that bad, but maybe she was wrong.

After the morning on the beach, whether they built sand castles or waded in the water or simply lounged in the sun or the shade of an umbrella, they'd go back upstairs to the condo. Grab something to eat. Frozen pizza, mostly, though Kaki was certainly tired of it by day three. After lunch, they crashed. Jordy watched TV, although mostly, it looked like he was asleep, sprawled out on the couch. And she read, tucked away in the big, comfy loveseat on the other side of the living room.

They spent their afternoons either in the condo pool or sightseeing. They'd driven down through Destin and into Panama Beach. Dinner was always a bigger deal that required more effort. Showers and makeup and real clothing. They'd put away a few beers, certainly, but they'd always been good at that.

Jordy always came back to the condo with her, but he'd gone out twice without her. Later. He'd waited until she'd gone to bed. Didn't tell her goodnight when he left, but he didn't try to hide the fact that he was going out, either. She'd dozed the first night when he was gone. Woke up after two to find him next to her in bed. The second time, she'd gone to bed with the intention of reading, but Owen had sent her a text, so she'd passed her alone time with him. In fact, she'd just said goodnight to him and put her phone on the nightstand on her side of the bed when Jordy had come in. He wasn't drunk. Didn't really even smell like liquor. Didn't smell like perfume or sex, but then, Kaki didn't get too close to him, either, so who knew?

She'd talked to a few guys. One on the beach the first day when Jordy had wandered down to the water to pout. She'd let him go. She hadn't been sure, exactly, what he'd had to pout about. He'd slammed her, not the other way around. She'd watched him for a while from behind her shades. Thought about the Halloweens she and Lauren had spent Trick-or-Treating with him. The year he'd dressed as *Scream*. Hadn't been scary, but he'd scared the bejesus out of a little boy in his neighborhood, and he'd taken the mask off and sat down right in the street with the kid to show him he wasn't really a ghost.

A couple of guys had walked past her, between the line of umbrellas and the water line, and they'd drawn her attention away from Jordy for a few minutes. Two of them were nice-looking, but when you were traveling with Jordan Steed, pulling off nice-looking just didn't cut it. The third was nerdy cute, and he'd happened to look back and catch her eye. He'd hesitated, and when his buddies stopped and looked back at him, he'd waved them on and approached her with a goofy smile.

Freddy, though he'd told her it was a nickname, short for his last name (Fredericks) had hung out with her for an hour, maybe. He'd stood for the longest time, and they'd talked about books. Finally, he'd squatted and eased himself into the sand just under the shade of her umbrella. He'd admitted to liking classic literature, and then they'd moved from the classics to sci-fi and horror. All perfectly appropriate. He hadn't even flinched when he'd finally noticed her wedding ring. Only asked if her husband was a reader. She'd laughed softly and said no. The only thing Jordy Steed ever read was the box scores and maybe an article or two in a sports magazine and maybe graffiti-like things scratched into girls' bathroom stalls, if the graffiti was about him.

She'd winced when she'd thought it. Hadn't said it aloud. Made Jordy sound a little bit like a jerk, and though Kaki would admit he had his moments, he was a good guy. Jordy had come back to the umbrella, trunks and cap sopping wet, when Freddy had taken her hand in a simple, kind gesture and shook it and said goodbye.

Jordy had watched him walk away with the obvious questions on his lips. *Who was he? What were you doing with him?* But he'd apparently thought better of asking, and he'd pulled his red towel from the beach bag and rubbed it over his head to dry his hat and his hair. Sat in the other chair and glanced at her.

"So. Beach. And then what? Should we do the pool today?" he asked her now as he crunched a mouthful of cereal. "Or did you wanna go see something else? Go shopping?"

"Nope." She had no interest in shopping. Not here. And not with him. Kaki liked shopping, but that was an activity better shared with Lauren.

"Mm-kay. Lunch out today? Or do you wanna stay with dinner out?"

She stretched her arms up over her head and took a deep breath. Let it out on a yawn and shrugged.

"I like lunch here and dinner out," she said simply. "What do you wanna do?"

He nodded. "That's fine."

He'd looked damned good when they'd first arrived here in Florida. Now with a few days of relaxation and the sun on his skin, he looked sexy.

Scratch that. She shook her head. *Healthy.* He looked *healthy.*

She snorted at herself and looked away. *Sexy.* Good grief. Jordy Steed was the hottest guy in Prior. Why whitewash that now that she was married to him? She'd scored the hottest guy in town. In name only.

"What's funny?"

He poked her when she didn't answer him.

"Nothing." She shook her head. "I'm gonna go change."

He nodded. Watched her as she stood up and gathered her breakfast dishes.

"Kaks?" He waited until she was at the door before saying her name.

"Hmm?"

"Do me a favor?"

"Yeah," she answered immediately. She'd married him as a favor, for God's sake. Wasn't like he could ask more of her than that. "What?"

"Wear the white bikini."

She tightened her fingers on the door handle. Tried to swallow, but her mouth went dry.

"Why?" Her voice was tiny. A little bit uncertain. She hated that.

"Why not?"

"Because it makes my hips look big," she answered. She tugged on the door, leaned to her right, into the door, when the dishes in her left hand started to teeter.

"Kaki."

"Hmm?"

"Wear the white bikini."

"I don't like—"

"I do." He wouldn't look at her, but she noticed the change in his voice. Little bit gravelly now, almost like it was painful for him to speak. "Please?"

Kaki narrowed her eyes at him. Shrugged when he didn't say anymore and went inside. Whatever. If he wanted her to wear it, maybe she'd wear it. They had today and tomorrow, and then they were headed back home. She'd told herself she wasn't going to do it, but she'd been toying with the idea of seeing Owen when they got back. When their fake married life became a fake routine.

She rinsed her dishes and set them in the sink. Went to the bedroom to grab her suit. Grabbed the multi-colored one with the halter-top. She loved its blue and green jewel tones. She stood for a moment, the halter in hand, and stared at the bed. Lost in thought. Wondered what Owen would say about the suit. The again, Owen made love with his eyes closed. All. The. Time. They'd clicked, and they'd been together for quite a while before things had gone south. Never so far south to let it all blow up, but far enough that it was a long distance to get back together.

With a deep breath, she tossed the halter down and stepped closer to her bag to find the string bikini. Maybe it would look better now, since she'd finally gotten some sun. She could hope anyway. She'd never wear the damned thing again when they got back to Prior. She and Owen had never gone anywhere together that called for swimwear. And he wasn't the kind of guy to appreciate sexy lingerie, either. She'd tried that. She'd been stunned when he'd glanced at her and turned out the lights without really looking.

Might as well get one more wear out of this thing. She carried it with her to the bathroom. Closed and locked the door. Used the bathroom, washed her hands and then her face. And then she stripped her pajamas off, stepped out of her underwear and stood in front of the mirror completely nude. *Passable.* But surely not Jordy Steed's regular fare. She leaned over the sink to see her face better in the mirror. Was that a zit? She brushed at the spot above her eyebrow and sighed in relief when whatever it was disappeared.

"You ready?" Jordy called and jiggled the doorknob. She jumped and spun around to stare suspiciously at the door.

"Almost."

She stood for a moment longer, eyes on the door. Wasn't like it was going to open. She could see that it was still locked, and Jordy wasn't going to bust the lock just to get to her. Unless he just needed to get inside to pee. She rolled her eyes as she turned back to the counter. Picked up the skimpy bottom and stepped into it. She eased it over her hips. Really, they weren't that big, and she was kind of proud of them, but seriously, why had he asked her to put this on after the scene the other day?

Quickly, before Jordy could say anything else, she held the bikini top up and twisted awkwardly to tie it at her back. Tied the strings around her neck and then checked herself in the mirror. Reached into the tiny triangular cups to lift her boobs a bit and move them around to look better. Wouldn't do to walk out with half of them falling out the bottom of the cups.

Jordy was in the living room when she opened the door and crossed the small hall to the bedroom. Perched on the arm of the couch, he'd looked at her and smiled, and then aimed the remote at the TV again and the sports broadcaster's voice had simply gone away.

"I'm gonna go on down," she called to him as he closed the bathroom door. She folded her pajamas haphazardly and set them on the end of the bed. Heard the door open again.

"What?"

"I'm gonna—"

"Gimme five minutes," he told her.

"I can—"

"Just wait for me." He'd moved from the bathroom doorway to the bedroom, and she felt his eyes on her now. She glanced at him over her shoulder and nodded.

"Okay."

He held her gaze for a few more minutes and then hurried back to the bathroom. Kaki finished tidying up the bedroom and moved back to the living area. She heard water running and assumed Jordy might be brushing his teeth. Rather than think about him in the bathroom, tugging the boxer briefs and the shorts off to trade for his trunks, she busied herself packing the beach bag again. Made sure she had the sunscreen and his cap. Their shades. Her book.

When the bag was ready, and she didn't want to think about Jordy changing clothes or the fact that she felt almost naked in the white suit, she picked up her phone and checked her messages. A text from Owen asking her if she was going to stick it to Jordy tonight and order surf and turf. She ignored it for now. For one thing, Jordy wouldn't blink if she ordered surf and turf, except he knew she hated seafood. The thought made her gag. She scrolled through her messages, read two from coworkers who teased her about how busy she must be. How rough it was going to be to come back to work after a week in paradise with her new husband.

Believers. She laughed softly and set the phone down on the dinette. Reached without looking for the ponytail holder she'd left on the table yesterday. Twisted her hair back into some kind of updo mess, didn't care as long as it was away from her face. Grinned when she read a text from Lauren about eating a half box of snack crackers last night.

Satisfied that her hair wouldn't bother her, she reached for her phone to tap out a response to Lauren. The grin had faded to a small smile. She missed Lauren. As she tapped letters to spell out *drank a six-pack yesterday*, she decided she might be having more fun if she'd come here on a honeymoon with Lauren instead of Jordy. She wouldn't have entertained any sexual thoughts if she were traveling with Lauren; therefore, no let down when absolutely nothing happened. She heard Jordy clear his throat. Looked up to find him in the hall watching her.

"Who ya talking to?" he asked quietly.

"Lauren."

"Mmm." He nodded.

"What?" she asked quickly.

"Nothing."

"What? What're you thinking?" she urged him. She tossed her phone in the bag on the chair and then grabbed the bag by the shoulder straps. "Ready?"

"Got everything?"

"I do."

They walked outside together, Kaki digging in the bag immediately for her shades. The sun made her eyes hurt; if she didn't put her sunglasses on, she'd end up with a headache.

"You looked happy."

She pulled her glasses from the small cloth bag and slipped them on before she looked up at him.

"What?"

"Talking to Lauren. You looked happy."

She nodded and looked away. "I am."

"You would've had more fun if you'd come here with her."

"Be kinda weird if I married her, though, wouldn't it?" she asked as they stopped at the outdoor elevator. She punched the down arrow.

"It happens now." He shrugged.

"Yeah, but I'm not into Lauren."

"You're not into me, either."

She looked up at him and grinned. "Heard anything from lover girl?"

He raised his eyebrows and nodded.

"Yeah. She actually sent a text last night."

"Mmm." Kaki nodded. Ignored the odd little jolt of pain that hit her in her belly.

The elevator stopped on their level, and the doors opened to reveal an empty car. They stepped on, and Jordy hit the main level button.

"Asked how the honeymoon was going."

Kaki leaned on the back wall of the elevator and studied her feet in her worn blue flip-flops. She'd had a fresh pedicure for the wedding. Still looked okay, but she figured if she looked closely, her toes would show some wear from the week in the sand.

"And what did you tell her?" she asked quietly.

"That we're having a good time."

He leaned on the wall of the car. From the corner of her eye, she saw him cross his arms over his chest. He wore an old Pirates t-shirt with the sleeves and collar cut out. He'd toss the shirt once they were by the water. Kaki had seen more than one girl watch him shrug the shirt off yesterday. A couple of them were young enough to be traveling with their parents. Kaki had watched Jordy strut down to the water's edge and wondered if he had any idea the effect he had on women, girls of all ages.

"That we're drinking champagne and kissing under the stars."

Kaki snorted and lifted her head to study him.

"You didn't. Did you?"

"Not a good thing to say?"

"To a woman like Brianna? No. Don't think so."

"What does that mean?"

She shook her head. "Trust me. If you really want her back, don't say weird crap like that to her."

"What's wrong with kissing under the stars?"

"Sounds like fun to me," she admitted, "but your girl-friend doesn't look like she'd be into that."

"Define *that*."

"Romance." She shrugged and stood up straight when the elevator car grinded to a halt at the main level. When the doors opened, she led him out and back through the tunnel way to the beach. She wondered if he had been sharing champagne and kisses under the stars with someone last night when Brianna had sent the text.

Wondered how many women he'd had down here on his honeymoon with her. What they looked like. Maybe she should've tried harder to hook up with someone. She'd bet Freddy would have been willing to play for a while. Shook her head as she walked. Okay, if that's what Jordy wanted out of this trip, that was one thing. Kaki didn't need true love for enjoyable sex, but then she hadn't come to Florida with promiscuity in mind, either. Just a time out. Some sunshine and sand. A few drinks. Some laughter with her friend.

The friend who was now her husband.

CHAPTER SEVEN

JORDY WALKED BEHIND HER, eyes on her ass, his mind on Brianna. She *had* sent him a text last night. And he'd answered with a simple yes to her question. He was enjoying the honeymoon. He hadn't used that cheesy line about champagne and kissing under the stars. He'd only thrown that out there for fun. But now he was intrigued by Kaki's comment. Girls like Brianna didn't go for romance.

Well. Yeah, he knew that. Brianna liked money and sex. She'd be bored stiff here with him. Then again, if he'd brought Brianna here, he'd be more interested in other things, too.

He watched Kaki's legs eat up the distance between the condo and the water. Her hips (where she got the idea that they looked big in that scrap of white stuff was beyond him) swayed invitingly. The toned muscles in her legs flexed as she moved. She turned her head and called something to him, followed it with a peal of laughter. When he finally caught up with her, she was smiling and laughing, and he had no idea what she was talking about, but she was beautiful and he was struck with the bizarre realization that he'd never noticed it before.

What would it be like? With Kaki? Not like Brianna, but he flicked his eyes down over his best friend's, his *wife's* body, and wondered if it might even be better. What would it be like to bury himself inside her and pump his hips over hers and make her throw her head back and fasten his open mouth on her exposed neck?

He grinned at her, wanted to ask her to repeat herself. But he couldn't just stand here and look at her and think about smoothing his hands over her soft, warm skin and cupping her breasts while she shared whatever she'd thought was funny.

Instead he cleared his throat and turned away from her.

"I'm gonna…" He shrugged.

"Go get in the water," she finished for him. "I know."

"Come with me," he suggested. The words were out of his mouth before he knew what the hell he was saying. Dragging her down to the water with him wasn't going to help the way his dick was poking around his swim trunks. Still. They'd been here all week. They'd walked on the beach, and they'd soaked up some sun together, but she hadn't gone in the gulf water with him even once.

"I'm fine."

"Kaks. C'mon." He glanced at her. Hoped she didn't look down, because he just remembered what she was wearing, and his trunks probably looked like one of these beach umbrellas right now.

"Mm-kay," she said quietly. She shrugged the straps of the bag off her shoulder and leaned a bit to let it fall to the sand.

"Really?"

"Sure."

He reached for her then, took her hand, and pulled her with him to the water's edge. She walked quickly to keep up with him, and he saw without being obvious about looking, that her breasts were bouncing in the white triangles.

Rather than look at her, but dammit, all he wanted was to

look, he turned his head the other way and watched a young family on the beach. A youngish mom and dad. Maybe a little bit older than he and Kaki, but not much. Two kids. One maybe four, and the other maybe just a year old. Jordy watched the guy sitting in the sand with the little one, patting a green plastic shovel on top of a mound of wet sand. Wondered if it was the little guy's first sand castle. Decided it wasn't so bad. The mom had the other kid by the hand, and they were walking in the water. The little kid walked a step and then giggled and shrieked at the cold water or the sand between his toes or who knew what. Jordy turned away with a small smile. He had nieces and nephews, and he was crazy about all of them.

He took a quick peek at Kaki to see if she was watching the family. She wasn't. She had her free hand at her visor, her face lifted to the endless blue sky above them. Before she would notice he was watching her, he looked back at the kids. He'd always just figured he would be a dad someday, since his brothers were all dads. But now he wondered how he thought he was going to have kids. He wasn't stupid enough to think a woman like Brianna was ever going to want to settle down with him and pop out a couple of kids and drive a minivan and sit in the stands at touch football games or dance recitals.

None of the women he spent his time with were the kind of woman to want that sort of future. None, except Lauren and maybe Kaki. Although it struck him as they stood there, hand in hand, gulf water lapping over their feet, he didn't really know what Kaki wanted from life. She'd studied history. Majored in history, but he didn't know what that meant exactly. He didn't know what period of history had fascinated her so much that she'd decided to spend years of her life studying history, and now she worked in the museum back in Prior, but he had no idea what that meant, what she actually did.

She'd been involved in a few relationships through the years. It had nearly killed him when she dated Tate Delaney their senior year of high school. Not that he'd had his eyes on Kaki, not like that, anyway. Just that Tate Delaney was a dick, and Jordy had worried he would hurt his friend. And he had, but Lauren had simply told him he had to let it go. Girls needed to get their hearts broken at least once. He'd asked her then who'd broken her heart, but she'd refused to say.

Kaki had lost her virginity to Delaney, and thinking about that still made his skin crawl. The guy was a year older than the three of them; he'd graduated from high school with honors, but flunked out of college immediately. Too much partying, not enough studying. And Kaki had been right in the middle of all of that.

She'd dated another guy a few months after Tate inevitably broke her heart. That one hadn't lasted long, but Jordy thought the next one had. He wasn't sure.

"What're you thinking about?" She tugged on his hand to get his attention.

"Hmm?" He finally turned his eyes to her, ready this time to find her looking at him, watching him curiously.

"What're you thinking about?" she asked again. She leaned into him. Reached up and brushed her fingertips over his forehead, between his shades and the bill of his cap. "You look so serious."

"I can be serious."

"Yeah, like seven seconds out of the year." She laughed softly. "Tell me."

"Hey." He grabbed her hand and then twisted her around to pull her against him, her back to his chest. *Serious seven seconds out of the year?* He could be serious when he wanted to be, when he needed to be serious. But now her back was pinned to his front, and she was warm and wiggling, and most importantly, at the moment, she was laughing as she struggled to get away from him.

This was missing. Since they'd started this charade, this fun part of their friendship had slowly slipped away. They'd both become so caught up in playing their roles and the expectations those roles carried, maybe they'd lost sight of who they really were to each other.

"Jordy!" She laughed and squealed as he lifted her off her feet and carried her further into the water. "Stop it! Put me down."

"Oh, I'll put you down." He pressed his lips close to her ear and growled playfully.

"No!" She stretched her neck and laid her head on his shoulder. Looked up at him; this close, he could see her wide eyes behind her sunglasses, and she laughed softly. "Please? Please don't."

"You can't go back to Prior and tell people you didn't go in the water," he told her. As soon as the words were out, he wished he could take them back. She was going back to Prior without her husband making love to her. Then again, wasn't like she wanted that anyway. Not to mention that she wouldn't tell anyone *that*. The whole relationship was a joke; she'd play the role of happy wife until they decided it was time to unravel things and go their separate ways.

"Please?"

Jordy lowered his eyes from her shades to her lips. Natural now, no gloss or color, they were the perfect shade of pink. They were parted, at the moment, and as he watched, she scraped her teeth over her bottom lip and laughed again.

"Please?"

He had a moment of regret that this plea was the only one he would hear from that sweet mouth. It would be easy to close his eyes and concentrate on her warm skin touching his, on the swell of her nearly nude breasts over his arm across her chest, on the press of her hip to his cock that she most certainly had to feel but was choosing to ignore.

He didn't, though. Didn't close his eyes, because who

knew what kind of idiot move he might make if he did. Instead, he grinned, kissed the tip of her nose, and walked her further into the water again.

"Jordy!" She yelped and laughed, and they were in the gulf up to their waists. He put her down, forgetting that she was just a bit shorter, that she was wearing that damned white bikini, and watched the water lap over her stomach and lick the little triangles that covered precious little of what he was just beginning to realize was definitely more than a handful.

He grinned and flicked his eyes up to hers.

"Cold?"

She gasped in surprise that he'd said it, and then laughing, she recovered quickly and lunged for him. He turned his back to her, but she threw her arms around his neck and hung on his back.

"You can't dunk me," he reminded her. "You have tried a million times, and you can't do it."

"First time for everything." She circled her legs around his waist and lifted herself higher. He ducked and tried to get away from her when she snatched the shell of his ear in her teeth.

"Ouch!" He laughed and jumped and tried to shake her off his back.

"Just go down." She let go of his ear and whispered to him like a siren. "Just take one for the team, Jordy."

"Dunking me by talking me into it doesn't count, Kaks."

"Doesn't it?"

Jesus. That butterscotch voice dropped an octave and lit a fire low in his gut. He groaned in protest when she pressed harder into his back and nipped at his ear again.

"Unfair play!"

"What?" She snorted. "Unfair? What? What the hell does that mean?"

"It means, that's a foul," he told her as he reached back to grab her. She fought him—he figured this spectacle was like their younger days, when the three of them passed blistering hot summer days and sticky nights in his family pool—but he managed to flip her around so that he was cradling her above the water.

"You can't call fouls on me," she said as she twisted to get away from him. "You can't—c'mon, stud. You can't—"

"Seems like I have the upper hand again, Kaks."

She stilled in his arms and met his gaze.

"Please don't do this."

"Oh, I'm gonna do it." He nodded. "My only regret is that I don't have my phone so I can get a picture of you as you come up for air."

She laughed softly, but she lifted her hand to touch his chest. He dropped then, took her under much the same as he had hundreds of times in the past. She came up sputtering, pushing her sopping hair out of her eyes.

"Payback," she said with a shrug.

"You've never been able to get payback in fifteen years!" He caught her hand in his fist when she moved toward him and reached out. "Why would that be different now?"

Her wicked grin made him shiver. In anticipation or fear, he wasn't sure.

"Seems like I'm in a damned good position to get revenge now." She arched her eyebrows. "Doncha think?"

He swallowed hard and looked back toward the sand. The row of umbrellas. Their abandoned bag a few feet behind the umbrella they'd been using all week.

"You know what?" he asked as he looked back at her. "You don't have any sunscreen on. Your back might burn."

"Did you hear that?" She turned her head and looked around. Made a show of searching in all directions. "Did you?"

"What?" he asked with a small smile as she walked closer to him. Droplets of water beaded her skin. She ducked her head under water again and then smoothed her hair back from her face.

"That." She cocked her head and then looked up at him again. "I think…wait…I think that was Jordy Steed calling uncle."

"Remember the night Lauren's family went to St. Louis for that family reunion thing?"

Her shoulders shook with that silent laughter he loved so much. There had been nights that she and Lauren kept him entertained just with the crazy things they said and the laughing and the silent laughter and shaking and clapping their hands together as if to say *bring it on.*

"Remember? You and I were in the pool for hours. What was the record? Seven? Did I dunk you seven times that night?"

"You wouldn't—"

"I would." He nodded. "And you know me well enough to know I will take you down again, woman. So behave."

"Be—? Are you kidding me right now? Behave?" She launched herself at him. He caught her easily against his chest, took a step back. Realized his thumbs were just under her curves now, and there was no easy way to move without drawing attention to the fact that he was almost touching parts that were off-limits.

"There's a family of four behind me," he said quietly. Decided he wasn't above fibbing to her to get her off him without any further contact. Contact she didn't want and that maybe he did. "Two little people. They probably think we're—"

She ducked her head to rest on his shoulder. She was shaking again, and for just a moment, Jordy panicked, thinking she was crying.

"Kaks?" He nuzzled her head with his chin. "You okay?"

She nodded, lifted her head, and snorted.

"What?" He looked at her, shocked when she dropped her head back and howled with laughter.

"Seriously?"

"What?" he said again. "What's funny? Why are you laughing at me now?"

"Well, for one thing, you're using that poor family to get away from me." She cleared her throat and tried to put a lid on the laughter. Clearly not going to happen as her shoulders shook again, and she turned her head. "What were you gonna say? Foreplay? The family back there is going to think this is our foreplay and we're gonna mate out here in the water?"

A little embarrassed, and yet pretty much caught red-handed on both counts, he eased her down over his body, made sure she was aware of what her near nudity was doing to him, and set her down in the water again.

"You sure you wanna go there?" He winked at her, but they were both laughing now.

"Biology," she mumbled, but he thought she was still laughing at him. She turned toward the beach and started walking. He stood for a moment, eyes on her retreating form, and wished for more of this in their marriage. If they weren't going to be lovers, and he could deal with that, they still needed to be friends. He needed Kaki Harper Steed as his friend, because he loved her way too damned much to lose that, too, when he divorced her. She looked over her shoulder at him and tilted her head. Reached her hand back for him.

"Will you put some sunscreen on my back?"

He stirred to life. Caught up with her and took her hand again.

The dad and the little kid were still in the sand, but now the little kid was crawling over the dad, and Jordy pictured them going home and the dad having big tan lines from where his kid was climbing on him. The mom and the other kid had wandered closer to them, and as they walked out of the water, she and Kaki made eye contact.

"Looks like you're having fun." The woman offered Kaki a tired smile.

"Honeymoon," Kaki answered simply, and the woman cast an appraising look at Jordy and then looked back at Kaki with a nod and a sly grin.

"We never made it out of our hotel room," she whispered, and then she hurried the little kid along and Jordy and Kaki were left looking at each other.

"It's a wonder they don't have ten kids," Kaki mumbled.

"Do you?" Jordy asked her, and then he realized she didn't know what he'd been thinking earlier and so she had no idea what he meant now. "Want kids? Do you want kids?"

Kaki dropped his hand and padded up through the warm sand to their bag. Jordy stared after her, but he ducked down to roll the umbrella out and watched her pull her towel from the bag. Much to his disappointment, she ruffled the towel over her hair and down over her body, drying the glistening beads of water from her sun-darkened skin.

CHAPTER EIGHT

KAKI TOOK her time as she draped her lime green towel over the chair under the umbrella. Jordy was watching her. Waiting for an answer, she supposed, but she didn't know what she was supposed to say. Was he just curious? Or was he about to up the ante? Offer her cash if she'd have a kid for him, with a bonus if it was a boy? Maybe even another bonus when the kid was eighteen, if he got a baseball or basketball scholarship to a Big Ten school.

She looked away, guilty for thinking it. He wouldn't make an offer like that. Jordy was a playboy. He was afraid of commitment, and he liked to have a good time. That didn't make him an asshole, like her thoughts made him out to be. When they'd put together this little scheme—her marrying him to get Brianna's attention—he hadn't offered to give her cash. Maybe it all came down to the fact that she was living a damned good life as his wife, because Jordy's family was wealthy by any means, and most certainly by Prior, Illinois' definition. But he hadn't been so crass as to suggest a payoff for her when it was over.

"No?" She sat down in the chair and took a deep breath, rubbed her knuckles over her chest when that deep breath turned into a sharp pain. She tried to avoid his eyes, but he'd moved, too, and he was sitting in the lounge chair right next to hers, watching her.

"No?" He sounded surprised. "You don't want kids?"

"What's wrong with my not wanting kids?"

"Nothing. I guess I just thought you would. You're so excited for Lauren and Tyler—"

She cleared her throat, let her eyes roam his way, though she was quick to look away.

"Oh." He nodded.

"Oh, what?"

"I get it."

"You get what?" she asked him. Might still be morning, but it was five o'clock somewhere, and she wished she had a drink. A margarita sounded good.

"You don't want kids with me."

Kaki opened her mouth to argue, to tell him he was wrong, but their eyes met and she couldn't find her voice. Jordy sighed. Sideways on the chair so he could face her, he propped his elbows on his knees and rested his chin in his hand.

"Jordy." She sighed.

"It's okay," he said quietly. "It's not what I meant, but it's okay."

She'd hurt his feelings. Of course she knew he had feelings, but it was rare for someone to hurt them, and she sure as heck didn't want to be the person to do it.

"I just..." She dragged her gaze away from him, looked out at the water and wished they were back out there, goofing off. "Marrying you like this is one thing. I can't do...that. I can't have a baby just to make—"

"Kaki, I'm not asking that."

She saw him shake his head.

"I'm sorry." His voice was gruff. He turned and swung his legs out to rest on the end of the chair.

Reached up and pulled the bill of his cap down low on his forehead.

"For what?"

"Doing this to you—"

"Dragging me down to beautiful sunny Florida for a week on the beach?"

"For taking away your first wedding. Should've been—"

"Don't." She cut him off. She saw him flinch, looked like he was going to turn and look at her, but he didn't. "That stuff doesn't matter to me—"

"It should matter to you. You were beautiful in that dress, and everything about the day should have been real for you."

The word *beautiful* touched her. Eyes suddenly filled with emotion, she turned away from him. Sat still for a moment and breathed. Waited for the feeling to pass.

"It doesn't matter," she finally said again. "I have no regrets. I just...I have to draw the line at the baby thing." She cleared her throat. "I mean...if you ever got married, and your wife couldn't...and I could...well, I don't know. Maybe that would be different, but—"

"Kaks."

"What?"

"Did you just offer to be a surrogate for me and my future wife who can't have children?"

She laughed softly.

"I love you, Jordy." She licked her lips and shrugged. Made sure not to look at him this time. "I'd do anything for you, but I can't have your baby now."

"Wow."

His breathless one word answer made her look at him.

"Wow, what?"

"I wouldn't ask that of you, but that's..." His smile was genuine. "That's so...generous of you—"

"Jordy." She rolled her eyes.

He laughed and rolled his head again to stare at the water.

"Okay, so all that mushy crap aside, I wasn't suggesting we go procreate. I just...wondered. If you want kids? Someday? With your real husband?"

Kaki pursed her lips and nodded slowly. *Procreate. Wow. He's so not into me that he has to use a word like procreate to describe what it might be like to make a baby with me?* Aware of the fact that he was waiting for her to say something, might possibly be looking at her, she still took her time in answering. First she had to swallow that word. *Procreate.* Why couldn't he have said he wasn't suggesting they have sex? She got that maybe Jordy Steed wasn't familiar with the phrase *making love*, but couldn't he have just said *have sex*, rather than *procreate*? If she was that unattractive to him, she could wear a burlap bag out here on the beach or just go nude, and he wouldn't notice anything out of the ordinary.

"Kaks?"

She cleared her throat, *procreate* still stuck at the base, making it hard for her to speak.

"Yeah." She nodded, unsure if he could hear her. "Yeah. Some day. With my real husband."

She saw him smile, but it took her another few seconds to look at him. To school her features into a mask. She wasn't sure what look she was going for, indifferent or amused, but she certainly didn't want him to see that he'd hurt her feelings again. She didn't want him groveling with apologies.

"You're gonna be an awesome mom," he told her, and she flinched yet again. Made herself look at him this time, met his eyes, though, thank God, they were both wearing sunglasses so the plastic lenses cut the intensity by about a billion percent, and smiled.

"Thanks."

"I always just..." She saw him frown, realized maybe he hadn't meant to insult her (although that sort of felt like even more of an insult) as he rushed on with what he was saying. "Figured I'd have kids. Like, when my brothers all started getting married and having babies—well," he laughed and glanced at her sheepishly, "—their wives were having babies, I just thought yeah, okay, I'm gonna do that one day."

Kaki nodded. Looked away. Watched the family of four that Jordy had referred to earlier, in the water, back before things got serious and depressing as hell, as they packed up to head back to their hotel or condo or to lunch or wherever.

Anywhere but here. Kaki was surprised to find herself wishing at the moment she were anywhere but here.

"But...it just hit me," Jordy continued. "I'm getting old. I'm not gonna have kids. I'm not...I don't know the first thing about women, except how to fuck them, and what woman in her right mind is gonna wanna settle down with me and have kids?"

Kaki pressed her lips together and drew in a deep breath through her nose.

Okay, so she'd been involved with Owen Matthews for nearly two years. Sure, they'd ended things and started them and ended them again not long before Kaki had agreed to marry Jordy. But even when they were sleeping together, even when they were *having sex*, they'd never talked about marriage. Never talked about kids. In a sense, Kaki was in the same boat as Jordy.

And if this trip was any indication, the two of them together weren't going to set anything in motion in order to make babies, wanted or not.

"You're young, Jordy," she said quietly. "There's time."

She wondered if she was talking to Jordy or reminding herself she still had time to meet Mr. Right and start a family. She was only twenty-five. As soon as she got away from Mr. Wrong, she glanced at Jordy and amended the thought to Mr. Just Kidding, she'd figure out what she had to do to find the right guy to start the rest of her life.

When he didn't say any more, and he didn't move for several minutes, Kaki decided he was sleeping. She took advantage of the moment, studied him in the quiet morning. The beach was coming to life around them, but the other families, the couples out there were separate from them, and Kaki was relieved their conversation was over. She couldn't see much of his face now, not with the ball cap and the shades. Her eyes roamed over his bare chest. His arms. Nice arms. She'd had to remind herself out there in the water that it was Jordy Steed holding her against his body. Best point-guard Prior High School's basketball team had ever seen. Good ball-handling skills—Kaki had heard several girls claim he had good hands and maybe he did—and a beautiful three-point shot. He'd been the baseball team's best starting pitcher their sophomore through senior years. Tied only by one for best batting average.

Her eyes lingered on the elastic waistline of his trunks as she considered that. Jordy hated Tate Delaney. He'd always hated the guy, but he'd become pretty vocal about it when she and Tate started dating. Was it the competition? On the diamond? Sure wasn't over her, she had no illusions about that.

She'd felt his erection when they were in the water. How could she not? She'd also reminded herself not to take it personally. He was a guy. Even if he didn't find her attractive, she had the biological parts to affect him. She'd brushed up against that part of his body more than once through the years, and they'd never made a big deal out of it before. She wasn't dumb enough to think it meant anything now.

Still. She couldn't help but wonder. When he got out of bed the morning after the wedding, his boxers and shorts had been pushed low on his hips, and she'd had to remind herself not to stare. She'd seen his bare ass a few times through the years; the baseball guys were big on mooning people. But she'd never seen anything more, never really wanted to. Until now. Right about now, she wanted more than an eyeful.

She groaned out loud. Moved gracefully and climbed to

her feet. Dug in her bag for her phone and walked away from the umbrella. At the moment, she couldn't shake the image of his underwear low on his hips and that dark swirl of hair on his stomach and the feel of him pressed up against her, his thumbs resting just under her breasts. Most guys—like, 99.99 percent of the guys she'd ever known in her life would have copped a feel out there in the water. Rubbed their thumbs up over her breasts, even over her nipples, and claimed it was an accident if she'd questioned them.

She wouldn't have questioned Jordy. But he hadn't done it. He'd simply put her down, as if being nearly naked with her in the water wasn't driving him out of his freaking mind.

If he woke up and she was gone, he wouldn't panic. She'd walked the other day when he was napping. She moved up the beach at a steady pace, though it wasn't easy walking bare foot in sand. Right now, she kind of wished she had running shoes on and she was on the pavement, like maybe back home, and she wasn't slowly turning into a sex-crazed Jordy Steed groupie.

When the walking hadn't calmed her down, she slowed her pace and headed back down the beach. From what she could tell, Jordy hadn't moved. Rather than return to the umbrella and the torture, she made a right and went back up to the building. Stood in the tunnel and looked at her phone. No messages. No calls. Her friends were respecting her right to privacy on her honeymoon. What a joke.

Except Lauren. But Lauren was working. She didn't want to bother her with a text when she was working, and Kaki sure couldn't call her. And say what, anyway? *I'm having second thoughts*? *I can't do this*? Because if she said that, Lauren would call her on it and ask why. And then she'd have to admit that Lauren was right. That this wasn't a good idea, and she'd have to admit to the fact that she wanted something to happen. She wanted Jordy Steed to pin her against a wall or the sand or the bed and take her.

TRACY BROEMMER

She laughed out loud at the thought. Not of Jordy pinning her to anything and taking or giving anything, but the phrase. *Take her.* Right out of a romance novel, the likes of which she hadn't read since she was fourteen, maybe.

This is stupid, she told herself. *Stupid, stupid, stupid. Two more days. Get through two more days on the beach, and then go back home and it will be a million times easier to deal with Jordy. Because you can ignore him. You can go your own way and do your own thing. And time will fly, and then it'll be over, and you'll be divorced.*

Except for next weekend. Every weekend. Until divorce did they part. Jordy's family was big on family. Sunday dinners. Every week. She'd have to deal with the hand-holding and the kissing and the teasing about the honeymoon.

With a long, frustrated sigh, she dialed Owen's number. Owen, if anything, was a lifelong scholar. At first, she'd thought it was sexy. Now she thought it was either lazy or his way of picking new women. He'd had them, she knew that, but she didn't think he'd been with anyone *while* they were together. He was a teacher's assistant, history, of course, so he didn't have a set work schedule like Lauren. Making this call was admitting desperation, but she needed a familiar voice.

Naturally, the phone rang once before going to his voice-mail. She hesitated. They'd been together the night of her bachelorette. Hadn't seen much of each other at all since then. Kaki wasn't sure she wanted to see him now, but she was desperate for a break from her husband's inattention.

"Hey." She cleared her throat when she heard the beep on the other end of the line. "I just wanted to say hi. I know we've been texting, but I just thought..."

Shut up, Kaki.

She sighed and tried again. "I'll talk to you later."

She ended the call and stood for a moment. Angry with herself. For letting Jordy get to her. For sinking low enough to call Owen. He'd moved on. God knew he had to have another girl by now, if not three or four. Might have been with someone when she called. He was into that. Lazy days spent in bed. A quick bang and a long nap.

On the verge of tears again, she swallowed them down and decided she'd call Lauren later. And maybe when she and Jordy got home, she and Lauren could go out for a drink or something and she would bow to Lauren and say *yes, dammit, you were right.*

Jordy hadn't moved when she returned to the umbrella. She studiously avoided looking at him as she sat down again. She almost dropped her phone back in the bag but decided against it. They'd talked about needing fun pictures to show family and friends when they were home. Pictures to convince everyone, including Jordy's slut, that they were indeed happily married. She turned to him then and took a shot of him out cold, ball cap still low over his forehead.

She glanced at the picture, refused to get caught up in it, and dropped her phone into her bag. Pulled her book out and sat back to relax. It was a thriller by one of her favorite authors, and it was good, but she wondered for a moment if she should find a smutty romance novel. A bodice ripper, she and Lauren had called them when they were younger. Would reading about hot, slippery skin and long, wet kisses and steamy, earth-moving sex help or send her over the edge?

CHAPTER NINE

SHE DIDN'T KNOW he was awake, so he watched her read for a while. Had no idea what she was reading, only that there was a picture of a knife on the cover, so he figured it wasn't trashy romance. Wondered if she knew her eyes grew wide sometimes, in disbelief or fear, maybe, as she read. That her lips twitched. Now and then, something apparently amused her, because she smiled. Twice, she laughed softly.

He closed his eyes again.

She didn't want to have his babies. Well. He would never have banked on it. Wouldn't have asked that of her. But still. Her reaction kind of stung. So he wasn't good enough for her; he got that. But c'mon. He wasn't like male hooker trash, was he? He'd been blessed with the best of both parents, and of their four sons, he'd been told he was the best looking. He wasn't sure about that. While he knew women everywhere turned to watch him walk by, he thought his bothers were all pretty easy on a girl's eyes, too.

So it wasn't like he had a face only a mother could love. He didn't have the build of a football player, but he was in good shape. He had some muscles. He didn't have the biggest damned dick out there, not that he'd ever engaged in comparison games but he was realistic, but he knew how to use what he had to give women a good time.

Apparently, Kaki just opposed the thought on moral grounds. He'd known she was reserved, conservative even, but he hadn't thought she was that uptight. Maybe it was her loss. That's what he told himself.

When his stomach rumbled the second time, he decided it was time to mosey up for lunch. Frozen pizza number six hundred eighteen. Or four, maybe, he'd lost count. Whatever. A couple more days and they would be winging their way back home. Back to the normal schedule, which unfortunately meant back to work at Steed Sporting Goods. Back to his regular run of women and casual sex, which he would be discreet about, but wouldn't necessarily give up. That thought brought his attention back to Kaki. He slitted his eyes open again and feasted on the view the skimpy suit gave him.

She laughed when his stomach growled again.

"Wow." Book still open, she turned to look at him. "Lunch time?"

He thought he wanted to argue with her, but that sweet smile reminded him she was his best friend. They shouldn't be having conversations about having babies together. He had no right to be pissed off at her for what she'd said. He was responsible for putting them in this situation, after all. Kaki was doing him a favor.

"Can you eat?"

She closed it now, finger holding her place and stretched her left hand up over her head. The deep breath lifted her breasts high, and Jordy let his eyes slide down over her smooth, tight belly to the strings tied in a bow on her hip. One tug. Just one quick tug would be all it took.

And then she'd probably slap him.

"Yeah." She nodded. "I'm hungry."

"Wanna go up?"

"Yeah. Let's." She pulled her bookmark from the back

pages and stuck it where her finger had been. He started to get up, but when she swung her legs off the opposite side of her chair and stood up, his eyes were drawn to her again. To her ass. Round and firm. Her suit was a bit twisted, and he noticed her tan line. Decided he really would like an opportunity to look at everything. Just one long, lingering look at her, from her head to her toes. He would notice things like tan lines and freckles. Birth marks, if she had any. The shape of her breasts. The color of her nipples. The scar he knew she had on her leg from a motorcycle accident she'd had when she was with the jerk, Tate Delaney. Luckily, they hadn't been moving fast, and according to an eyewitness, Tate had laid the bike down gently. She'd walked away with abrasions on her hands and a burn on her leg from the muffler. Tate broke his arm, and lucky for him, Lauren hadn't let Jordy near him or he would have broken his teeth, too.

"You coming?" She looked back at him over her shoulder as she picked up the bag.

"Yep." He moved quickly. Grabbed his towel from the chair and followed her across the sand. "How long was I out?"

"I don't know." She shrugged and looked up at him as he walked. "I went for a walk."

"You did? Without me?"

She smiled. Reached for his hand. His eyes traveled from hers down to their linked fingers. Funny how she'd all but ripped his heart out and killed his pride earlier about the baby thing, but one touch like this soothed him.

"I didn't wanna wake you."

He nodded. Probably he should thank her. But he didn't. They dodged two little kids racing down the beach, but Jordy didn't watch them. Not this time. Watching kids this morning had made him feel a little down, and they only had a couple days left here. No need to waste the sun and water and beach. He and Kaki should be laughing more. Having more fun.

How many best friends got to vacation together like this? So what if they were married? The rings and the paperwork didn't have to change their friendship.

"Frozen pizza?" she asked at the door of the condo, as she dug around in the bag for the key card.

"Sounds delicious, huh?" He grinned when she lifted her eyes to look at him. Propped a shoulder on the building while she stuck the key in the card reader and opened the door.

"Kinda makes me wanna barf," she answered honestly. They laughed as Kaki led them inside. She set the beach bag down by the door and fished her phone out. Looked at it as she headed to the bathroom. Jordy shivered in the air conditioning. He went the opposite way, to the kitchen, and turned the oven on. He had to pee, too, and standing here in the cold room only made it worse.

He grabbed the pizza from the freezer and set the box on the counter. Heard her come out of the bathroom so he headed in to take care of business. Kaki stood in the small hall between the bedroom and bathroom. Glanced up from her phone and smirked.

"What?" he asked quickly.

"Cold?"

She lowered her eyes to his chest, and Jordy looked down to find that his nipples were tight little beads. He stuck his tongue out at her and ducked on into the bathroom. He closed and locked the door, pushed his trucks down and then had to stand there for a few minutes because he was thinking about Kaki looking at his chest.

When he was finished and he'd washed his hands, he opened the bathroom door half hoping Kaki had put the pizza in the oven. Instead, he found her in the bedroom on her phone. He braced his arms over his head, against the doorframe. Raised his eyebrows when she turned to look at him.

She mouthed the words *my mom* when their eyes met. He

nodded. Stood for a moment longer, and then decided to have some fun with her. After all, if they were really newlyweds, wouldn't her mom expect him to bug her when she was on the phone? What would it hurt to pat her butt or nibble on her neck? She'd put her teeth on his ear earlier; he owed her something. She'd turned her back to him again, so when he moved up behind her and slid his hands around her hips and her belly, she jumped. He thought she moaned softly but decided probably she was going to say something to her mom and surprising her like this made her lose her train of thought.

Still. She dropped her hand to cover his. Slid her fingers down over the back of his hand and gave him a gentle squeeze. Jordy had been about to kiss her, to press his lips to the back of her neck, but he hesitated for a second. Long enough to wonder why she'd done it. Wasn't like her mom could *see* them. And then, rather than wonder about it, he decided to enjoy it for a second.

Kaki kept talking. Something about her brother. A job offer. Jordy closed his eyes, blocked her words but let her thick buttery voice wash over him. Kissed her. Just a sweet kiss on her neck. Parted his lips and breathed over her, traced a line up to her hairline. Still in his arms, still in the skimpy swimsuit, he felt her shiver. When he opened his eyes, he saw goose bumps on her skin. Wondered if she was cold.

Still talking, so he kissed her yet again. This time, he trailed his tongue over her neck to her ear. She did moan this time. Scrunched her shoulders up and dropped her head back.

"Jordy!" she hissed, but when he peeked, he saw that she was smiling. Laughing softly. Her fingers still holding his right hand in place, he moved his left. Up over her bare stomach. She jumped again when he stroked his fingertips over the triangle of material over her breast. Her nipple was already firm, definitely cold, but fire exploded in his groin when he felt it tighten against his fingers.

He nibbled on her ear.

"Cold?" he whispered.

She laughed again. He was disappointed when she moved her hand from his, but before he could step away from her, she touched him. Closed her fingers around his other hand, the one at her breast. He shifted behind her, because the thought of her nipples under the damp suit brought his dick to life again. He couldn't hide it, but he could take care where it rubbed against her.

Brain fried, his thoughts in Kaki's suit, his hand hovering over her breast with her hand holding him there, he didn't realize she'd ended the call until she turned to him with a smile. Laughing again, not at him but with him, she pulled the phone away from her ear.

"I can't believe you—"

He raised his eyebrows as he lifted his other hand from her belly to cup her chin. Raked those fingers under her jawbone and up into her messy ponytail as he leaned in to kiss her. A real kiss. No one watching or listening but to hell with it. He *wanted* to kiss her. He wanted to lick her lips and see what the perfect natural pink tasted like.

"Jord—"

He cut her off. Her lips still parted, he took advantage and slipped his tongue between them. So far, natural pink tasted pretty fucking good, and he wanted more. His fingers cupped the back of her head as he rubbed his lips over hers.

"Kaki?" he breathed her name. Scared to death she would say *no* and terrified she would say *yes*.

She didn't say a word. She lifted his free hand to their mouths and broke their kiss long enough to kiss the palm of his hand.

Go.

Surely, that meant *go*.

He forgot who he was and the reputation he had for finesse, and he plunged his tongue inside her mouth, greedy for more of her. Part of him worried that she would think he was a jerk, or worse, that she wouldn't think he was a good kisser, but part of him was desperate for more. For his tongue on her skin. Her hands on him.

She was breathing heavy when he ended the kiss. He waited. Scared that was it. That she would send his ass packing or tell him to go eat his lunch. To leave her alone. Fire burned through him, down low in the pit of his gut and his inner thighs and made his cock throb with need when she kissed him again. A quick, desperate kiss. She turned then, tossed her phone at the bed, and then looked back at him.

"Fuck." He groaned when she pressed into him. Her hot silky mouth claimed his, and she wound her arms around his neck. Scraped her fingernails over his skin, up into his hair as their tongues danced and slicked and rubbed. He dragged his hands down her sides, fascinated with her smooth skin. Rested them on her hips and toyed with the strings on her bikini. One tug and they would fall away. He could slide his hands over her bare skin. Cup her in the palm of his hand. Tease her. Slip his fingers inside her hot, wet center.

They walked backward to the bed, and then they were falling together, holding onto each other. Kaki kissed him back. She didn't sit back and wait for him to move; she took what she wanted. She sucked his lip into her mouth and then stroked her tongue into his mouth, her hands still in his hair, her body supple and warm now beneath his.

He kissed the corner of her mouth. Moved to flick his tongue over her pulse below her ear. Sucked her skin into his mouth. Nipped his way lower, her hands smoothing over his shoulders. Molding his muscles.

"Jordy," she whispered.

Head poised over her breast, he lifted his eyes to look at her. Head thrown back, he saw her parted lips, heard her shallow breathing and her soft moans. Let his eyes move over her bare neck and her breasts, barely covered by the wicked little swimsuit he'd pay a million bucks just to see her wear again.

Eyes still watching her, he lowered his mouth to her breast. Nipped at her nipple through the white material.

"Oh my god, Jordy," she hissed. Drew her knees up and lifted her hips to grind against him.

"Jesus, Kak—-"

"Jordy." She combed her fingers up through his hair again and pushed him gently back to her breast. He opened his mouth, nudged her nipple and the suit with his tongue and was rewarded with a whimper and a shiver that tore through her whole body.

He lifted his head and moved back up to kiss her. The press of their bodies together, the warm skin-to-skin contact made his heart pound in his throat. In his tongue. His ears.

She met his eyes and parted her lips to kiss him again. All tongue this time. Jordy rocked up in the v of her thighs, his erection snug against her. He tugged gently at the string around her neck. Breathed deeply when he felt it give. His fingertips tingled as he pushed the scrap of material out of his way. Traced his fingers over the swell of her breast and felt her nipple bead at his fingertips.

"Please," she whispered.

He lifted his head when he heard her phone buzz. Fingers still pinching her nipple just slightly, he glanced at the screen and saw the name Owen. Owen? Who the fuck was Owen?

"Jordy." She lifted her head to look at him, her face a mix of need and desire.

The guy on the beach? The nerd on the beach? Calling Kaki? Seriously?

He rolled off her and stood up.

"What—?" She lifted herself to rest on her elbows. "What's...what're you—?"

He covered his face with his hands, turned his back to her, and paced away from the bed. His cock throbbed in protest when he heard her frustrated groan. She wanted it. Right now, Kaki Harper Steed wanted him.

No, she didn't. She might want sex right at this very second, but that didn't mean she wanted him. He could climb back on top of her and put his hands and mouth all over her scorching hot body. He knew he would enjoy it, and he was confident he would make it good for her. But what then? She would hate him. She would hate him for taking advantage of this whole asinine situation.

And besides that, if she was down here hooking up with a dickhead she met on the beach, some dickhead named Owen, she could fucking have him. Jordy wasn't hard up for sex. He hadn't done it. The whole week he'd left her here in the condo late at night and strolled the beach in the moonlight. Flirted. Hell yes, he'd flirted with more girls than he could count. But he'd behaved, kept his dick tucked away, all zipped and locked up.

And now to think maybe Kaki was banging somebody? Maybe some dumbass sci-fi guy thought he was a hotshot because he'd laid a hot babe like Kaki? Jordy wished he'd have decked the fuckwad when he'd considered it the other day by the water.

"Are you kidding me?"

When Kaki finally managed to get a complete sentence out, he scrubbed his hands over his face and back up over his head. Turned to look at her, nearly nude on the bed they were sharing, bikini top untied and her left breast spilling out.

"We can't do this."

"What?"

He shrugged. "We weren't gonna do this, remember?"

When she only gaped at him—shocked that Jordy Steed could say no when offered the perfect blend of curves and heat and generosity?—he shook his head and paced back to the window, back to her.

"No?" She huffed out a huge breath, heavy with frustration. Anger. "You're saying no? Now?"

"Kaks." He took a deep breath. "You're my best friend."

Would his best friend screw around on their honeymoon? What the hell did she see in that guy, anyway? He looked like every overgrown fifteen-year-old geek guy in all the stupid romance movies. Jordy grinded his teeth together and bit off another string of four letter words. If the geek on the beach were like a romance movie guy, that meant he'd get the girl.

Jordy propped his hands on his hips and hung his head. Hit him like a fastball between the eyeballs. He didn't want someone else to have her; he didn't want *anyone* else to have her. She was his. Right now, Kaki Harper Steed was his woman, his wife, and therefore no other man out there had the right to look at her, let alone entertain thoughts about what he'd just been doing to her.

"Did you forget that? When you started this?" Her voice was huskier than normal. He glanced at her to find her sitting up now, right hand pinning the loose side of the bikini to her chest.

He nodded when their eyes met. Turned away again.

"If we add this to what we've already done..." He turned to her but kept his distance. "If we add sex to this...joke of a marriage...there's no way we'll still be friends when it's over."

She drew her knees up, prim and proper, legs together now, instead of wide open to accommodate him as they had been only moments before. Rested her elbow on her knee and covered her eyes with her hand.

"Kaks—"

She shook her head.

"Just..."

Was she crying? What the hell?

"Kaks, are you okay?"

"Jordy." She lifted her head to look at him. No tears. In fact, she looked pissed. Good. This was her damned fault. Slinking around in that skimpy bikini, turning him on like he hadn't sex in a year, and then having that dumbass guy on the beach call right in the middle of it. What guy could lay here and make love to her wondering what the hell was going on between her and *Owen*?

"Look—"

"Just gimme a minute?" she snapped. "Please?"

While he watched, she reached back and yanked the pony-tail holder from her hair, still holding the suit up to cover her breasts.

"Yeah." He shrugged when she looked at him again. "Yeah. I'll be out..."

He nodded to the door, but she wasn't looking at him. She'd already dismissed him. He stalked out of the bedroom, out the short hallway, to the living area. The whole place smelled a little like pizza from all the previous days he'd thrown the frozen pies in the oven.

CHAPTER TEN

KAKI FLOPPED backwards on the bed when Jordy walked out. Her thighs were still quivering with anticipation, and no matter how hard her brain tried to tell her body it wasn't happening, she couldn't catch her breath. She was pissed, too, so it was sort of hard to tell where the desire stopped and the pissed off kicked in.

What the hell had he been thinking? Coming on to her like that only to walk away? Had he done it on purpose? Wasn't like he'd just been overcome with lust for her and made a play thinking he would get lucky. Kaki doubted Jordy would consider sex with her getting lucky. So what did that leave? Why would he dick around with her like that?

Okay, sure. She'd been on the phone with her mom. He'd wanted her to make a little noise to make it sound like they were typical newlyweds enjoying each other's company. But he'd kept it going when she ended the call. Why hadn't he walked away then? God, okay, they were best friends. She loved the guy to the moon and back, but did he not realize this was a really sucky thing to do?

He'd been hard. She'd felt his erection sliding over her

center. Apparently, he'd just come to his senses and realized he was about to do her. His wife. His plain little friend from grade school.

"Kaks?" He knocked on the still open door, but to his credit, he didn't step inside. She looked at him over her head, without turning to him.

"Go away."

"Do you want some of this?"

She snorted sarcastically, and Jordy cleared his throat.

"Pizza," he asked quietly. "Do you want some of the pizza?"

"I dunno."

"I could—"

"Jordy."

"Sorry."

She sighed again when he walked away. Decided to shower. Put some real clothes on. Maybe rip the white bikini to shreds and toss it. Burn it. She sat up and scooted to the edge of the bed. Picked up her phone as she stood and then fished in her suitcase for clean clothes. She saw him from the corner of her eye when she passed from the bedroom to the bathroom, but she didn't look at him.

Door closed and locked, she shucked the suit and turned the shower on. Didn't take a second for self-scrutiny. She'd known from day one Jordy had no interest in her, not that kind of interest, and she'd let herself get caught up in the possibilities. She laughed out loud as she climbed into the shower.

Possibilities of what, Kaki? Joining the ranks of women Jordy had fucked and forgotten? She didn't want to be on that list, anyway. Ever. He'd done her a favor, coming to his senses like that.

She didn't hurry through the shower, but she didn't linger, either. Yes, she was still a little irritated with Jordy for what had happened, but on the other hand, she'd been all in, willing (okay, desperate) for him to touch her. To make love to her. She snorted again at her word choice. Okay, she'd wanted Jordy to do her, that list of his women be damned. She couldn't take it all out on him. She could have stopped it before it ever got that far.

She shut the water off and toweled herself dry. Rubbed lotion over her body, again without paying any attention to her nice tan or her girl parts that had been begging for Jordy's touch only a half hour ago, if that. Combed through her hair and sprayed a bit of mousse in it. She didn't bother with drying or styling it, no makeup. Because she sure wasn't trying to impress anyone here, especially not her husband.

The condo felt empty when she opened the bathroom door. She stood for a moment, the stupid bikini in hand, and listened. Nothing. So he'd slammed down some of the pizza and left her alone. She sighed in defeat and slumped in the doorway.

It hurt, and the fact that it hurt told her that even though she didn't think Jordy had stopped out of chivalry and friendship, she was glad he had stopped. Five minutes of ecstasy with him wasn't worth killing their friendship. Now the rest of their honeymoon would suck. He'd go his way, and do God knows what. Sure, he was leaving her alone at night to get some action, but at least they'd been hanging out together and having some fun during the day. That was over now.

She dragged her hand back through her hair and crossed the hall to the bedroom. Put the suit in the plastic bag she'd packed for dirty clothes. No need to let it hang and dry if she was going to toss it. And she didn't want to have to look at it and be reminded of how humiliated she'd been, lying on their bed, boobs falling out of her top, pleading with Jordy to come back. Not her finest moment and one that would surely haunt her for the next five years.

When she left the bedroom, her mind on what she could eat for lunch, because she sure didn't want to sit up here alone and eat what was left of Jordy's stupid frozen sausage pizza, she heard the sliding door to the balcony open and glanced that way.

"Hey." He offered her a small, pained smile. "You okay?'

Just right at the moment, she was. He hadn't left her up here alone to stew over what had or hadn't happened. That was something, anyway.

She nodded, but she was quick to look away, embarrassed still by the scene in the bedroom. Maybe he should feel the same. After all, her nipples got hard and she'd been breathing heavy, but that was all he could see. His excitement, even if it was simply biology, had been obvious like a flagpole in his trunks.

"Yeah."

"Wanna sit outside with me?" he asked hopefully as he carried his empty paper plate across the room. "It's nice and hot."

She laughed softly and shrugged. "Yeah, I guess."

"Wanna beer?"

"Yep." She didn't have to think about that one. She needed a beer. Maybe two. Or six.

She grabbed the two smallest slices of pizza and put them on a paper plate. Grabbed a napkin, because if he thought he was going to lick pizza sauce off her face now, she might throat punch him. With a glance his way, he was grabbing a beer for her, she turned and headed toward the door.

He was behind her, so she left the door open when she stepped outside. Put her plate on the little table and then moved to the railing again. Looked out at the people on the beach; it was crowded now. Lifted her gaze further out to the water.

"Kaks."

He sidled up to her at the railing, but she didn't look at him.

"I'm sorry."

The words went a long way toward soothing her hurt feelings, taking the sting out of the humiliation. Nothing would erase that feeling, but knowing he meant it, knowing he felt bad for what had happened—after all, he might not be into her as a girl, but they'd been too damned close through the years for him not to mean it—made her feel somewhat better.

She acknowledged his words with a slight nod.

"It should—"

"Don't." She closed her eyes for a second. "Just...let it go."

When he didn't say anything, she finally opened her eyes and glanced at him. He looked contrite. Like a puppy she'd kicked in the teeth, actually, and she felt a flash of guilt. Then again, why should she be sorry? What had she done wrong?

"K." He nodded.

She moved when he did. To sit down. Took a long drink of the beer and decided it tasted damned good.

"So." He shoved half a piece of pizza in his mouth and grinned as he chewed and tried to talk at the same time. "You showered? You're not going back down?"

"No." She picked a piece of sausage from one of her slices and popped it in her mouth.

"Kaki—"

"It's fine, Jordy." She raised her eyebrows in a dare for him to say more. "Maybe I'll take a nap. Or read."

He shrugged. Folded the remainder of his piece in half and took another big bite.

"K. It's just more fun with you around."

"Right." She nodded and turned her attention back to her beer.

"We could go..." He leaned his chair back and balanced it on the back legs. "Buy goofy souvenirs for Lauren and Tyler."

"No."

"Or we could get something for the baby. Like one of those cheesy suit things that says something about my aunt and uncle went to the beach and all I got was this damned onesie."

Okay, that got her. Good idea. And she was touched that Jordy was thinking about Lauren and Tyler's baby.

"Except we're not the baby's aunt and uncle," she pointed out.

"So just now." He wiped his mouth with his napkin, chewed the last bite of pizza, and downed a swallow of beer. Pointed at her with his bottle in hand. "You're making me think of the time when we were in eighth grade. And there were like five of us who ditched afternoon classes. Remember?"

She did remember, but she didn't want to sit here and reminisce with him. Not now.

"We skipped out of school after lunch hour. We were all in. And when we got caught, when they pressured you, you ratted me and Dalton Kretzer out."

She had to laugh, but she didn't want to.

"A smile." He leaned across the table, bottle in hand, as if he wanted to high five her. "You have a gorgeous resting bitch face, but it's so much prettier when you smile."

"Shut up." She laughed out loud this time. "You've used your up *being a dick* rations for today. Don't push me."

"Me? Be a dick?" he argued quickly. Set his beer on the table. "Kaks, I was trying to be a gentleman."

"Then you shouldn't have started it."

"You shouldn't have let me."

She held her hand up to stop him. "I know. It was stupid. Shouldn't have happened. I don't wanna talk about it."

"But you brought it up."

"Shut up."

"Women." He groaned. "Never thought I'd say that about you."

"You never noticed I had boobs before?" She blurted the words out before she could stop herself.

Jordy curled his lips and stared at her for a moment. "I'm not touching that one." He shook his head.

"Yeah, you already did," she mumbled.

Jordy threw his head back and laughed. "I don't know this side of you near as well as I know it in Lauren."

Kaki eyed him curiously. "Define *this side* of me."

He opened his mouth to answer her. Stopped. Closed his mouth. Frowned. Opened it again and closed it again immediately.

"*The* Jordy Steed." She grinned. "Speechless."

"Wait, wait." He held up his hand and shook his head. "Lauren always spoke very freely about sex. And the things she did. You don't. You never have."

"And yet, surely you realize, I'm a woman, and I do have sex."

"Well, yeah. But." He shrugged. "It's not something I spend a lot of time thinking about."

"But you do spend time thinking about Lauren? And her sex life?"

"There's more to visualize?" he suggested.

"Oh my God." She rolled her eyes. "I hope you don't do that now. She's married!"

"I'm kidding."

"You're not." She stood up and picked up their plates. Hooked her finger around the neck of her bottle.

"What're you gonna do?"

"Read."

"Let's go do something. Together." He looked up at her with that puppy dog face again. "Let me take a quick shower, and we can go play putt putt or something."

She stared at him for a moment and finally shrugged in defeat.

"Whatever."

Jordy climbed to his feet as she pulled the door open.

"Your enthusiasm overwhelms me."

"Yeah, well you took earth-moving sex off the table and replaced it with miniature golf." She looked back at him over her shoulder. "Do you blame me?"

"How do you know it would be earth-moving?"

"I've heard lots of stories about you. Women all over town talking about riding Steed."

"I have three brothers," he reminded her. "They could be talking about them."

"Um..." She narrowed her eyes in thought as she tossed the paper plates and napkins in the garbage can under the sink. "Let me think. What else have I heard about you? Oh. Jordo the Dildo."

"What?" he yelped. "Are you kidding me?"

"Nope."

"That's insulting."

"Why? I thought you liked your playboy lifestyle."

"Well..." He shrugged as she drained her beer and rinsed the bottle out. "But there's more to me than..."

"Hey." She shook her head. "I didn't make it up. You've earned your reputation."

He took a deep breath. Looked at her silently for a moment.

"What?" She looked around for the beach bag and crossed the room to grab her book from it when she found it.

"Did your mom..." He cleared his throat. "You know..."

"Did my mom think that my husband was messing around trying to get in my pants on our honeymoon?"

Their eyes met. Jordy's Adam's apple bobbed when he swallowed.

"Yeah."

"Yep. She fell for it just the same as I did."

"Kaks." He raised his hands and shoved his fingers back

through his hair. "Dammit. Don't. I wanted...to do it. I want...but—"

"It's okay, Jordy," she said quietly. "Anyone asks me about the honeymoon, I'll tell them we hardly saw the beach because we were so busy in the bedroom."

Jordy stared a moment longer. Pressed his lips in a grim line and finally gave her a curt nod.

CHAPTER ELEVEN

THE OUTBACK FELT a little too small to Jordy. He was packed in too tightly with Kaki, and he wasn't sure if that bothered him because an hour ago, he'd been grinding on her, with his mouth all but sucking on her breast or if it was because he knew she was still mad about the whole thing or if that because she was still peeved about what he'd started and walked away from, she'd taken a shot at him. Well, more than one, really.

As he navigated the black SUV out of the condo's parking lot and out to US-98, his mind kept dragging him back to the condo and the things she'd said. More than what she said, it was how it had affected him that bothered him. Maybe when he was younger, he thought he was a hotshot. Maybe knowing women liked riding the steed or that they called him Jordo the Dildo would have stroked his ego. Before. Now that he was married to Kaki, even if it wasn't real, he was embarrassed. He'd wanted to dig a hole in the floor of the condo right down to the sand and ground under it, where he could bury himself when his wife-*his best friend*-filled him in on the things she'd heard other women say about him.

As if that wasn't enough to brood over, he was stuck on

what she'd said on the deck. Yeah, the thing about him starting something he wasn't willing to finish bothered him, but she'd had to go and say that thing about how she was a woman and she had sex. She hadn't *said* she liked it, but he'd be willing to bet from the brazen way she'd reminded him she's a woman and her aggressiveness in the bedroom before that she enjoyed sex. God, maybe as much as Lauren, and dammit to hell if Jordy wasn't intrigued by the thought. He wanted to know more.

He didn't just want to take Kaki back to the bedroom and rub his body all over hers and then undress her one piece of clothing at a time and then lick her from head to toe, he wanted to hear about her adventures in the bedroom. Or the car. Or the gym or locker room or movie theater or wherever the hell she'd done the deed. He wanted to know it all.

He wanted to know Kaki the way they both knew Lauren. The way both girls knew him.

And if he asked her a question like that—if he asked her if she'd ever gone down on someone at a movie or hitched her skirt up in a bathroom stall, if he asked if she'd ever watched porn and touched herself as Lauren had admitted to more than once—she'd probably throat punch him all the way to next year.

"Do you?"

He turned his eyes to her now when she bumped his arm. The right one stretched out, wrist slung over the steering wheel.

"What?" He shook his head.

"I asked if you like it."

Jordy cleared his throat. He had no idea what the hell she was referring to, because he wasn't listening to her, and the only thing on his mind right now was sex. If he told her that, if he said yes, he most certainly did like sex in any fashion, shape, or form, he'd only be validating her already low opinion of him.

He frowned. Wasn't like that. Well. Okay. It was like that. But right now, his mind was on Kaki. Making love with Kaki. He coughed. He'd never thought those words before, not just adding Kaki on at the end, but *making love*. He'd never considered the things he did to women, the things they did to him as *making love*. And right now, he was consumed with the idea of making slow, sweet love to her and lingering in bed with her all day. Kissing her. Holding her.

What the hell was wrong with him? God, but he needed to get home and get back to normal. So he hadn't been able to do it here. To pull the trigger. Well, no, he hadn't pulled that trigger with Kaks, but he hadn't been interested enough in the girls he'd seen down here to hook up. Maybe on some level, the thought made him feel a little guilty. They'd traveled here together; it would be really jerkish of him to sneak away and spend an afternoon or evening with another woman. But when they got home? Fair game. There were girls he *could* call who would drop everything and run to him.

He grunted an answer that meant nothing, hoping she'd let it go. Didn't want to admit to her that he hadn't been paying attention.

"The song, Jordy."

He wasn't looking at her, but he could hear her roll her eyes with that tone of voice.

"Um." He rubbed his forehead with his free hand and shook his head. "What is it?"

"I dunno. I thought you would." She reached over to turn the volume down a bit. "I think it's Jack White, but I'm not sure."

"Mmm." He shrugged. "You could Shazam it."

She nodded, but she didn't dig for her phone. He wondered if she'd seen that Owen had called. If the guy had left her a message. If she'd made plans to meet him later or something.

She rode the rest of the way in silence, which made Jordy

feel bad. He'd insisted they do something together this afternoon, and now he was spaced out and not listening to her when she talked. Edgy and a little defensive about how he was acting. Not a good combination.

Thankfully, they were in the SUV for no more than twenty minutes. Jordy had been ready to turn the radio up and sing with Billy Squier when he'd seen the big neon sign for the mini golf place they'd staked out on his phone. As much as he liked Billy Squier, he doubted Kaki would like his version of any Billy Squier song, so he climbed out of the SUV with a smile on his face and watched Kaki lean back into the car to paw through her purse for her phone. She wore a scoop neck tee and leaning like that afforded him a peek at her sweet breasts, and he felt a rush of regret for earlier. For walking away from her, from what would be his only chance to be with her. But also for starting anything in the first place.

How long was the picture of her, lounging on the bed, half of her bikini falling off and her breast spilling out going to haunt him? Bigger than he'd thought, a perfect round globe, with just the hint of a pert little pink nipple peeking out at him. Her lips parted as she panted and watched him move away from her.

He'd never get that image out of his head.

Not in a million years, not in two or five or ten girls.

Never.

He'd had a taste of perfection, and now he had the sick feeling she'd ruined him for everyone else.

"Ready?" She scooted back out of the SUV and closed the door. He nodded as she tucked her phone in the back pocket of her denim shorts.

"You wanna put your purse in the back?"

"No. I left my billfold in the safe at the condo."

"Okay."

As she stepped up beside him, he started walking. It startled him when she reached for his hand.

"I'm sorry," she said quietly. "For…all of it."

He looked at her as they walked. "It's not your fault."

"I said things I shouldn't have."

He considered her words, her tone. Thought if she was apologizing, and he'd apologized, they were reaffirming their friendship, and he wanted to seal it with a kiss. But that would only lead them right back to where they were.

Instead, he only nodded in response.

"Have you gotten any better at this?" he asked, pointing ahead at the twisty, hilly putt putt course.

"You're thinking of Lauren," she reminded him. "Lauren has the three digit scores."

He laughed softly. "Yeah, but you're not very good, either. Maybe I'll play left handed."

"Remember when she sort of teed off? On hole fifteen at home?"

"And sailed her ball across the parking lot and hit the Harley motorcycle?" he deadpanned. "No."

"And the time she lost her putter?"

"She didn't lose it!" Jordy laughed as he pulled the door open for her, and they stepped inside. He shivered when the blast of cold air hit him. Almost looked at Kaki to remark on the fact that air conditioning in the summer was a cruel necessity, but he thought better of it. He didn't want to know if she was cold. "She threw it."

Kaki snorted. As he stepped up to pay for the two of them to play, he saw her nod.

"You don't have to buy everything," she told him.

"My parents could buy the course," he reminded her. "Besides, I got you into this mess."

"It's not a mess."

She studied the balls on the counter and selected light green. He'd known she wouldn't take pink. Lauren was the pink girl; Kaks hated the color on anything. He grabbed the navy blue ball, thought his balls might have been about that color earlier in the day, and they took the putters the kid at the counter handed them.

"You know what we should do?" he said as they walked outside to the first hole. The place was busy, but not packed, and Jordy didn't see anyone on the first three holes. Hoped there wouldn't be anyone following too closely, because while it was true that Lauren had scored in triple digits before, Kaki wasn't a great putter, either.

"Go to that beach art store and see if we can sign up for pottery lessons?"

"So close, but no." He watched her set her ball down on the mat and then study the hole at the end of the twisty first green. As if it mattered. She could study it for hours and still score a seven.

"I give."

"When we get home, we should go golfing."

"Yeah? You're having such a blast now you wanna do it again already when we get home?"

"Not miniature golf. Real golf."

Kaki laughed and took her shot at the same time. Jordy watched the ball roll to a stop on the lip of the hole.

"Damn." He nodded at her, impressed. "Almost got lucky."

"No kidding." She cleared her throat.

Their eyes met, and a hundred emotions rushed between them. Finally they both laughed and looked away. Jordy took his turn, sent his ball a little too hard to the wrong corner before the twist and into the far corner by the hole. He looked up to find Kaki studying the goofy stuff around the golf course. Made him think about those kids again on the beach. His nieces and nephews. The fact that if he didn't grow up and find the right woman soon, he might never be a dad.

"So. I suck at putt putt," Kaki absently dragged her eyes from the course décor and brought them around to look at him, "but you want me to go play real golf. Because why?"

He grinned.

"Might be fun."

"For you," she agreed.

"We could go to lessons," he suggested. Kaki tapped her ball in and then watched him putt his in from the corner.

"Lessons."

"Golf lessons. We could go to the pro. At the course."

"Why would we do that?" She shook her head.

He didn't answer her. Wondered if she thought the idea of golf was a bad one, or if she was opposed to spending time with him. They played on, kept the pace steady and stayed a few holes behind the people ahead of them. Jordy noticed when another couple started on the first hole, but he and Kaki were far enough along, it wouldn't be a big deal.

"So." He studied his putter on the eighth hole. Eyed the water all around them. Located the net he'd have to use to fetch his or her ball if they putted into the water, which he figured one of them would do. "Michael got a job offer?"

"He did, yep. In San Antonio."

"Oh!" Jordy putted his turn and looked up at Kaki. "How's Mom taking that?"

"She's not happy."

"What's the offer?"

"I don't know. Some entry level accounting position."

"He can't find an entry level position closer to home?"

"I'm sure he could, but he doesn't want to."

Jordy raised his eyebrows. Couldn't say he blamed him. Kaki's younger brother was the adventurous type. Nothing like Kaki. Well. Nothing like the woman Jordy had assumed her to be. Seemed there was a lot more to his wife than he'd ever guessed.

"Is he gonna take it?"

"I don't know." Kaki frowned and shrugged. "I'm kind of surprised that he hasn't called me about it."

"You'll tell him to stay."

Kaki eyed him curiously. "Why would you say that?"

"If he asked you for advice, you wouldn't tell him to stay?"

"No. I think I'd tell him to go. At least for a while."

"Ever been?" Jordy asked. He watched her tap her ball in, and then they walked together to the next hole.

"To San Antonio?"

"Yeah."

"Been to Texas but not San Antonio. Why?" She looked at him quickly. "Have you?"

"Dallas. Fort Worth. Houston. Never San Antonio."

"Well, there ya go. Put a trip to San Antonio on our bucket list right under golf lessons."

They stood toe-to-toe at the mat for the next hole. Close enough that he could smell her perfume. If he leaned forward just a bit, he could kiss her. He wouldn't, but he could. Kind of figured he was going to notice every possible opportunity to kiss her now that he couldn't do it anymore. Worse than a breakup, really. In a breakup, at least you had the right to kiss someone, touch her. In an effort to win her back. Kaki was his wife, but she'd never been his to lose and so he had no rights to kiss her to win her back. In fact, if he kissed her now, she might throw in the towel and walk away from their charade. He didn't much give a damn now about getting Brianna back, didn't really give a damn about making her jealous. But he wasn't in any hurry to call the marriage shenanigans off.

"I will." He held her gaze for a long moment, the look almost more intimate than a kiss would have been.

CHAPTER TWELVE

THEY SLEPT LATE the next morning. Kaki was exhausted, possibly more so than she had been when she'd gone to bed. Had nothing to do with the hot guy in bed beside her. Maybe they'd played too hard yesterday. Thirty-six holes of miniature golf and laser tag. Ice cream treats. Jordy had suggested bumper boats, but she'd refused, so they'd driven go-carts instead. Topped it all off with early evening bowling, perhaps the one thing Jordy wasn't terribly good at, and then a seafood dinner on the beach. They'd buried the incident, and they'd been having so much fun that when they got back to the condo, they'd walked on the beach. They'd both slipped their flip-flops off and carried them; Jordy had reached for her hand as they walked. Even that wasn't enough, so they'd sat on the balcony again, and they'd each killed a couple of beers, and Kaki hadn't been drunk when she'd gone to bed. But she'd been mellow.

She suspected, though, that she was just tired. It had been a busy engagement. Hadn't been a one-act play. Jordy had put the ring on her finger, but she'd had starring roles in other acts. She'd had to convince their families and friends, other than Lauren and Tyler, that they were very much in love and so happy they'd realized their true feelings for each other. She'd had to do the dress shopping and picking out bridesmaids' dresses, and she'd handled a lot of the catering and cake details. Jordy had done a lot, but Kaki carried most of that weight. She'd had to dazzle her guests at the wedding shower Jordy's brothers' wives had thrown for her. And she'd had to show up for the award winning acting the day of the wedding. The walk down the church aisle had seemed miles long. Add in the vows she'd made. The walk back down the aisle with her husband. All of the pictures had been taxing enough to give her a headache. She'd had a hell of a time smiling for the photographer when she knew she had no intention of ordering a mega package of photos. The reception had been exhausting. Fun, yes, but tiring. And now the week on the beach. The sun had drained her. Fighting with Jordy yesterday had really sucked the life out of her. And playing all day yesterday after the fight had worn her out.

Thinking about flying tomorrow. Going home to that big brick bungalow she now shared with Jordy. Turning it from a nice house to a home was going to take a lot of work. And heart. As much as she loved Jordy, she wasn't sure she had the heart for the job. And the thought of going back to work on Tuesday, thankfully, they'd given her one last day to recover, and having all of her friends cornering her and asking questions about Florida and the beach and the honeymoon promised for another day that would completely drain her.

"What's wrong?"

She lay on her side with her back to him. The drapes were pulled, but morning light pushed through the slight opening in the panels and lit the room in shades of gray. Kaki took a deep breath.

"Nothing."

How could he tell something was wrong? And what could she tell him?

"You've been tossing and turning for awhile now."

"I'm just tired." She rolled back just enough to look at him.

"Ready to go home tomorrow? Or would you stay another week if we could?"

Kaki laughed softly and flopped over on her back. "Jordy, you're you. If I said I wanted to stay another week, you'd pull strings and we'd stay another week."

On his back, hands stacked under his head, he grinned at the ceiling.

"Do you? Wanna stay?"

"No."

"Did you like it?" He turned his head just enough to look at her. "It was fun, wasn't it?"

"Yeah. It was great." She nodded. "Nice to get away."

"What should we do today?"

"Well. I'm thinking we could go to the beach."

The slow grin that crossed his face stole her breath away. When he looked back at the ceiling, she let her eyes slide over his bare chest and arms. Folded as they were, his arms looked bigger. Kaki caught herself before she could reach out and touch him. Stroke the skin over his muscle. Try and wrap her fingers around his bicep.

"The beach it is," he agreed.

"Yesterday was fun," she told him. She'd said so last night, and he'd said so, and she felt stupid now for saying it again. But she didn't want the bad feeling to linger and follow them home.

"Kaks?"

"Hmm?"

"Will we still do that stuff at home?"

"What stuff?"

He shrugged, but he seemed to be trying hard not to look at her.

"The fun stuff. We'll still hang out, won't we?"

"Jordy, our whole world thinks we're madly in love. We have to."

"Ouch." He locked his gaze with hers. "Is that how you feel about it? Being together? That we have—"

"No." She shook her head. "You know I didn't mean it like that."

"I mean, I guess…I know you have your own life. At home. And I have mine. And I'm gonna miss it being just you and me down here."

Kaki blinked and looked away. Stupid. Stupid. Stupid. To let his words get to her. For one thing, it hadn't been just the two of them down here, or else he wouldn't have had to leave the condo alone at night when he had. Still. Sometimes, with Jordy especially, her heart listened harder than her brain.

"Me too." She nodded, but she looked away quickly, afraid he might see something in her eyes that she didn't care to admit.

"Can I tell you something?" He rolled to his side now to face her. Brought his left hand down to stroke his fingers over her face.

"What?"

"You're the first woman I've slept with."

He had such a sweet look on his face. His eyes were wistful, and a tiny smile tugged at his lips, and Kaki's eyes were drawn back to his. Who needed blue bedroom eyes? Jordy's green eyes were so sexy and warm.

And yet, what he'd just said made her laugh. Maybe she was the first woman he'd slept with, but she'd bet she was next to the last woman in Prior that he didn't know in a biblical sense.

"You're not supposed to laugh," he scolded her.

"Sorry."

"I was gonna tell you I like sleeping next to you." He lifted himself on his elbow to look at her. "I think I sleep better when I know you're here."

She didn't know what to make of what he said, let alone how to answer him. Before she could make up her mind if she was supposed to say anything at all, he leaned over and touched his lips to hers in a sweet kiss, there and gone so fast she wondered if she'd imagined it.

He sat up, stretched his arms up over his head. Kaki raked her eyes over his back, desperately wanted to touch him. Just to skim her fingernails lightly up his spine and see him shiver. She didn't. She didn't linger on that kiss, either. It had been a completely different kind of kiss than yesterday's. Sweet and soft and friendly, even. Made her smile.

She rolled back to her side as he scooted to his side of the bed and stood up.

Yesterday's kisses had left her body aching in all the wrong spots. Right spots. Depended on how she looked at it, she guessed. This one kind of made her heart hurt, but she only swallowed that feeling down and watched him round the bed and head out of the bedroom to the bathroom.

She missed Lauren and Tyler. Not Owen, though yesterday she'd missed him something fierce just because he'd have been good for the ten or fifteen minutes she'd have needed here in this bed. At the moment, she doubted she'd even call him right away when they got home. Maybe she just wouldn't call. Time to put an end to that, anyway. She didn't need him. Who said any woman needed a man to be happy?

She did miss Lauren, though. And her family. Even Jordy's family, although they made her nervous now like they never had before. His sisters-in-law had teased her mercilessly at her bachelorette party. Given her naughty gifts. Silky negligees. Lacy thongs. Black, nude tones, pale pearly pink.

They'd roared with laughter when she'd opened the crotch-less panties from Lauren. Made sure Jordy's brothers knew about them, too, so Kaki had been teased to the nth degree about it.

Still. As hard as this week alone with Jordy had been, she hated to leave. They'd spent a lot of time together, the way they had years ago when they were kids. Going home meant going back to reality. And reality, even if they were happily, really married and certainly since they were fake married, meant sharing Jordy with everyone else. Including letting him run with other women or girls or however he liked his females. And letting him go back to Brianna if and when she started sniffing around again. The thought made her sad.

"Hey."

She blinked and looked at the doorway, at Jordy, leaning in it like he had the day before.

"Hmm?"

"I made coffee for you."

"You made coffee for me?" she asked quietly. She tried to school her face into a hopeful smile but figured she was frowning. What did a guy who drank a Mountain Dew with his breakfast every morning know about making coffee?

"Mm-hmm."

"How do you know how to make coffee?" She pushed herself up to her elbow to look at him.

"I texted Lauren."

"You texted—what?" She sat up. "You can't text Lauren. She's at work."

"Yeah, well, I did. Caught her on her break. So she told me."

"Hmm." Kaki pursed her lips. "Thanks."

"She thinks that I should get brownie points for making you coffee."

"Yeah? And what does our friend who knows the detailed

arrangements of this marriage say you get with those brownie points?"

"Well, she reminded me that you make really good peanut butter cookies."

Kaki slid her elbow back down the sheet and buried her face in her pillow.

"I do. She's right."

"You could maybe make some later this week."

"Maybe."

"So. Half a bagel?"

"I don't know. What's that gonna cost me?"

When he didn't answer her, she lifted her head to look at him. His face was a mask of anxiety.

"I'm kidding," she said quietly.

"Get up, lazy bones. Sit on the balcony with me."

"How can I resist that invitation?" she mumbled, but she sat up with a smile on her face. "I'll be out in a minute."

When he nodded, she turned to the side of the bed and stretched. Yawned and then rolled her head on her neck. Stood up and padded barefoot to the bathroom. In no rush to get to the beach today, she used the restroom, washed her face and brushed her teeth, and then joined Jordy in the kitchen.

"Really?" She eyed his bagel, slathered in cream cheese and looked up at him in disbelief. "Is there any left?"

"I already did yours," he told her. He pointed to the other plate, where indeed, there was half a bagel with a generous amount of cream cheese spread on it. "Figured we need to use it up since we leave tomorrow."

"And we're not eating tomorrow morning? Before we leave?"

"I think we should splurge and get a donut when we head out."

"I don't eat donuts."

"Why not?"

She watched him pour her coffee, mix in a little cream, and then took it from him when he handed it to her.

"Because I don't need the extra calories."

Jordy lowered an eyebrow at her. "Don't be one of those girls, Kaks. Live a little."

"I have lived to the tune of frozen pizza and too much beer and that huge Mexican dinner and the steak when you had seafood—"

"Okay, so live one more day and have a donut with me in the morning."

Kaki held his gaze. Finally nodded.

"Let's go sit outside," he suggested.

She picked up her plate and followed him to the door. Noticed when he set his paper plate on the table that he had a handful of napkins. Again with that little twinge of sadness. She wished yesterday hadn't happened, so that maybe he'd steal more of those innocent yet sexy kisses.

"What?" He noticed her staring as he pulled his chair out to sit down. "I haven't even eaten anything. I can't..." He patted his chin and his lips checking to see if he had food on his face.

On the other hand, she was glad yesterday had happened, because it was probably her only make out session with him. Hadn't been near enough, but it was something. She'd tasted Jordy Steed. His lips and his tongue. She felt his body pressing hers into the mattress at her back, and he'd played just for a moment with her body. She hadn't ever considered it a possibility, hadn't ever thought she'd want something like that to happen.

She was embarrassed to admit, even to herself, that she was glad it had.

"Nothing." She shook her head. Offered him a small smile when he finally sat down opposite her.

"Have you thought at all about what you wanna do?"

Bagel at her mouth now, Kaki froze and stared at him in a

panic. What the hell? She swallowed hard, moved the bagel an inch from her face, and cocked her head at him. Oh hell yes, she'd been doing nothing but thinking about what she wanted to do. She'd start with straddling his lap. Pull her pajama top off and offer him her breasts. Scoot in close and grind her middle over him—

"What?" She sounded breathless, and she prayed that he didn't notice. If he did, he wisely chose to ignore it.

"With the house. I mean…when we bought it, we talked about…painting a few rooms—"

"Mmm." She shrugged, took the bite of the bagel, and set it down slowly. Nervous energy tingled in her hands, her fingers. They hadn't put a timetable on this game when they'd started. She wondered now how long she would last. "It's your house, Jordy."

"Kaks, don't do that. We picked it out together."

"It was Steed money that paid for it—"

"And you're a Steed," he reminded her.

"In name only."

He groaned, obviously frustrated, and pushed his plate out of the way. Plopped his elbows on the table and hung his head. Kaki watched him drag his fingers back through his hair over and over again.

"What?" she finally whispered. "What did I do now?"

"Money." When he looked at her, the wear and exhaustion on his face stunned her. "Every woman I've ever been with has made a big deal out of the money."

"I'm not every woman, Jordy. I'm your best friend."

"And you're making a big deal about the money."

"You bought a house—"

"For you and me to live in. While we're married. Okay, we're not going to have a physical marriage, but we're living together. We love each other, and we're friends, and we're gonna live in that house for a while. I dunno. Maybe I'll live there after…" He shrugged. "Maybe you'll keep the house."

"I'm not keeping your house."

"Dammit, Kaks. Take from me. I have it to give. You married me. You threw away your first wedding. Your chance to feel like a princess. Or a queen, whatever girls want on their big day. You gave me your first vows in front of everyone important in your life. You gave me the first dance at your wedding. You gave me everything. Just so I could make Brianna want to come back—"

"I felt like a princess," she said quietly.

"What?"

"On our wedding day." She shrugged. "I felt like a princess. It was the perfect day, Jordy. And the best part is, when we get divorced, I'll still have you. Because we'll always be friends."

He stared at her in silence. She watched the frustration and what looked like regret move over his face. Saw the moment when he accepted what she'd said to be truth. His shoulders sagged. He lowered his gaze.

"The worst part," he said in a small, tight voice, "is that you were a beautiful bride, and none of it's real."

She licked her lips. "Except that we're friends?"

Jordy sighed. Reached across the table to take her hand. "Always."

She nodded. Wished when he'd brought this hare-brained idea up all those months ago, that they'd looked at each other and laughed it off. Because she sort of felt like friends or not, Jordy Steed might just break her heart after all.

"But Kaks?"

"What, Jordy?"

"You're decorating the damned house. Because you're a girl, and that's a girl thing."

She pressed her lips together and sat back. Stared at him long enough to make him shake his head and toss his hands up as if to ask her what now?

"You know what else is a girl thing?"

"What?"

"Chocolate icing on donuts."

His smile warmed her, made her forget that she'd just wished this whole play marriage away.

"I'll get you a donut with chocolate icing," he promised her. "Two of them."

"Nah, that's pushing it."

CHAPTER THIRTEEN

IF THIS MARRIAGE WAS REAL, Jordy decided he would feel excited about going home. Leaving the scene of the honeymoon and starting their new married life. But there wasn't anything real about the marriage, nor had there been anything real about the honeymoon. Going home meant going back to work. Seeing his dad and brothers every day at the store, listening to them rag on him about married life. They'd tell him they hoped he'd enjoyed the honeymoon, because now that he'd married Kaki, she would quit putting out. All of his brothers had moaned and groaned about the same through the years. And Jordy would eye all of his sisters-in-law and know his brothers were bullshitting because their wives were crazy about them, and he'd seen plenty of stolen kisses and ass grabbing through the past few years.

He'd been a little bit afraid they'd mope the whole way home, but the return trip had been okay. He still worried, though, that once back to real life, they'd drift apart. Which, technically, was how it was supposed to go for them. But now that they were at this point in the plan, he wanted to call it off. Just hold things steady where they were. He could live with her, sleep beside her, hang out with her and be happy as hell. Score a little action on the side. Hell, maybe he'd get to the point where knowing she had someone on the side wouldn't bother him.

Stranger things had happened.

Didn't matter. It wasn't fair to her to even consider it. Eventually, he would have to call it quits. With or without Brianna, he'd have to let Kaki go find her true happiness. And yes, as she'd said, they would always be friends. But they'd be the sort of friends who might grab a beer after work on a Friday night or hang out at his niece's softball game or some such thing. Not the close, intimately acquainted sort of friends who slept together (fully clothed) and had breakfast together in the morning.

She'd devoured the donut, and she'd laughed and snorted and wrestled with him for his phone when he'd taken a picture of her enjoying it. Luckily, he hadn't even started the Outback, so it wasn't hazardous when she nearly climbed over the console in the SUV struggling to get the phone from him to delete the picture. Well. Wasn't hazardous to anything but his dick. Entirely possible the whole package might explode if he didn't find someone to take care of the perpetual wood for him soon. Preferably a pretty, brown-eyed blonde, with a voice like honey and sex, and a healthy, hearty laugh.

Jordy wasn't sure there were any more of such a thing than the woman who had driven him wild the past week.

She'd read at the airport. Sipped her coffee. When she caught him staring at her, she'd asked if he wanted to read the book when she was finished. He'd grinned but backed away and turned his attention back to his iPad and the article he was reading about the latest fad in fitness. Hadn't read anything more, though, because he'd thought of that jerkwad on the beach who'd flirted with Kaki. The nerd who'd sat under his umbrella, talking to his wife about sci-fi and fantasy books all day. Jordy was overcome with the idea of that dumbass fantasizing even now about his wife.

Owen.

Maybe the woman beside him wasn't his in the traditional sense of the word, but he loved her and he would protect her from dumbass nerdy guys and mean guys and rude guys. And he was pretty sure Owen didn't deserve her.

When they lined up to board the plane, Jordy stood behind her and reached for her hand. Much to his surprise, she'd leaned into him and turned her face to his neck.

"I love you," she'd said quietly. "Don't forget that, 'kay?"

No one had heard her, so he knew she wasn't pretending. She wasn't boning up on her acting skills, or lying skills, maybe, was the better word for it. But he also knew she hadn't meant it in any sort of romantic way. Just a reminder that their friendship was the most important piece of this marriage pact.

He'd tucked his arm around her middle and kissed her forehead.

"Love you, too, Kaks," he'd promised her.

She'd slept for a while on the plane. When she woke, they'd talked some. Made up stories about the two guys across the aisle from them. Talked about what to do for supper once they got home to Prior. Decided they didn't want to cook, and Kaki had decided that even though she'd eaten a donut earlier, Gomer's Pizza sounded good. Delivery. A cold beer. Crashing in their new house.

Jordy knew their family and friends would crowd in soon. Press them for details about the honeymoon. Not *those* sorts of details, but about the beach and the dinners they'd had and if they'd gone parasailing or done anything else out of the ordinary. His brothers and their wives would tease them; even Kaki knew that. But everyone would want to share the basic fun of a beach vacation, and everyone would want to see pictures.

Jordy just hoped they'd all give them just one more night alone. Not like anything would come of it. No long, soft kisses. No sighs of pleasure. No touching. But he didn't want to share her yet. Even if they crashed on opposite ends of the couch, which was currently setting crooked, half in the living room and half in the dining room, and ate pizza from the box and watched basic programming on TV because they didn't have any cable service hooked up yet, he didn't want to share Kaki with anyone.

"So. Dad's sending Jackson to Chicago tomorrow," he announced when they were waiting at the baggage claim at Lambert International Airport in St. Louis. Their flight had landed at least twenty minutes ago, still had to get their bags and get to the car and then another two hours, give or take, on the road before they were back home in Prior.

"How come?" She looked at him. Kept her eyes on him as if was the only person in the airport.

"Some showcase." He shrugged. "New line of football equipment and gear."

"So, Jackson's going as a buyer?"

"I guess." Jordy shook his head. Unnerved by her intense gaze, he looked around the baggage claim area. Didn't recognize a soul, but he hadn't expected to, either.

"Does that bother you?" she asked quietly.

His dad and his granddad had owned the sporting goods place for what felt like a thousand years. Maybe his great granddad and another great, too. Jordy and his brothers were all jacks-of-all-trades. Maybe if he hadn't been away on his honeymoon, he might have been the one his dad had chosen to send to Chicago. Maybe he was thinking about the next thing coming up, somewhere out of town. If his dad chose him, Kaki couldn't go with him, because she had a job, too. Their marriage vows weren't real, but the thought of going somewhere and leaving his young bride at home made it hard to breathe. His hands itched like his skin was on too tight.

But maybe it was better to let Kaki think he was jealous of his brother, so he answered her with a half shrug.

"Yeah, but your dad put you in charge of the whole spring seasonal stuff. The displays and the ads. That was pretty huge."

Jordy nodded. Stepped around her when he saw one of their bags on the carousel. He grabbed it, saw the other way down at the other end, and glanced at Kaki. She nodded. When he'd grabbed the second bag, they headed outside. Talked about the store again as they boarded the van for the parking deck. Tired of talking about his brothers, all older and all pains in his ass through the years, he asked Kaki if she knew what she would be returning to at work. She said Karen, her boss, had told her before she left someone had unearthed a huge assortment of old dishes and kitchen items from some old, abandoned house in the county, so she figured she'd be cataloguing those things.

Crossed his mind that he might have found a job like that boring. Well. No might about it. But anyone else telling him about such a job would bore him. Not Kaki. Her eyes all but sparkled at the prospect.

The drive had been uneventful. He'd tossed her the keys, so she'd driven all the way to Prior. He had to pee so bad his eyeballs were probably yellow by the time Kaki had opened the door and led him inside.

"Wait!" He edged around in front of her in the nearly dark kitchen. "Hang on."

"Why?" She looked around. "Did someone set a trip wire or something? A bucket of water's gonna fall on my head?"

"Stay right there. I'll be right back."

"Jordy." She laughed but shrugged and mumbled *okay* as he dashed through the house gray with twilight to the bathroom half way down the hall from the kitchen to the front of the house. He pushed the door closed and strained to listen. Hoped she'd wait in the kitchen where he'd left her. Felt like he peed for two days, so he was surprised when he found her waiting obediently in the kitchen, their luggage at her feet.

"Okay." He grinned.

"What?" She wriggled her eyebrows. "Did you have a stripper stashed away that you had to get rid of?"

"Close." He rolled his eyes and then slipped around behind her again. "C'mere."

"What? What are you doing?"

He took her hand and pulled her back to the door. She yelped when he scooped her up in his arms and carried her over the threshold into the kitchen.

"What was that?" She laughed. Still in his arms, she looked up at him. "What are you doing?"

"Well, I wanted to carry my bride inside, because I didn't do it on our wedding night."

"If you'd tried, we'd have both crashed. Probably woulda broke something."

"We weren't drunk," he argued.

"Decidedly close, though."

Jordy eyed her with a frown. "Decidedly?"

She laughed and then squirmed in his arms, threw her head back.

"Put me down. This is goofy."

"Well." He finally set her feet on the floor, but he pulled her in gently against his chest. "You didn't get the real honeymoon treatment."

"Jordy," she whispered as he leaned in to kiss her. He telegraphed his purpose. Tucked her chin in his thumb and fingers. She didn't struggle, though. Didn't try to get away. In fact, he'd swear she rose up on her tiptoes and pressed into him further. She tasted like the mint gum she'd chewed on her drive home. The snapping of the gum and the way she'd sung along to every song on satellite radio had been an odd turn on. Now he took his time and devoured every inch of her lips, her tongue. Rubbed his tongue over hers in long, languid strokes that did nothing for the fire that had been burning in his groin for the week. Nothing but kindle it, anyway.

When he let her go, she sighed. He opened his eyes and studied her sweet face in the dim light in the kitchen. Felt her breath fan his lips. Wanted very much to kiss her again. Decided he wouldn't. No sense in starting that fight again.

"That's it?" she whispered as she opened her eyes.

"I like kissing you," he said quietly.

Kaki looked around, and then twisted in his arms and took a moment to survey the whole kitchen, for all the good it did her. She couldn't possibly see whatever it was she might be looking for, and Jordy had no idea what that might be.

"What're you doing?" he finally asked her.

"Looking for…" Her words trailed off as she turned back to him. "Are we alone?"

"I think so." He nodded.

"Hmm." She frowned and then nodded. "Um. Okay." She stepped away from him and hung her head. Rubbed the back of her neck. "Why don't I dump the luggage? Sort everything to be washed. You order pizza."

"Why don't we just order pizza and relax?"

"Because then I have to do all of that tomorrow. Might as well start tonight."

"Ill help," he told her. "Don't think I'm gonna be a dick about this and never do anything around the house."

She nodded and stepped back. Turned to get the luggage.

"Good."

"Kaks?"

"Hmm?"

"I wish…" He lost his nerve when she lifted her head and their eyes met. "I wish we were still in Florida."

"Me too."

He watched her grab the handles on the bags. "I have an idea."

She stood up straight and eyed him wearily. "That makes me nervous."

He grinned. "Let's hang out in the dark."

"Why?"

"So..." He shrugged and shifted his weight from one foot to the other. "So that if any of our nosey family and friends drive by, they won't know for sure if we're home, and we can just have one more night to ourselves."

Her smile was a little bit soft and dreamy.

"Sounds great, Jordy, but the car's out there in the driveway."

"Then if the lights are off, they'll think we're in here doing private things that newlyweds do."

CHAPTER FOURTEEN

JUNE 22, 2015

"What do you mean, it sucked?" Lauren handed Kaki a stack of dishtowels. Leaned her elbows on the counter when Kaki squatted down in front of the cabinets to put the towels away. "What happened to the free beach vacation and soaking up the sun and the fruity little drinks with the umbrellas in them?"

"I didn't get any of those." Kaki looked up at Lauren now, surprised to realize she hadn't had a single fruity drink with a cute little umbrella the whole week.

"And that's why it sucked? The whole week with Jordy?"

Kaki laughed and nodded to the box on the counter behind her friend, and Lauren drew herself up to stand. Took another pile of towels from the box and handed it to Kaki.

"Woah, that's pretty." Lauren tugged the top towel off the pile and unfolded it to admire it. Kaki eyed the brown and tan towel and then frowned at Lauren. "What?"

"Really? This is who we've become? Friends who used to ride our bikes no hands down Shelby's Hill and friends who ran from the cops to get away from underage drinking charges and now we're marveling at pretty dishtowels?"

"No, we're not." Lauren shook her head. "You were telling me why your honeymoon sucked."

Kaki laughed softly. Hoped Jordy would either call before he came home or make enough noise that she heard him coming, and he wouldn't overhear her complaining about the week at Fort Walton.

"Aren't there any dishrags?" Still squatting, she looked up at Lauren again.

"Mmm." Lauren leaned on her left elbow and dug through the box. "Yeah. Here." She handed Kaki a stack of rags. "Did your mom have towels that looked like calendars? With the days of the week—"

"I know." Kaki waved Lauren's explanation away. "I grew up in your house. Hello?"

"Well?"

"No, you know that. Mom's kitchen is all color-coordinated."

"That's right." Lauren pointed at Kaki as if to award her a point. "Seriously? Why did it suck?'

Kaki slowly stood. Looked over her shoulder at the closed back door. Lauren had pressed her on this earlier on the phone, but Kaki had refused to discuss it. It had been a ply to get her buddy to come and visit her, and it had worked.

"Why do you think?"

Lauren snapped her head back in surprise, like Kaki had popped her in the nose.

"You said that you were okay with this," Lauren reminded her.

"Don't." Kaki shook her head. She stepped over to the refrigerator and grabbed a beer and a bottle of water. Handed the water to Lauren and twisted the top off the beer.

"Don't what?" Lauren set the water down and hoisted herself up to sit on Kaki's counter.

"Oh. Don't do that. You'll hurt yourself."

"I'm pregnant, not disabled!" Lauren groaned. "You sound like Ty. He follows me around, fretting about everything I do. Like I'm gonna go into labor or something."

Kaki shrugged her lips. Still no kitchen chairs or table in the room, she backed up and then slid her back down the trim on the doorway. Huffed out a deep breath when her butt hit the floor.

"So?" Lauren arched her eyebrows.

Now that she had Lauren's undivided attention, Kaki didn't know what to say.

"Don't be that friend who says I told you so."

"I've always been that friend, Kaki Steed. How could you forget that?"

Kaki laughed softly.

"Was he that bad?"

"No. It was fun. *He* was fun—"

"I mean with other women. When I talked to him about this—"

"Wait." Kaki held her hand up, took a drink, and then lowered the bottle, other hand still holding Lauren off. "When you *talked to him about this*? What does that mean?"

Lauren tilted her head and sent her long auburn curls cascading over her shoulder. She pursed her lips and then sighed.

"Before the wedding. The week before the wedding. He came by."

Nothing new. The three of them were close, always had been.

"But what talk?" Kaki circled her hand in the air to urge Lauren to continue.

"About this. About you. He wanted to make sure it wouldn't…bother you…if he…"

"If he hooked up with random women while he was on a honeymoon with me."

"Fake honeymoon. With you. His friend."

Kaki shrugged and stared at Lauren expectantly.

"And you said…"

"I told him just to be respectful. Not to put it in your face."

"Hmm." Kaki nodded and rested her head on the wood-work behind her.

"Was I wrong?" Lauren took a drink of her water. "I mean, if it had been me with him, I would have expected the flirting, and I would've expected him to…be out with other women. Same as you."

"Yeah."

"But I still wouldn't want to have to watch it. Especially when I was sitting there with his ring on, with all these strangers knowing I'm his wife, and he's out fooling around with everyone else."

"Pretty much," Kaki agreed.

"So? He wasn't? Discreet?"

"Oh yeah, he was." Kaki nodded quickly. "Left the condo late at night a few times. Never came in stumbling drunk or anything."

"Okay." Lauren nibbled on her lower lip. "So what's wrong then? Why did your beach vacation suck?"

Kaki sighed. Stared at Lauren silently.

"Because you didn't get any." When Kaki didn't flinch, didn't move a muscle, Lauren leaned way forward, arms out wide at her sides. "Is that it?"

"Lauren, don't do that!"

"Oh my God!" Lauren groaned. She scooted as far back on the counter as she could and leaned on the wall. "Is this better?"

"Am I stupid?" Kaki rested her head on the door trim again and closed her eyes.

"Um." Lauren cleared her throat, and Kaki opened her eyes and shot her a look of disbelief. "In reference to me falling off the counter? Or…"

"Not funny."

"Mmm." Lauren pursed her lips.

"Great." Kaki sighed. "I am stupid."

"No, no, I didn't meant that, Kaki. I just…it's not your thing."

"*What* isn't my thing? What do you mean? I like sex."

"Sex with strangers. You and I both know you had no intention of strolling the beach, looking to get laid."

Kaki rolled her eyes and bent her knees. "That's so gross!"

"See?" Lauren shrugged her eyebrows. "You don't even like the words. *You* don't contribute to these talks when Jordy and I have them."

"And yet I am still attracted to the opposite sex, and I do like to *have* sex occasionally."

"So you're telling me your whole honeymoon, such as it was, sucked because you didn't have the balls to flirt your way into someone's bed?"

"I don't have balls, nor have I ever, nor will I ever," Kaki mumbled. She rested her head on the wall again and rolled it back and forth. "And no, that's not what I'm telling you."

Lauren shook her head. "'Kay. I give up. *What* are you telling me? What are you *not* telling me?"

"It was a honeymoon!" Kaki yelped.

Lauren's mouth gaped open, and she stared at Kaki in wide-eyed surprise.

"You…" She laughed. "Oh my God. You…"

"This isn't funny."

"You wanted to have sex with Jordy!"

"It was a *honeymoon*."

Lauren covered her mouth with her fingertips, but Kaki knew she was laughing.

"This isn't funny."

"Wait." Lauren dropped her hand and took a deep breath. "Let me clarify. You aren't upset about not hooking up with someone. You're really upset that you guys...that you and Jordy...didn't do it. On your honeymoon."

Kaki stared at her stoically. Maybe if their roles were reversed and she was happily married, she would think Lauren's situation was funny. At the moment, this wasn't funny.

"Mmm. Yeah. And I know." Kaki nodded. She set her beer down and heaved a big sigh.

"What? You know? You know what? How funny this is to me?"

"Lauren."

"Because it's really damned funny. I *so* told you so, Kaki Steed!"

The back door swung open, and the object of their conversation strolled in, phone at his ear. He grinned a hello to Lauren and then turned to Kaki, still sitting on the floor. Waved his free hand at his phone and rolled his eyes.

Not in the mood for playboy Jordy and not really in the mood to laugh at all, Kaki offered him a small, tired smile.

"Yep. Whatever, Jackson. I'll tell her. Yep. Bye." He ended the call and moved to set his phone on the counter. He nudged Lauren's leg with his fist and then turned to Kaki. "Big brother sends his love to my blushing bride."

Kaki nodded and groaned. Wondered what stories Jordy had told him on his drive home from work. Decided maybe it didn't matter. Apparently, she was too uptight about this stuff anyway. Even Lauren had hinted at that.

Hinted. Kaki gave herself a mental shake.

"How are you?" Jordy turned to look at Lauren again. Kaki chewed nervously on her lip when she realized Lauren was still trying to control her laughter.

"Good." Lauren nodded. "Tired. I feel like I could sleep like, twenty-seven hours a day, and pee the other five, but ya know, other than that, it's all good."

"That and your math sucks," Jordy mumbled. "What're you giggling about?"

"Nothing."

Jordy leaned on the counter and looked at Kaki.

"Is my wife sharing funny honeymoon stories with you?"

Lauren snorted, but when Kaki narrowed her eyes at her, she cleared her throat and offered Jordy a sweet smile.

"Yeah. She is." Lauren nodded. Clamped her hand over her mouth when another bit of laughter bubbled out.

Jordy shot Kaki a panicked look. "Are you telling our secrets?"

He sounded like he was joking, but he wasn't. He didn't want her to tell Lauren about what had almost happened the other day. Wow. *So* unattracted to her, he didn't want their best friend to think something might have happened.

"Nope." She took another drink of her beer. Felt Lauren's eyes on her as Jordy stretched. He wore sexy jeans with thread-bare pockets. They snugged around his waist and cupped his ass, and Kaki looked away rather than be jealous about it. His gray Steed Sporting Good's shirt slipped from the waistband. He rubbed his hand over his head and looked at Kaki again.

"I'm gonna go change clothes."

"Okay."

"What do you wanna do for supper tonight?" he asked as he headed out of the room.

"I don't care."

Kaki watched him disappear down the hall. Thought about last night. The way he'd made a big deal of carrying her over the threshold and the lingering kiss he'd laid on her. What he'd said to her. He liked kissing her. She'd assumed someone was either in the house watching them or coming up to the door outside.

Still. It had been a nice kiss. Enough to stir her desire. Again. But not so much that he'd left her wrecked and frustrated again. She glanced at Lauren again when they were alone.

"What happened?"

She couldn't talk now. Not with Jordy upstairs. Doubtful he'd hear anything. The house was solid; he wouldn't overhear her through a crack in the wall. But it felt funny. She was irritated with Lauren, and it would take too long to lead her through the whole story, and she wasn't in the mood to wallow anymore.

Beach vacation. Good food. A scorching hot make out session that lasted all of seven or eight minutes and now a pretty perfect house to share with one of her best friends. Why should she complain?

She climbed to her feet and snatched her beer from the floor.

"Nothing." She shook her head.

"Are you gonna tell me another time, or is this where it starts?" Lauren flipped her hair over her shoulder and stared at Kaki defiantly.

"Where what starts?"

"You and Jordy keeping me out of the loop."

"There's no loop, Lauren." Kaki shrugged and shook her head. "I'm being bitchy because he got some on our honeymoon, and I didn't."

Lauren reached for her. Tucked a chunk of hair behind her ear.

"You're sure?"

"Yeah. I'm fine."

"Don't call Owen. Promise? Don't be so desperate that you call him. He's a prick."

"He is," Kaki agreed. "But I'm certainly no catch, either."

"Shut up." Lauren shook her head. "You were the prettiest bride ever."

"Painting party next weekend," Kaki reminded her as

Lauren scooted forward and executed a graceful jump from the counter.

"I can't be around paint fumes." Lauren rubbed her belly. "Bad for the baby."

"'Kay. Send Tyler."

"How about if Tyler comes to help, and I'll fix dinner for everyone. You guys can come by when you quit for the day."

Kaki considered Lauren's offer and nodded. "That sounds good."

"Okay." Lauren leaned in to hug her. "You sure you're okay?"

"Yep."

"You're not, because you say yep when you mean no, but you don't feel like going into it."

"I'm fine," Kaki whispered. She kissed Lauren's cheek. "Thanks for coming by."

"I'll call you tomorrow."

Kaki stood at the back door as her friend hurried down the back steps and around the corner of the house. Lauren looked fresh and sweet even in the Midwestern June heat. No baby bump yet, but she already had that soft, feminine glow that pregnant women always acquired.

"Where'd she go?" Jordy asked as he returned to the kitchen. Kaki looked over her shoulder at him. Noted the gray Hurley t-shirt and the khaki shorts. Sexy. Not as sexy as the jeans, but not bad. Then again, she decided she liked him in trunks. And nothing else. Maybe that's why she'd been mopey today. Because she missed the lazy afternoons with him on the beach. Probably had nothing at all to do with what their marriage wasn't.

"Home."

"How come?"

"I'm guessing Tyler's home." Kaki closed the big door and turned to him.

"Did you remind her of the painting party next weekend?"

"Yeah. She can't be around paint. Said she'd send Tyler over to help, and she'd fix something to eat."

Jordy nodded. "Good idea."

She cleared her throat and leaned on the door at her back. "Did you talk to Brianna today?"

CHAPTER FIFTEEN

JORDY RUBBED HIS EYES. Pushed his fingers as far into them as he dared. Dropped his hands and looked at her again. No use. She was wearing cut off denim shorts and a loose fitting tank, but all he could see was her breast falling out of that white bikini top.

"What's wrong with you?" Kaki asked him now. "Do your eyes itch or are you tired?"

"Yeah." He shook his head. No way in hell he could tell her the real issue. "And yeah."

She stared at him silently for a moment. Finally gave him a stiff nod and pressed her lips together.

"So." She cleared her throat. "Sounds like it's working then."

He shrugged. Didn't want to waste time talking about Brianna right now.

"I don't know. She isn't begging me to take her back."

"Yeah, but she texted you on your honeymoon."

"Probably more to bother you than anything."

Kaki flinched and nodded reluctantly. "Maybe." She stood up straight and breezed by him, giving him a whiff of her perfume. He breathed deeply. Wished he could press his face to her neck right about now and smell that scent that was so distinctly Kaki it made him weak in the knees.

"What do you mean?" He turned and watched her as she pulled the refrigerator door open and stared at the six-pack of beer and box of taco shells on the top shelf.

Eyes still on the beer and shells, like they might morph into margaritas and tacos, she drummed her fingers on the refrigerator door. Nibbled on her lip.

"What, Kaks? What're you thinking?"

"She texted you on your honeymoon," she said again. "That means something, Jordy. Even if she is trying to rile me, she's doing it for a reason. Otherwise, she'd just walk away."

He stared at her for a second. Nodded. "Maybe."

"What did she want today?"

"Um." He shook his head. He couldn't tell Kaki what Brianna had said today. He couldn't tell her Brianna had asked about how he'd enjoyed sex with his sweet, little vanilla wife. Instead he nodded at the refrigerator. "Let's go—"

"No. I don't wanna eat out every night."

"Okay. So we're having taco shells?"

She looked at him with a smirk. "There's some peanut butter in the cabinet. Canned peaches. And a can of lima beans."

"Um. Okay. First?" He tossed his hands up and frowned. "Lima beans? How? Who the hell bought lima beans? Because we don't eat them."

He and Kaki and Lauren used to feed their lima beans to Lauren's dog when they were kids, and Lauren's mom fixed dinner for them. Delbert the dog liked lima beans. Any human child, any human he'd ever known, not so much. Well, apparently, except for Lauren's parents.

"No idea." She shrugged.

"And peanut butter? On taco shells?"

"Might be a new taste sensation." She pointed at him. "You never know."

"I was gonna say let's go eat something and then go to the grocery store."

Kaki blinked at him. "Seriously?"

"What? You don't think we need some groceries?"

"No, I do." She frowned. "I just figured you...I figured I would end up going—"

"I told you last night I don't plan on being a dick while we're living together. I'll do my part."

"Okay." She held her hands up in surrender.

"Okay. So dinner. And then the store."

"Or the store and then we can come home and throw something together," she offered. She pressed her lips together and gave him a tiny shrug. "Because then...we don't have to talk to anyone."

Jordy was all for that. He still wasn't ready to share his wife with anyone. Hell, he'd been annoyed to come home and find Lauren here, and he *liked* Lauren. She was as much a fixture in his life as Kaki was. But he wondered now if Kaki didn't want to go out because she didn't want to be seen with him. They'd had a spectacle of a wedding, sure, but out of sight, out of mind. Maybe she was hoping people forgot she was now married to him.

"Sure." He nodded. "Wanna go now?"

"Yeah."

He watched her drop her phone into her purse, and then he followed her to the back door. Wondered what she and Lauren had been talking about. He didn't think she'd tell Lauren about making out with him. Unless she felt the need to confess it to someone so she could forget about it and move on.

Then again, wouldn't matter if Lauren knew. Lauren was the least judgmental person he knew. She'd probably shrug and ask Kaki if she'd had a Mai Tai or if she'd gone shopping while they were gone and gloss right over the make out thing.

Did he want Lauren to know? Did he want to talk to Lauren about it? Well, no, because she might not judge them for what happened, but she'd be the first person to stand up and say I told you so. She'd warned him about his scheme. Told him he was playing with fire and someone was going to burn. *Probably* she didn't mean that restless fire that still raged in his groin. Then again, maybe Lauren had meant exactly that.

"What're you thinking about?" Kaki asked as they walked to the drive. Her car was pulled up close to the house; his Wrangler was out by the street. He took her hand and led her out to the Wrangler.

"Lauren."

Kaki didn't seem surprised.

"Is she doing okay?"

"Seems to be."

"I still can't wrap my brain around her and Tyler being parents."

"I know," Kaki agreed. She climbed up into the passenger side of the Jeep and he patted her butt, suddenly a little bit happy to be home. Here in Prior, people knew they were married, so he had to play with her hair and squeeze her butt and steal kisses to keep up the charade. He just hoped she didn't get sick of it and decide she wanted out.

"She doesn't sugar coat anything." Jordy settled into his seat and put the key in the ignition. "It's nice, but maybe... harsh for kids."

Kaki leaned forward and fiddled with the stereo when he started the Jeep. Settled on PRD 105, country music, Pride of Prior.

"Really?" He shot her a frown when he heard the old Neal McCoy song "The Shake." She shrugged and nodded. The three of them had gone through a country music phase, obsessed to the point of cutting out everything else, but they'd long since gone back to listening to pretty much everything. Except jazz and Sinatra. Jordy might boot Kaki out if she got hooked on that stuff.

"I think she'll be different then. Life changes you sometimes. Sort of molds you into a softer, more pliant version of yourself."

He looked at her for a moment and decided she might be partially right. Life might soften some people, but it might make others hard and bitter. He hoped to hell he hadn't set things in motion that would hurt Kaki and make her hard and jaded about love.

"You're absolutely right, Dr. Steed."

She laughed. Lifted her hand to frame his face when he leaned in for a kiss. They were getting good at this. Maybe they should move to Hollywood. When they ended the kiss, and her lips hovered near his, he gave her another quick peck and turned his attention back to the errand they had to run. Backed out of the drive and headed east on Lincoln.

"So." She looked around, tucked a wild hunk of hair behind her ear when the wind lifted it from her face. "You never told me what Brianna said."

"You don't wanna know, Kaks."

"I *do* wanna know, Jordy. How am I supposed to get you back with her if I don't know what's going on?"

He glanced at her as he slowed to a stop at Twenty-Fourth and Lincoln. He hit the blinker and looked to his left. To his right, and back to his left, more to avoid her eyes than watching for traffic.

"She asked if you like it like she does," he mumbled wishing the wind would carry his words away as he accelerated and turned left on Twenty-Fourth.

"And how does she like it?"

No such luck.

Jordy pursed his lips and sighed. "Please don't make me

say this, Kaki."

"Do you want my help?"

"She likes it dirty. Like…porn stuff."

"Whips and chains?"

"No."

"Handcuffs."

"Not what I meant, but yeah, she gets off on that."

"So do I need to go watch some porn to figure out what you're too chicken to say to me?"

"She likes threesomes." He grinded the words out. "She likes to deep throat…when she—"

"Got it." Kaki nodded.

"She likes me to slap her ass when we're doing it, and she has a lot of sex…toys she likes to play with."

"Are you blushing?" Kaki leaned toward him and laid her hand on his shoulder.

"Shut up." He laughed and pushed her hand away.

"First. Do sex toys necessarily mean you like porn quality sex?"

Jordy snuck a quick peek at her as he drove by Reilly Park. Shook his head quickly when she looked his way.

"Don't."

"I don't own a lot, but I've—"

"Please? Don't?" He clamped the fingers of his left hand around the steering wheel and rubbed under his eyes and down over his mouth with his free hand. "Don't tell me stories."

Kaki watched him so closely, he couldn't even wiggle around in his seat to fix his dick, which felt like it was about to burst out of his zipper. Imagine that. Driving through Prior, top off the Jeep. Top off the dick. Arrested for indecent exposure.

"'Kay." She looked away and shrugged as if to say *suit yourself*. He wanted to know. Hell yes, he wanted to know every damned thing she'd ever done. What she liked. But not *now*. Not in a conversation about Brianna. And not in his Jeep. On the way to the *grocery store*. How the hell was he going to walk around the store and buy produce and meat and chips and cereal when all he could think about was taking this woman to bed and making her forget any other man had ever touched her?

"So?" she finally asked.

Jordy made a right turn onto Broadway and looked at her again. What? What did she want now? What was he supposed to say?

"What?" He shook his head.

"What'd you tell her?"

"Kaks."

"Jordy, this is why we got married. C'mon. Tell me."

"I told her you like it all."

"Threesomes?" she winced. "Really? You think I'd be into that?"

Jordy groaned. Waved at his brother Jason when he honked at him from his truck at the stop sign on Twenty-Eighth and Broadway. Kaki twisted around in her seat to wave at Jason and then looked back at Jordy as if to tell him she had no intention of dropping the subject.

"I didn't tell her anything, Kaks," he finally admitted. "I figured it's none of her business, and even if you and I were hot and heavy, a gentleman, someone in love with his wife wouldn't kiss and tell."

Kaki stared at him with the same look a fifth grade teacher might give a kid who finally mastered long division.

"Wow." She nodded. "That's impressive, Jordy."

"Are you being sarcastic?"

"No, I'm not," she said simply. "That was a nice thing to say. I hope it killed her."

He laughed softly.

When he pulled into the lot and parked, he sat still. Took a deep breath. Felt her eyes on him, but he didn't look at her.

"Are we like...taking a moment to pray?" she finally asked him.

He laughed. Leaned sideways, hooked his arm around her neck and pulled her close. Took advantage of the moment to close his eyes and breathe her in. The perfume he loved, the wind in her hair.

"Jackson asked me if you're really that into me," he said quietly.

"What?" She pulled away from him and stared at him with big eyes. "Like he doesn't believe—"

"No. Like he thinks I'm a jerk with women, and he thinks you deserve better."

"Jordy." She flinched.

"And I have to admit to you that I did tell him that you're incredible in bed."

She laughed and rolled her eyes.

"You're not angry?"

"That you lied to your brother about me?" She shrugged. Jordy's heart skipped and slipped a good inch his chest. Scared he was having a heart attack, he stared in disbelief as Kaki brushed her fingertips over his lips. Followed that caress with a soft brush of her lips. And then sank in deep for a long, wet kiss.

Hell yes, she was getting good at this. He was willing to let her fool *him* into believing.

"I'm thinking BLT sandwiches," she announced as she pulled away from him.

"You're thinking..." He shook his head. "You're rubbing your tongue all over mine and making me crazy, and you're thinking about bacon and lettuce?"

"And tomatoes." She nodded. "Let's go. I'm hungry."

Jordy watched her jump down from the Wrangler. He huffed out a sigh, reached down to adjust things so he could maybe hide what was going on in his shorts, and then climbed out of the Jeep to walk with her into the store.

CHAPTER SIXTEEN

KAKI COULDN'T SAY she'd never had fun in a grocery store before. There was the time when she and Lauren and Tyler made a guacamole run before the Super Bowl party two years ago. Tyler had been running commentary on every person they met in every aisle, and he'd mumbled something sassy in aisle three and an older lady had heard him. Rather than take offense, she'd flirted with him. Wrapped her hand around his forearm and patted his biceps appreciatively. Wagged her eyebrows and looked at her and Lauren with a smug grin. They'd zoomed the hell out of aisle three thinking the lady thought they were a threesome and might want to be added to the roster.

There was the time, also, when she and Lauren and Jordy had come in one night to get a twelve-pack of Mountain Dew. At sixteen, it was Jordy's drug of choice, unless he could sweet-talk his oldest brother into buying alcohol for them. Didn't happen often, but now and then. That night, though, they'd come for Mountain Dew, and Lauren had gone AWOL on them. She and Jordy had raced through the aisles looking for her. Kaki had climbed on the front of the shopping cart, and Jordy had pushed her and the cart around cutting corners short and barely missing knocking over a display of Halloween candy. They'd found Lauren in the junk food aisle and watched wordlessly as she tossed boxes of sweets and chips into the cart.

She'd caught them sneaking peeks at each other and announced that she wasn't pregnant, but she'd started her period that morning and she'd been wanting to eat a pound of chocolate since. Used to Lauren's personal information dumps, neither of them flinched. Simply laughed and helped her toss a few more boxes of chocolate goodies into the cart.

The first grocery-shopping trip as husband and wife–well, the first official one, the honeymoon one didn't count–was fun. No stupid, uncontrollable laughter. But fun. They hadn't raced through the aisles. In fact, they'd moseyed. Looked at tofu and dragon fruit and pickled herring and bought bread and lunchmeat and Doritos. She had insisted they get some fresh produce and some meat. Told him she was serious about not going out for dinner every night. Mumbled that she'd like to leave the marriage either at her current weight or less and then wished she could take the words back. They'd made a deal, and eventually, this fun little escape from every day would end and they'd go their separate ways. But she was surprised to realize she wasn't in a big hurry to do that, and she didn't want to remind Jordy that it was all part of the plan.

He'd played with her butt in the bread aisle, and embarrassed, she'd ducked her head to his shoulder and told him to stop.

"Too much?" he'd asked sincerely. She'd simply nodded, and he'd kissed her head and backed away with a promise to behave. And then he had, and Kaki had been a little disappointed. Still. A pat on her butt was one thing, but he couldn't walk around behind her squeezing her ass cheeks every five minutes.

When they'd loaded the groceries in the backseat of the Jeep, he'd tossed her the keys.

"You want me to drive?"

"Why not?" He shrugged as he climbed up to the passenger seat.

"You just want to see if I can get home without breaking the eggs."

He laughed and shrugged. "Takes some skill."

"I've got mad skills, Jordy Steed," she'd told him. She climbed up in her seat and put the keys in the ignition. Looked up to find him watching her with hungry eyes. She'd raised her eyebrows in question.

"I am sure you do," he'd finally mumbled and turned away.

Kaki felt that same nervous energy roll over her that she'd felt a few times on the honeymoon. Maybe sexual awareness was the right word, although she doubted it, because Jordy had made it clear he wasn't interested in her that way. And why would he be if Brianna was into threesomes? Seventh heaven for him. As much as Kaki didn't like Brianna, she certainly recognized her sex appeal to someone like Jordy. Add in another girl who looked anything like Brianna, Jordy might die of a heart attack in bed with them. She supposed he'd at least die happy if it happened that way.

"What's wrong?"

"Hmm?" She shot him a look as she hit the gas and turned left on Thirty-Sixth.

"You look sad." He reached for her hand. Kaki squeezed his fingers and then turned to look over her right shoulder so she could ease into the right lane.

"I'm fine."

"Kaks."

"What?" She shrugged. "It's nothing, Jordy. I'm hungry."

"Me too. Dad bought me lunch today."

"Yeah?" She eyed him expectantly.

"Mmm. Yeah. They had Boats deliver sandwiches to the store."

"That sounds good. I had peanut butter."

"On what?"

"A spoon," she answered, and she laughed when Jordy stared at her like she'd spoken in a foreign language.

"You had peanut butter on a spoon for lunch?"

"Yep."

"Like ten spoonfuls? Twelve?"

"One."

"One?" He shook his head. "You're gonna waste away. Do you do that often?"

"No. But you saw the contents of the kitchen," she reminded him.

"You could've gone out—"

"I was busy. I got a lot of the kitchen stuff put away."

"Which was important because we had no food."

"Well, now we do." She shrugged and slowed at President to make a right turn.

"Did you lick it?"

"What?" She blinked and glanced at him.

"The peanut butter."

"Did I what?"

"Like...did you lick it from the spoon? Or just...put the whole thing in your mouth?"

Laughter rolled up from low in her belly, and she shook her head.

"You didn't wanna talk about this stuff earlier."

"Yeah, I was driving, and we were walking into a public place."

"Well, I hate to disappoint you, Jordy, but I don't stand around by myself and try to be sexy."

"You don't have to try."

"And you don't have to say stuff like that."

"So." He cleared his throat. "You didn't lick it?"

"No. And you know what else?"

She felt him staring at her, but she kept her eyes on the road.

"When I shower—"

"Oh Jesus, Kaks." He blew out a deep breath and turned his head away.

"Do you wanna hear this?"

"Yes?" He shrugged.

"I don't stand with one foot forward and thrust my boobs up and out and picture what my silhouette would look like on the other side of the door."

"And yet, I'm sure you in the shower are sexy as fuck."

He mumbled it, but she heard him. When their eyes met briefly, she saw that he was embarrassed. He arched his eyebrows and grinned, looked the other way.

A little embarrassed herself, Kaki cleared her throat and shook her head.

"You don't have to say that," she said quietly. She didn't look at him to gauge his reaction, so she had no idea if he heard her over the music and wind or not. That sexual awareness throbbed inside her now, and she wondered as she turned left on Twenty-Fourth and flew down the street to Lincoln, how she was going to get through night after night next to Jordy in bed. She didn't want to look elsewhere for sex. Even if she and Jordy didn't have a traditional marriage, she didn't want to cheat. She respected him too much to do that to him. If anyone found out and told Jordy, it would embarrass him in front of his family. She didn't want to do that.

But good grief. How the hell was she supposed to deal with this? With the need? The desire? And not just for sex, but for Jordy? They'd only just started, and there was no end in sight.

"I'll fry the bacon," he offered as she slowed to pull into their driveway. Still too wound up and still a little embarrassed—and yeah, okay, this conversation had dredged up the humiliation she'd felt last week when Jordy had laid her down and walked away—Kaki only nodded. Kept her eyes straight forward.

Since they had groceries to carry in, Kaki pulled the Wrangler further down the driveway. Pocketed his keys, jumped out of the seat, and grabbed as many bags as she could carry. Jordy eyed her with amusement as he did the same.

"Damn, Kaks. You got muscles, too." He whistled as he followed to the back door. Kaki rolled her eyes and then stood at the door. Realized the keys were in her pocket and sighed. She started to shift her arms, to let a few bags slide off, but Jordy set his down first. Shot her a wicked grin as he stepped up behind her and slid his fingers into her pocket. He could easily have grabbed the keys, but he eased his whole hand inside her pocket.

She laughed. Jumped and dropped her head back to his shoulder when his fingertips crept close to her inner thigh.

"Jordy."

He leaned into her; she felt his breath on the back of her neck. Felt her skin break out in goose bumps when he pressed his parted lips there and then flicked the tip of his tongue against her skin. More than willing to enjoy this moment, she stood still and hoped he wouldn't quit.

Except that he would. And she'd be left to shut down the feelings he'd stirred to life in her again.

"Jordy." She laughed softly as he licked a trail up the back of her neck and rubbed his fingers up and down her thigh, still hidden in her pocket. "It's one thing to flirt so people see it, but we're gonna get arrested."

"Might be fun until the cops show up."

He pulled the keys from her pocket and moved back around her to unlock the door. She watched him pick up the bags he'd discarded and then usher her inside in front of him.

She put the bags on the counter and then shook her hands to kill the tingles his lips had chased through her.

"Hands numb?" he asked her.

She looked at him, considered how to answer him, and decided it was better to leave that question alone.

"Want a beer?" She cleared her throat. Fetched two from the refrigerator and opened them before he answered her.

"You're cute when you're flustered." He took the bottle she offered him and took a long drink. "Wanna tell me now?"

"Tell you what?" She narrowed her eyes at him and wondered what he would say now.

"About the sex toys. I'm assuming you have a—"

Two could play this game. She shrugged, took a long drink, and then licked her lips. Maybe he wasn't attracted to her, but she had a feeling she would make him damned uncomfortable talking about her sexual experiences.

"You really wanna talk about this?"

Jordy took a deep breath. Lifted his hand and stroked his thumb over her lip.

"No." He leaned in and kissed her. A simple peck on her lips. "I don't have sisters, but I think you telling me about… that…stuff would be an awful lot like listening to a little sister talk."

"Little sister? Really?"

She was hurt, but she swallowed it. How was it he could listen to Lauren talk about giving some guy a blow job at an office party, but listening to Kaki tell the same story would be like hearing a little sister talk? She turned away from him. Well, that was easy enough. Lauren was sexy. Alluring. That long hair and those green eyes. Plus she was confident in ways Kaki wasn't. She'd thrown her virginity away with little care when she was seventeen, and as far as Kaki knew, she hadn't changed much since then. Of course Jordy would find her sexy. And see Kaki as a kid.

"Yeah. You feel like a little sister sometimes."

She nodded. Took a deep breath.

Play the game, Kaki.

"That's because you're older than me. You turned twenty-five in January. And I haven't yet."

"I've got a few months on you." He shrugged when she turned to look at him.

"And you always will." She flashed him a grin. "Let's get this done. I'm hungry."

"Me too," he agreed. Kaki turned her attention to the bags. Handed him the package of bacon when she found it so he could get it started while she put stuff away.

"Kaks?"

"Hmm?"

"Thanks."

She slowed in the process of putting a jar of mayonnaise and a bottle of ketchup in the refrigerator.

"For what?"

"Marrying me."

Kaki looked at him over her shoulder, body in the V of the open fridge door. She nodded and shrugged her eyebrows.

"What're friends for?"

"Lauren wouldn't have done it."

"Lauren's married," she reminded him.

He shook his head and turned back to the stove, where he'd set a skillet on the big burner.

"She wouldn't have done it anyway," he mumbled.

Kaki sighed. Wondered if Jordy wished it had been Lauren he'd married instead of her. If Lauren was his fake bride, would he have given her honeymoon sex? No doubt in her mind. She swung the refrigerator door closed and hurried out of the room.

"What're you—?" Jordy called after her.

"Be right back!" she answered. She hurried up the steps and into the bathroom. Closed the door and leaned against it. She needed a moment. Not to calm the libido this time. But to swallow all the green stuff. The jealousy that had hit her downstairs. It was ridiculous to feel this way. She was crazy about Lauren and Jordy. Loved them both. Always would. So why did she have to create competition, tension where there wasn't any?

"Kaks?" He knocked on the door. "You okay?"

She took a deep breath. Nodded to herself.

"Yeah. I'll be down in a sec."

She stood still, waited to hear his footsteps move away from the door before she stood up straight. She moved to stand in front of the mirror.

"Okay, Kaki. You're not sexy enough to score a night with Jordy Steed." She huffed out a deep breath and shrugged. "But you're not stupid, either. You knew it going in, and nothing's changed."

Her reflection didn't say anything. Kaki studied her eyes, her hair. Decided neither was particularly lacking, and she *was* stupid to let Jordy make her feel so unattractive.

CHAPTER SEVENTEEN

"DAD START with the grandkids talks yet?"

Jordy choked on a mouthful of Mountain Dew and scowled at Jackson. He swiped the back of his free hand over his mouth and coughed.

"What the hell did you just say?"

Jackson leaned back against the front checkout counter and folded his arms over his chest. He was laughing and looking around, most likely hoping to find Jason or Jamie to tell them he'd just nearly killed their baby brother.

Jordy expected him to point at him and say *gotcha*! So when he took another drink and Jackson shrugged innocently and instead said, "Well? Did he?" Jordy sputtered and choked again. He leaned over, set the Dew on the counter, and pounded his chest with his fist. Coughed up a bit of the warm, oversweet soda and then coughed and swallowed wrong and coughed again.

"Don't be an ass."

"Not kidding." Jackson shrugged when Jordy finally unfolded to stand up straight and look at him. He cleared his now raw throat and rubbed his neck. "I think Dad gave me a day or two after Diana and I got home from Cancun before he started hinting that he and Mom were ready for more grandkids."

Jordy groaned and dropped his hand. "No. He hasn't started and don't remind him."

"Like hell I won't," Jackson said simply. "We each took our turn. It's yours now."

"We just got married. Just got home," Jordy argued. And he hadn't made love to his wife, and never would, and how the hell did his family think he and Kaks were going to make babies when they'd blundered the one make out session he shouldn't have started?

Well. He'd blundered it. She'd been ready and willing, and he gave himself holy hell over that every day. Their friendship was strong enough to make love and stay friends. At least once. He'd like more, sure, but he was an idiot for blowing that perfect opportunity.

"Yeah." Jackson nodded. "'Bout time."

"For God's sake, Jackson. They have seven grandkids. That's enough to keep them busy for awhile."

"What's the matter? You don't think you can make babies? That wife of yours would have some darling kids. Not sure about your ugly mug."

Jordy glanced at the front doors as a woman tugged them open and walked inside.

"Good morning," he called, amazed that he could sound normal while he was standing here taking a verbal beating from his brother. "How are you?"

The woman looked up with a smile. "Fine. Thanks."

"Anything we can help you find?" Jordy asked. Please, he thought. Please let me help you so I can get away from this jackass who's ribbing me about my fake wife.

"Just looking, thanks."

Jordy felt his shoulders fall. Figured Jackson had noticed, and he'd comment on that, too.

"My ugly mug is too busy in that bed with my beautiful

wife," he turned to Jackson and lied through his teeth. Felt a little guilty for it, but he'd told Kaki last night that he'd said something about this to Jackson. Told Jackson Kaki was incredible in bed. What had she said? Was she mad at him for lying about her?

Lying about her? He hadn't lied about her. He'd lied about them. About the nature of their relationship.

He rubbed the bridge of his nose now. Wondered if there was some hidden meaning in what she'd said. Hell of it was, Jordy thought there was always some kind of hidden meaning in what women said. Which is one reason why he kept things easy and loose with his women. Enjoy the sex, forget the rest.

Except with Kaks it was exactly the opposite. Forget the sex, enjoy the rest.

"I thought she was smarter than that," Jackson mumbled, but his grin took the edge off his words.

Did he enjoy the rest? Well. Yeah, he had fun with Kaki. He loved hanging out with her. But things had damned sure gotten complicated.

"Hey. Jordo."

He cringed when he heard his brother Jason call him *Jordo*. After Kaki had told him that girls around town referred to him as Jordo the Dildo. Sounded like a stage name. Be great if he was a stripper. He turned now and snagged the bottle of soda. Met Jason's eyes as he took another drink.

"Dad hit ya with the grandkids thing yet?" Jason asked. Jordy heard Jackson snort behind him. He coughed again, swallowed the soda wrong, and thumped his chest.

"I'm leaving."

"You're not, though." Jason made a show of looking at his phone screen before sliding it back in his pocket. "You have another six hours, bro."

Jordy sighed.

"Tired?" Jason popped him in the bicep with a firm fist.

"Lots of late night lovin' goin' on at the new Steed household?"

"I drove by last night." Jackson busied himself at the register now. Straightened a stack of ads and then checked the tape in the register printer. "I think I heard some Barry White blaring."

Jason snorted. "She model that thing Beth got her yet? For her bachelorette?"

Jordy's mouth went dry. What thing? What thing had his sister-in-law given her that night? He had no idea. They hadn't talked that much about their parties, although Jordy remembered now that Kaki had told him she'd had sex that night. He wondered yet again who the guy was. If Kaki had modeled something sexy for that guy. Something that was supposed to be for his eyes. His pleasure.

Except that they were just pretending.

Besides. Kaki couldn't possibly put anything on that could be hotter than that white bikini.

And look at how he'd handled that.

"Yo. Bro."

Jordy gave himself a mental shake and saw Jason snapping his fingers in front of his face. Jason laughed and looked at Jackson.

"Oh man. He's got it." He nodded.

"Got what?" Jordy asked quickly.

"You're still in honeymoon mode, man," Jason told him. He looked to Jackson for confirmation. "You might be here at work, but your brain is back at home in that nice, warm bed with that pretty little wife."

Jordy cleared his throat and cocked his head to look at Jason.

"Do you blame me?"

"Hell no!" Jackson answered. "And Jason doesn't either. He was ten minutes late to work this morning."

Jordy looked from Jason to Jackson and back at Jason with a grin.

"Take what you can get with kids in the house."

"Hey!" Jamie hollered from the fishing and hunting supplies. "Can one of you ladies get me a new pricing gun? This one just up and died."

"Yep." Jordy nodded and took a step back from Jason. He turned to head back to the office to find Jamie a new gun. "I'm on it."

"Nope, you're on her," Jason mumbled.

"Jordy, you guys ready for kids yet?" Jamie asked when Jordy walked by, already shaking his head at Jason's comment.

"I'm gonna go apply for a job at a fast food place." He tossed his hands in the air and then muttered a string of swear words when he spilled what was left of his Dew.

––––––––

HE STEWED ABOUT IT ALL DAY. WORKING ON THE NEW GOLF display. Double-checking inventory as he built the display. Setting the signs Diana had written for them; Jackson's wife was an artist, so she did a lot of their in-store signage, whether just pretty calligraphy letters or actual cartoons or other drawings. Jordy knew his dad paid her well on a free-lance basis, but she earned the money, no doubt. Jonathon Steed was a slave driver, but he was fair and generous with his wealth and his praise.

Maybe stewed wasn't the right word for it. Obsessed. Over Kaki. And the things his brothers teased him about. About the fact that they weren't true, and that he wanted them to be true—he thought—and they were married, and they could have *been* true. And yet, if they'd slept together—if they did it once, it *wouldn't* be enough—they would surely ruin their friendship. When they divorced, if he ended up with Brianna or not, he would hate the thought of another man doing things to Kaki's body that he'd once been allowed to do. He already hated the thought, dammit, and he hadn't been allowed to do much of anything.

Frustrating.

He sat back on his heels and studied the ball and cup he'd put on the display. Looked stupid in his opinion. He'd set out a golf bag, stick some clubs in it, and stand a mannequin there in a golf shirt and pants and be done. Jason always had to get cutesy with this crap, and it drove Jordy to distraction. Wondered why his dad didn't turn some of this stuff over to him. Either the traveling part or the advertising stuff. Sure, he dealt with the agents who visited from the local papers and TV studios, but Jason lorded it over him that *he* was in charge of advertising and his was the last say.

Jordy shrugged as if to say *I give up* and stood. The displays weren't what sold their merchandise to locals anyway.

Would this be an issue? If he'd married Lauren? She'd have laughed in his face if he'd suggested this crazy idea to her instead of Kaki. If Lauren had been single, though, would he have wanted to ask her before Kaki? If he and Lauren had been alone in Florida, if he'd have started that little bedroom thing with Lauren and they'd ended up half-naked together on that bed, would they have done it?

Yes. Absolutely he would have taken everything Lauren put on the table. He'd have pinned her to that bed and ridden her long and hard. It might have been fan-fucking-tastic, too. But then, maybe not. If Lauren had been single, he wouldn't have asked her. He'd have asked Kaks.

Why was that? He cared about both of them. Always had, always would. Both pretty, both sexy, and both smart. Funny and generous, both of them had always had his back. Lauren would be wild in bed; he knew that. Hell, everyone who knew her knew that about her. But Kaki was mysterious. Alluring. Sweet, but not innocent. Sly, but not cunning.

He gave himself a mental shake and wondered why he was debating this with himself. For one thing, didn't matter because Lauren was married. He liked her husband. They were all good friends. And second, he was currently married to Kaki, fake or not, and he still didn't get the way thinking about Kaks made him feel all tangled and hollow inside.

He needed a sounding board. Looked around the store. Heard his dad and Jackson talking somewhere nearby. Heard the broadcast of a Cubs game from the overhead speaker. Wasn't like he could talk to his brothers about it. They'd die laughing at him. All of them. And they'd tell their wives, and they would all get a damned belly laugh at his expense. Couldn't tell his Dad. He'd skin him alive for wasting all the money on a fake wedding. Who the hell even knew what his mom would say? She'd probably tell him to love the wife he had.

Lauren. He could take Lauren out for a beer; well, no, he couldn't do that, either. He could take Lauren out for ice cream and lay it all out for her. She'd laugh. She'd say I told you so. But then she might offer a suggestion. Not sure what it would be. Not sure what he wanted it to be.

What if she told him he needed to grow the hell up, cut Kaks loose, and move on with or without Brianna?

CHAPTER EIGHTEEN

THE PRIOR CITY Museum was a quiet building, people tended to tiptoe through and murmur quietly to each other, much like they were in a library. But Kaki knew when her lunch hour rolled around, her coworkers would bombard her in the break room. She'd run into Connie Morgan first thing this morning. Connie being some indeterminate age, married for a couple hundred years, and the mother of six grown children, Kaki hadn't been expecting the woman to grill her about the honeymoon. Connie had asked after her, of course: if she was well, if she and her young man had enjoyed the beach, and how were they getting settled now that they were home. Kaki had stood for a moment with the woman and shared sweet stories, some partially true and some totally fabricated. She told Connie that Jordy was such a gentleman; usually he was, but Kaki didn't add that she said so because he didn't flaunt his other women in front of her face in Florida. She also told Connie the beach and the gulf and Florida in general were beautiful and peaceful and that she missed it already and wished they could go back.

She'd clocked in and exchanged pleasantries with Bruce, the security guard at the front door. He'd asked if Jordy had taken in any baseball on the honeymoon. Kaki had told him no, and Bruce (again, she couldn't gauge his age and didn't want to try) had roared with laughter and patted her shoulder and said *of course not, kid. You probably wore him out.*

Kaki had simply stared at him, shocked by the teasing, and nodded as she hurried without appearing to hurry away from him. She made her round of the museum floor, as was her habit. Walked slowly, fingers trailing over the display cases as if she was greeting old friends. Read bits and pieces of the plaques and displays, though she could probably recite everything by heart if pressed. She'd loved history since she was a kid, and she'd known even then that she was the odd girl out in school. Lauren hated history. Always told Kaki history was in the past and therefore not important. Kaki had tried to argue that history repeated itself and she'd tried to point out examples from history, but Lauren had stared at her, almost catatonic, and finally Kaki had offered her a shot of tequila and revived her. She hadn't tried again. Lauren stopped complaining about Kaki's obsession with the past.

She'd prefer to work in a museum in New York or DC. National history. Ancient civilizations. European history. The Chinese dynasties. All of it fascinated her. She'd love to be knee deep in a museum that showcased Civil War items or World War artifacts. But to do that, she'd have to leave Prior. Pick up her life and go somewhere else. She didn't want to. Wasn't that she was afraid. She didn't think she'd get homesick. She just wasn't particularly adventurous, and she liked her life here, and so she worked in the Prior City Museum and happily visited the museums in any city she visited.

Maybe that's why Jordy had been certain she'd talk her brother out of leaving, heading to San Antonio. Maybe he thought she was afraid. Uninspired. Obviously, he thought that about her in other areas of her life.

She'd pursed her lips and folded her arms over her chest.

Slipped out of the main show room and moseyed down the hall to her workroom. Took a deep breath as she surveyed the boxes of things someone had delivered while she was gone, the items unearthed from a house in the county long-since abandoned. Lauren would hate this. Lauren might walk out on the job if she was greeted with something like this when she came back from her honeymoon. Junk, she'd say. She wasn't a garbage girl; why did she have to sort through someone's trash?

Kaki nibbled on her lip. Considered grabbing a cup of coffee before she got started. Decided against it, because she felt like she'd put on a few pounds last week and certainly hadn't had any exercise, say in the form of crazy, mind-blowing sex during the same week, and she didn't want to pack on even another pound or inch. Not that Jordy would notice, but one day, there would be no fake husband and she'd be back on the market.

Lauren's trash was her treasure. She'd tucked her hair behind her ears and moved to the tables covered in another family's life and dug in. One thing that struck her time and again was that people were people across all times and ages. The world and political environments might change, but people, their basic needs and desires, remained constant. People in ancient times and people in colonial America and people in the eighties were the same as people now. A twenty-five-year old woman in colonial America probably worked a heck of a lot harder than Kaki. She'd be keeping a household, doing the wash, and cooking and caring for her children. Kaki worked outside the home, and sure, she did laundry and cleaned house, but she had a washing machine and dryer and a vacuum cleaner and life was easier. But that twenty-five-year old woman from history had loved some-one. Maybe she'd been very much in love with her husband, or maybe she'd feared him. But if she had children, she'd loved them. Kaki had a husband she loved, albeit in a different way. But one day she hoped to have that forever, romantic love. And children.

That thought brought to mind the little kids on the beach and playing in the gulf with Jordy and the way her stomach had dropped when Jordy had asked if she wanted kids and she'd reacted and said no, she wouldn't carry his baby.

Jordy had seven nieces and nephews. He was crazy about all of them, and Kaki had no doubt he'd make a good dad. But his brothers had all been settled down by his age. Real love, real marriages. Jordy had time, but that day on the beach, he'd sounded a little bit desperate and that had made her feel panicked because going along with marrying him was one thing. She'd even been willing to (willing, hell, she'd begged for it) have sex with him, but having his baby was a step too far. Imagine if they got pregnant and one day their child heard the story of how they scammed their family and friends to make some femme fetal jealous.

Nope. Not happening.

In fact, after last night, when Jordy had kissed her on the back step and then intimated that she was like a little sister to him, she'd vowed to not let things even sort of get out of hand again. Ever. She'd play along when someone else was around, but she was drawing the line on that stuff when it was just the two of them in the house.

She managed to slink through the morning with relative ease, but a couple of her coworkers she considered friends cornered her in the break room at lunchtime. They asked about mundane things, like the flight, the beach, whether the water was cold, and the very personal things she'd known they would ask. She didn't blame them. They were close; maybe not quite like she and Lauren and Jordy, but they were close friends, and they minded each other's business often. Luckily, the questions about the beach and what the water was like sent Kaki's mind shooting back to the morning she and Jordy had played in the gulf together, when he'd come onto her when she was on the phone, just to get her to make a little noise.

Kaki wore a rosy blush as she hit them with a mix of fictional and nonfictional details. She wasn't sure what embarrassed her more: remembering the thing with Jordy, wishing she could rewind and do that day over, the fact that they knew Jordy and she didn't know Jordy—biblically— though she didn't *think* either of them did, either, or just the fact that she was flat out lying to her good friends. She sucked down a quick drink of water while they ruminated over the story she'd told about the last night they were on the beach. Felt a moment of pity for Jordy if all of his brothers and sisters-in-law were giving him this kind of grief. And then changed her mind immediately. This had been Jordy's hare-brained scheme, so he could handle the ribbing.

Then again, what if Jordy was saying the same kinds of things to them as she'd just said? What if at Jordy's parents' house Sunday for dinner, the bunch of them were looking at her, envisioning her...

Suddenly warm, she set her water bottle down and patted her cheeks. Leisha and Megan eyed her curiously, but before she could even try to make up a story for why she was suddenly blushing again, they both burst out laughing and wagged their eyebrows suggestively and mourned the fact that Jordy Steed was a married man.

Though they were probably kidding, the idea that maybe they weren't, that maybe one of them had been with Jordy, made her feel a little funny. Made her stomach feel hollow, like she was back in high school and there were mean girls laughing at her because they knew something she didn't. Leisha and Megan weren't mean girls, by any definition, but they were both young and sexy. Leisha had honey blond hair down to her butt and Kaki knew Jordy had a thing for long hair, and Megan had boobs the size of bowling balls, another of Jordy's weaknesses. What if one of them had been with him? Didn't that make something…weird? Should she have asked Jordy for a list of women he'd been with before they got married? Maybe a list of local women he *hadn't* been with would be simpler.

Maybe she'd ask him. Tonight. If they were at home, she could just casually mention this conversation and ask. Not about every woman he'd been with, because she didn't need or care to know about that. But maybe just about her friends. She could just feel her way around and see if her husband had been with any of her friends.

What she wanted to tell them, or maybe, what she needed to talk about and not necessarily what she wanted to tell *them*, was that she'd talked to Owen. They both knew she'd been involved with him back when it was going on. They didn't mind him, but neither of them knew him as well as Lauren did (Lauren didn't like him much) and they didn't know she'd hooked up with him the night of her bachelorette (Lauren did) and so she didn't want to tell them that she'd been texting with him while she was on her honeymoon. That would make her the bad guy.

Kaki said her goodbyes to them as they cleaned up the break area. She ducked into the women's room. Took a few extra moments in front of the mirror hoping to calm herself. She'd rushed through a roller coaster of emotions during her lunch hour, and now heading back to her workstation, she felt overstuffed, though she'd only played with her yogurt and apple. She figured the uncomfortably full feeling she had was more about Jordy and the situation she'd allowed herself to be in than the meager lunch she'd had.

Maybe instead of rushing straight home to get to work with more unpacking, she'd drive by Lauren and Tyler's place. Then again, she'd only be rehashing what they'd already said, wouldn't she? She'd complained enough; even she was tired of hearing herself complain about being married to Jordy. She'd agreed to this to help him out, no more, no less. Jordy had left her shortchanged in the bedroom the other day, but he hadn't promised her any such thing to begin with.

Maybe she needed to find a way to see Owen without being found out. Not that Jordy would care, but she didn't want to embarrass him. She'd let him set the pace for their pretend marriage and pretend breakup. After all, it was all about Jordy and his fight to get Brianna back.

CHAPTER NINETEEN

JORDY FOUND Kaki teetering on a chair, a stool, actually, with no back, in the kitchen when he came home. He might have taken a few seconds to admire her lean, muscled calves and her smooth, sun-kissed skin, but instead he dragged his eyes up over her waist and the sun-kissed skin exposed between the waistband of her white athletic shorts and the navy tank and over the curve of her breast—not the one that had almost fallen from the bikini top the day they'd made out—and up over her lean, muscled arm to her fingertip, painted clear with that white tip. Jordy thought it was a French manicure, and he liked it, and right about now a French kiss sounded particularly good.

"What are you doing?" He rushed to the back of the chair, afraid it would wobble and Kaki might fall.

She eased back from her tiptoes to stand flat-footed on the chair and looked down at him.

"Putting stuff away," she answered simply. "The house isn't gonna sort itself out."

"Well. No." He shrugged. "I know that. But…"

"What?" She jumped down, drawing his eyes from hers to the little bounce in her breasts.

"Well. The chair was wobbling. You could've fallen."

"The chair was not wobbling," she argued. She turned her back to him and wandered over to the high top pub table they'd had delivered earlier this morning. Because Kaki had gone back to work, Jordy's sister-in-law, Diana, had come by and waited around for the furniture delivery. They'd ordered the pub table and chairs and a few pieces for the living room; the rest of their furnishings were a combination of his and hers.

"It could have wobbled," he mumbled. "You could've fallen."

Kaki cut him a smartass grin over her shoulder and then turned back to the box on the table.

"Worried about me?"

He took a moment to look at her. Really look at her. At his best friend. The wedding ring he'd put on her finger just over a week ago. Found himself wishing for half a crazy second that things could just stay like this. He'd almost be able to handle no sex if he could share every day with Kaki Harper. Kaki Harper Steed.

"What?" She turned and caught him looking at her.

He shook his head. Took a few steps toward her and shoved his hands in his pockets.

"How was your day?"

"Fine." She shrugged.

"Lucky you."

She arched her eyebrows. "Why? Yours was bad?"

"All of my brothers took turns asking today if Dad has hit me with the *need more grandkids* conversation."

She grimaced. No other word for it. The little laugh that escaped her cut the edge a bit, but it still got to him. Still bothered him that she'd flat out said no to having a baby with him. Well. No. Not that she'd said no, because *that* would be a disaster, and he knew it. But the way she'd acted as if making a baby with him, parenting a child with him was a ridiculous idea. *That* hurt. Still.

"Oh boy." She cleared her throat. "And has he?"

"Well, as of each brother asking me, no," he answered. He stepped closer to her. "But when I grabbed a drink on my afternoon break, yes. He let me know that he and Mom would be tickled pink to welcome more grandchildren into the fold."

Kaki worked her mouth as if she had something to say, and she was trying desperately not to say it.

"Kaks."

"Hmm?"

"What're you thinking?"

She shook her head and turned her eyes to the box on the table. Jordy noticed she'd laid a white sheet over the table to protect it from scratches. While she was busy looking at the box, he slipped his hand from his pocket and stroked his fingers up over her arm.

"I think we need to get the kitchen situated tonight," she said quietly. She didn't flinch, but Jordy couldn't miss the way she pulled her arm back from his reach.

"I was thinking…" He stopped talking when she lifted her eyes to his again. Gave him that look that said they were going to get the kitchen situated tonight if it killed them. He answered with an eager nod. "Yeah, yeah, that's fine. Let me go change my clothes."

She nodded but looked away again as he turned to slip out of the room.

"What?" she asked just before he could go down the hall.

"What?" He stopped walking but didn't turn around to look at her.

"What were you thinking?"

"Um." He'd been on the verge of suggesting they get a puppy. Offer the puppy as a replacement grandchild, never mind that the puppy would be company for him when he and Kaki split up. He turned to look at her and shook his head. "Nothing." Maybe it was stupid to suggest it. They were busy; they both worked and if they had a puppy, one of them would have to come home through the day to check on it. Too much extra work right now.

She pursed her lips and watched him walk away. He heard her moving again as he climbed the steps.

"Don't climb on those chairs!" he hollered as he dashed up the last of the stairs. He heard her yell something back at him, probably arguing, if he knew Kaki, but he couldn't make out what she'd said. He unzipped his pants as he walked into the bedroom. Glanced at the bed they were sleeping in and wished just once he'd find it wrecked from their activities. She hadn't made the bed, but you'd never know from looking at it in the mornings that two newlyweds slept in it.

He turned his back to it and kicked out of his jeans. Picked them up and tossed them in the hamper. If he didn't do it, she'd do it later, and Jordy didn't want her to have to pick up after him. He grabbed a pair of athletic shorts from the pile on his side of the bed; they hadn't unpacked this room, either, and he considered telling her maybe it should be next. But if they were working side by side in the bedroom, he wouldn't be able to keep his hands off her.

He stepped into the shorts, whipped his work shirt over his head and dropped it in the hamper, too. Went down the hall to the bathroom and took care of business. Eyed Kaki's stuff as he did so. Again, they hadn't put things away in here, and Kaki's make up and hair stuff was pushed up in the corner of the vanity by the wall. He noticed her perfume bottle and considered picking it up to take a big whiff but decided that was a little creepy. He washed his hands and then looked around for a towel. When he found it, his eyes locked on something skimpy and satiny and beige hanging on the back of the door.

His mouth went dry. He envisioned the satiny material

against her breasts. Adjusted his cock before tossing down the towel on the vanity and leaving the room. He hesitated at the bedroom. Would it bug her if he went downstairs shirtless? Probably. He didn't kid himself. It wasn't that she wouldn't be able to keep her hands to herself, unfortunately. But she might think he was rude if he didn't put a shirt on. Besides, he couldn't go down in sock feet if he was going to be climbing on anything. He'd end up being the one to fall and break his arm, and then everybody'd get a good laugh at his expense. So he needed to grab shoes, too.

When he did get back downstairs to the kitchen, the stool was still in place, but Kaki was squatting this time in front of a cabinet. Again he watched her for a moment. Admired the smooth slide of her healthy tan skin over her muscles as she reached in to arrange the skillets and pots and pans, all from his place, neatly in the cabinet.

"Are you hungry?" she asked without looking at him.

Her question took him by surprise and since he was eyeing her butt, he felt a flash of guilt and then he realized she was asking if he was ready for dinner. He cleared his throat and rolled his head on his neck.

"Kind of."

She nodded and stood, still without looking at him.

"I made fruit salad since it's so hot out, and I was thinking maybe we could just do burgers." She stopped talking when he stepped up right in front of her. In her space, no apologies. "What're you doing?"

Overcome by the flecks of gold in her brown eyes—they made him think of a sunrise—he only stared.

"I don't know what you're used to doing," she tried again, but Jordy dropped his eyes from hers to her parted lips. That perfect pink he'd noticed that day on the beach. In the gulf. The day he'd tasted her lips again.

She shivered; he felt goose bumps on her arm as he slid his fingers over her again. Leaned into her and flicked his tongue over the center of her lips. She sighed, he hoped with pleasure, but in the next instant, when he pressed his lips to hers, she took a step back and shook her head.

"Jordy."

"No?"

"It's just…" She ducked her head. "It's one thing when we're out and people are seeing us. But I can't keep…"

"Can't keep playing around with me," he mumbled. Nodded. "Okay. I'm sorry."

He heard her sigh, thought she sounded upset. Decided maybe he should wait her out and see if she had more to say.

"Can I ask you something?" She cleared her throat, but she spoke quietly.

"Of course."

"You know the girls I work with?"

"I know who they are," he answered.

She took a quick breath and lifted her chin. Met his gaze.

"Have you slept with either of them?"

"No."

He hadn't. Sure, the blonde had gorgeous hair, and what guy wouldn't want to play with the other one's tits, but he hadn't been with either of them. Didn't know their names, never saw them when he was out on the weekends. He only knew of them through Kaki.

She nodded.

"Why? Did they say—"

"No." She snapped out of her thoughts and shook her head. "No. It's just…knowing…your reputation. I don't wanna just find out from a friend that she's been with you like that. It would make things kind of weird for me."

His *reputation*. God, but he hated when she said things like that. All true, and yet, it made him feel ashamed when she had to bring it up like that.

"I have not been with any of your friends."

"None of them?'

He hesitated. Maybe now would be a good time to admit to those twenty minutes with her college girlfriend the night before the wedding. But that wasn't what she was talking about, was it? She meant girls right here in Prior that she might run into in the grocery store or at work.

And Lauren. Did she mean Lauren, too? Well, he couldn't admit that to her, no matter what.

"No."

"Okay." She nodded. Backed away from him and turned her attention to a now empty box on the table. She picked it up and carried it to the back door.

"What about you?" he asked as he lifted another box from the floor and hefted it up to put it on the table.

"Have I been with any of my friends?"

The thought struck him as particularly sexy. Not Kaki and Lauren. That was just too weird. But Kaki with another—he counted to ten. Gave himself a mental shake.

"Or have I been with any of your friends?"

"No." He pulled the box open. "That's not what I meant."

"What'd you mean?"

"Well." He reached into the box and grabbed a cup wrapped in newspaper. "What the hell?"

She rolled her eyes and took it from him. Unwrapped it to reveal a big rust-colored coffee mug.

"Looks like something you just took off the pottery wheel." He shrugged.

"You have no imagination."

He raked his eyes over her from head to toe and back up to meet her eyes. "I think I do."

She shook her head and carried the cup to the counter. "Hand me the stuff."

"You're not climbing on the stool again. I'll put stuff up there."

"You're not that much taller than me," she reminded him.

"Wanna bet?" He laughed as he pulled another cup from

the box and took the newspaper from it. He carried it over to her and then stood toe-to-toe with her and looked down at her.

"Yeah, but your reach isn't that much longer." She tugged on his arm when he reached up over their heads to the cabinet. "Besides, the dishes need to be right here on the first shelf. Where I can easily reach them."

He looked at the shelf in the open cabinet. There were mixing bowls and plastic containers on the higher shelves, but the bottom shelf was bare. She'd been planning.

When their eyes met, he saw her sink her teeth into her lower lip. Felt them on his tongue the day they'd kissed with that hunger that had led them to the bed. Remembered the name Owen and wondered now if she'd heard from him again.

He backed away from her, ignored her little sigh because it sounded like disappointment, and turned back to the box.

"Have you?" He hoped he sounded nonchalant. The thought of Kaki rolling around naked with one of his friends made his skin crawl. The thought that one of them might have touched her, been inside her pounded in his head. Made him jealous, yes, but also he wanted to punch that guy's lights out because Kaki wasn't that kind of girl.

"Have I what?"

"Been with any of my friends?"

"Not since I handed my virginity over to Tate." She shrugged when he looked at her. Took the cup from his outstretched hand.

"We weren't friends."

She shrugged again. "Maybe not, but you were all in that crowd, Jordy."

"Was he good?"

"What?" She looked at him with wide eyes, obviously surprised by his question.

"Tate. Was he good?"

She snorted. "No. Of course not. I didn't know what good sex was until…"

"Until what?" he prompted her. Stood with his back to the table now, the box full of dishes and folded his arms over his chest.

She looked away from him. Made a show of studying the cabinet, though she wouldn't actually put anything in it until he started handing her plates.

"Until I got older," she mumbled. He saw the twinge of pink in her cheeks. "Away from guys like…"

He nodded. And turned around yet again. He wasn't dizzy, though. Maybe a little pissed off. Definitely a little stung. She was going to say *guys like you*. Wasn't fair of her to judge him if she'd never been with him, was it?

CHAPTER TWENTY

HER PHONE RANG as she climbed the ladder. Kaki groaned and shot a look over her shoulder at Jackson's wife, Diana. Her sister-in-law grabbed it from the tarp-covered dresser and handed it to her without looking at the screen. Kaki glanced at it and felt her heart skip a beat when she saw Owen's name on the screen. Wasn't the fact that Owen was calling that flustered her, but that Diana could have seen a guy's name on her phone. And no, she didn't sleep with every guy who called her, but *Kaki had called him* on her honeymoon, and she sure as hell couldn't explain that away. She ignored the call and stuffed the phone in the back pocket of her old denim cutoffs. When she felt Diana watching her, she ignored her and eyed the ceiling in the spare bedroom.

She and Jordy had accomplished a lot this week, but they'd worked quietly, separately after Tuesday night. In fact, it felt like Jordy had gone out of his way all week since then to avoid her. She'd wondered several times what she'd done to make him mad, considered asking him, and decided for now this worked better. They got more done when they weren't pawing at each other, and while she'd be all about that fun stuff if they were really married, she'd meant it the other night when she'd said she couldn't do it anymore.

After giving it some thought, she decided maybe that was why he'd quit talking to her. No more free kisses. Then again, he'd had access to everything in Florida, and he'd turned her down, so who knew what his deal was?

The house was full today, and while it was technically a painting party, not everyone was painting. Her mother-in-law was in her kitchen, dishing up sandwiches and snacks, as Lauren and her mom were at her house fixing dinner for everyone for later. Kaki had no idea what they were making, but she'd felt more than one stab of guilt over the fact that their friends and family were all gathering around to help, and she and Jordy were only playing games.

"So." Diana cleared her throat. She'd climbed a ladder in the opposite corner of the room. Kaki shot her a quick glance. "How's married life?"

Kaki had been asked the same question hundreds of times this week. She'd started out with a cheery answer, something along the lines of *great* or depending on who asked, *he keeps me busy*, but as the week wore on and Jordy spent his evenings in any room where she wasn't, she'd grown tired of the question. Tired of the lie she had to tell.

"It's good," she said now, her back to Diana.

"Mm-hmm."

"What?" She twisted around on the ladder to look at her.

"That almost sounded sincere." Diana nodded. Kaki watched her dip her brush in the paint tray and turn her attention to the wall. She dabbed at it high up near the ceiling.

"What do you mean?"

"Hmm?"

Kaki wondered if Diana was trying for that prissy tone. *"Almost sounded sincere.* What does that mean?"

Diana looked at her again and turned back to the wall.

"Evelyn and I think something's up," Diana said with a shrug.

"Up?"

"Yeah. This isn't real. You and Jordy."

"Why would you say that?"

She should sound outraged that anyone would question their love. If they were really in love. But she was too curious about how Diana and her mother-in-law would know something was up to play the worried new bride, desperately in love with her husband.

"You guys are besties." Diana shook her head. "The vibe's totally off."

"Di—"

"Which—"

"You can't fall in love with your best friend?" Kaki asked with a laugh that was so obnoxiously fake, she rolled her eyes at herself. Sure, people fell in love with best friends. Happened all the time. Happened in all the rom-com movies. She'd thrown it out there as a joke, but she wanted Diana's opinion.

"Well, yeah, but that's not you guys," Diana answered simply. "Ev's planning to wait you out. Play along to the end of game. But I wanna know what's going on."

Kaki swallowed hard and let her gaze fall to her own paint tray. She dipped her brush and got started on the wall where it met the ceiling. Of course no one would believe she and Jordy were really in love. She wasn't his type. Never in a million years would a plain girl like Kaki be the object of a guy like Jordy's affection. She wasn't sure he could fall in love with anyone, but she damned sure ought to know better than if he did, to think she'd be the one.

"Nothing's going on, Di," she mumbled, and sadly, that was one truth. Maybe not the one Diana was fishing for, but certainly the truth about what was going on inside her sham of a marriage.

They worked in silence for a while, with Jordy and his brothers traipsing in and out to check on them. She heard them down the hall the first time when they all came upstairs together. His brothers were ribbing him about their bedroom. The big bed they slept in. Except of course, they thought she and Jordy did a lot more in that bed. Jordy had actually destroyed it earlier, to make it look like they'd had crazy sex before they got up. She didn't care, exactly, though she did tell him most women would make the bed anyway, especially if they were expecting people at the house.

"What color are you doing in here?"

Kaki looked over her shoulder now at Jordy and Jackson. They stood just inside the door, both of them with their feet spread wide and their hands on their hips as they surveyed the room.

"Some grayish green color," Jordy told his brother. Kaki rolled her eyes. She wouldn't tell him the color on the can was *kale green*, because then they'd be hung up on kale, and though Kaki had nothing against kale, she didn't want to stand here and debate health benefits as if she actually ate it on a regular basis.

"I think you should do yellow," Jackson announced.

"Why yellow?" Diana asked her husband.

"Then they're covered when the baby comes. Won't matter if it's a boy or girl. Yellow is neutral."

"So's green," Diana argued.

"No baby coming," Jordy talked over the top of them.

"No baby." Kaki put in her two cents. She looked at Diana again, but her sister-in-law was busy with the wall.

"We need another girl," Jackson went on as if no one had spoken.

"Jack," Diana scolded him.

"What?"

"You promised you wouldn't do this to them."

"I know." Jackson almost hit sincere, but then his wild

laugh tore through the room. "But it's just too damned fun. I had to put up with it from Jason and Jamie."

"You guys hungry?" Jordy asked. "Mom's got some killer subs going down there."

"Nope." Kaki doubted she'd be able to eat all day or night now. Diana's comments had left her stomach feeling sour.

"I might grab a bite of one," Diana decided. She'd worked her way across one wall. Kaki turned and watched her climb down the ladder. She shot Kaki a quick smile and then followed Jackson out of the room. Kaki sighed and looked at Jordy.

"What's wrong?"

She watched Jordy approach the ladder. Saw him reach to touch her leg and still jumped when he skimmed his finger-tips over the back of her knee.

"Why aren't you working?"

"I am." He nodded. "Jamie and I just put that new sink thing in the bathroom downstairs."

"Yeah?" She arched her eyebrows. "Does it work?"

"Hey." He cupped his hand around her calf muscle. She backed down the ladder a few rungs, stopped nearly even with him. "Of course it works."

He stroked his thumb over her cheek. Flinched in apology when she met his eyes. Apparently, she looked as shocked and breathless as she felt. He hadn't touched her. Since Tuesday when he'd kissed her and she'd backed away, Jordy hadn't touched her until now. Her leg. And now her face.

"You had...paint..." He pointed at his face where he'd touched hers.

"Your sister-in-law," she said quietly in case there was someone in the hallway, "doesn't believe this is real."

"What?"

"Diana told me she doesn't believe what we're doing."

"Well, she can be wrong—"

"And neither does your mom."

"My…" Jordy raised his eyebrows. "My mom. My mom thinks we're scamming people?"

"Jordy, we are," she reminded him. "They're onto us."

"So." He shrugged. "Does that mean you just wanna come clean now?"

"No!" she answered quickly. "No. Not at all!"

"Then what—"

She kissed him. Without a second thought, she hooked her arm around his neck and dragged him closer to kiss him. Her teeth bumped his, and she laughed and then Jordy moved in closer and slid his hands over her waist. There was a tiny part of her that wanted to cry. The only reason he was game to make out like this right now was the hope that someone would catch them at it. Kaki figured they looked too methodical about it when people were watching. They needed to make out. To *feel* something. To light each other up like they had for that few seconds in Florida to make it believable.

The rest of her was willing to forget that Jordy only wanted her to play the game through to the end. To get Brianna back. And enjoy what his tongue on hers felt like. To savor the taste of his drink of choice on his tongue. The press of their bodies.

He finally decided to get in the game. She gasped out loud when he moved his hands and she felt them on her back, under her t-shirt. She let him go, wondered how far they'd have to take this before they got caught. She hoped not far, because this wasn't really how she'd like for this to happen if it was going to happen. But on the other hand, this seemed to be the only way she was going to get what she wanted from him.

Did she want this from him? When had her need for something physical, for sex, become an obsession with *sex with Jordy*?

"Jordy." Her breath caught as he moved his hands up over her breasts. She felt his fingers stroke her nipples through her bra. He groaned softly when they beaded with excitement. She wanted more, but not like this. Knowing that as soon as someone walked into the room, he'd turn it off and walk away.

"Is this the bra that was hanging in the bathroom Tuesday?"

"What?"

"Slinky, silky, beige."

"No."

"No. Because it feels like…" He did it again. Rubbed the pad of his thumb over her already hard nipple. She felt his lips curve under hers. "I wish I could see what I'm doing to you-"

"God, leave them alone for five minutes," Jackson groaned loud and long, and Jordy jumped away from Kaki. Let his hands fall to his sides. Kaki swiped the back of her hand over her mouth and climbed back up the ladder without looking at him or Diana. She was more embarrassed to be caught by Diana than Jordy's brother.

Jordy hung out by her ladder for a few minutes, even after Jackson moseyed back out of the room. She caught him watching her once, and she frowned and asked him quietly, so Diana couldn't hear her, what was wrong. He made a show of fixing his shorts, as if to tell her he couldn't just walk downstairs right now with a boner like his. She wondered if he thought of Brianna when he kissed her. If that was what had happened in Florida. The one time he'd gotten carried away with her, had he been wishing, pretending she was someone else?

Because the thought hurt, and because being hurt by Jordy Steed made her feel stupid, she turned back to her job with the wall without comment. Eventually, he wandered back out of the room, and she supposed, back downstairs to work on something. She had no idea what her house might look like this evening when all their family left. Figured she had no particular décor in mind and no particular right to complain if she didn't care for how it turned out. She was a temporary figure here, nothing more.

The thought made her paintbrush feel much heavier than it was. She let loose with a wistful sigh and then remembered she wasn't alone. Shot a peek at Diana, thankful her sister-in-law wasn't looking at her.

Her parents would be crushed if they found out the whole wedding was a sham. They loved Jordy. Sure, they'd been as surprised as everyone else when she'd come home wearing his ring and announced they were getting married. But her mom had been ecstatic; even Michael was happy about it. They'd all be so disappointed for her, in her. Angry, too. She hadn't let them put much money toward the wedding; she'd felt responsible for her part, since she was walking into the church knowing at some point she and Jordy would call it quits. And Jordy had insisted on paying for quite a bit of the wedding details. They'd argued about it, but in the end, he won. He'd assured her that his family had put in a lot when each of his brothers got married, and then he'd hammered away at the fact that Kaki was doing him a favor and hope-fully soon, he'd be holed up somewhere with Brianna and Kaki would be somewhere with someone she loved.

The thought made her sick now. Not the worry over what her parents would say. Not even the idea that Evelyn knew they were just pretending. How could Jordy's mom suspect they were pretending all of this stuff and let them go through with it? No, what made her sick was thinking about Jordy holed up somewhere with Brianna. She wondered what Brianna did to turn him on. What it would take for her to do it.

Diana was right, though. They'd been friends far too long for him to see her that way. And maybe if they did have sex now, Jordy would walk away and be okay with going back to just friends. But Kaki didn't think she could.

She'd see him with another woman, *Brianna*, and it would all come rushing back to her. So, this was best. Just play the game.

Still. How was she to play the game, the physical game, without getting caught up?

"Kaki?"

"Hmm?" She roused herself from her thoughts and looked at Diana, who was now standing at the foot of her ladder.

"You okay?"

"Yeah, I'm fine." Kaki shrugged. "Why?" She cleared her throat and beamed what she hoped was a *boy, I'm so happy to be married to Jordy Steed* smile down at her sister-in-law.

"You just painted right over the doorframe." Diana nodded her head to the woodwork behind Kaki. Kaki looked back at it and mumbled a few choice words.

"It's okay, ya know?" Diana said quietly.

"What is?" Kaki turned and leaned to look at the trim. They'd taped it, so hopefully they could just peel the tape away and the woodwork itself would be okay. Still. She hated that Jordy would see it. She wasn't stupid. She knew how to paint.

"Whatever it is you guys are doing." Diana raised her eyebrows. "I'm sure there's a reason, and even if it was one night that put you in this situation, it'll all work out. It's okay to end up loving him."

Kaki blinked. What the hell had Diana just said? Did she think Kaki was pregnant? For God's sake, they'd been engaged forever. It wasn't like they'd thrown together a shotgun wedding so they could give a baby married parents and one last name.

"Diana, I'm not pregnant." She shook her head.

Diana only shrugged.

"We've been engaged for a long time," Kaki reminded her. "And while I put on a few pounds on the honeymoon, this isn't a baby bump."

"Oh for Pete's sake!" Diana laughed and squeezed Kaki's hand as she climbed down the ladder. "I don't think that."

"But you said—"

"Baby bump." Diana shook her head. "You don't have a baby bump. You're too thin."

Kaki stared at her silently, not sure where she was going with anything she'd said.

"You don't act very happy, Kaki," she continued. "And I wondered if you rushed to get engaged because..." She shrugged her eyebrows dramatically. "A lot of pregnancies end with miscarriage."

"Oh my God. Seriously?" Kaki covered her mouth. "Oh my God. No. Diana, no. I've never been pregnant. That's not...what this is about."

"Then what is it?" Diana asked her.

Kaki swallowed hard. Summoned up her best acting and said simply, "I'm in love with him."

The words made her feel a little shaky. A little bit cold. Sick to her stomach.

Diana cocked her head and studied her face for a long moment. Finally she nodded and stepped away.

"Maybe you are," she mumbled as she walked out of the room. Kaki stared after her, wondering what the hell she was supposed to take away from the discussion. That the only reason Jordy might marry her would be because she was pregnant? Was that really any different from him marrying her to make his ex jealous? Not for her, not really. Was she supposed to think that she'd pulled off the acting moment of her life to make Diana believe she might indeed be in love with Jordy Steed? And if so, why did Diana walk out of here then as if someone had died right here in this room?

Or *did* Kaki have feelings for Jordy Steed?

CHAPTER TWENTY-ONE

JORDY WASN'T sure the house was completely finished when the gang headed out for Lauren and Tyler's, but it was close enough. They'd done a first coat of paint in the spare bedroom upstairs and the room downstairs they weren't sure yet what to call. Maybe a den. Maybe an office. Except that neither of them needed an office. He and Jason had set the pedestal sink in the first floor bathroom. Jordy thought it looked nice. And it did work; he'd acted affronted when Kaki questioned him, but he would admit to himself he wasn't sure he'd known what the hell he was doing. He hadn't excelled in college, not when he knew he had the family business to fall back on. But he wasn't particularly mechanically inclined, either, so the sink had been an experiment. He'd wondered, though, when the sink was done if Kaki would want new tile flooring. The linoleum in the small room was worn and faded.

The kitchen was finished. All their kitchen utensils and spices and dishes and pots and pans had been put away. The pub table and stools looked great with the fancy little flower centerpiece thing Kaki's mom had brought over. He'd walked her through the house, taking his time showing off the big rooms, the hardwood floors and the high ceilings as if he and Kaki were very much in love and very much a new happily married couple, and he wanted to impress his mother-in-law. Lanna had beamed; she'd seemed so happy all day, he'd had a few moments of guilt so strong, it had burned up his throat like acid reflux.

He and his brothers had moved the furniture around until Beth reminded them it didn't matter what any of them thought, because it was Kaki's house and it was her decision. Jordy agreed; even above the games, he wanted Kaki to like the way the house was set up, so he'd gone upstairs to drag her down to supervise. She'd been a little quiet at first, a little distant, and he'd wondered what was wrong. He couldn't ask her then, not with a house full of people. Instead he'd stepped up behind her and put his arms around her. Kissed her neck just below her ear and reminded her they would both live here and he wanted her to decide on stuff like where to put the couch and the recliner and the bookshelf.

Finally, she'd relaxed against him, still in his arms. Pointed out to Jason and Jamie that the bookshelf couldn't go where they'd set it because the door bumped it. The TV needed to be in that spot. The couch definitely needed to be across from the TV; as avid sports watchers, the guys all knew that.

When they'd called it quits for the night and headed to Lauren and Tyler's for dinner, he'd grabbed Kaki's hand and tugged her gently back through the kitchen door.

"What?" she'd asked with a small frown.

"Just hang on." He shook his head. They watched everyone else leave, and naturally, Jordy's brothers were mumbling and groaning about Jordy getting a quickie when they'd worked hard all day, too. Jordy had seen his parents exchange a look and a smile as they sauntered out to the drive.

"What's wrong?" he'd asked Kaki when he was sure they were alone.

"Just tired."

"No, you're not." Still holding her hand, he rubbed his thumb over her bare ring finger. He kissed her knuckles and looked up at her with a frown. "Where's your ring?'

"Took it off to paint," she answered simply. "Figured I'd end up—"

She stopped talking when he nodded. "Yeah. Saw where you painted the doorframe."

She grinned. "Of course you did."

"You look sad, Kaks. What's the matter?"

He watched her swallow hard. Knew her well enough to know something was bugging her. Before they were married, he'd have been able to coax it out of her easily. Now he wasn't so sure. Why had that changed? She was still his best friend, she and Lauren; he didn't want her to just clam up and stop talking to him, no matter what was bugging her.

She took a deep breath then. Looked around the kitchen and back at him with a smile.

"Looks good."

"It does. The house looks great," he agreed. "So, what's wrong?"

The silence around them was loud after a day of laughter and constant chatter and yelling from down here to upstairs.

"Maybe we should talk about it later," she suggested.

Jordy drew back to study her. "I'd rather know now."

"It's not…" She shook her head. "No, Jordy, it's fine. We should be over there with our families."

He nodded.

"I know. I just hate seeing you like this."

"It's nothing," she repeated. "Just kind of bothered me. What Diana said."

"What she said?" he asked her. Pinned her in place with his eyes. "Or what I did?"

She blushed, and something tightened in the backs of

Jordy's knees. Made him stand up straight and struggle for a deep breath.

"No," she whispered with a soft laugh. "Just...what she said."

He nodded. Relieved at her answer, though he didn't want to take much time to think about what that meant.

"Okay." He sighed. "Are you hungry? Do you wanna go to Lauren and Tyler's?"

"Of course I do," she answered as if he was crazy to think otherwise.

"Because I'm hungry, but I'd be happy to stay right here with you and do that again."

She laughed and shook her head.

"You don't have to say that, Jordy." She leaned in and kissed his cheek. "Let's go."

———

Lauren and Tyler's house smelled like lasagna, and Jordy's stomach growled as he and Kaki walked in the back door. Kaki shot him a glance as his brothers and friends all whistled at the entrance.

"Damn, little brother, that was fast for fast." Jamie held his hand out for a high five. Jordy draped his arm over Kaki's shoulder, felt a rush of relief when Kaki laughed at them. He ducked his head to kiss her and gave her a breast a playful squeeze when she kissed him back. When she parted her lips to laugh at him, he took advantage of the moment and rubbed his tongue over hers. Thank God, she played along for the audience.

And for him.

He'd missed this. She'd shut him down the other night, and so he'd backed away from her. He had to respect her wishes, but he didn't have to like it. Hated that they were only messing around for show, but he'd take it if that was all she would offer.

"Hey guys." Lauren moved in on Kaki to hug her. Slugged Jordy as she did so and then winked at him. Jordy moved on away from his best friends and joined his brothers at Lauren and Tyler's big ass kitchen table. He'd teased her about it, asked her if they planned to have six or seven kids like Lauren's parents. When she'd only shrugged, he'd been stunned into silence. He couldn't quite imagine Lauren with one child, let alone six or seven, but she hadn't shushed him or argued with him, so Jordy decided it might be best not to question their plans. As long as Lauren and Tyler were on the same page, nothing else, certainly not his opinion, mattered.

Tyler offered him a cold beer. Jordy twisted the top off the bottle and looked back just in time to see Jackson snag his wife for a hug. He watched them tease; Jackson pulling her in for a big hug and then dropping a sweet kiss on Kaki's cheek. Pissed him off; not because he was jealous, but because everything about this marriage was right. Except for the fact that they weren't in love. That they were just friends, and they'd started this whole thing with an end date in mind.

Kaki moved from Jackson to Jason, and Jordy reminded himself to smile. To laugh along with their antics, because this is what his family did when they took someone in. This is how they'd all treated each of his brother's wives when they'd married into the family. His bothers were accepting Kaki as the newest sister-in-law. He turned his head in time to catch his mom watching him. He felt a moment of panicked guilt—the same as when he was a kid and she caught him drawing pictures on his bedroom wall—and wondered what she would say to him. About Kaki. But she only arched an eyebrow. Gave him a small smile.

Dinner was delicious, but then, he hadn't expected anything less. Lauren's mom had perfected the art with her brood at home, and that was one thing that had rubbed off on Lauren. He and Kaki sat together, one part of their bodies constantly touching, whether it was their hands or legs or shoulders. He appreciated that she'd apparently upped the effort; she could have just folded and called it quits on the whole thing. Then again, he supposed that would be a cruel thing to do to her parents.

Lauren had to be exhausted, but true to form, she was a trooper. After slaving all day on dinner, she and her mom worked together to clean the kitchen and dining room. Kaki had offered to help, but Lauren's mom had waved her away and told her to enjoy their party. Kaki hadn't done it, but he'd read the intention. She wanted to look at him; she was afraid someone, maybe his mom or Diana, was paying too much attention to them.

Later, when some of their friends and family had cleared out, Jordy found himself outside with Jackson and Tyler. They were sprawled on patio furniture, all three nursing cold beers, talking baseball. Perfect night as far as Jordy was concerned. He'd worked hard today; he'd eaten a damned good meal, and now he was kicked back with a cold beer, good company, and talk about baseball.

His mind was on the women inside. One woman, specifically. What else had Diana said to her that upset her? He wanted to take her home and talk. Well. He wanted to take her home and take her to bed. Make love to her. God, he wanted to put his hands and his mouth all over her sweet little body, see if she tasted like the Florida sun. The way she had the day he'd kissed her and fallen in so deep, he was still drowning.

Once he'd made love to her, he wanted to lie with her in his arms and talk to her. Ask her what was going on in her life. What had happened Tuesday that made her pull away from him? He wanted to ask her what Diana had said to upset her. He wanted her so badly, it was an ache in his gut and his groin. He wanted to undress her. Slowly. Reveal that beautiful body inch by inch. Then again, he liked the idea of watching her do it. Watching her shimmy out of her shorts. The panties he assumed she was wearing.

Holy fuck. The thought that she might be traipsing around inside with nothing but smooth skin and hot silky Kaki under the shorts made his dick throb to life. He imagined sliding the palms of his hands over her slender hips. Running his fingers down over her curls and between her thighs—

"Jordy?"

"Hmm?" He stood up. Paced around the patio, wishing it was full dark.

"You okay, bro?"

He looked at Jackson quickly and shrugged. Took a drink of his beer.

"Yep. Why wouldn't I be?"

"You shot outta that chair like someone lit your ass on fire, dude." Jackson chuckled. Jordy saw him look to Tyler for confirmation. Jordy held his breath, but he needn't have worried. They hadn't known Tyler through high school. He'd moved to Prior after college and met Lauren at an after hours work event. After hours for Lauren; Tyler was waiting tables at Le Plat Delicieux, the fanciest restaurant in Prior. Little did any of them know, least of all Lauren, he worked there by nights and at a marketing firm by day. Tyler, though a kick ass waiter if Jordy had any say and though the tips rolled in for good-looking male waiters at places like Le Plat, had since quit the night job and now seemed to cater to Lauren's every whim. He was completely on board with Jordy and Kaki's scheme.

Tyler's laugh, even with the slight shoulder shake, looked completely genuine.

"Something bite you?" Jackson suggested, still with that dumbass grin on his face.

"Shut up."

"Thinking about what you're gonna do with that beautiful bride when you get her home?"

Jordy felt like an ass for saying yes, especially when he'd been thinking exactly that. But he nodded, laughed quietly, and said a silent apology to Kaki. As much as he wanted her, as much as he wanted to brag up their sex life and have it be true, it wasn't, and he wondered if that bothered her more than she would admit.

"What'd you think of that number Diana and Beth gave her for the bachelorette?" Jackson whistled. Jordy didn't have clue one what she'd gotten for the bachelorette, except laid when it was over. Wondering again who she'd been with made him so angry, so jealous that his head hurt. But wondering what number exactly his sisters-in-law had given her made his mouth water. Still. What to say to that? He turned his back to them and fixed the situation in his shorts yet again.

"I heard about it," Tyler said, and Jordy wondered if he was going to clue him in. "Love the sweet, sexy stuff like that, but Lauren knocked it out of the ballpark."

"Lauren's gift beat the lacy thong?"

Jordy squeezed his eyes closed. Imagined Kaki in nothing but a lacy thong.

"Red crotchless panties," Tyler told Jackson, but again, Jordy thought he was broadcasting details to help Jordy out.

He bit his lip. Changed his mental image to Kaki in crotch-less panties. Deep, sexy red. Maybe some red lipstick on those perfect lips.

"Jesus," he groaned and turned to his brother with a sigh. "What do you think I thought about it?"

Jackson grinned. "Which do you like better?"

"Seriously?" Jordy rolled his eyes. "Depends on the day of the week, man. I like her best in nothing at all."

Jackson nodded at him as if to award him a point. "Amen. Just..." He swallowed the last of his beer and stared off at nothing as if he were deep in thought. "I mean, it's Kaki. The kid who always had a ball cap on. I think she wore a ball cap until she was sixteen."

Jordy nodded his agreement when Jackson looked at him.

"Yeah. Pretty crazy that I'm so crazy about her," he mumbled.

"And that's what women do to ya." Jackson stood. Tapped his empty against Tyler's and then knuckled Jordy. "I'm gonna go gather my woman and take her home."

Jordy dropped back in his seat when Jackson disappeared inside the house. He let out a huge, disgruntled sigh. Tyler looked torn between commiserating and laughing.

"You guys doing okay?" he asked Jordy. Jordy leaned forward in his chair and looked around. Found that they were alone and looked back at Tyler.

"I dunno."

"Dunno why?"

"She's my best friend," Jordy said quietly. "I feel like a first class prick thinking about her, talking about her like this."

"She's also gorgeous," Tyler pointed out. "And sexy. I love those shorts—"

Jordy cut him off with a pointed look.

"Anything happening?"

"You mean are we doing it?" Jordy asked with a groan. He wouldn't do this. He wouldn't discuss this if Tyler weren't married to his other best friend. If Lauren and Tyler weren't completely in on the whole thing, he would keep his mouth shut. But living with Kaki was making him crazy.

Tyler shrugged and nodded his head to the side.

"No."

"You're kidding me?" Tyler leaned so far forward in his chair, Jordy thought he might fall out of it. "You're sleeping with her? Night after night? And nothing?"

"Nothing."

"Did you try...or you just...aren't attracted to her?"

"She's sexy as hell."

"You're both adults," Tyler reminded him.

"I know." Jordy leaned forward and rested his elbows on his knees. Rubbed the back of his neck. "I just don't want to take advantage of her. She didn't have to do any of this for me. I was hoping she could get out of it unscathed. I don't even know if she could have the marriage annulled, but it's what I wanted for her. Ya know? I hate that she's gonna be so young and have a failed marriage around her neck, when it's all for me."

Tyler blinked at him and shrugged. "I don't know how any of that church stuff works, but let me just remind you, she knew all of this walking into this with you. She was willing. She's been having fun. The idea of being a divorced woman doesn't seem to bother her."

Jordy sighed. He had no idea what the causes, the grounds for an annulment were, but he did get divorce. Such an ugly word after such a big wedding and Kaki being such a beautiful bride.

"She might be wanting sex as much as you are," Tyler continued.

"Not with me, she's not," Jordy mumbled.

"You hooking up with Brianna? Anyone? On the side?"

"No." Jordy sighed. "No." He heard how pathetic that sounded and rushed for something to cover up the fact that he'd married Kaki to get back at another woman and now the joke was on him. "Too much going on right now to think about it."

"Look, Jordy," Tyler stood up, "I know you don't wanna hurt her. I get that. But she's not fragile."

CHAPTER TWENTY-TWO

PAINTING all day had put a mean crick in her neck, and she was tired after drinking two beers. Only the wind in her face as Jordy drove the Jeep back across town to their house kept her awake. And even that, in an odd way, still made her sleepy. When Jordy pulled into the drive, she led the way inside, thinking a hot shower and cool sheets sounded good.

She hesitated once inside, though. Took a few minutes to wander the first floor, in love with the way the guys had placed their furniture and the pictures and framed art on the walls. They didn't have a ton of stuff for decoration, nothing to make the house look cluttered, but they had enough that the rooms didn't look stark and boring, either.

"Looks good, doesn't it?" Jordy asked from behind her.

She turned to him and smiled. Gave him a silent nod. The house looked like a home, and she supposed it would be. They were roommates, so it was home to them. But it sucked that it wasn't real. That they weren't going to really sink into that comfort of love and family that both Jordy's parents and her parents had.

"I'm gonna go up and shower."

"I thought we were going to talk." He reached for her hand, linked his fingers with hers.

She laughed softly. "We don't have to do that, Jordy. This isn't real."

"I care about you." He stepped toward her. "Remember that? And I know something upset you."

"I think I'm just tired," she lied. "And Diana just…really caught me off guard. That's all."

"Kaks."

"She insinuated that maybe we'd rushed into an engagement because I was pregnant."

"And what? You've been hiding a baby away in here somewhere for ten or eleven months?" He strummed the back of his knuckles over her belly. Kaki caught her breath and stepped back.

"I asked her the same." She met Jordy's eyes.

"And?"

"She wondered if I'd miscarried."

"Really?"

Kaki shrugged. Nodded and stepped back. "I told you it's not a big deal. Just all sort of hit me weird today."

"Kaks?"

"Hmm?"

She watched him struggle with something, like he wasn't sure how to bring up a particular conversation.

"Just say it." She squeezed his fingers.

"Jackson asked me what I thought of the gift the girls gave you for your bachelorette."

Kaki stared at him, blindsided by the question.

"I'm sorry. I never thought about showing it to you or at least telling you—"

"Tyler covered," Jordy shook his head, "but can I ask you one thing?"

The intensity in his eyes unnerved her. She answered with a reluctant nod.

"You said you were with someone? The night of your bachelorette?"

She dropped her gaze as heat flooded her face.

"Yeah."

"Did you…wear…it for him?"

She tried to imagine modeling any lingerie for Owen. Laughed softly.

"No." She lifted her chin and looked at him boldly. "I didn't, Jordy. It's all tucked away in my drawer upstairs. Tags still on everything."

He stared at her a moment longer and finally nodded.

"Okay."

"So you guys were outside talking about…" She cleared her throat. "That stuff?"

He flinched, nodded curtly.

"I'm sorry, Kaks. Does it bother you?"

She frowned. It didn't, really. They were all adults now. Sex was just a small part of a relationship. But what did bother her was that Jordy could sit out there and talk about her that way and not want to come home and undress her and take her on the dining room floor. Of course she and Lauren and Diana had talked and joked about the same things. If Diana hadn't been there, Kaki might have told Lauren about what had almost happened in Florida. She was wired now, exhausted, but she wanted Jordy so badly right now, she considered undressing for him.

The thought that he might dismiss her, tell her to get some clothes on kept her from moving.

"No," she said simply. "It's fine."

"Did my mom say anything to you?" he asked her.

She laughed out loud and rolled her eyes. "Um, no. Not specifically about operation wedding scam—"

"Shenanigans."

"What?"

"Sounds better than scam."

"There were no wedding day shenanigans, Jordy. The closest we came to that was you using your teeth to take my garter off."

He turned away but not before she saw his face flush.

"She talked my ear off," Kaki continued about his mom, "but not about the sincerity of our vows."

"Good."

"Yeah." She nodded. "I'm gonna go take a shower. I have a kink in my neck."

"Where at?"

"Um." She raised her eyebrows and smiled. "In my neck."

He grinned. Pulled her to the living room with him and nodded to the couch.

"Let me rub it for you."

She gave in and sat down. She could shower after he rubbed her neck for a few minutes. Nothing to complain about there.

He sat down behind her without turning a lamp on. Only the streetlight from the transom above the front door shone in on the floor, just a small rectangle of silver light. The house felt unnaturally quiet now after having a house full earlier today.

"Here?" he asked as he sank his thumbs into her neck and rubbed.

She gasped out loud and then moaned her approval.

"You know I love you, right?" He continued the magic on her neck, but Kaki shivered when he dropped a kiss in her hair.

"I know."

"Don't ever forget that, Kaks. Okay? Nothing is more important than that."

"Talked to Brianna lately?"

"She called me last night on the way home from work."

"Yeah? And?" She turned her head to look at him.

"Turn around." He laughed. "I'm being the good doctor."

"Are you gonna see her?"

"What?"

"Did she ask you to see you?"

"She did, yes," he answered after a slight hesitation. "But I told her I wasn't sure if I could."

"Jordy, you want this. I'm not gonna stop you from being—"

Her brain switched off when he traced his fingers up over her neck and into her hair. She forgot what she was saying. Possibly her middle name. The date. Afraid to move, she waited for him to do something. Almost crossed her fingers that he would kiss her or something. She wasn't going to be picky. Another mini make out session was preferable to going up to shower alone and climbing into bed alone.

He played with her hair for several long seconds and then scraped his stubby nails back down over her neck. She shivered and closed her eyes. Sighed when he dug into her tired, achy muscles again.

"Feel good?" He rested his chin on top of her head. It did, yes, but her mind was on other things he could do to make her feel good.

"Mmm." She nodded, hung her head forward when he tickled her again with his fingertips. This time he played with her longer. Rubbed her neck up into her hair. She pressed her lips together and lifted her head again. "Thanks."

"Kaks?"

"Hmm?" She turned her head to him again. Closed her eyes when he leaned into her. Parted her lips in anticipation of his kiss. He was hesitant. Careful. She was a little bit surprised by his reticence, but then again, they'd just been talking about Brianna. Maybe it was hard for him to get into her if he was thinking about the woman he really wanted.

"I know you don't—"

She cut him off. Lifted her left hand to cup the back of his head. Traced his lips with her tongue and caught the tip of his in her teeth. Jordy moved his hand. Down over her shoulder to squeeze her upper arm. Her bicep, which was a little bit sore from painting. She tangled her fingers in his hair as he slid his hand further down her arm.

The kisses were soft and slow. Deep and wet. Everything Kaki had wanted. Her belly quaked, and her thighs were tingly warm. Her hand in his hair almost vibrated with energy. She moaned softly when she felt his hand slide under her t-shirt again to smooth over her skin. His palm was heavy on her belly, but she gasped against his lips when he rubbed his fingertips over her nipple again.

Lips parted, their tongues danced in a slow, rhythmic motion. She felt a jolt of heat shoot through her, straight to her core when he pushed her bra up out of his way and rubbed his finger over her nipple.

"Jordy," she whispered. "Please."

"Sshh." He dragged his mouth from her lips over her cheek to her neck. Drew a circle over her nipple and then pinched her gently when it beaded with desire.

She wanted to touch him. To feel his skin under her hands. To smooth her palms over his abs and his chest and his arms. To feel the muscles she'd been watching develop over the years. To taste him. To learn the contours of his body, to see if she fit against him when they were lying side by side.

But she was afraid to move. Afraid he'd remember who she was, and who they were to each other. Afraid he'd stop.

"Please don't stop," she whispered when he cupped her breast in the palm of his hand and then rolled her nipple again. He captured her mouth again as he moved his hand to her other breast. Sighed in appreciation when he found her already excited and ready for him.

"Kaks, are you sure?"

She nodded. And then she hesitated. Did he not want this? Was he humoring her? God, the only thing worse than marrying Jordy to do him a favor was begging him to do her before he left her for someone like Brianna Fleer.

She kissed him again. One last long kiss. Stilled her mouth over his to concentrate on his hand on her breasts. Finally, out of breath, she shook her head. If she begged him to do it, and he did and even if it was the best sex she'd ever had, it would destroy her, destroy their friendship when he left. Nothing he was doing to her right now was worth losing a lifelong friendship for.

Maybe it would be different if they both wanted it. Begging made it pathetic. He'd be embarrassed for her.

"No."

"No?" he repeated. He groaned and in the deep grays of the room, she saw him squeeze his eyes closed. There was a commotion outside. Car doors slamming. People laughing and talking. She covered his hand with hers, hers outside her t-shirt.

"We shouldn't do this."

"Okay." He nodded. He was breathing heavy, enough so that Kaki wondered if she'd made the right decision.

"Jordy."

"Just gimme a minute, Kaks," he mumbled. She'd said the same to him that day on their honeymoon. She cleared her throat. Started to stand and Jordy let his hand fall away from her.

"I'm—"

"I'm fine." He nodded. Someone banged on their front door, and then the doorbell rang. They stayed as they were, Kaki standing in the front of the couch and Jordy sitting. He scrubbed his hands over his face and back over his hair and stood up. "It's okay. I'll get it."

He kissed her. A quick peck on her forehead. She stood for a moment, torn between the need to run like hell to get away from him and the need to shove him back down on the couch and straddle him.

"Jordy?"

"What?"

"I love you, too."

The light through the door transom threw a rectangle over his green eyes. He nodded. Kaki hurried upstairs as he flipped on the lamp.

She took a few extra moments in the shower to get a hold of herself. She didn't cry, but she wanted to. No need for it. She'd done this to herself. The hot water did feel good on her stiff muscles. Not quite like the neck rub Jordy had given her, but she felt a bit more relaxed when she crawled into bed a little later. It was quiet downstairs. She could hear the TV, but no one else. Whoever had come by, probably one of Jordy's brothers, had already gone.

Any hope that he would come up and try to interest her in sex again was out the window. She breathed deeply and frowned at the big whiff of fresh paint. Turned her head to Jordy's side of the bed and reached for his pillow. It smelled of his cologne.

CHAPTER TWENTY-THREE

JORDY SUPPOSED it was a good thing Kaki had put the brakes on last night. Otherwise, they'd have ended up naked on the couch and five minutes later, their marriage, their friendship over, Kaki would have trudged up the steps alone and lumped him in the group of amateur lovers like Tate Delaney. He wanted her; he wanted to bury his balls so deep inside her he'd never find his way back out. But he didn't want something that she'd remember as mediocre. He didn't want to be tossed into the same group as Delaney.

He wasn't proud of it, but he'd jacked off in the shower after he'd seen that she was asleep. Didn't need to think about what she'd look like in a lacy thong or crotchless panties. He'd simply remembered the feel of her breasts in his hand. The smell of her shampoo and her perfume as he'd rubbed her back and then played with her nipples. The stroke of her tongue over his. He'd come fast and hard, and he worried that he might have woke her, that she might have heard him.

She was sound asleep when he'd slipped between the sheets a half hour later. He'd watched her sleep, felt the tension, the heat build in his groin again as he watched her chest rise and fall. Wondered if she'd had to resort to what he'd just done since they'd been married. Or if she still had her guy on the side.

Maybe that was it. Why she was able to just turn it off and come upstairs. Because she had plans to see him. What kind of guy could he be, though, if he was okay with her marrying Jordy? No, they weren't burning up the sheets or anything for that matter, but still, she slept beside him every night. Jordy wouldn't want her lying beside another man if he was in love with her.

He'd flopped over on his back and stared at the ceiling then. Tossed and turned before finally settling into a fitful sleep. When he awoke the next morning, the bed was cold and her side was empty. Jordy pulled shorts on over his boxer briefs (he'd slept without shorts, and she hadn't even noticed) and wandered downstairs. He found her in the kitchen. Dressed already in another pair of short shorts and a tank. She was at the kitchen table, a mug of coffee at hand, eyes on her iPad.

He took a deep breath in appreciation for something that smelled damned good. She looked up when she heard him and flashed him her trademark smile.

"Hey." She picked up her mug and took a sip of her coffee. The overhead light sparkled in her wedding ring.

"Hey. What time is it?" he asked. Rubbed his eyes and shuffled over to join her at the table.

"Just after eight. Why'd you get up?"

He shrugged. "I woke up, and..." He stopped himself. Couldn't say he'd noticed she was gone and had to come looking for her.

"Smelled the cinnamon rolls?" she prompted him with a grin.

"Yeah." He nodded. "Yeah. I did."

"Stomach growling?"

He laughed sheepishly. He watched her put her mug

down and then slide off the stool. Not realizing she was waiting on him, he picked up her iPad.

"What're you reading?"

"The new Karl Morgan book."

He cut his eyes to her and then looked back at the iPad. "Translation?"

"Thriller."

"Don't you read trashy romance novels anymore?"

She laughed as she carried a bottle of Mountain Dew to him.

"Kaks, you don't have to wait on me—"

"I do sometimes," she said with a shrug.

"Have to wait on me?"

"Read trashy novels."

He grinned and twisted the top off the bottle. Took a long swig. Kaki grimaced and looked away.

"I don't know how you can drink that in the morning."

"We all have our vices."

"Try my coffee."

He watched her bend over to take something from the oven. Felt his eyes pop open in disbelief when she pulled a pan of cinnamon rolls out and set it on one of the front burners. When she glanced at him, he rolled his eyes and reached for her mug. Took a drink. Made a face of disgust before he actually tasted it. She watched him expectantly when he set the mug down.

"Well?" She carried a potholder to the table and then set the cinnamon rolls on it. Jordy reached for her, pulled her in for a kiss and then let her draw away from him so he could look at her.

"I like it better like that," he said honestly. Kaki shook her head and laughed. "Kaki?"

"Hmm?"

"C'mere." He pulled her in close to him again and put his arms around her. He'd hugged her less since they'd been married than when they were just friends. "We're okay? About last night?"

"Of course we are." She hugged him back.

"Can I ask you something?"

"No, I'm not going to butter your cinnamon roll."

He smiled sadly. Sort of hated to do this. But it was the point of the whole wedding, after all. And anyway, why would Kaki care if he saw Brianna? Maybe it would be a good night for her to see her guy.

"You really don't care?" He lifted his hand and brushed her hair from her shoulder. "If I see Brianna?"

She stared at him silently for a moment. Straight face.

"No." She shrugged. "No. Of course not."

He nodded. Let his eyes roam down over her face, over her lips because they looked delicious and he wanted to lick them. He'd wanted her to rage at him. To tell him hell yes, she cared.

"Did she call again? When I went to bed last night?"

"Um." He cleared his throat. Shook his head. Avoided her eyes. "No. I just thought I might…call her later."

Kaki stood for a moment, her hand resting on his knee.

"Okay, but remember you're married. Like you want her to think you're happily married. So…"

Jordy watched her walk back to the cabinets to get plates. He *was* happily married. Minus the physical part of their relationship. Why did Kaki say that kind of thing? Last night, she'd told him they didn't *have* to do it, *to talk*, like most married couples.

"So keep my pants zipped?" He aimed for funny, but he could tell from Kaki's hesitation that he missed. She nodded finally. Smiled. And then grabbed the butter and a knife.

"Tell me about your guy," he said when she sat down again.

"What guy?" She flashed him a look.

"The one you were with the night of the bachelorette."

"Oh." She shrugged. "Eh. He's not my guy."

"Random?"

"No. We used to…"

"Mmm." Jordy nodded. "Got it."

"Who came by last night?" she asked. He watched her dip the knife into the tub of butter and then slather it over the top of the roll she'd put on her plate.

"Jason and Jackson."

Kaki raised her eyebrows as if to say *surprise, surprise.*

"Where were the girls?"

"Probably at home being sensible."

"Were they here to teepee the yard or were they hoping to catch you with your pants down?"

"Two references to my pants already this morning." He wiggled his eyebrows. "Interested in a moonshot, lovely lady?'

"Put it out there, and I'll kick it, Jordy Steed."

He laughed and shivered in mock fright. "Actually, I believe you."

"Good." She nodded.

"What're we gonna do today?"

Jordy watched Kaki almost take a bite of her roll and then stop, fork poised near her mouth. She stared at him with wide eyes and smiled uncertainly.

"Um. I don't know?"

"Well, what do you wanna do today?"

"Like." She shrugged. "You wanna spend the day with me?"

"Yeah. I do." He leaned forward and rested his elbows on the table. "That okay?"

"Sure." She nodded.

"Wanna go fishing?"

"Not really, no." She laughed. He watched her as she finally slipped her fork in her mouth. The way she breathed deeply as she chewed the sweet treat. "What?" She laughed when she realized he was staring. "It's good. I haven't eaten this kind of stuff in months."

"Why?"

"Why?" she yelped. "Are you kidding me? I had to look good in that dress."

"Your wedding dress?"

"Yes." She tossed her hands up as if to say *what other dress?* "Might be someone out there interested in this package."

"I'm sure there are all kinds of men interested in you, Kaki Steed," Jordy agreed. "And you were drop dead gorgeous in that dress. But I'm sure you would've been even if you'd eaten a cinnamon roll before the wedding."

She snorted and took another bite.

"And why not go fishing? We used to have fun at the lake."

"Yeah, when I was, like, fifteen." She frowned and shook her head. "I'm not into worms and fish now."

"We could go for a swim," he suggested.

"In the lake?"

"Used to do that, too."

"Nope."

"How about a bike ride?"

"Maybe." She nodded slowly. "But I'm not gonna take an eight hour bike ride."

"Yeah, me neither. Bike seats aren't comfortable."

"We could go to a movie later." She picked up her coffee and sipped it.

"We could," he agreed. "What's on?"

"No idea."

"What if we ride our bikes to the lake and then take a walk?"

Kaki took a deep breath and finally shrugged. "Sure."

"And then go to a movie later this afternoon."

"Okay."

"Kaks?"

"Hmm?"

"If you wanna call him..." Jordy cleared his throat. "Your guy..."

"Not my guy," she reminded him. "We aren't seeing each other anymore."

He nodded. Took a big bite of his own roll. It was hard to swallow, though, with the guilt creeping up his throat. How could he sit here and tell his wife he wanted to see his ex-girl-friend? Maybe it would be different if she weren't his best friend. Wouldn't matter so much how she felt. Then again, she wouldn't have married him if they weren't close.

"Jordy."

Still chewing, he met her gaze.

"Don't worry about me, okay? This whole thing," she opened her arms to include their marriage and their house and their life together, "is all about you getting her back. You don't have to keep me happy."

He slowed his chewing. Wondered if that was her way of telling him to get on with it. If she was already tired of their arrangement. If she wanted out.

CHAPTER TWENTY-FOUR

"I LOVE IT. SERIOUSLY." Lauren folded her arms over her chest and leaned in the doorway of the spare bedroom. Kaki watched her crane her neck around looking at the room. She and Jordy had put the second coat on it the other day before heading out for a marathon bike ride. They'd followed the bike ride with a walk by the lake. Jordy had been quiet at first, and Kaki had wondered if he was thinking about Brianna. She wondered if he really thought Brianna was going to end up taking him back. Coming back to him. However he saw it playing out in his head. Kaki kind of thought the woman was toying with him. Maybe she just wanted to break him. Get him away from his wife and then leave him again. She'd hinted at that possibility before, and Jordy had studiously ignored her, and now she was afraid to bring it up again. She didn't want to hurt him.

"I love the color," Kaki agreed. "I wish we'd have done this in our bedroom."

"Mmm." Lauren nodded.

Kaki, back to her friend, heard the funny tone in Lauren's response. She turned slowly to look at her. The room was a bit smaller than theirs, but at the moment, it looked huge. There was only the body of a dresser—no mirror—shoved to one wall. No other furniture. Not yet. Kaki supposed everyone that thought they were really married—well, that they planned to stay together—would use the bedroom for a nursery eventually. Kaki had no idea what they'd use it for, but since she didn't plan on having babies with Jordy, she'd flat out said no to any hint of baby furniture. Not that Jordy had pushed it. Evelyn had brought it up the other day, and Kaki's mom had jumped on the idea.

"What?"

"Hmm?"

"What?" Kaki asked. She crossed the room to stand almost toe-to-toe with Lauren. Their eyes met. "You said *mmm*. What does that mean?"

Lauren's grin was ornery, but she looked tired. She rested her head on the doorframe and nibbled at her lower lip. Kaki knew her well enough to know she'd started the day with her mouth coated in her signature shade of fiery reddish brown lipstick—even Kaki thought it made Lauren's lips look smoking hot—but by now, it had faded and she nibbled at the last of it.

"Your bedroom." She shrugged. "Just sounds weird to hear you talk about your bedroom. That you share with Jordy."

"Yeah, it's like one giant sleepover." Kaki nodded.

"He really hasn't touched you?"

Kaki blinked. Let out a slow breath and looked away.

"He has?" Lauren stood up straight. "Seriously? And you didn't tell me?"

"He'll be home from work soon—"

"Kaki."

"When we were in Florida." Kaki cleared her throat. She paced across the room to the window on the east wall.

"On the honeymoon? But you said—"

205

"I mean..." Kaki kept her back to her friend. "You've seen him kiss me."

"Yeah. Looks like he finds it a real pain in the ass to have to kiss you."

"Shut up." Kaki dropped her head back and sighed, but she laughed. "We had been out on the beach. Playing in the water—"

"Did you wear that suit? The string bikini?"

Kaki nodded. "He dunked me. A few times."

"Oooh." Lauren wagged her eyebrows and licked her lips.

"Yeah, not so much." Kaki shook her head. "When we went up to grab something to eat, I called Mom just to check in. Hadn't talked to her since we'd left." She made eye contact with Lauren and then let her eyes roam when Lauren nodded. "He came on to me. Like he wanted Mom to think..."

"What if he came on to you because you were dripping wet in a white string bikini?"

"Yeah, I believed it for a minute."

"So what happened?"

Kaki frowned. "Are you sure you wanna hear this? I mean...isn't this weird"—

"Kaki, I'm happy with Tyler. You know that. And you know I made out with Jordy once, and..." Lauren shrugged helplessly.

"Yeah, but you had cold feet."

"Still. It felt like I was kissing my brother." Lauren licked her lips now. "Is that how you feel when he kisses you?"

"No, but..." Kaki sighed. Hadn't he said as much to her? That she was like a little sister to him?

"Tyler and me? We're the real deal." Lauren rubbed her belly. "I love that guy to the moon." She took a few steps toward Kaki. "You being with Jordy doesn't bother me. And I don't think there's anything wrong with it. I just don't wanna see either one of you get hurt."

Kaki swallowed hard. Turned to look out the window again.

"I kissed him. We ended up on the bed, and he was untying my top, and he had his mouth…" Kaki waved her hand toward her chest. "And then he just stopped. Got up and walked away."

"And?"

"He reminded me that we're friends. And that sex would complicate that."

"You don't agree?"

"I do!" Kaki groaned. "But ya know, when a guy's putting the moves on you, and he suddenly backs off, it's—"

"You were into it."

"I was."

"Is that it?"

"What?" Kaki shook her head. "That wouldn't bother you?"

"I mean, has it happened since?"

"Things haven't gone that far, but…"

"Take your clothes off and see what he does."

Kaki heard the door open downstairs. "I won't throw myself at him, Lauren. I don't want him to feel like it's part of the plan. Not that hard up."

"I don't think you're hard up," Lauren said quietly. "I think you're into him."

"Then the joke's on me."

"Maybe he's into you, but he's trying to play by the rules you guys made when you started. Remember that? You were both adamant that you would live like roommates."

Kaki sighed. "I know. I do. But."

"Hey." Jordy appeared in the doorway behind Lauren. "My two favorite ladies!"

"Hey Jordy." Lauren turned to him. Kaki watched her friends hug. No tug of jealousy there. She believed Lauren and Tyler were the absolute real thing. Believed her husband might never be anyone's real thing.

The thought made her sick with guilt. And something else. Something that tasted like heartache and what if. Disappointment. Kaki was disappointed in the marriage scheme she'd been behind one hundred percent as little as a month ago.

Jordy offered her a smile.

"How was your day?"

He asked her that every night. They usually talked over dinner, whether that was spaghetti or burgers or chicken he'd grilled out on their patio. They shared their days. Talked about people at work—Jordy had shocked her the other day when he'd told her Jason and Beth were expecting again. They'd shared a relieved laugh; they were off the hook with his parents if Beth and Jason were pregnant. They talked about mutual friends and shared things they heard on the news.

Like a married couple.

"Good." She looked up as he approached her and dropped a quick kiss on her upturned lips. She saw Lauren raise her eyebrows behind him. Tamped down the smile that played at her mouth.

"I'm thinking homemade pizza," he suggested. She nodded. She did most of the cooking, but now and then Jordy wanted to jump in and do something. She was more than happy to let him help. "Wanna stay?"

Lauren snapped her head around to look at the north wall when Jordy looked at her over his shoulder. "Um. No. Thanks. I have…a thing. I have a thing I need…to do."

Kaki smiled when Lauren met her gaze.

"Just wanted to see the house after you guys did your thing the other day."

"What do you think?"

"I think it's perfect," she said simply. "You know, I was

just telling Kaki. Since you guys aren't planning to do the kid thing, you could get a queen bed for this room. And then one of you could sleep in here. You know? So you wouldn't be in each other's space. You could just be roommates. And no one would have to know."

Kaki snuck a peek at Jordy to see what he thought of Lauren's suggestion. She hadn't said any such thing to her; she was pushing Jordy to see what he would do.

"Yeah." He nodded. Tossed his hands out, palms up. "Yeah, that's a good idea."

Lauren glanced at Kaki again. "Call me? Later?"

Kaki nodded. "I'll walk you down." She crossed the room and then turned back to look at Jordy.

"I'm gonna…" He looked down at his jeans. "Change clothes. I'll be down in a minute."

"Mm-kay."

Lauren waited until they were in the kitchen before she turned to Kaki.

"What do you think?"

Kaki avoided her eyes. Took a moment to breathe, to think. Did she want to admit this to Lauren? Because once she said it, it would be too late to ever take it back.

"I like sleeping next to him," she whispered.

But Lauren only nodded. "He didn't look too excited about one of you moving out of the bedroom, Kaki. Do something about this."

"About what?"

"You love him—"

"Oh my God, no, I don't. I don't love—"

"Yeah?" Lauren cocked her head and studied Kaki's face. "How long are you gonna live like this? You're miserable."

She was, and she wasn't, but she knew exactly what Lauren meant. That didn't mean she was in love with him, though. Living in his space, sleeping next to him, she'd suddenly realized she was attracted to him. That was all. And giving in to that attraction would blow up not only their marriage, but their friendship.

"Yeah, but at least I'm in the boat, Lauren."

Lauren hugged her, pressed her lips to her ear and whispered, "You deserve better than that. So much more."

"Did you tell Lauren the big news?" Jordy asked, and Kaki understood why Lauren had moved in close to whisper to her.

"What big news?" Lauren backed up. Kaki watched her gather her purse and her keys form the counter. She slipped her purse strap over her shoulder and looked up at Jordy.

"Beth and Jason are pregnant again."

"You Steeds sure are good at reproducing."

Kaki snorted. Lauren winked at her.

"Night, guys."

Kaki watched Jordy move around the kitchen. He grabbed a bowl from the cabinet. The pizza crust mix from another cabinet.

"We need a pantry," he mumbled. Looked at her quickly when she laughed. "What?"

"Never thought I'd see the day you settled in to married life and started cooking."

"I used to cook. When I had my apartment."

"Frozen pizza and popcorn don't count."

He grinned. Shrugged nonchalantly and glanced at the back door.

"What were you guys talking about?"

Kaki sat down. She needed to buy time, because she didn't know what to say to him.

"The house. She asked if she could move in."

Truth. Sort of. Lauren had jokingly announced she was moving in. But they'd quickly moved on to other things.

"It really is a great house," he said softly. "I liked it, but now…that everything's done…" He looked up at her and then shrugged and looked back at the crust mix he was now kneading. "It's...even better."

"I love that green paint."

He nodded, looked as if he wanted to say something, but he was quiet for a while. Kaki wondered why he'd stopped talking. She wanted to say they should have painted their room that color. She wouldn't now. For one thing, it would be a pain in the butt trying to do it and finding a place to sleep for a couple of nights. Not to mention, she didn't want both bedrooms the same color and the upstairs hallway something else.

"Did you tell her?" he finally asked.

"Tell her what?"

"About Florida? Did you ever tell her that?"

"Does it matter? If I did?"

"Um." He nodded his head back and forth and pursed his lips. "No? I guess not."

"Do you have secrets from me? With Lauren?"

"So you told her," he ignored her question with one of his own. "Did she flip out?"

Kaki was stunned. Was it so out of the question that they screw around? Was she that unattractive that it was laughable he might be attracted to her?

"I didn't really tell her much," she mumbled. "Just...I didn't..." She shook her head. Scooted off the stool and headed out of the kitchen.

"Kaks?" he called. "Where're you going?"

"I didn't, Jordy." She spoke so quietly, she knew he couldn't hear her. Lauren was right. Happy to miserable in 0.5 seconds. This pretend marriage with Jordy was the scariest roller coaster she'd ever ridden. What the hell would a real marriage feel like?

CHAPTER TWENTY-FIVE

THE UPS and downs of his fake married life gave him a new respect for his brothers, if nothing else. Jordy had never paid much attention to his brothers, regarding their wives and their family lives. He liked working with them, and he enjoyed their family days. Loved hanging outside with the kids, having water balloon fights or splashing with the little ones in the pool. But he hadn't paid attention to the work his brothers and sisters-in-law put into what they shared. He appreciated it now. Wished some of the happiness, the family togetherness would rub off on him and Kaki.

She'd turned off again completely the other night. Jordy didn't know what to make of it. They'd been talking about Lauren, and then suddenly Kaki had walked out. He'd found her on the front porch, and she'd come inside to eat. She'd even talked to him, but she'd clammed up. No more mention of those private things they'd shared. No discussion on Lauren and anything she might have told her.

Jordy wondered if maybe Kaki had been talking to her about the other guy, the one she insisted to Jordy she wasn't seeing anymore. He'd even gone so far as to wonder if she'd heard from that guy in Florida again. *Owen.* The take away was that his wife wasn't happy, and though they weren't husband and wife in the traditional sense, Jordy wanted her to be happy.

He'd suggested they go furniture shopping again a couple of nights ago. She'd given him a blank look. Asked what other furniture they could need. When he'd mentioned getting another bed for the spare room, she'd only mumbled *okay*. Jordy wasn't sure what that hell that meant, either. He had assumed that since Lauren brought it up, it was something Kaki had discussed with her. Maybe she was sick of sharing a room with him. A bed with him. Maybe he snored. Maybe she wanted a full bed to herself to do things she didn't want or need him for. When she'd said something about loving the new paint color, he'd assumed that was her way of claiming the new room as her own.

So why had she seemed so unhappy when they'd walked hand in hand through Daniels Furniture Company shopping for a new bedroom set? They'd found one they both liked, and they'd arranged for six months same as cash financing and delivery next week. And still Kaki had seemed sad when they left.

He'd considered talking to Lauren. He could pry it out of her. It wasn't that he cared more for Lauren. Never that. But communication between them had always been a bit more open and easy, and if he asked if she knew what was bugging Kaki, she'd tell him. Kaki told Lauren everything. He'd always known she confided more in Lauren than him. Hadn't ever bothered him all that much, but it sure as hell did now.

"Penny for your thoughts."

Jordy eyed the red and khaki tent they were assembling for display. It was lopsided, hung a little to the left. The thought made him laugh to himself. They were sporting goods people, and they'd screwed something up in the setup of this tent.

"It's crooked."

"That it is," Jamie agreed. His oldest brother, Jamie, had been married almost ten years. He and Shawn had married young; she'd attended grad school after they were married. They'd had a long distance relationship for not quite two full years before she finished school. Jordy wondered now how they'd survived it. "What else?"

"What?" Jordy looked at his brother and stepped away from the tent to study it.

"Your mind is a hundred miles from here." Jamie stuck his hands in his pockets. He teased Jordy, often and about every-thing, but never quite so much as Jason and Jackson. Right now, hands in his jeans pockets, shoulders hunched, he looked like their dad. Jordy sighed and shook his head. "Trouble in paradise?"

"I don't even know," Jordy mumbled.

"Wanna talk about it?"

"Nope. I don't." He walked a circle around the tent and then stood in front of it again. "We should do this."

"What?" Jamie moved. Rested his elbow on the huge stack of boxed tents to his left.

"Go camping again. Fishing. Sleeping in tents."

Jamie whistled softly. "That didn't take long."

"What?" Jordy looked back at his brother.

"The new and shiny already wear off?" Jamie narrowed his eyes in thought. "What's it been? A month? Six weeks?"

"Kaks isn't happy."

"With you?"

"I dunno."

"What'd you do?"

"Nothing!" Jordy snapped. "Nothing." Okay, that wasn't fair. No, he hadn't done anything specific to upset her, not that he could remember, but it wasn't fair of him to shove the blame for this sham of a marriage off on her.

"You cheating on her?"

"No." Jordy shot Jamie a look of anger. "I wouldn't do that to her."

"Say something stupid?"

Jordy shrugged, but Jamie laughed.

"You did. Always just assume you said something stupid."

"Okay, so if I assume that, what do I do?"

"Ever send her flowers? Just because you're thinking about her?"

"No."

Jamie shrugged. He stepped up in front of Jordy and eyed the tent. Jordy watched him move to one of the poles on the left and twist it enough to extend it upward. The whole tent perked up and stood tall.

"Remind her you love her?"

Well, he did, but he wasn't sure that one counted. Then again, maybe it was important that he tell her that. Even if it wasn't the same kind of love.

He nodded, though, because he couldn't just say that to Jamie. Any of his brothers would blow the whistle on them. He was curious why Diana hadn't. What she and his mom were doing, sitting back and watching he and Kaki play house.

"Things still okay in the bedroom?" Jamie avoided looking at him this time. Things were most definitely not okay in the bedroom, but again he couldn't just say that to Jamie. And he sure as hell couldn't pretend there was another problem in the bedroom. All the parts in his plumbing worked just fine; he sure as hell didn't need his brothers ripping on him about something like that.

He mumbled a yes, and then repeated it louder when Jamie shot him a doubtful look.

"What's her favorite flower?" Jamie asked him.

Jordy didn't have a clue what her favorite flower was. She liked lilies. But were they her favorite? Why didn't he know that? He should know that just because they'd grown up together.

"Send her roses," Jamie suggested when he realized Jordy was lost. "Pink roses."

"Pink?"

"Yeah, she'll love them."

"And that's just gonna fix everything? Flowers?"

Jamie shrugged and moved to the side of the tent. He squatted down to fasten it to the display base.

"Depends on how stupid whatever you said was."

"Damn." Jordy sighed.

"Tell her to go out with some friends. Let her hair down and have some fun."

"She has fun with me."

"I'm sure she does," Jamie agreed with a slow nod. Jordy rolled his eyes, felt like Jamie was talking to him like he was ten instead of an adult. "But girls like time with their friends. I'll say something to Shawn."

"No." Jordy's voice was so loud, it almost echoed off the walls of the store. Jamie, still squatting, looked around to see if anyone was watching them.

"Get the chairs to set out," Jamie instructed him. "And I didn't say I'd tell Shawn you guys are having problems."

"We're not having problems," Jordy corrected him. "Kaki's just…"

"I'll suggest that she and the girls take Kaki out for a drink this weekend."

"This weekend?"

"Oh." Jamie stood up slowly. He took the folded lawn chairs Jordy handed him. "So it's an emergency. Girls' night out, stat."

"Jamie."

"She'll have a blast," Jamie assured him. "Shawn comes home recharged and happy as hell anytime she's out with Beth and Diana."

Jordy thought maybe the last thing he and Kaki needed was her out with their sisters-in-law for a night of drinking and girl talk, but he finally agreed that Kaki would probably enjoy it. Called Isles' Flowers the minute Jamie walked away to fetch the camp stove they were featuring in the display and asked to have a dozen red roses—he wasn't crazy about pink, nothing out there could touch the perfect pink of Kaki's lips—delivered to her at work.

———

SHE GREETED HIM AT THE DOOR WHEN HE GOT HOME AND THREW her arms around him and kissed his cheek. Stunned that his brother was right and to feel her warm, supple body pressed up against his again after so many days of space between them, it took him a minute to grab on and hug her back.

"Thank you."

He was thrilled to see the smile on her face, but it sliced right through him at the same time. God, she was beautiful. And this was temporary. One day he would come home from work to an empty house again, and some other lucky guy would come home to her.

He'd sort of wanted to see the flowers, a vase of red roses with *Love, Jordy* written on the card, but she said she left them at her workstation. Told him it brightened up the room, and she'd decided to leave them where she'd be spending her days. The idea of something he'd given her making her days happy made him feel good, so he only nodded.

"What was the occasion?" she asked, still wrapped up in his arms. Jordy turned his face into her neck and breathed in her delicious, rich perfume. He smelled it every night when he lay beside her. In the mornings when she'd just dabbed it on and come downstairs for a bagel before she headed to work. But there was something so heady and so sexy about being this close to her and breathing her scent.

"What?"

"Why the flowers?"

She pulled back from him, enough that she could look him in the eyes.

"Because I was thinking about you," he said simply. She was always with him now in thought. Since they'd been married, engaged, really. He liked that; he liked having these special memories of Kaki that he could call up at will. The look on her face in the mornings when she sipped her coffee and read from her book or iPad. The sound of her laughter carrying through the house when she was on the phone with someone. The feel of her lips on his cheek when she surprised him with a sweet kiss now and then. But today, she'd been front and center in his head, and it had been the look of hurt, betrayal she wore now and then that haunted him at work.

She grinned. "You're gonna make someone a great husband some day."

"You think so?"

"I do." She nodded. Before she turned away, he saw the sadness steal over her face.

"Dinner?"

She shrugged. "I don't know. I got busy at work and didn't take time to think about it before I got home."

"It's okay." He grabbed a couple of beers from the fridge and offered one to her. She took it with a smile of gratitude, and they leaned on the counter as they twisted them open. "Chinese delivery?"

"Yes." She nodded enthusiastically and managed to not spill her beer as she took a drink. "That sounds perfect."

"Good. So what were you so busy with? At work?" He wanted to keep her talking. He much preferred spending his evenings with her, talking and laughing or watching a movie, than just living side by side in the same house.

"Still finishing up that huge delivery from when we got home from Florida. It's a process, and it all takes time. And when the roses were delivered today, I had people slinking out of the shadows, people I didn't even know were at the museum coming in to see them."

He grinned. He'd never sent a woman flowers before. It surprised him that it felt so good to see her gush about them.

"We're getting ready to change the displays, too. The end of summer."

"It's July."

"Planning phases, though," she said simply.

"Kaks?"

She looked at him with big eyes, bottle half way to her mouth. "What?"

"What's your favorite flower?"

"Why?"

He drummed his fingers on the cabinet he leaned on and sighed. "I wanted to send you flowers, but it hit me I don't even know what your favorite flower is."

"The roses are beautiful, Jordy. Every women loves red roses—"

"But if I want to send you flowers again, I want to send what *you* love. Not every woman."

"Calla lilies."

"And what's your favorite color?"

She turned to him, hip resting against the counter, and ducked her head sheepishly.

"You don't have to do this," she said quietly. "I don't expect—"

"You've been unhappy. Upset with me about something all week—"

"Jordy, I'm moody. I know that. And this is…anything but…normal. Between us. But I don't expect you to do this."

"I've never sent anyone flowers." He lifted his hand and cupped her chin. "It's kind of nice knowing that something I did made you happy."

"You make me happy," she whispered. "I just need you to remember this is...hard sometimes."

Jordy swallowed hard. Nodded. "Tap out, Kaks. Anytime you need to, tap out."

They stood like that for a moment. Eyes locked, Jordy's fingers curled under her chin. Finally, she cleared her throat. Took a drink of her beer.

He held his breath when she opened her mouth to speak, afraid this was it.

"Do you want egg rolls or crab rangoon?"

CHAPTER TWENTY-SIX

KAKI DECIDED as Friday nights go, the one they'd spent last night was just about perfect. They'd come home from work right around the same time; Jordy had followed her into the house. Both of them had changed clothes, and then Kaki had hung out on the patio with him while he grilled pork chops. She'd sat on the picnic table while he stood at the grill, and they'd talked about the old days. Shared a lot of old stories about mutual friends, laughed about the good times. When the chops were done, they'd thrown them on paper plates, added leftover pasta salad to the plates and sat outside at the picnic table to eat. Their walk down memory lane lasted through dinner. Kaki had wondered when they went back inside to clean up their small mess if he'd rather be out somewhere, if he'd contacted Brianna yet. But she hadn't wanted to ruin the mood.

When he suggested watching a movie, she willingly followed him to the living room. Claimed the couch, knowing he preferred the recliner anyway. Rather than go to the popular movies on Netflix, he browsed through titles she'd never heard of. Picked something that sounded remotely interesting. Started out as a film about a family and ended with a lot of action and violence. She liked it. She liked the company more.

They'd watched TV when the movie was over. Jordy flipped through the channels too fast for her to catch what was on, but she'd let him control the remote. She was too lazy, too content to complain. When they'd gone upstairs to bed, she'd kissed him goodnight. Just a kiss on his cheek. And then she'd turned her back to him.

"Jordy?"

"Hmm?"

"Are you bored?'

"I'm tired," he answered her.

She turned over to lie on her stomach and looked his way. Couldn't really see him in the dark, but she could feel him there beside her.

"Staying around the house all the time? With me?"

He took such a long time to answer her, she worried that he was bored. That maybe she'd bored him to sleep already. Finally, though, before she could give him her back again, he'd reached out and rubbed his hand up her arm.

"I like being at home with you," he said quietly. "But I'd like to go out sometimes."

"Okay." She took his hand and kissed his knuckles. The bittersweet answer was better than him flat out saying he was bored with her. But she hated the thought of Jordy Steed on the prowl while she was stuck at home.

"Kaks?" He'd snuggled up to her when she did finally flip back over to her side.

"Hmm?" She closed her eyes. It was nice to have him plastered up against her back, but she knew by now not to read anything into it.

"I meant with you."

"What?"

"I love being here with you, but I think we should go out. Go to dinner or see a movie. Go to a club."

She grinned, laughed softly. "You wanna take your wife clubbin'? That's gonna kill your reputation. You know that, right?"

"Think about it." He kissed her head.

He'd told her Jamie's wife might be calling her about going out with the girls. Kaki thought it sounded like fun, but when Jordy didn't appear to be thrilled with the idea, she'd told him she'd stay home. He'd insisted she go, though, and so when Shawn did text her, Kaki said yes, she'd go out this Saturday. Jordy had read Shawn's text over Kaki's shoulder. Rested his forehead on her and took a deep breath. Kaki assumed he was worried she'd spill the beans.

"I'm not gonna tell any of them what's going on," she'd promised him again this morning.

Jordy, half his face buried in his pillow, had answered her with a lazy grin. He'd lifted his arm over his head, and Kaki had taken a moment to let her eyes travel over his firm bicep and forearm and then she'd met his eyes, and they'd laughed.

"I dated this guy once," she'd said and she'd reached out to skim her fingertip over Jordy's arm, "with really big arms. He liked handcuffs." Eyes still on her finger on his arm, she'd smiled at the memory and then held her breath when she looked back at him and realized what she'd said. "Sorry."

"He liked handcuffs," Jordy repeated. "As in some big guy with really big arms held you down."

"Um." She'd squirmed a bit. "No." Sighed and avoided further eye contact. "He liked…to be handcuffed…while I…"

When she let her eyes jump to his, he arched his eyebrows impatiently.

"While you what?" he'd asked with a big grin. "C'mon. You've heard stories about me."

"Are they stories if they're true?"

"Kaks."

"He liked me on top. While he was handcuffed."

"So."

Kaki felt a wave of warmth rush her as Jordy's eyes took a quick trip down over her shoulders and her breasts. She wore a modest pajama set, but she felt naked when he looked at her that way.

"You gave him private lap dances, and he couldn't touch."

She blushed and ducked her head into her pillow. "Something like that."

"Sounds interesting," he'd decided and before Kaki felt his brush off down to her toes, he continued, "I would certainly try it. But I think I'd tear my arms up trying to get to you."

She'd blushed again. "You're funny."

They had breakfast together, and a couple of times Jordy referenced her handcuff story. Asked her if she'd by chance been given a pair of cuffs as a gift at the bachelorette. She hadn't, thankfully. She'd have hated to say yes and then watch Jordy's face as he realized he'd walked right into his own trap.

After a leisurely breakfast consisting of a bagel and cream cheese for her and pancakes for him, they'd lingered at the table for a while. She hadn't even realized he was drinking coffee until he refilled her cup.

"What are you doing?" she asked suddenly.

"Playing Scrabble," he announced. "I suck."

Confused by the Scrabble remark and the coffee, Kaki had leaned over to look at his phone. He was indeed playing Words With Friends and getting his butt kicked by nearly two hundred points. She eyed the scoreboard.

"Wait." She held up a hand and tilted her head to look at him in disbelief. "You're playing Words With Friends with Beth?"

"Yeah. Why?" He blinked. "We've played for like... twenty-seven years."

"Yeah? Before it was an app?" Kaki winked at him. "You

don't strike me as a words kind of guy. You're more of a sports guy."

"We all have our secrets," he'd said with a shrug. Kaki had narrowed her eyes at him.

"What else do you keep secret from me?"

Jordy snatched his hand away from her to hide his phone. "I'm not telling. You're learning all my secrets, and you don't tell me anything."

"Don't play that word, by the way," she advised him. "It's three points. I'm sure you can do better."

Jordy eyed her suspiciously and then turned sideways on his stool to look at his phone. She heard him groan.

"And you know about the handcuffs," she reminded him.

"Thank you." He stood up and set his phone on the table and picked up his coffee. She watched with a grin as he took a drink. Impressed that he didn't make a face when he swallowed, she nodded and gave him a thumbs up.

"For saving you from the three letter word? Want me to help you find—"

"For putting that mental image back in my head." He propped his hands on the table and took a deep breath. "Some guy that I don't even wanna think about lying under you while you sit on him, bare breasted—"

Kaki roared with laughter. Shocked at her own outburst, she slapped her hand over her mouth and then ducked her head and rested it on the table.

"What?"

She rolled her head on the table, still laughing too hard to say anything.

"What?" He grabbed her hand. She squeezed his fingers and tried to sit up. Jordy moved around the table until he could sidle up right behind her. "What're you laughing about?"

Kaki tucked her hair behind her ears and wiped at her eyes as she looked at him.

"Have you been reading my trashy romance novels?"

He grinned. "I will. If there's something in there about bare-breasted women riding—"

"Oh, there is." She nodded. "And then some."

"Then some," he repeated. "Like what?"

"Scrabble, though? Really?"

"I can beat her," he said with a small smile.

Kaki cupped his face in her hands and leaned in to drop a quick kiss on his lips.

"I just figured you for sports games."

"I kinda like the farm games, actually."

"I'm going outside," she'd announced. She'd kissed him once more and then ducked under his arms and headed out the back door. Jordy had followed her out, though it had taken him a few moments. Kaki assumed he was cleaning up the kitchen. She pulled the mower out of their one car garage. Wished she'd have pulled her hair back; she couldn't keep it in a neat ponytail, but it was already hot and humid this early, and she'd be soaked through with sweat by the time she was finished.

Didn't matter. The yard needed to be mowed. She worked at a good pace. When Jordy came outside, he offered to take over for her. She waved him away. Noticed him getting the weed eater out to trim. When the yard was finished, Kaki rinsed the mower off and sat down for a moment with the cold beer Jordy fetched from the kitchen for her. He took a long swig from his, but rather than sit with her, he filled a bucket up with soapy water and sprayed her car off. Kaki leaned forward in her lawn chair on the patio and rested her elbows on her knees, the bottle dangling from one of her hands.

She watched him for a while as he worked. Laughed when he did a little dance for her. Pointed out a spot he'd missed and then ran from him as he threatened to spray her with the hose.

When both cars were washed and the yard was mowed and trimmed, they ate cold cut sandwiches on the patio. Sat for a while and then when they decided their lunch was settled, they took a bike ride. The sun was hot enough they could have fried eggs on the sidewalk, but Kaki figured what the heck. She couldn't sweat anymore than she already had, and she loved riding her bike. They didn't go far. Just enough to stretch their legs. They rode from Lincoln to Cleveland and then cut over to Twenty-Fourth. Kaki followed Jordy when he took the lead. Out Twenty-Fourth to Shenandoah Drive, where his family had lived when he was a kid.

Her legs felt like dead weight when they pedaled back toward Lincoln. Even though they hadn't gone terribly far, she was beat. The beer before lunch probably hadn't been a good idea.

"Hot out here," Jordy mumbled as they walked their bikes into the garage.

"Yep. It is." She lifted the tail of her t-shirt and wiped the sweat off her face. "I'm gonna go take a shower."

"Okay." She tried not to watch him when he pulled his cut off t-shirt over his head. Did it anyway, though she looked away before he caught her checking him out. "I think I'm gonna trim that bush out front."

"What bush?"

"The one in front of the house. On the right side. It's like double the size of the other one. On the other side."

She nodded slowly and backed up a few steps. "You mean the hedge?"

Jordy rolled his eyes. "Hedge. Bush. Tree. It's all the same to me."

He tossed his soaked t-shirt on the driveway. Kaki headed to the house, but she turned twice to eye him as he reached for the hedge trimmer hanging on the garage wall. Took just a moment before he turned to admire his arms. His obliques.

Pictured him handcuffed in their bed upstairs, her straddling that hot, muscled body.

She turned and rushed into the house, hoping he hadn't known she was watching him. Then again, even if he'd known she was there watching, it was doubtful he'd guess what she was thinking. She chuckled to herself again as she climbed the stairs. The Jordy she'd grown up with would have said something sleazy about a *girl riding someone with her tits in his face*. Not the whole *bare-breasted woman* thing.

As she gathered clean clothes to put on after her shower, she eyed their bed. Neatly made. Wished just once they could tear it up. Wondered how much damage they could do if they had one shot at it. She figured he was hard and fast, and though she preferred slow and deep, she'd take what she could get.

Reminded herself it wasn't going to happen in any way and headed to the bathroom. She peeled her sweat-soaked shirt off the second she closed the door. Dropped it on the floor for now. Leaned into the shower stall to turn the water on. Stripped off the wet sports bra and shorts. Wiped at a smudge on the glass shower door as she waited for the water to warm a bit. Sure, she was hotter than hell, but she didn't want to just climb into ice-cold water, either.

Once it was warmer, she stepped out of her wet underwear and into the shower. The water felt good. The perfect temperature. Needled her shoulders and the back of her neck just so. She closed her eyes and stood still for a moment.

The yard looked great. The house was so perfect. She and Jordy were so perfect together, except that they weren't in love. Didn't have that mutual attraction that could sustain a physical relationship. She thought again of the bed that was to be delivered next week. That hurt, but once she remembered it, she couldn't push it out of her mind. Apparently, Jordy had loved Lauren's idea that they furnish that room so they didn't have to sleep together anymore. She had a feeling she wouldn't sleep as peacefully once she moved as she did now.

Thoughts on the future, on where she'd be and what she would do when Jordy got Brianna back and gave Kaki the boot, she grabbed her shampoo bottle and poured a bit in her hand. Scrubbed her hair thoroughly, again marveling at how good a shower felt when you'd been outside doing something hot and strenuous all day.

Rinsed it just as thoroughly. Only because she was in no hurry to get out. The girls weren't going out until later. Jordy was outside working on the hedge in front of the house. She had a few minutes to herself, might as well take that time. The door opened suddenly, and Kaki heard laughter and then Jordy stepped inside, closed the door, and fell against it.

Kaki stared at him in shock. Their eyes met. She lowered her hands from her hair to cover herself, but she felt like she was moving in slow motion.

"Jordy!"

He squeezed his eyes closed and shrugged apologetically.

"What're you—?"

She stopped when he put his finger over his lips. Tried to make sure her breasts were covered, at least the main parts, as he crossed the room to stand next to the glass door.

"I'm sorry." He pushed the door open a smidge so he could speak quietly to her. "Beth and Diana are out there. They showed up with a gift for you and insisted I come in and tell you."

He'd looked. Before, when she'd jumped to cover herself, when she'd squealed at him, she'd seen his eyes take a fast once over her body. He'd seen it all. Now she wondered if she dropped her hands what he would do. He was talking to her, eyes on hers, as if she had a turtleneck sweater on under a snowsuit.

"A gift," Kaki repeated. "For me."

He nodded.

"I couldn't make a big deal out of walking in on you in the shower."

"Yeah. Yeah. It's..." She shrugged her eyebrows and laughed. Wondered if he heard the nervous edge in her laughter or if she did only because her stomach was suddenly a jittery mess.

"So, it's a scarf." He rubbed his eyes. Dragged one hand back over the top of his head. Kept his eyes on hers.

"They brought me a scarf."

"To wear tonight."

Kaki frowned. It was July. The high today was ninety. It wouldn't cool off much at all when the sun went down.

"They could have given it to me tonight."

Kaki saw his Adam's apple bob when he swallowed. "I think this was...."

"A test." She nodded. "Do you think Diana told Beth?"

"No." He shrugged. "I don't know. I hope not."

"So." She cleared her throat. "Should I do some stupid high-pitched girlish giggles?"

He huffed out a sharp, brittle laugh. "I love you, Kaks."

"Jordy."

"Hmm?" He sighed.

"Naked and cold here."

"Sorry." He started to back away so she could close the door and finish her shower. But she thought about Lauren. Her suggestion that she just take her clothes off and see what happened. Kaki had said she wouldn't do that. But at the moment, she was already naked with good reason to be. And there were two people in the hall that either expected to hear them carrying on like newlyweds or for Kaki to kick his ass out of the bathroom.

"C'mere." She leaned toward him.

"You don't wanna touch me," he warned her. "I'm disgusting right now—"

She kissed him. A soft simple kiss. Her wet lips against his.

"Kaki Steed, you're killing me," he groaned.

"Just go back out there thinking about what you could be doing in the shower right now."

He lifted his eyes to hers with a slow, lazy grin.

"What do you think?" he asked her. She thought it was a pretty good idea. It would be fun; they could pass some time if he shucked his shorts off and climbed into the shower with her and put his hands on her. But she didn't think that's what he meant.

"About what?" she asked quietly. He hadn't so much as dropped his eyes once. She knew him too well to think he had that kind of discipline. The Jordy Steed she knew would not only be peeking; he'd be reaching, pawing at something.

"Do I look turned on?"

She ducked back under the water, but kept her back to him. Wasn't like he was going to waste time looking at her butt anyway.

"I don't know, Jordy," she mumbled. "I don't know what you look like when you're turned on."

CHAPTER TWENTY-SEVEN

HE'D NEVER BEEN SO happy in his life when Kaki left the house with Diana. He'd been walking around with a loaded gun in his pants since he'd walked in on her in the shower. He hadn't wanted to do it; well, he'd wanted to. Hell yes, he'd wanted to get a good long look at those luscious curves and her Florida tan and the beads of water sliding over her breasts. He'd wanted his hands on those curves. His tongue licking the drops of water from her skin.

But he'd known it would embarrass her. And he hadn't wanted to do that. She always seemed to be angry after anything remotely sexual happened between them, and he'd figured this would be no different. She'd scrambled to cover her breasts—not before he got an eyeful—and then she'd calmed down when he'd explained the situation to her. The test. He'd known in a heartbeat Diana was testing them; he was glad Kaki had thought the same.

Still. Now she was probably pissed at him again. Marrying her hadn't given him that freedom to waltz in on her in private moments. Maybe in most marriages, but not theirs, and he'd known that. Still. His sisters-in-law were probably used to his brothers doing ornery stuff like that, and it would have looked suspicious if he'd refused to walk into the bathroom and say something to his wife when she was in the shower.

So Kaki was probably pissed. Or she would be once she got home and looked at him again. Once she was reminded his eyes had seen something he wasn't supposed to see. And until then, he had a granite dick that hurt like hell and nowhere to go with it. Jason had texted him. Told him to get his ass over to his and Beth's house; they were going to order pizza and watch baseball. Sounded fine, but Jordy couldn't go like this.

Another night of jacking off didn't appeal to him, either. He wanted the woman. He wanted that soft, warm skin. The breasts she'd tried to hide. Her strawberry pink nipples that might just beat her lips for the perfect pink. He'd love to taste them and find out.

That kind of thinking wasn't going to help. He drank a soda. Perched on the edge of the sofa and watched a documentary about some painter he'd never heard of. Sent Jason a text and told him he'd be over in a bit; that he'd worked outside all day and needed to shower. By the time he'd killed the soda, the documentary had killed his wood. He showered. Wondered what the girls were doing as he dressed in khaki shorts and an old Prior Pirates t-shirt. Kaki had looked smoking hot when they left. Dolled up in skinny jeans and black heels and a black tank. He had to admit the filmy silver, purple and white scarf Diana and Beth had brought her to wear added a sexy little flair to the outfit, but he'd also argue that she didn't need it. She wore only her wedding ring, no other jewelry. She'd left her hair down, so she hadn't even bothered with earrings.

Before they left, she'd kissed him goodbye. A long, wet kiss in the kitchen that they both knew would draw Diana's attention. She'd been waiting in the living room, but she'd come looking for Kaki when she took too long with the goodbye. Jordy had made sure to ruin her lipstick, so Diana had given him a playful punch when Kaki ducked into the first floor bathroom to fix it.

He worried now that someone else would catch her eye. That while she was having a drink with his brothers' wives, some guy would catch her attention. He didn't think Kaki was the type to slink off with a stranger to get some, but then he still didn't know if anything had happened with that Owen guy on the beach in Florida. He had no room to be jealous anyway. She had every right to be loved, to be treated to a whole hell of a lot more than he was giving her. Jordy knew she was way too much woman to be wasting time with him in this pretend marriage.

He shoved his wallet in his back pocket and then hurried down the steps. Hesitated at the bottom trying to remember where he'd left his phone. Had he carried it upstairs or left it in the kitchen? Hell, for all he knew, Kaki's kiss had scorched a few thousand brain cells and he'd tossed his phone in the oven or flushed it down the toilet. He laughed, but it bugged him, too. The way he felt about her. He didn't know what the hell to call it, but it was making him crazy.

As he entered the kitchen and spotted his phone on the table, the doorbell rang. He groaned under his breath. Grabbed his phone and slipped it in his pocket as he headed back to the front door. Probably one or more of his brothers here to collect him since he'd taken so long to get ready. He laughed again as he reached to open the door. If they asked, he'd tell them. Kaki's goodbye kiss had left him wound so frigging tight, he'd had to spend time in front of educational television to decompress.

His heart nearly exploded in his chest when he pulled the door open and found Brianna on the porch. Dressed in a tight black dress that left nothing to the imagination and stiletto heels that made Kaki's look like dress up toys, she was a walking fantasy. When their eyes met, she flicked the tip of her tongue over the middle of her fire engine red lip and arched an eyebrow suggestively.

"Is your wife home?"

Jordy felt his stomach fall, and his dick spring to life again. He groaned. He could lie, but at the moment his mouth was so dry, he couldn't speak. Brianna took his silence as a no, apparently, and invited herself inside. Jordy catalogued her long, squared red nails, the zipper on the front of her dress (he knew if he tugged it, he'd find nothing but skin underneath) and the *do you wanna fuck me* look in her eyes.

Did he? Want to fuck her? He couldn't deny that the woman was hot. One look at her and his blood all went straight to his groin, and his brain shut off. The last time they'd been together, she'd deep-throated him, swallowed everything and licked her lips.

"She's out with friends," he finally managed to answer her. His voice sounded solid, no hint that she'd sucked the breath, the life out of him just by showing up.

"Her mistake." Brianna nodded. "Do you wanna pretend to be happily married and show me around your cute little house?"

"I am happily married, Brianna."

Nevertheless, he led her through the first floor, no intentions of taking her upstairs. He didn't want her in their bedroom. Didn't want her near Kaki's things. She almost seemed interested in the décor, the colors he and Kaki had used to accent the living room. She'd trailed a hand over the pub table in the kitchen and then turned to him. Raked her eyes over his body. He was dressed for a night of pizza and baseball with his brothers; Brianna liked him in tight jeans.

"So…" She shrugged. Licked her lip again. "If you're happily married, you're just not interested in…"

Jordy's chest tightened, and he had to gulp a quick breath of air. Brianna toyed with him for a moment, played with the zipper and finally gave it a tiny pull. He watched with baited breath as she inched it down so slowly he thought Kaki might get home before she presented herself to him.

Kaki would tell him to do this, wouldn't she? That this was the whole reason she'd married him? To make Brianna come back to him? He hadn't thought they were there yet; that Brianna would come this quickly. They'd been texting. A little bit of sexting, though Jordy wasn't really into it. He'd rather hang out with Kaki and watch old movies or take a bike ride than flirt with Brianna.

But now that she was here…

Then again, Kaki might tell him to play it cool. If he ran right to Brianna like a lapdog, she'd probably treat him like a lapdog. Sounded like something Kaki might say.

"Brianna." He sighed. She tugged the zipper open and parted the dress. All skin, just as he'd expected. Her breasts were high and proud, her nipples dark and hard. He wasn't fooled. It wasn't that she wanted him. She wanted control.

"What if she came home and found you fucking me on your kitchen table?"

That wasn't going to happen.

"I think you need to go," he told her. Her eyebrows shot up in surprise. Rather than deter her, it spurred her into action. Rather than offer her breasts to him, she held his gaze and slipped her fingers between her legs. Rubbed herself suggestively. Jordy moved quickly, but he wasn't sure what he intended to do. Part of him wanted to touch her. To push her hand away and replace it with his. Part of him wanted to sink his teeth into her breast. Part of him wanted to zip her up and send her back out the front door.

"She doesn't need to know," she reminded him. Jordy swallowed hard as he stood in front of her. Close enough to feel her breath on his face. His hand moved as if it was disconnected. Cupped her breast. He stroked his thumb up over her nipple, eyes still on hers. He'd been expecting the flash of surprise, the pleasure Kaki always seemed to convey when he touched her. Whether it be a soft whimper, a moan, or just the way her eyes widened and warmed, he knew he turned her on.

He wasn't sure what turned Brianna on. Other than control.

Her breasts were fake. He'd known it and loved them anyway. Before Kaki. As he stroked the back of his knuckles over Brianna now, he thought of Kaki in the shower earlier. The way she'd pressed her hands over herself. He remembered that when he'd seen her in the bikini, he'd been floored to see how perfect she was. Now he knew that for sure.

Perfectly natural.

And pretty.

"I'm not going to do this," he announced. He stepped back from Brianna. Dropped his hands. Wished like hell he hadn't touched her. Not like this. Okay, so maybe he'd wanted her back, but it felt completely wrong to do this in his house. The house he shared with Kaki. To touch her with his wedding ring on.

"You're kidding me."

"Nope."

"You sure about that, Jordy?" She leaned in and pressed her lips to his ear. "This offer isn't gonna stand forever. I might be gone when you get bored with plain Jane."

"Pretty sure I'm not gonna get bored," he answered simply.

"Well, while you're here waiting for Jane to get home—"

"Her name is Kaki," Jordy told her.

"I'll be at home. Naked. Playing. Thinking about you."

He held his breath while she zipped her dress. She tugged it up just under her breasts, so that every time she moved, he was treated to another eyeful. He followed her to the front door. Tried to pull away from her and turn his head the other way when she kissed him. When she finally walked out, he nearly slammed the door. Hurried back to the first floor bathroom. He almost laughed since Kaki had to fix her lipstick before she left, and he had to wipe Brianna's off his mouth before he left. But he didn't. It wasn't funny. He leaned over the sink and threw water on his face. Rubbed his hand over his mouth and wondered how he'd ever thought Brianna Fleer cramming her tongue down his throat was sexy.

Kaki might find that interesting, but he wasn't sure how to tell her. Because if she asked what sort of kisses he did find sexy, he'd have to say hers. Any kiss that involved any part of Kaki's body, whether it was her mouth on his or his mouth on her, was sexy as hell. Those were the kisses he wanted more of.

How the hell did a guy tell his wife something crazy like that?

———

"Where the hell have you been?" Jason asked when Jordy walked into his brother's house. "My wife gets ready faster than you do."

"Something came up," he mumbled. He'd debated the whole drive here whether or not to tell them about Brianna. If he and Kaki were really married, if it was real to them, would he mention it? Confide in them? Or would he try to hide it? The thing was, any number of people could have seen her car at his house earlier. She hadn't been there long, no, but still. On the other hand, he planned to tell Kaki. So it wasn't like he was going to try and hide it.

He hadn't come to a decision when he pulled into Jason's drive and climbed out of the Jeep. Decided he was going to wing it. The lies he and Kaki were telling were getting complicated. His head was pounding. Jamie's slap on his back followed by Jackson's punch in the shoulder didn't help.

"Pizza and beer, man." Jason waved him on into the living

room. Jordy rubbed the back of his neck and dropped to sit on the couch.

"What came up?" Jamie asked him as Jackson disappeared from the room. Jordy rested his elbows on his knees and rubbed his eyes vigorously.

"I'll bet on that," Jackson announced as he returned, an open bottle of Miller Lite in hand. He offered it to Jordy.

"His wife wasn't home," Jamie reminded Jackson.

"So maybe he was wishing she was. Spent a little too much time in the shower?" Jackson directed his shrug at Jamie.

"Actually, yeah. When Kaks left the house with Diana, she laid such a smoking hot kiss on me, I had to decompress with a documentary about some painter named Ralph Mannard."

"Never heard of him." Jason shook his head.

"Yeah, me neither. He's from Arkansas. He paints animals."

"Like dogs? Or zebras?"

"Dogs would maybe be easier," Jackson offered. "Maybe one color. Zebras..."

"Really?" Jason frowned up at Jackson. "I'd think you'd have to really mix a lot of colors to get a dog's fur—"

"Jordy?" Jamie cleared his throat. Jordy huffed out a quick breath and then rubbed his hand over his eyes again.

"I...um." He pursed his lips. Once upon a time, he'd have flaunted Brianna Fleer in anyone's face. Now he was a little bit embarrassed by what he'd had with her. "I was getting ready to leave the house, and Brianna showed up."

His words were met with silence. Only a disembodied voice on Jason's big screen TV spoke, listing the side effects of a new drug for heart disease. Jordy was sort of afraid to look at his brothers. None of them were crazy about Brianna, but he'd expected some display of support.

"Dammit, Jordy." Jamie tossed down his paper plate as he stood up. Jordy watched the plate hit the coffee table and slide off. Flutter to the floor. A small piece of crust rolled off to the hardwood floor.

"Wait." Jason frowned. Drew back and looked down his nose at Jordy as if he was a slug. "You...cheated? You get a woman like Kaki to marry you and then you cheat the first chance you get?"

It wasn't the first chance he'd had, but he couldn't go into the honeymoon nights when he'd left Kaki alone in their bed and prowled the beaches looking, albeit half-heartedly, for someone to hook up with.

"Wow. Diana is in love with Kaks. She's gonna be so pissed—"

"I didn't cheat." Jordy stood up. "Nothing happened."

Jamie stalked around the low, circular coffee table to get in Jordy's face.

"Then why are your lips so red?" Jamie drilled his finger into Jordy's shoulder, just under his collarbone. "You son-of-a-bitch. You set it up so our wives would take her out so you could screw around with—"

"I did not cheat." Jordy gritted his teeth.

Jamie nodded. Poked him again. Jordy saw him ball that same hand into a fist.

"You're gonna hit me?" He laughed. "Are you kidding me? I didn't cheat. I wouldn't do that to Kaks."

"Then explain why you look like a clown after family hour at The Post."

"Because she kissed me."

"Grow up, Jordy." Jason sounded tired.

"She came inside. And she waltzed around the house like she owned it. Unzipped her dress and pretty much asked if I was interested."

When Jordy turned to Jason and Jackson, their stares were cold. He felt a rush of gratitude. His brothers loved his wife unquestionably already. But how ironic that he had to defend himself about cheating on her when in reality, Kaki had married him to help him get Brianna back.

"What? A thong? Fishnet stockings?"

"Nothing."

Jason cleared his throat. "Your ex-girlfriend showed up naked to try and seduce you?"

"Well, she had a dress on, but yeah." Jordy shrugged. "It pissed her off when I said no."

"You said no?" Jackson eyed him suspiciously. "Really?"

"After being with Kaki like that..." He let his words trail off. Couldn't go into detail there. Not now. Not when he really, honest to God, meant it.

"So she just laid one on you?"

"Yeah. I walked her to the door and told her I wasn't interested, and she decided to jam her tongue down my throat for old time's sake."

"And you swear that's all that happened?"

"I swear to God, that's all that happened." He tossed his hands up helplessly, careful not to spill beer on Beth's floor. There'd be hell of a different kind to pay if he got something on his sister-in-law's floor.

"I'll be damned, guys." Jamie laughed softly. "Little brother *is* in love."

CHAPTER TWENTY-EIGHT

IT WAS fun hanging out with the girls. She'd known them all as long as they'd been married to Jordy's brothers, since she technically predated all of them. She and Jordy had been friends long before Jamie met Shawn to get the ball rolling. They had dinner at La Gran Cantina, easily Kaki's favorite Mexican restaurant in town. They'd shared a couple of pitchers of margaritas, though Beth guzzled water and raced to the bathroom several times, and some girl talk. Nachos. Beth talked about the woes of the early days of a pregnancy. From what Kaki gathered, they all agreed that the first several weeks exhausted a woman even more maybe than the month before delivery. They'd asked about Lauren, then, and Diana had even called her to invite her to join them. Lauren had thanked her for calling, and they'd talked and laughed for a few minutes and then Diana had disconnected and said Lauren had asked for a rain check because she was at one of her niece's ball games.

The girls had teased her about her newlywed status. Teased her about their in-laws harping already about needing more grandbabies. Beth, who'd just returned from the bathroom again, had patted her belly and told Kaki they'd tried to take the pressure off her and Jordy. After dinner, they'd headed to Jazz Moon, an upscale bar that Kaki doubted Jordy had ever set foot in. He would hate the place's hip, modern look. Neon lighting around the bar, low-slung couches lined the walls. High top and bistro tables filtered in and around the couches and coffee tables. They'd snagged a high top. Hung out there most of the night. Kaki was feeling no pain, but she didn't care to slide much past the nice buzz. She didn't want to spend Sunday dinner at the Steeds' tomorrow with a hangover.

She hoped when Beth dropped her off near midnight that she'd been a convincing blushing bride. She hadn't told a ton of stories; the more she told, the harder it became to keep everything straight. She gathered from their talk, though, that Jordy's brothers all had a voracious appetite for sex, and that none of them left their wives unattended to, and she'd wished yet again that there was more to her and Jordy. Diana had quizzed her on the drive earlier, when she'd picked her up. Asked her about the scar on Jordy's leg. Kaki didn't point out that she'd been friends with him when he'd cut his leg on the playground equipment at school and had to have stitches. She'd simply described the shape of the scar, nearly a two inch long slice, the placement of the scar (high on the back of his thigh) and she'd told Diana that she and Jordy had compared scars. Related to her the story of the motorcycle wreck when she was dating Tate Delaney.

She was surprised to find Jordy at home when she walked inside. The house was mostly dark, but the TV was on. Kaki had tossed her keys on the counter and carried her purse in through the living room. He was stretched out on the couch, one arm slung up over his head.

He looked at her through slitted eyes and offered her a smile. Kaki looked from him to the TV and found he was watching an old horror movie.

"Hey." He scooted around on the couch to make room for

her to sit. Patted the cushion by his waist. She dropped her purse to the table and sank gratefully to the couch. "How was your night?"

"It was fun," she answered. She'd enjoyed it, and she'd promised she'd go next time, whenever that might be. But she'd missed Jordy. Even with all the laughing going on and the girl talk about Diana's new jeans and Shawn's mom's battle with cancer and Beth's pregnancy and all their kids' crazy antics, she'd been surprised to realize she was thinking about Jordy. Wondering what he was doing. Thinking it would be nice to be at home with him.

"Good." He rested his hand on her leg.

"What'd you do?" She reached down to take her shoes off and moaned softly when her bare feet touched the floor.

"Watched baseball with my brothers."

She nodded. She should have known he'd hang out with them. She hated to admit it, even to herself, but she had this fantasy where Jordy saw Brianna, even spent some time with her, and realized he just wasn't that into her after all. Pretty junior high of her, and she covered her face now to hide her blush from him.

"What's wrong?"

"Um." She yawned. Rubbed her face to convince him she was beat. "Tired. Been a long day."

"It has," he agreed.

"I'm gonna go to bed."

"What'd you guys do?"

"Went to El Gran Cantina."

Kaki dropped her hands and looked at him. Felt a ripple of desire slide through her belly when that sexy grin crossed his face.

"So you had margaritas."

"Yeah."

"And you ate chicken fajitas."

"How do you know that?"

"It's what you've ordered there for the past ten years."

She turned sideways on the couch and drew her right foot up under her other leg. She studied him silently.

"What?"

"Am I that predictable?"

"Are you kidding me?" He laughed. Took her hand in his and pulled it to his mouth. Kissed her knuckles. "I'm happy that I knew that. A little mystery is nice, but I like knowing things about you."

"Because knowing I like chicken fajitas is fascinating."

"Kinda." He nodded.

"On that note—"

"What else?"

"What?"

"What else did you do?"

"Went to Jazz Moon."

"The slinky bar in that old warehouse? What was it? An old hardware store or something?"

"I think so."

"How was it?"

"Kind of cool," she answered simply. "It was a lot of fun."

Jordy scooted around again and then propped himself up on his elbow. He still held her fingers in his.

"Would you go there with me sometime?"

The hunger in his eyes zapped her. No little ripples this time. Just a straight shot of electricity down through her belly to her inner thighs. She took a quick breath and summoned up a shred of sarcasm.

"You?" She laughed softly. "You wanna go there? To Jazz Moon?"

"If it meant taking you out on a date, and you dressing like that and wearing those shoes…" He sounded dead serious. "And dancing. Do they have a dance floor there?"

A wave of nerves scraped over her, leaving her insides

trembling and her skin chilled. When she couldn't make her mouth work, she only nodded.

"Dancing with you. Yes. I would go there."

He held her gaze. The thought of dancing with him again made her think of their reception. The wedding night. All the nights since then when he hadn't touched her. She cleared her throat and looked away.

"How much did you have to drink?" She grinned and arched her eyebrows. "I mean, the Jeep was in the driveway. You didn't tear up the yard, but that—"

"Kaks."

"Hmm?"

"I need to tell you something."

Just like that, the flame of desire in his eyes was gone. He shifted his gaze to the TV. Kaki held her breath. What the hell was he going to tell her? Had Brianna come running? Had he lied about hanging out with his brothers? Not that there was a damned thing in the world she could do about it. It was the end game, after all. Operation *get the slutty ex back*. Kaki squeezed her eyes closed. She didn't like Brianna, but she didn't have to be hateful about it.

Except that she did kind of hate her. Now. Because Jordy wanted her.

"Okay." Her voice was small. She dipped her head and nodded. "What?"

"Brianna showed up here tonight."

Kaki managed to hide the sharp pain in her chest. Eyes lowered to her lap, she simply closed them again and nodded. She'd known it would come to this. Of course it was going to happen. Even if all Brianna wanted was to break them up and make Jordy miserable, he was into her and it was going to happen.

She wondered if they'd been in her bed. The thought made her head spin. She swallowed hard; her throat burned with the taste of tequila and lime.

"Okay."

"Nothing happened."

She looked up at him and shook her head. "You don't need to tell me that." She squeezed his fingers. Lifted them to her mouth and kissed them, lowered his hand to the couch and then stood. "That's your business."

"Kaks."

"Just tell me she wasn't in my bed—"

"Nothing happened." He scrambled to get up. Kaki watched him pace the living room, shoving his hands back through his hair. "I mean…she tried. But…"

Just that bothered Kaki. *She* tried. Now she would go to bed and lay awake wondering what exactly that meant. What had Brianna done to try and seduce him? Didn't matter that he claimed nothing had happened. He'd wanted her. Jordy was a stud, but for whatever reason that woman turned him into a puddle of desire.

She crossed the living room, but when she looked back, she saw her shoes on the floor in front of the couch. She should take them upstairs. But she didn't want to take the time. She didn't want to walk back into the zone, anywhere near Jordy. Not right now. Her chest felt tight, full of tears she didn't want to cry. Especially not in front of him. That whole feeling no pain thing was out the window, because right now, her head pounded with a drum solo. She was angry.

Not with Jordy. With herself.

How could she have been so stupid to fall for Jordy? She knew him better than anyone, and she knew just exactly who and what he was. One thing to love him as a friend. Something completely different to fall in love with him when sex was only a game to him.

"Okay." She nodded again. She looked around the room, sort of wishing he'd just sleep down here tonight. She couldn't imagine lying next to him right now. Wondering what Brianna's seduction attempt had included. Wondering how much had happened for Jordy to say nothing had happened. He'd probably say nothing had ever happened between them, too, so odds were he'd had his hands on Brianna somewhere. "I'm gonna...go upstairs."

"Kaki, I need to talk to you."

She backed up a step when he walked toward her. Lifted her chin and met his eyes. Would he see the tears? In the dimly lit room, would he even notice?

"I can't, Jordy," she said softly. "Not right now."

Maybe she had had too much to drink. Jordy sighed and groaned out loud as he ducked his head. When he lifted his head again and made a show of avoiding eye contact, Kaki's eyes roamed his face. The deep groove between his eyebrows. The sad, downturn twist of his lips, and the puckered bags under his eyes.

"Okay." He nodded. "Okay."

It wasn't okay. Nothing was okay, but Kaki turned and moved to the steps. In her mind, she raced up the steps to get away from him. But she forced herself to move slowly. Casually. He loved her. Jordy loved a woman who would break him. Again and again and again. It hurt her to know that whenever this was over, when Jordy decided he was finished with her and Brianna was ready to take him back, she would tear him down all over again.

She'd told Jordy on their honeymoon that he wasn't like Brianna. That he wasn't cruel. He didn't want control over women; he simply liked sex. She decided now as she peeled her clothes off and groped around the bed for her pajamas that maybe he was worse. He wasn't cruel. He was clueless. He'd been sleeping with Kaki for a month now. Toying with her with the steamy kisses and the tender strokes. Laughing and playing the way they'd always done as friends, and yet, he was looking right at her and he couldn't see what he was doing to her.

CHAPTER TWENTY-NINE

HE'D DEBATED over not going to bed. Just crashing on the couch to give her some space. He'd even stayed on the couch until after two. Eyes on the TV now and then, but he wasn't watching anything. The horror movie he'd had on had ended, and another had started. Jordy tuned the gore and the nudity out and thought about his wife. Alone. Upstairs.

He wasn't sure what had happened. He'd pissed her off with the Brianna thing. Well. He wasn't even sure pissed off were the right words for it. He'd hurt her. He just didn't get how. Or why.

Cold, and if he was honest, just desperate to be close to her, he'd finally turned the TV off and trudged upstairs. He tried to be quiet, but naturally, he hit his elbow on the doorframe and then knocked her hairspray over in the bathroom when he brushed his teeth. He'd stood still for a second, waiting to hear her move. When he didn't, he hurriedly wiped the sink out, hung up the hand towel, and then flipped the light off. She was sound asleep on her side, her back to him. He'd sat gingerly on his side of the bed and watched her for a few long moments. Wanted to touch her. To brush her hair off her face. Run his fingers through her hair. Kiss her goodnight.

He didn't. In fact, when he did lie down, he'd hugged his side of the bed so he wouldn't bother her. Sleep had been a long time coming. His mind raced over the night. The whole night. From walking in on her in the shower to that goodbye kiss she teased him with before she left with Diana. The shock of finding Brianna on the porch, and the even bigger shock that when she'd bared herself to him, his brain had automatically compared her to Kaki and found her lacking.

The kiss with Brianna didn't phase him. In the big scheme of things, that didn't matter. Except to remind him of Kaki's sweet kisses. Even the steamy ones, when she stroked her tongue over his again and again, when she got so wrapped up in it she scraped her fingernails up over his arms and his shoulders and into his hair, even those kisses were sweet. Sexy as fuck, but there was more to them. Something he'd never felt with Brianna. Or any other woman, for that matter.

The scene with his brothers played out over and over in his head, too. The way they'd all jumped to conclusions. All so quick to believe he'd screw around on Kaki and hurt her. He loved that they wanted to protect her, but the way they'd banded together had felt like a personal attack against him. Maybe it was, but it left him feeling like it was them and Kaki against him. He'd finally convinced them he hadn't cheated, that he didn't want to hurt Kaki. And then Jamie had gone and thrown down that word.

He knew before he opened his eyes this morning that he was alone in bed. He lay for several long moments wishing she were beside him. Wishing he could roll over and take her in his arms and kiss her. He'd kiss her face, her forehead, her cheekbones, her nose. Her hair. He loved her hair. The flowery scent of her shampoo. The soft silky threads against his face when he held her. Her lips. God, would he kiss those lips. He'd lick them and then suck on them. Nibble. Stroke.

And when she'd finally open her mouth—he loved how she did that. How she sighed with pleasure when he kissed her, the way her lips parted and he could feel that first slow panting breath over his face. The blind desire in her hooded eyes when she looked at him—he'd slide his tongue over hers. Warm and velvety soft, the thought of her tongue on other parts of his body drove him out of bed.

He'd gone straight to the shower, simply because he couldn't stroll downstairs with his cock at attention like this. Then again, wouldn't have mattered because she wasn't downstairs. He'd expected to find her in the kitchen. Felt a shot of panic rip through his chest, his heart, when he found the room tidy and empty. She hadn't made coffee. No breakfast. Nothing in the kitchen that resembled a note. Suddenly the panic throbbed from head to toe. What if she'd left? He'd told her to tap out when she couldn't do it anymore. What if this was it? What if she thought Brianna showing up last night was enough, that she could finally move on with her life?

Heart heavy, he hurried up the steps to check the closet. He'd have heard her. Right? If she had packed her stuff to leave this morning, he'd have heard her. His stomach cramped up like someone had reached down his throat and grabbed a handful of his guts and squeezed the hell out of him. He yanked the closet door open and then slumped in relief when he saw all of her things still there. Embarrassed for being such an idiot, he rubbed his hands on his shorts and then lifted his left hand to look at his wedding ring.

What if…

What if he wanted to keep it? To keep her?

Where the hell was she? Okay, he'd quelled the panic. Even if she'd gone out for a drive to clear her head and she came home to pack and leave him, he might have a shot at changing her mind.

He paced the bedroom, his eyes never leaving the bed.

Dammit, he wanted to make love to her. How the hell was he supposed to keep this up? To sleep by her night after night and keep his hands off her? The smell of her perfume always in the sheets. In her hair. The sound of her laugh echoed in the house even when she wasn't here. Her smile. Her voice. Everything about her haunted him.

He made the bed, but not because she'd want him to. Because it was an excuse to touch the sheets on her side. He folded her pajamas, but he was thinking about the things she'd been given for her bachelorette. Things she'd been given to wear for him.

Had he really thought this was a good idea? Marrying his best friend? Just to make a dime a dozen ex jealous?

Back downstairs, he paced in the living room. Went over the scene from last night again. What if she and her ex had left things on hold for this idiotic marriage thing? What if living with him ended up costing her true happiness?

When he heard the car in the driveway, he almost ran out the front door. Almost. Remembered, suddenly, that just because he'd missed her all morning—it was almost noon now, and she hadn't come home—didn't mean she'd been desperate to get home to him. Reminded himself to play it cool. So maybe he felt something for Kaki. Didn't mean she felt a damned thing for him.

He bit off a mouthful of expletives when the doorbell rang. Wasn't Kaki after all. He huffed out an irritated sigh as he yanked the front door open. If it was Brianna, he'd shut it. No hello. No goodbye. Just shut the door and go back to waiting for Kaki. If it was one of his brothers, odds were he was going to take a swing. Just hoped to hell he connected, because he needed the satisfaction of hitting something solid. The aching knuckles. The cracked skin and the blood on his hand.

"Hey Jordy."

Well, he sure couldn't take a swing at Lauren. He lifted his arm, wrapped his fingers in a white-knuckle grip around the edge of the door, and hung his head.

"Do you know where she is?"

"What?"

He tossed his hand up to invite Lauren inside. She slipped by him, all sunshine and hearts. The baby on the way had started to soften her. Dulled the edge on her sharp tongue. She smiled more now. Tempered her blunt comments with polite, positive crap. The hell of it was, Jordy thought it was real. Genuine. Pregnant Lauren was beautiful. He wasn't in the mood for it.

He gave the door a push and nodded when it crashed closed with a loud thud.

"Remember when I did that? When I was seventeen? Slammed the door so hard, two picture frames fell off the wall. Shattered the glass. Dad grounded me for a month."

Jordy crossed his arms over his chest and shrugged. "Point?"

"Jeez." She arched her eyebrows and looked around. "What's up your butt today?"

"Do you know where she is?"

"Who?" she asked quickly. She shook her head. "No. Kaki said I could borrow your crockpot. Tyler's family is coming in later."

"His family?"

"His parents. And his grandfather. I need the crockpot to throw some stuff in. For dinner."

"What's wrong with yours?"

"Um." She laughed softly, and again, Jordy thought of how she'd changed. Light trills of laughter now, in addition to the big hearty laugh he knew and loved. For half a second, he was jealous. Lauren was happy. This was Lauren's life now. Happily married. Madly in love with Tyler. He'd known that when she'd kissed him the night before her wedding, just a case of nerves. She and Tyler were happy, anxiously awaiting their baby's arrival.

Who the hell would ever have thought Jordy Steed could be jealous of the American dream?

"I dropped it."

"What?"

"The crockpot." She closed her eyes. "Don't get pregnant, Jordy."

"Don't plan to."

Another sweet little laugh. "Kills brain cells. Makes you clumsy. Dropped the damned thing outside. Shattered it. Took a chunk out of the cement on the patio."

"Why did you have it outside?"

"Took it out to dump the...greasy stuff...from a pork roast in the back of the yard." She shook her head and gave him a deadpan look. "Again, I don't recommend—"

"Getting pregnant." He nodded. "Noted."

"Carrying that damned thing."

"Use the garbage disposal in the sink."

"Broken."

He had to laugh.

"So?" She bit her lip. "Can I? Borrow yours?"

"Yeah, but let me carry it to your car for you."

She followed him to the kitchen.

"The sex is still good, though," she mumbled.

"Lauren."

"Hmm?"

"Maybe we'll file that under things you don't need to tell me."

"Just...giving you tips for the future."

He opened cabinets one by one until he found Kaki's crockpot.

"You don't know? Where she is?" He glanced at her over

his shoulder as he picked it up. Gave a gentle tug when the cord got stuck on something.

"No." She shook her head. "Why?"

He shrugged in defeat and shook his head. "I don't know. Things are so good, Lauren. I love living with her. I love being around her."

"You love her."

"Well, yeah." Crockpot in hand, he shrugged and lifted it toward the front of the house. "I love you guys, but…"

Lauren rolled her eyes and made a tssking sound. As if she was scolding him.

"I think she wants out." He pushed the words out over the tightness in his throat. Avoided Lauren's eyes and then started walking when she led him out of the kitchen.

"Wanna know what I think?" she asked with her back to him.

"I'll probably be sorry for saying so, but yes."

"Fuck her." She turned as she walked so she could look at him.

"What?" He nearly dropped the crockpot. The thought of gouging the hardwood and having to explain that to Kaki made him feel faint.

"How long have you been married now?"

"But. Lauren, she's—but—"

"She's a woman, Jordy. I'm not sure what you're thinking. But she's not gonna break. You're killing her with the shows you're putting on. It's just sex. Give it to her."

"We agreed to not…do that…before we got married."

Lauren snorted. "Really? You're a smoking hot guy with a reputation for great hands and a wild ride. She's pretty smoking hot, too, and she's put her life on hold. For you. The least you can do is make it fun for her."

"She doesn't want me—"

"Don't be stupid, Jordy." She shook her head and then turned her back to him again. "She'll be back."

He hefted the crockpot to the side and watched the drive as he followed Lauren to her car.

"Then you do know where she is."

"I don't." Lauren shrugged. "Maybe she needed a little Kaki time. Maybe she went for a drive. Maybe she went shopping."

"It's Sunday morning. There's nothing—"

"Jordy!" Lauren snapped.

Chagrined, he turned away from her. She opened her car door and stepped out of the way so Jordy could lean in and set the crockpot on the passenger seat.

"She's committed to this," Lauren told him when he backed out of the car to stand up straight. "For you. She'll see it through. For you. But she invested a lot in this...scheme, too. A lot of hard earned money. And pride. I mean, give her six months at least, before you go back to that woman you want. Her family believes in this. They think you're madly in love with her and that you're gonna spend the rest of your life making her happy."

Jordy swallowed hard. He wanted to spend the rest of his life working his ass off for Kaki. Just to see her smile. If he said so, Lauren might either deck him or laugh from now until she checked into labor and delivery in six months.

"Don't embarrass her. Please? I love you, Jordy, you know that."

He finally looked at her. Met her gaze. Sighed and nodded. "I know."

"But I love her, too. I'm crazy about both of you, and I'm gonna kill you. If you hurt her."

"Yeah." Jordy pursed his lips and raised his eyebrows. "Yeah. Thanks for the warning."

Lauren nodded. "You bet. It'll be ugly, too. Grisly. Painful."

"Got it." He nodded.

He shoved his hands in his pockets as she slid into the driver's seat of her little white Malibu. She buckled her seatbelt, so prim and proper now, and then tossed him a wave and backed out of the drive. Jordy waved. And then turned and wandered back to the house.

CHAPTER THIRTY

HANDS FULL, Kaki bumped the back door open with her hip. She heard music when she stepped into the kitchen and looked around the empty room. She kicked her foot out to close the door but missed. With a frustrated grumble, she carried the grocery bags to the counter and set them down. Pulled her keys from the pocket of her shorts as she crossed back to the door to close it.

"Hey."

She set her purse and keys on the counter and looked over her shoulder to find Jordy watching her uncertainly from the door to the dining room. The music, she realized, was coming from the entertainment center in the living room.

He'd looked so harmless this morning when she left him in bed. Tiptoed out of the room to shower and get dressed. Curled away from her, hugging his side of the bed—maybe after seeing Brianna, the idea of sleeping beside Kaki bothered him—he'd looked like an overgrown kid. She'd stolen just a moment to watch him sleep. His thick eyelashes and eyebrows were sexy, but she'd half hoped he'd open his eyes and look at her. Find her watching him and reach for her.

Might as well shoot for the moon, if she was going to start wishing on stars.

Now he'd showered and dressed in a different pair of khaki shorts (he had several, she'd laundered them now, so she knew) and a collared maroon shirt and shaved. He stood with his hands up at his sides on the doorframe, one bare foot stacked over the other.

"Hi." She offered him a smile. Not quite an olive branch, but then they hadn't quite fought last night. Most likely, Jordy hadn't had a clue she'd gone to bed so upset, and there wasn't a need for peace offers.

"Where were you?"

"I got groceries," she answered as she started taking things from the plastic bags. She glanced at him when he moseyed into the room with her but turned her attention back to the deli meats and cheese and bread.

"You've been gone a long time."

Hand still in a bag, she looked up quickly and stared at him. Surprised he'd noticed. That he cared enough to ask. Uncertain what to say, and afraid her voice might wobble if she tried to speak, she finally pressed her lips together and shrugged.

"I went to get coffee first." Okay, her voice was quiet, but not breathless or timid. She grabbed the meats and cheeses now and sidestepped him to get to the refrigerator.

"Mmm."

She felt that telltale flutter in her belly. Her fingers. He was making her feel a little tingly and nervous. And that pissed her off.

"What time did you come to bed?"

The question sounded so normal. For a wife to ask a husband. And yet, everything about it was wrong, and Kaki continued to put the groceries away while he stood, apparently rooted to the spot, and watched her.

"After two."

"I…" She cleared her throat. "I didn't want to wake you."

He shrugged one shoulder from his slouched position. Kaki decided he didn't look refreshed or happy this morning. He looked like a schoolboy, pouting that he'd been denied something fun. Maybe he was sore about having to turn Brianna down. Maybe he blamed Kaki for suggesting that he play a little hard to get with her.

"Who'd you have coffee with?" Rather than look at her, he studied his feet. Kaki watched him scrunch his toes up, as if he was trying to take up less space in the room. Or maybe just get away from her.

"Just me," she said simply. "And my book."

"I'd have gone with you."

"You don't have to."

"Have to what?"

"Keep me company at all hours. I'm fine being alone."

He hissed something and then lifted his hands and linked his fingers behind his neck. He looked pained, his face twisted in a scowl.

"What…about…" He shook his head. Looked at her, but looked away quickly.

"What?"

"Dinner? At Mom's?"

"What about it?" she asked him.

"Are you going?"

Now she hesitated. She'd been going to the Sunday dinners at Evelyn and Jonathan's house since they were engaged. Why would that change now?

"I…planned to." She worried her bottom lip with her teeth. "You don't want me to go?"

"Of course I do. Just thought maybe you had something else to do."

"No." She shook her head. She wasn't sure how long she'd last out there now. Not with this Jordy-sized headache banging around. She could use another back rub. The night he'd worked at her neck, he'd eased her headache. Then again, he'd touched her somewhere else. Somewhere he shouldn't have his hands. And she had to remember that now. No more messing around. The starts and stops and the need that was never quenched was making her crazy. And her being crazy was going to drive them apart.

She didn't want to be responsible for that. Breaking up their marriage didn't matter so much to her. But she would hate herself if she was the one to ruin their friendship.

———

THE AFTERNOON WAS FUN BUT EXHAUSTING. JORDY'S NIECES AND nephews most certainly didn't suspect that she was a fake aunt, and they kept her busy all day. She tossed a football with Jamie and Shawn's eight-year-old son, and she played countless games of Ring Around the Rosie with Mia and Chessie, Jason and Beth's beautiful stair-step girls, Mia being four and Chessie three. Not to be forgotten, Jamie's other two demanded she play with their Barbie dolls with them, and before the evening was over, she'd read Jackson's kids three stories each.

Her sisters-in-law apologized all over themselves for their kids climbing all over her. She didn't care. She liked kids, though she would admit to being a little bit relieved that she wasn't in the Steed family for the long haul, because she wasn't sure she could pop out three or four kids for Jordy. She might end up pulling her hair out.

Beth tossed her cookies, too. She made it to the bathroom, but still, Kaki must have turned white when Beth hurried out of the kitchen after dinner and Shawn and Diana moaned in support for her, because they all rushed to assure her it wasn't that bad. All worth it in the end, blah blah blah. Kaki had heard that before. Even before she and Jordy were engaged, she'd heard them and other friends say the delivery of a healthy baby was worth anything experienced in a pregnancy. Since she and Jordy weren't planning to take their deceit to the next level, she decided not to worry about it. Wasn't something in her future at this point in her life.

She'd dried dishes, and Shawn had washed, because Beth couldn't deal with putting her hands in warm water because apparently, that triggered the vomiting and Kaki chose not to question them since she was the odd one out. Diana put the dishes away. They all gave Beth a pass, let her sit at the table with her feet up.

Evelyn wandered through from time to time, but the girls wouldn't let her lift a finger to help. Kaki knew Evelyn did the cooking. Every last dish for the Sunday dinner. Always. So the girls did the clean up. When Mia climbed up in Beth's lap, Shawn suggested she go find Daddy.

That did it. She'd been fine. Enjoying herself, even. She'd put last night out of her mind. The whole headache over Jordy and Brianna. The worry that Brianna was going to hurt him again. The ugly green jealousy that had gripped her at the thought of Jordy with Brianna.

She'd taken time out this morning at Lotsa Latte. She'd taken her book, but she hadn't even opened it. Instead she'd let her mind drift. Stared out the window at the cars rushing back and forth on Broadway and remembered all the fun times and the hard times and the best times of her friendship with Jordy and Lauren. Drank her coffee, plain, black coffee, and remembered nothing in her world was more important than that friendship.

But now. That daddy thing. Shawn had just put an arrow through her heart. Jordy Steed was going to make a good daddy some day. He was crazy about his brother's kids, and it showed, and for just a moment, Kaki let herself dream of what could be. Of the day she and Jordy announced to this family that they were expecting a baby. When the girls would take care of her. When she and Jordy would go home together with their baby and tuck him in and then go to bed together and lay in each other's arms. Instead of side by side, like awkward but polite strangers sharing a bed.

When they got home from his parent's house, Kaki paced for a while. Jordy watched her for a minute and then disappeared. She heard the TV then. Rolled her eyes. He hadn't talked much to her today after the thing in the kitchen, when she thought he'd been trying to uninvite her to the family dinner. He'd been over the top at said dinner. Flirting. Loving. Always touching her. Little kisses on her forehead or her cheek. Squeezing her butt when she was drying dishes and he came inside to grab a couple of beers. Egging her on to get in the pool with him and his bothers after the kitchen was clean. Groaning in mock disappointment when she didn't, the same as his brothers did when their wives didn't join them.

He'd only told her on the drive home that he was tired. No dissection of their Sunday performances. No sharing funny stories. Just a quiet that Kaki couldn't label awkward or contented, because it was sort of both.

"What're you doing?" he asked when she trotted down the staircase. She'd gone up to go to the bathroom. Pulled her hair back in a messy, loose knot and then come downstairs. Jordy had been studiously ignoring her most of the evening, since they'd been home, but now he seemed to be hyper alert to her movements.

"I think I'm gonna go see Lauren," she lied. She looked at him, made eye contact, and then slipped down the hall to the kitchen. Before she could grab her keys and her purse, Jordy wandered into the room with her.

"Now?"

"Why not now?" She put her purse on her shoulder and glanced at him.

"I dunno." He shrugged. "I thought we could…watch a movie."

She wanted to. She wanted to throw her keys and her

purse down and throw herself into his arms and hold on. But she was afraid that he wouldn't catch her. She missed him, and, yet, she thought they were spending too much time together. She'd never be able to walk away when the time came if she didn't make a change now.

"I need...to get out of the house." She stumbled over her words. Swallowed the guilt she felt for blowing him off.

"We could—"

She shook her head, took a deep breath, and met his gaze.

"I need to get away from you for a while, Jordy."

He worked his mouth, as if he was going to say something, but finally gave up and shrugged. Threw in a nod and took a step back from her.

"I'm sorry," she whispered.

"No." He shrugged. "I get it. It's...it's fine, Kaks. You don't have to explain yourself to me."

"I just..." She sighed. Looked away from his sad eyes and shifted her weight from foot to foot. "I need Lauren. I just need Lauren right now."

"Okay." He shoved his hands in his pockets and hunched his shoulders. "Just...be...careful."

She needed to breathe, but she was afraid she might lose it. Might end up in tears. So she nodded at him, flashed him a smile that probably looked sick, and turned to hurry out of the house. She wasn't going to see Lauren. She just needed to get away from their fake house. And her fake husband.

CHAPTER THIRTY-ONE

SHE WASN'T WITH LAUREN.

He'd had a sharp pain in his chest and then just a slow burn when he found that out. He hadn't called to check up on her. Lauren had called him. She said she'd called Kaki only to get voicemail. Assuming they were together, she'd called him instead. To say thanks for letting her borrow the crockpot and that the day had gone off without a hitch. Jordy had squeezed his eyes closed at that. Rubbed his fingers over the bridge of his nose. She'd also asked him if he'd thrown Kaki down and had his way with her yet, and the question had been followed by a loud, hearty streak of laughter, reminiscent of their years of friendship and the crazy things they'd done through the years.

When he said no, Lauren had asked if everything was okay. It wasn't, obviously, but he wasn't about to rehash it all again for her. He didn't believe for a second that Kaki wanted to be with him that way, and he sure as hell didn't want to talk about the fact that she'd apparently gone out to meet someone else. Fake marriage or no, he'd thought they were going to be open with each other. He'd told her about Brianna showing up last night. He wanted to know if Kaki was feeling something for someone else. So he could let her go.

He didn't, though. Not really. Knowing she was out all night with someone else made him so angry he wanted to throw things. Like the TV. The microwave. The crockpot Lauren had borrowed. Big things that would crash and bang and shatter, so he wouldn't feel like the only broken thing in the house. He kind of wanted to know who he was, the guy who might have undressed his wife and made love to her tonight, so he could punch him.

He wanted to ask her. Just ask her why.

And then again, he didn't. Because if he pretended he didn't know, they could go on as if everything was all fake and happy and perfect. Jordy thought the fake thing would beat the hell out of simply losing her. Of facing the house day after day without her.

She got home just before ten. He considered meeting her at the door, but that felt too confrontational. After all, she had the right to do whatever she wanted. The vows they'd made were for other people's sake, not theirs. He sat in the living room instead with the TV on, but that felt dumb. Posed.

Instead, he hurried upstairs as he heard her open the back door. Stupid. He was playing stupid junior high games. What if he just told her how he felt? He slipped into the bathroom and closed the door. Stood for a moment. Flushed the toilet and then felt like an idiot all over again.

He could talk to her. He had to talk to her. If nothing else, he had to at least tell her it was okay. If she'd met someone or if she wanted to go back to the other guy, it was okay. He'd let her go.

He loved her too much to hold her in this marriage when it wasn't what she wanted.

His hand shook when he opened the door. *Holy shit!* He'd *thought* it. He'd just thought *that* word, and it was exploding inside him right now and he didn't know what to do with himself.

The house was empty when he went back downstairs. He wandered from room to room. The lights were on, as he'd left them. But Kaki was nowhere to be found. He stood in the kitchen for a moment, eyes on her purse, where she'd put it on the counter. Wondered if he'd missed her upstairs. Had she been in the bedroom when he walked by? He glanced at the back door and then crossed the room quickly, thinking she might have gone out to sit on the patio. The door was locked, the outside lights off.

Deciding he must have missed her upstairs, he headed down the hall to go up. No clue what he'd say when he found her, but he had to look. He noticed the front door wasn't closed all the way. Pulled it open and saw her hunched over, sitting on the top step of the porch.

With a deep, shaky breath, he pulled the door open and stepped outside. He saw her shoulders tense up, but she didn't greet him. Didn't ask him to leave her alone. He shuffled up to stand at her side, and encouraged when she didn't reach out and sweep his legs out from under him, he lowered himself to sit by her.

She didn't look at him. Stared straight ahead.

"Hey."

She lifted her chin to acknowledge him, but she didn't answer him.

"You okay?"

She nodded.

He hung his hands between his knees and looked away from her. Studied the light on in the house across the street. They hadn't met most of their neighbors yet, only the family to the east. Accountant dad, nurse mom and two kids, one boy and one girl. A dog. A cat. And a classic car hidden away in the garage. Jordy had gone over to talk to the dad just to get a peek at the '55 Ford

Thunderbird. He'd been glad he had. The car was gorgeous. He'd never seen it out in the open yet, though the dad said they traveled to car shows in the area in the fall.

"Kaks?"

She blinked. Turned her head to look at him. He flinched when he realized she'd been crying.

"Hey." He leaned into her, but she stiffened and pulled away. "Where were you?"

"I told you—"

"You weren't with Lauren. She called here looking for you."

She didn't panic at being caught in the lie. Why would she? Instead, she turned back to the street and arched her eyebrows.

"Are you cheating on me?" His tone was light and teasing, but her answer meant everything to him. If there was someone else, if Kaki was in love with someone else, he had to let her go.

"No." She shook her head.

He swallowed hard. Rested his elbows on his knees and folded his arms over the empty space between his legs.

"Then why did you lie to me?"

She glanced at him again.

"I mean, you shot me down anyway. Why not just hit me with everything at once?"

It had hurt. Knowing she'd been gone first thing in the morning, that she'd chosen to leave and go sit alone somewhere to have her coffee, had hurt. When she'd told him earlier that she had to get away from the house, away from him, her words had sliced him open. He wanted to be with her. It hurt that she didn't feel the same way.

"I'm sorry." She licked her lips.

"Don't be sorry. I get it." He nudged her again. "I wouldn't wanna live with me either."

"Jordy." She rubbed her eyes. "I don't know…if I can do this…anymore."

Her words pounded him between the eyes. In his gut. But he hurt everywhere.

"Be married to me," he clarified.

She reached out to him, cupped her hand around his arm for a second. "Be fake married to you."

He nodded. "Did I do something? Do you think I'm lying about—"

"Can I ask you something?" She pushed her hair up off her forehead, away from her face.

"Of course." He shrugged when she looked at him.

Forehead resting on her palm, she looked at him sideways. Took a deep breath and then ducked her head and rubbed her eyes again.

"Do you really find me that unattractive?" She spoke quietly, but he heard exactly what she said. The meaning of her words, the things Lauren had said to him earlier, hit him in the groin. His dick twitched, but he scooched around impatiently. This conversation was more important than the things those words brought to mind.

"What?"

She sniffled, and he realized she was crying again.

"You heard me."

"I did." He nodded. "Have you been drinking?"

"Yep." She looked at him boldly. "But I'm not drunk. And I want to know."

"You think I'm…" He squeezed his eyes closed and shook his head. "You think I'm not attracted to you."

She nodded. "I do."

"Kaks." He groaned. Hung his head and muttered under his breath.

"I mean…I know you and Lauren—"

"What?" He looked up quickly.

"I get it." She shrugged. "She's sexy as hell. But I mean…

sometimes I think you've been with every woman in Prior. But me."

"Wait." He shook his head. "What do you know about me and Lauren? Like me and Lauren what?"

Kaki looked at him and raised her eyebrows. "She told me. That she panicked before the wedding."

"But we didn't do it."

"I know."

"Damn." He took a deep breath. "How long have you known about that?"

"Since she left your place that night."

Jordy leaned back on his hands and stretched his legs out.

"Would you rather I didn't know?"

"No, it's just…" He shook his head.

"Tyler knows, Jordy."

"What?"

"She felt so horrible about it, she told him. It's…not a big deal."

Jordy met Kaki's eyes. "Tyler. Tyler knows. That I had my hands all over his wife the night before they got married."

Kaki nodded.

"He knows it didn't mean anything, either."

"Still." Jordy turned away from her. "That's just…I thought…that was our secret. Me and Lauren's."

Kaki studied him for a moment, but he was careful not to look at her.

"Are you into her?"

"No," he said honestly. "I'm not. But it's just…something I thought the rest of the world didn't know about."

Kaki cleared her throat. "So you were attracted to her, but…what is it with me?"

"What makes you think I don't—that I'm not—"

"You didn't touch me on our wedding night."

"We agreed not to do that. Not to add that to an already complicated situation."

"When you finally did start something, you just switched it off and walked away."

"What?"

"On the honeymoon."

Angry now, he sat up straight and then slowly climbed to his feet. Frantic, she looked up at him, as if she thought he was going to walk away from the conversation.

"Who's Owen?"

"What?"

"Who is Owen?'

"Why are you asking me about Owen?'

"Who is he?" He stepped off the porch and paced in front of her.

"My ex."

"Your—?" He plunged his fingers back through his hair and turned to look at her in disbelief. "Your—your ex? Owen? Is the guy you used to date?"

"Yes." She nodded.

"You were with him the night of your bachelorette?"

"Yes." Now she sounded frustrated.

"This is pretty great," he mumbled, fingers now linked behind his neck. "Fucking. A. Mazing."

"What?"

"When I was in the middle of undressing you? Remember that? Remember how you had on that skimpy white string bikini that made my dick so hard it hurt?" He looked at her and shrugged his shoulders and eyebrows. "And you were on the bed, and I was on top of you. And I untied your top? Just about had my mouth on you?"

"Do you think I could forget that? Do you know how humiliating that was?"

"Owen called you. Right in the middle of...us...doing that, your phone screen lit up and all I see is the name Owen. And I thought—"

"What?"

271

He watched her, saw her swallow hard and rub her eyes again.

"I didn't know who Owen was, because you never told me. You never mentioned a guy by name. You never told me about a boyfriend named *Owen*. I thought it was someone you met on the beach. I thought it was that nerdy guy who hung out under the umbrella with you when you were on your honeymoon with me."

"You seriously thought I would hook up with someone like that?"

"No!" he snapped. "But what was I supposed to do? I wanted you. I wanted you naked. I wanted my mouth and my hands on you. I wanted to be inside you, and then your phone lights up with some other guy's name."

Kaki avoided his eyes. She pulled the elastic out of her hair and shook it out. He wondered if she knew that made it hard for him to breathe. That his chest tightened when she shook her hair out like that and made him think he was having a heart attack.

"Why did he call you? On your honeymoon? If things are over between you?"

"Because I called him."

"Kaki."

"Are you kidding me? It was okay for you to leave me at night? To screw around with I don't know how many girls? And you're gonna be pissed off at me for talking to him? We weren't sexting, Jordy. We just talked."

He held up a hand to stop her.

"First of all, I didn't do that."

"What?"

"I didn't hook up with anyone in Florida."

"I wasn't sleeping those nights you left."

"I left the condo, yes." He shrugged and shook his head. Rolled it on his neck. Took a deep breath. "I left. I walked the beach. I had a few drinks. I flirted with I don't even know how many girls. But I didn't do that."

"Why not?"

"Because I wanted you."

Kaki nodded. He watched her stand up.

"Where are you going?"

"I don't believe you," she said simply. "I don't believe you, Jordy."

"Kaki, I haven't had sex since the night before the wedding—"

"I don't believe you want me." She turned around and went inside. Jordy sighed. Growled out loud and then hurried in after her.

"What do you mean you don't believe me?" he roared. He leaned back to push the door closed. "Where are you?"

"Right here." She appeared in the hallway and then ducked back into the kitchen, Jordy hot on her heels. "What about the fact that you're all over me in front of your family?"

"I kiss you when no one's around."

"And you walk away."

Jordy watched her plug her phone in and leave it on the counter. He scrambled to keep up with her as she rushed up the steps and into their bedroom.

"You stopped me last time," he reminded her. "Remember? I touched you. When I was rubbing your neck. I touched you. And I could hear you breathing heavier. Like you liked it. And then you kissed me. And when I asked if you were sure, you said no. You stopped me."

"Because I know you aren't interested. This is a game. It's all a game to you."

"I can't believe this." He dropped to sit on the edge of the bed and hung his head. "I never thought I'd have to argue with a woman that I think she's hot."

"You walked into the bathroom yesterday when I was in

the shower. You had the perfect opportunity to look. And you didn't. You didn't try to touch—"

"I looked," he argued quietly. He scrubbed his head again and then dragged his hands over his face. "I looked. I didn't wanna be a dick about it, because I felt guilty for barging in on you. But I looked. Before you covered yourself, I saw something I've wanted for a very long time, and when you left to go out with the girls, I had to sit and stare at a documentary about some stupid painter just to settle the fuck down."

"Yeah?" She stood at her side of the bed now and tossed her hands up. "Why not jack off? If you were that—"

"I did that the night you shut me down with the backrub," he informed her. He looked up at her. "Happy? Yes, I got in the shower, and I thought about how soft your skin is and how good you always smell, and I thought about the way your nipples got hard when I touched them, and I jacked off. It gets old, Kaks. I want *you*. Not my hand."

Kaki sobbed out loud. He watched her slump against the wall at her back.

"When Brianna showed up here?" He moved closer to her.

"Please don't." She shook her head. "Please? I can't hear about her right now. You don't get it, Jordy. You don't get anything."

"She offered herself to me," he ignored her pleas. Stopped when he stood toe-to-toe with her. Cupped her chin in his hand and held her still to make her look at him. "Opened her dress to all skin. Heels that could kill a guy. Red lipstick."

She nodded, jerked free of his hand, and planted hers on his chest.

"You need to let me go."

"What?"

"You told me to tap out when I needed to."

"Kaks—"

"I need out, Jordy. I need this to be over."

CHAPTER THIRTY-TWO

"NOW?" Jordy stepped sideways to cut off her escape. "You want out of this now?"

"Please?"

He moved. Backed out of her way and watched her stalk across the room to the closet.

"Kaki."

She turned to look at him. The distance between them gave her a little strength.

"What?"

"Don't do this."

"She's interested." Kaki rubbed her hands over her face. Tucked her hair behind her ears. "You've got her attention. Please let that be enough."

"I told her no last night because she's not you."

His words hung in the sudden silence. Kaki's stomach ached, and her eyes burned, and her throat was so tight she could hardly breathe. Exactly the words she'd wanted to hear. But by now, they weren't enough. It wasn't enough if Jordy wanted to take her to bed. She was in love with him, with her best friend, and sleeping with him now would only complicate things in a hundred different ways.

"Kaks, I—"

"The thing is, Jordy." She pressed her lips together and shook her head. "It isn't even about sex. There's so much more—"

She stopped talking when he closed the distance between them.

"I love you."

She nodded. "Me too. That's why I have to leave."

"Kaki, I love you."

She watched his eyes as they roamed down over her face and her shoulders. She had to look like a sad clown; she'd been crying on and off since she'd left the house earlier. If Jordy hadn't wanted her in the string bikini in Florida, he sure wouldn't want her in old cut-off shorts, a t-shirt, and eyeliner tracked over her cheeks.

She gasped in surprise when he leaned toward her and slipped his finger under her chin to lift her lips to his. Kissed her with a sweet tenderness that made her sad. She resolved to be strong. To push him away, but his lips and his tongue were persistent, and he stroked her mouth like he had all the time in the world for her.

Like she was the only woman in the world.

"Jordy, I don't think—"

"We're not thinking," he agreed with her. "Way too much damned thinking going on."

He eased away from her, but instead of leaving her alone, instead of patting her on the butt and then heading downstairs to watch a movie, he reached for the hem of her shirt. Her heartbeat hammered in her throat, and she struggled to swallow. To breathe. Their eyes met, and he hesitated. Not asking permission, but giving her time to accept that he was in control. When he tugged gently, she lifted her arms and let him pull it off her. He dropped the shirt; his eyes raked over her, heavy and hungry on her eyes and then down over her lips and her bare shoulders. The curves of her breasts over the silk bra she wore.

Before she could say no, before there was any wiggle room for either of them to pretend this wasn't happening, he reached around her and unhooked the bra. Slid the straps off her shoulders and tossed it aside, too.

Self-conscious now to be standing in front of him half naked, after crying on him because he wasn't attracted to her, she held her breath as he dipped his head again. His lips made a quick pass over hers, and she breathed over his chin, desperate to taste him. This time, he was slower. Soft, sweet kisses. Barely there on her lips and then gone. The corner of her mouth and then her chin and then he licked her upper lip, and suddenly, he stroked his hand up the center of her belly and her chest. Over the curve of her breast to her nipple. He stayed with the playful kisses, eventually licked a trail from her lips to her ear and still, his fingers explored her nipples.

"Jordy," she breathed, and before she could say more, he slid his tongue inside her mouth. Over hers. In and out in a slow, delicious rhythm, as if they were making love. He smoothed his hands over her bare stomach and up her sides to her back, and then his fingers were working the button of her shorts. Somewhere in the midst of the soft touches and sweet kisses, she'd lifted her hands to rest on his arms. Rubbed her fingers ever so slightly over his skin, felt the ripple of muscles and now, as he eased her shorts over her hips, she lifted her arms to circle his neck.

When he stepped away from her, she moaned in protest. But he grabbed the collar of his shirt and yanked it off over his head. Let it fall. Reached for her hand and pulled her to the bed they'd been sleeping in. She swept her eyes over his chest. Remembered the warmth of his skin when they'd played in the gulf.

"You don't have to do this." Her voice was tight and

small, because she desperately wanted him to do exactly what he was doing.

He took her hand and pulled it gently to his mouth.

"Lay down," he told her. "I wanna look at you."

"Jordy."

He raised his eyebrows as if pleading with her. She fell back across the bed, her knees weak and trembling. She watched him unbutton his shorts. Their eyes met as he unzipped them.

"Do you want this?" he asked quietly.

"You don't have to touch me."

He shook his head and swept his gaze over her bare breasts.

"I want this." He knelt between her legs and trailed his hand down over the small triangular patch of silk that covered her. "I want to taste this. And I want to get inside you, Kaki."

On her elbows, she dropped her head back and sighed.

"Don't do that."

"Do what?" she whispered as she lifted her head to look at him.

"Don't hide from me. I wanna see your face. I wanna see your eyes."

She licked her lips. Watched him again as he looked at her. Her heart beat so fast it hurt as he traced his finger up her inner thigh.

"Jordy."

He rubbed his thumb over her core, the silk a soft barrier between them.

"I'm not gonna hurry." He shook his head. Rubbed over her again and lifted his eyes to hers. "I'm gonna make this last."

She caught her breath when he scooted backwards off the bed to kick his shorts off. Her mouth went dry as she took in his broad shoulders. His chest. The small dark disks, flat and soft now. She wanted to put her lips there. Suck that dark skin into her mouth.

She'd seen this part of his body often through the years. But she let her eyes roam lower, to the swirl of dark hair that disappeared at the black elastic of his gray boxer briefs. Breathless, she let her eyes linger on his hips. The delicious place where he let his jeans hang low sometimes when they were home alone. She tried to swallow when she finally let her eyes slide over to admire the bulge hidden by his briefs, but she was parched.

She liked the way the briefs hugged him. Outlined the package she so desperately wanted. But she wanted them gone. She wanted to look at him. Touch him. She needed to cup his erection in her hand and curl her fingers around him. To feel him throb against the palm of her hand.

She wanted him inside her.

When she lifted her eyes to his, he was watching her.

She was scared to move. Afraid the moment would shatter and he would put his clothes on and walk out. Afraid of all the other women he'd been with, mostly Brianna, but Lauren, too. Afraid she wouldn't measure up to his expectations.

Thinking about him with Lauren had never bothered her. Not until now.

"Jordy, touch me," she whispered.

He moved then. Put one knee on the bed and stretched over her. Hungry for his mouth on hers, she lifted up on her elbows again and kissed him. More of those simple kisses. Sweet and soft. Until suddenly, her arms quivering, the kisses were longer. And wet. Jordy rubbed his tongue over hers again in that same rhythm as before.

Finally ready to cave, she lifted her left hand to cup the back of his neck, pulled him with her when she fell back to lay on the bed. She moaned softly when he sank into her, his body warm and hard over hers. He shifted between her legs, until his erection was pressed hard against her center, and she lifted her hips to rub over him.

"Don't do that." He shook his head. "Kaks, you say the word, I'm gonna embarrass myself before I ever get inside you."

"What word?"

When he lifted his head to look at her, she grinned.

"I wanna take you every way I can," he told her. "But I'm trying really hard to control myself right now."

"I really need you to touch me." She squeezed the back of his neck.

"Where at?" He pressed his lips to hers. "What do you like?"

She wiggled under him again, and he cut loose with a loud, drawn out groan. He slid off to her side, and she felt his cock pressed painfully hard against her hip. She breathed deeply as he danced his fingers over her thighs and dipped them inside her panties.

"Jordy." She closed her eyes, but she whimpered when he moved again. Traced his fingers heavily from her knees to her belly. She squirmed and shivered as goose bumps broke out over her skin. "Oh my god." She caught her breath and moaned with pleasure when she felt his lips close over her nipple.

"I've been thinking about this since I saw you in that wedding dress."

"Mmm." She combed her fingers through his hair and pressed his head to hold him at her breast.

"When we were dancing, I could tell you—"

"Jordy."

"Hmm?" He nudged her nipple with the tip of his tongue. Traced circles over it and then licked around the center of her breast.

"Touch me."

"You want me to make you come."

"God, yes!" she hissed. "Please. Put your fingers on me and make me come."

He toyed with her still. Fingers teasing, hand rubbing over her belly and her thighs. She sighed his name again when he sucked her nipple into his mouth and tugged at her and then scraped his teeth over her.

Tired of waiting for him, she moved her right hand to the aching spot between her legs. He turned his attention to her other breast and feasted again, while their hands played together at the silk between her thighs.

He let her slide her fingers under the silk, even let her touch herself, before he shifted to look. To watch her. She panted, out of breath and shaking with need.

"Are you wet?" His gravelly voice stoked her fire.

Eyes locked on his, still breathless, she nodded.

"Show me."

She lifted her head to look down their bodies. Shivered at the sight of her own hand in her panties, Jordy's covering hers outside the silk, his body pressed intimately to her side.

"Show me, Kaki." He pressed his face to hers and nibbled on her ear. "I wanna feel how wet you are."

She dropped her hand from where it now rested on his shoulder. Reached to cover his at the apex of her thighs and lifted it. Urged him to put his hand inside her panties. He covered hers instantly, their fingers slipping over her core. His eyes held hers as she stroked herself. He moved his fingers slightly and pushed them inside her.

"Hot and wet." He dropped his head to kiss her. Moved his fingers inside her and used his thumb to move her fingers. "Let me."

Kaki kissed him. Rubbed her hand up over his back and then smoothed it around his side to rub her fingertips over his nipple.

"Like this?" he whispered against her lips. She moved

with him, moved her hips to meet him, to add to the friction, the fire.

"Just like that." She nodded. She let her eyes close and then opened them again when she felt his mouth on her shoulder.

"I love the way you breathe when I'm touching you."

"Don't stop, Jordy." She arched her back when he closed his lips over her nipple again. Rode the first wave of heat that sighed through her thighs and her center. "Just...gimme..."

"Faster?" he offered.

"No." She covered his hand again with hers. "Just...like that. Just..."

"Come for me, Kaki. I wanna make you moan my name."

"Right there." She bit her lip, lifted her right hip from the bed and then caught her breath again.

"Here?"

"Yes." She felt him looking at her. Met his eyes, panted softly and pumped her hips faster as that heat climbed inside her again. "Faster, please. Now."

"You're beautiful," he whispered as she stretched and moaned and felt the orgasm rip through her. She breathed fast and hard and lifted her head to kiss him. To feel his tongue on hers as he continued to stroke her center, and her body quivered beneath him.

"Jordy?"

"What?"

"Did you make her come?'

"Who?"

"Lauren."

"You really wanna ask me that now?" He frowned down at her. She flopped back on the bed and tried to catch her breath.

"I love you guys, but I want this. Just for me. I need this for me. I need you to be mine."

"No." He shook his head. "No. It never got—I thought she told you what happened."

"She said you made out."

"Yeah, it was junior high stuff. A few dangerous kisses, and she let me put my hand on her breasts. By then we both figured out it wasn't—"

"Okay." She rubbed her thumb over his lips. "I'm sorry. It's just that I want this. I need this to mean something, Jordy."

"Kaki, I told you that I—"

She lifted her head again. Kissed him.

"You don't have to tell me lies," she whispered. "It's enough to know this is just something between me and you."

"Can I be inside you, Kaks? Please?"

She nodded. Watched him when he moved backwards off the bed again and shoved the briefs down over his hips.

"Jordy Steed," she breathed as his erection sprung free. She swept her eyes over him again. His shoulders and the arms she'd decided long ago were just right. His slender hips and his obvious desire to finish what they'd started.

"Are you on the pill?" His voice was gruff.

"Yes." She reached for him.

"I had all the blood work done."

"What?" She sat up. Curled her fingers around his cock and looked up at him. "I want you inside me."

"I'm clean."

"Jordy."

She smoothed her thumb over the tip of his penis. Felt a jolt of want zap her low in the belly. When she lay back this time, he moved with her. Drove into her slowly and she lifted her hips to press against him.

"This okay?"

He was hard and hot inside her, but it was the look of ecstasy on his face that took her breath away.

"Yes."

Kaki sighed with pleasure when he began to move, his hips pumping over hers in a slow, rhythmic motion. Eyes locked again, they moved together, Jordy's body hard and controlled.

She touched him. Claimed his skin, his body as hers. Hands roamed over him, her fingers kneading his muscles. And still he rocked against her, in slow, deep movements.

"Do you always do it like this?" She stroked her fingers up over her stomach and cupped her breasts. She'd expected him to move fast, to ravish her body, and explode, completely out of control. Instead, he was savoring her; from the look on his face, he appeared to be riding the pleasure as far as he could while desperately pacing himself, forcing himself to move slowly.

"No." Sweat curled the ends of his hair, and his breaths were ragged and heavy as he labored over her. "I'm trying to make this good for you."

"Jordy."

"I want this to mean something, too, Kaki." He flicked his eyes down over her shoulders, watched her play with her nipples and then met her eyes again. "I don't wanna be one of those guys who…doesn't…."

"You." She pushed herself up on her elbow again and kissed his chest. "Inside me. This is perfect, Jordy."

"Can you come again?"

"Yes."

"Then I'll try to wait."

She slipped her fingers between their bodies again and touched herself.

"Hurry," he told her.

He pinned her in place with his eyes again as he moved inside her, and she rubbed her core slowly and then faster and finally she let her head fall back and she moaned with her release.

"Oh my God." She heard him, but she let her eyes close as

the pleasure washed over her again. She felt him shudder and tense as he came inside her.

He collapsed beside her on the bed, both of them panting to breathe. The house was quiet now, but in her head, Kaki could still hear them whispering and moaning and chanting each other's names. He'd been so determined to make slow, passionate love to her, she hadn't heard the bed creak once, and she knew for a fact, the damned bed could make a hell of a lot of noise at times.

Jordy moved when the central air kicked on to blow frigid air over their sweat-slicked skin, and Kaki shivered. He pulled the sheet over them, and they scooted to lie together on the pillows.

"We should have done that on our wedding night," he whispered. Kissed her hair. "I'm so sorry I didn't. I just thought…you might have hated me if I'd tried something."

"I have to tell you, you broke my heart when you bought that new bed."

He lifted his head to look at her. "I thought you'd just been telling Lauren you didn't want to sleep with me. I've been so afraid you would decide you couldn't stay, I thought maybe if we lived like roommates, you would be okay with it."

"Does that mean I can stay?" She framed his face with her hands. "In this bed? With you?"

"Do you wanna stay?"

"If we live like husband and wife."

CHAPTER THIRTY-THREE

THEY'D GONE to sleep in each other's arms. He'd fought it; hell yes, he'd fought it. He didn't want to waste a second sleeping when he finally had Kaki's delicious, warm body naked and pressed to his. They'd made love again. Twice, before he'd gotten so cozy and warm and satiated next to her, that his eyes had finally closed, even while his hand continued to strum her skin, to acquaint itself with her curves and her freckles and the tender spots that made her purr like a kitten. He awoke after three and stretched away from her for just a moment to turn the lamp on the nightstand off. Her soft whimper, his whispered name on her lips, the way she reached for him in her sleep zapped him straight in the heart. He'd turned back to her, waited while she'd snuggled up to him again, her back to his chest, and dropped his arm possessively over her waist.

When he next opened his eyes, she was still pressed against him, head to toe. Only she was awake, drawing circles on his chest with her fingertips. When she lifted her eyes to meet his and he shot her a lazy smile, she trailed her hand lower, down over his gut. He arched his back as she scraped her fingernails lightly over his thighs and finally over the length of his cock. Already aroused just from waking with her naked in his arms, he stirred to life under her fingers.

"Kaks?" He lifted his left hand from her back and played with her hair. "You're playing with fire."

Rather than slow her down, his words seemed to embolden her. She closed her fingers around him and slid her hand up and down. Lifted her eyes to look at him again.

"Should I put that fire out?" Her already thick, buttery voice was husky with sleep. She kept her eyes on his, bold and intense, and then dipped her head forward to press her open mouth to his chest.

"I don't think you're ever gonna put this fire out," he groaned as he reached for her. She moved with him, lifted her head and shimmied further up his body. He tangled his fingers in her hair as their teeth clashed in a hungry, demanding kiss. He wanted his mouth on her. He wanted to suck her skin, her neck and her breasts into his mouth. He wanted to nibble at her lips and then caress them with his tongue. He wanted to lick her, to slide his tongue over her, inside her and hear her gasp his name out loud. But she continued to stroke him with her elegant, capable fingers, and his brain timed out.

"Do you really wanna do that?" He managed to spit the words out, though he figured it had taken ninety-seven percent of his brain to tack the sentence together and spit it out intelligently.

"You don't want me to?"

"Fuck, yes, I want you to." He squeezed his eyes closed and gritted his teeth. "But what about you?"

He opened his eyes, looked at her in askance. He was far enough gone that if he flipped her over now to drive into her, he'd explode in ten seconds. He wanted this. He wanted her to jerk him off. She was breathing hard, and her nipples were beaded and tight, and her eyes were glazed with need, but he wanted to make her scream before they had to get up and face Monday morning.

She increased the pressure just enough to take him to the edge. It crossed his mind that she'd done it before, driven a guy out of his mind with her hand, and probably her mouth. She flicked the tip of her tongue over her lip and arched her eyebrows.

"I think there's probably something you can do for me." Her seductive whisper, her tongue on her lips and her fingers coiled around him, the pad of her thumb on the head of his cock sent him reeling, gasping to breathe.

"Jesus, Kaks. Oh God." He lifted his hips from the bed as she stroked him one last time, and he lost control.

"I love this," she whispered as she clutched his shoulder and pressed her breasts into his chest.

"What?" he asked, out of breath, his brain in that post-orgasm blur, his cock still pulsing in her fingers.

He opened his eyes when he felt her lips whispering just under his chin. Over his lips and then back to that spot under his chin, and she licked a hot wet groove to the hollow at his neck and finally lifted her head to look at him.

"Your hair."

"My—?" He frowned. Still coming down from the brain fog, he lifted his head from the pillow to look down at himself, where her hand was still on him, though his damned dick had started to shrivel up. He couldn't see it anyway. Just her beautiful face and the curves of her breasts now flattened against his chest. "What?"

She smiled. Shifted again to straddle him, though she rode him high, her center pressed over his stomach. She dropped a quick kiss on his lips and then smoothed his hair back from his forehead. He still had no idea what she meant, but when she leaned over to kiss him, his forehead and his hair, her breasts rubbed his lips, his cheeks.

"Your hair curls when you sweat."

"And that's sexy?" he asked in disbelief. Didn't most women find sweat offensive and gross? He wouldn't complain, though. Not about the way she'd draped her body over his. Instead he stroked his hands up over the backs of her thighs and then smoothed them over her bottom.

He heard the hitch in her breathing.

"It's curly now. Little ringlets. Last night, too."

"And that's sexy?" he asked again.

"That I make you sweat?" She started to sit up straight, but he shook his head, still buried in his pillow, and rushed to press her upper body back down.

"Don't move. This is a fantasy." He fingered the ends of her hair.

She leaned in again and moved her lips over his. Teased his apart with the tip of her tongue.

"I think it's fuckin'…" she whispered. "Hot as hell that I make you sweat, Jordy Steed."

Why that turned him on, he didn't know. He'd known Kaki since they were in grade school. He'd heard her drop the F bomb hundreds of times. But having his hands on her bare ass, his fingertips grazing her center, her breasts swaying in his face, her tongue licking his lip and hearing that butterscotch voice tell him it was fuckin' hot as hell that she made him sweat shot every drop of blood in his body straight to his cock again.

Hotter than hell in the room, in the bed, Jordy kissed her. Sucked her lower lip into his mouth and moved his hands over her legs. Kaki arched her back to allow him room to touch her, but she gasped in surprise when he reached around her bottom to stroke his fingers over her. She threw her head back as he moved again, slid his hand between their bodies, between her thighs.

He lifted his head, fingers still sliding over her and then inside her, his brain marveling at how wet she was for him, and gently caught her nipple in his teeth.

"Damn, Jordy," she moaned as if she was uncertain whether it was pleasure or pain she was supposed to feel. He saw her arms trembling when he sucked on her nipple, pressed it flat between the tip of his tongue and the roof of his mouth and then rolled it again and again with his tongue.

"I'm...gonna....almost..." He felt her tense up and then she gasped out loud and whispered something again with the F bomb, and Jordy shifted her backwards enough to push into her again. She looked at him then, a hazy mix of pleasure and surprise in her eyes, as she shivered and sobbed and tensed over him again.

"What did you say?" he asked her.

"What?" She sank over him now, breathless and boneless. He stroked his hand up over her back and her head. Played with her hair again.

"When I made you come? What did you say?" he whispered as he kissed the top of her head, strands of her silky hair.

"I said I've never been so fucking hot," she answered on a long, uneven breath. "You make me burn, Jordy. You make me want to burn up."

He opened his mouth. To say *I love you*. To say, *I love you so much it hurts*. And then he closed it, because in the daylight, those words scared the absolute hell out of him. What if he and his best friend wife had just fucked each other senseless and hoped to come back and do it again tonight, and the next night and the next, and still, some day she left? He could be mature about letting her go. Staying friends. He had to have her in his life. One way or another.

A low, sarcastic laugh bubbled inside him. Who the fuck was he kidding? He couldn't fall all in with a woman like Kaki and then step aside when she got bored and not have hard feelings. No way. He loved her. Wasn't sure when that had happened, but he was shell-shocked and desperate to keep her around and scared to death that Kaki might have just needed a night of wild, crazy sex.

Hadn't Lauren pretty much said so?

Hadn't Lauren told him Kaki would be fine if he took her to bed?

"What?" She lifted her head to look at him.

Not ready to dump his feelings, he shook his head.

"Nothing."

"No, don't do that." She pushed his hair off his face again and kissed him. A heavy kiss on his lips, on his cheek, between his eyebrows. "You were gonna say something."

He didn't know what to say. If he told her he was in love with her, right here, right now, she would think he was lying. She might even suggest he'd said it to all of the women he'd been with, and how would he convince her he'd never said those words out loud to anyone in his life?

How would he convince her he was sincere?

"I wish we were still in Florida," he said softly. Moved to flip her on her back and kiss her.

She grinned.

"Eight hours. You can hold out for eight hours, can't you?"

He cupped her face in his hand and dragged his thumb down the column of her neck. She thought he meant sex. That he wanted to still be in Florida so they could stay in bed all day, for days on end.

It sounded like heaven. But what would be better would be not sharing her with anyone else for the next seven days. He kissed her again. A soft, tender kiss that spoke of love, not lust.

"I miss it being just the two of us."

Eyes locked on his, she nodded. "Me too."

———

Jordy felt like he was twelve feet tall and maybe even bulletproof. He worried that his dad and his brothers were going to notice a difference and demand to know what was up. Wasn't like he could spill the beans about spending the night in Kaki's arms. He wouldn't, anyway, but if he suddenly started spouting lines from love poems and discussing Kaki's soft, smooth skin and her firm breasts and her hot, tight sweet spot they might all decide he was crazy. He was supposed to be very damned familiar with all of her physical attributes already; they'd question why he was suddenly overwhelmed by how insanely lucky he was.

He'd had good sex before. Hell, he'd had pretty great sex pretty often. He'd had it all, including two or three at a time and back door sex, and he'd had girls sending him videos of themselves begging him to come back and do them again, long after he'd gone.

None of it compared to Kaki. He should've known it would be better than fan-fucking-tastic because kissing her lit him up inside. The first time he'd done it, kissed her in front of his family, his body had vibrated like a tuning fork the second their tongues touched. He'd walked around with his dick jacking around with his briefs for days. Had a couple of dreams about her, and while they'd been scorchers, he now knew they paled when compared to the real woman.

When she'd turned those doe eyes on him and asked if he found her that unattractive, he'd been struck dumb. Absolutely speechless. Here he'd been walking around with a wedding ring on and a beautiful wife for over a month, and he'd thought they'd agreed that for the sake of their friendship they wouldn't add sex to the fake marriage. He'd fantasized about her more than once, whether it was hard and fast with her straddling his lap in his Jeep or the steamy, sensual burn they'd shared last night. He'd had every inappropriate thought about his best friend a guy could have, and he'd swallowed gallons of guilt for thinking about her that way, and then he'd found himself in the hot seat for not wanting her, for not finding her attractive.

She'd stunned him with that bit about Lauren. About knowing he and Lauren had made out before Lauren got married. Thank God it hadn't meant anything to either of them. Hadn't hurt the friendship, hadn't kindled a need for more. It had been a ten-minute thing, and Jordy had known when it happened that Lauren was panicking. Testing herself. But still. He hadn't wanted Kaks to know about it. Just made him out to be an ass. She didn't need any more reason to believe that of him.

He'd been so relieved to finally find out who the hell Owen was. Hated that she'd talked to him on their honeymoon, but then again, he had left her alone several nights, and she'd known what he was thinking about when he'd left the condo.

Kaki had always been more reserved than Lauren, yes, but he'd always thought she was pretty, and her reserve had intrigued him as much or more, even, than Lauren's brazen, carefree personality. That she'd let him see her last night, not her body, but her vulnerability, her desire for him and her disappointment at what she'd seen as his disinterest had squeezed his heart painfully hard, and those first kisses he'd meant to soothe, to comfort, to love. They'd ignited his own passion, though, and once he'd started undressing her, it might have taken a freight train to stop him from proving to her just how sexy, how beautiful she was.

He'd have stopped. If she'd have said no, it would have hurt to high heaven, but he'd have stopped. Instead, she'd asked him to touch her, and he'd found her wet and ready, and now, he hoped like hell she wouldn't find something about it today to regret. That when they got home from work tonight, they would spend their usual time together, having dinner and drinking a beer and sharing their days and then they would turn on something soft and sexy and christen the couch.

Or the kitchen counter.

Or the floor.

He wasn't particular.

But last night and this morning had only whet his appetite, and he hoped it had only been the beginning of a lifetime together.

CHAPTER THIRTY-FOUR

SHE SUPPOSED that even though they'd been married for a little over a month now, in the big scheme of things, they were still technically newlyweds. It was okay for her to walk around in a fog, wasn't it? Still dreamy in love with her new husband? Okay, not even Jordy knew that part, and Kaki thought maybe she'd never tell him how much she loved him. Be easier when this had to end when he had Brianna's full attention and he was ready to move on. The wedding, the marriage, involving family and friends, and the new house was all complicated enough. Even at that level, their plan had the potential to blow their friendship apart. What if they had a recurring fight about laundry or toothpaste tubes or how to put a bread tie on a bread package that ended up making them hateful and resentful to each other? Now they'd gone and thrown in sex and upped the level of explosiveness. Kaki would admit, if pressed, that once they split up and moved on, it would make her whole body Christmas tree green to know Jordy was using his goods and services to pleasure someone else, whether it was Brianna or the next girl.

If she were to tell him now that she was in love with him, that maybe he was the one—*her one and only*—and that when they split up and he was with Brianna or the next girl, it would tear her heart out, the whole thing might go up in smoke.

The way he'd made her go up in smoke last night. She'd been timid at first. Afraid that he was only humoring her. Sure, any guy would jump at the chance to take a willing woman to bed. She had never doubted that Jordy could get it up for her. Just that he might much prefer to do someone else.

Except there was something raw and intimate between them. Something so much more than sex. Than the friction. The heat.

He hadn't fucked her. He'd made love to her. Slow, steamy, sliding, sticky, desperate-to-please her, love.

She'd dismissed that thought fifteen times today, and she'd pushed it out of her mind another fifteen times. For one thing, thinking about him, about the sweat-dampened ringlets of hair on his neck and the look of concentration and pleasure in his eyes, and the way he'd moved over her, inside her had her wet and ready before lunch time rolled around. Besides, she couldn't, wouldn't assume that every time would be that way. Maybe he'd just been that into pleasing her because she'd been such a basket case out on the porch. Maybe it had been a pity fuck that he'd kind of enjoyed, too.

It wasn't. She knew it.

Still. Best not to rock the boat. The bed, sure. The boat, no. Best to enjoy her husband as her lover as long as she could. So what if the thought of going back to someone like Owen, who wouldn't notice if she'd worn a burlap bag or the string bikini on the beach, who thought fast was best (sure, he'd sealed the deal for her, too, but all as if on a tight schedule that only set aside seven minutes for foreplay and sex) made her want to swear off men, buy a new vibrator dildo combo and name it Jordo, and get a dog or five and be a single dog lady forever.

Great.

She was so in love with him, it hurt to be at work. To be

without him. To miss him. To need him. She'd never tell him, because not loving her back would kill him. He'd never want to hurt her; he'd never want to hurt her or Lauren, and he'd told her flat out from day one of the engagement scheme that had led to their wedding day fraud and the late but better than never honeymoon shenanigans that he did not expect any sort of physical relationship with her at all.

Twice while working on a new display that would focus on architecture in late 1800s Prior, Kaki had zoned out on Leisha. She didn't do it often. She loved history, and while she'd always enjoyed sex, she'd never had a night quite like last night and she'd never been in love. But she'd let herself get caught up first in the memories and then in thoughts of what tonight would hold. If they'd follow the regular routine. Swapping stories over dinner, hanging out and having a beer and then maybe they would move to the living room and rather than watch a movie, they'd act out a naughty scene from any number of movies or the trashy romance novels Kaki used to read.

Leisha had had to snap her fingers in her face and nudge her shoulder to get her attention. Kaki had blushed terribly; judging from the heat she'd felt pounding in her cheeks, she figured she'd looked like a tomato. Leisha had whistled softly and then when Kaki blushed yet again, she'd laughed.

Kaki had almost dumped the details. Not the kind about how he'd undressed her save the silk underwear and rubbed his thumb over her through the silk, but the ones about how they hadn't been lovers before last night. She'd caught herself, though. Bit her lip and arched her eyebrows and dove back into the open glass display case where they were mounting old black and white pictures of the police station in old downtown Prior.

She decided she would run by Lauren and Tyler's house on the way home. Lauren knew the whole story, and really, there was no one she'd rather tell than Lauren, anyway. But when she started her car and pulled her phone from her purse, she found a text Lauren had sent earlier in the afternoon.

So did he do you?

Kaki had laughed out loud, and she'd started moving her thumbs over her keyboard when it hit her that the question was sort of out of the blue. Why would Lauren randomly ask her that? After the things they'd discussed, wouldn't it be more along the lines of *is anything happening yet*? *Did you seduce him*? She'd huffed out an uneasy breath and sat for a moment in the lot, fingers drumming the steering wheel.

She didn't know how to answer Lauren, and that bothered her. She'd never not known what to say to Lauren in all the years they'd been friends.

Finally she'd texted back and asked Lauren why she would ask.

She'd tossed her phone down like a hot potato, put her car in drive, and headed home. The undercurrents of what they'd done just this morning beat in her blood along with sexy speculation about what tonight might bring. And yet, she felt unsettled. What had Lauren meant by that? She heard her phone buzz and told herself she would wait until she got home before she touched it.

And then at the stoplight at Twelfth and President, she picked it up to peek.

Meet you at your house.

She shrugged her eyebrows, but this time she set the phone down gingerly. Fingers sliding off it slowly. Still uneasy. Sure, she and Lauren could and would talk, and she'd wanted to talk to her anyway. But the memories of last night and this morning felt just a tiny bit distorted now.

Relief pounded through her when she pulled into the driveway and found it empty. Jordy never parked his Jeep in the garage; he saved it for her. She hit the remote on her sun visor, waited in the drive for the door to go up, and then eased into the tight little space. Climbed out, reached back for her phone and purse, and then hurried to the house. The sky was hazy; the sun hadn't even bothered to put in an appearance today. But it was still hot and soupy outside, and Kaki's blue oxford blouse stuck to her back.

She tossed her keys and purse on the counter and rushed on through the hall to the steps. She was ready to peel her work attire off and slip into some shorts.

Or the sheets, she decided when she stepped into the bedroom and laid eyes on the bed where she and Jordy had become biblically acquainted. For once, the bed looked a little bit destroyed. No doubt they could and would do a better job dismantling it, being that last night had been that slow, tender pace rather than wild and desperate groping and clawing. Still. She liked the look of it.

"Oooh."

She turned when she heard Lauren behind her.

"Nice." Lauren nodded. Kaki watched her silently as Lauren slipped by her into the room and walked around the bed studying it from different angles. "Not bad."

When she looked back for confirmation, Kaki only blinked.

"Well?" Lauren shrugged dramatically. "Did he fuck you?"

"You should put earplugs on your belly." Kaki approached her and smoothed her hand over Lauren's tiny baby bump. "Your baby's gonna come out asking what he has to do to get a fucking bottle of milk."

Lauren snorted.

"Why do you ask like that?"

"What?" Lauren shook her head. She eyed the bed again and then tugged the comforter up and sat down. "Did he?"

"Yes." Kaki nodded and shrugged. "Yes. But…"

"Good." Lauren sighed with relief. Kaki unbuttoned her

blouse slowly, her brain crunching what Lauren had just said again.

"When I called last night, I was hoping he'd fixed it. But I could tell something was—"

"What?"

"I called. To talk to you, but Jordy—"

"Hoping he fixed it?" Kaki narrowed her eyes and shook her head. She shrugged out of her blouse and tossed it in the hamper.

"Points to you." Lauren gave her a nod and eyed her appreciatively.

"What?"

"Whisker burn." She waved her fingers over her own chest. "Both boobs. A coupla hickeys on your neck."

"Whatever." Kaki rolled her eyes and pulled a tank top on.

"Yeah, rub it in," Lauren mumbled. "I don't have *any* hickeys, but yes, I'd love to stare at yours—"

"Shut up." Kaki laughed. "You've been married a lot longer."

"And too damned tired to want sex."

"So?"

"When I came over here yesterday," Lauren explained, "you were gone. And he was...he asked if I knew where you were. Told him no, and he seemed...upset."

Kaki snorted. "Yeah, because Brianna was here the night before."

Lauren cringed. "Eh. Really?"

Kaki nodded. "He said nothing happened."

Well, he'd also said he'd told Brianna no. Because he'd wanted Kaki. Now she wondered.

"Well. Anyway, I told him to fuck you."

"You." Kaki felt her happiness, her overwhelming happiness that had bubbled over all day, drain just as if someone had pulled a plug from the back of her knee or something to empty her out and put her away. "You told him." She licked her lips. "You told him to fuck me?"

Lauren stared at her wide-eyed.

"I just…" She swallowed hard. "I thought I was helping. I told him you're not kids. That you're a woman, and you guys have been living in close quarters, and that he didn't need to treat you like a china doll."

Kaki nodded.

"Yeah," she agreed. A huge pit of nothingness yawned inside her. Erased her. She turned her back to Lauren and unzipped her slacks.

"Right? I mean…you wanted him?"

"I did," Kaki answered quickly.

"And it was good?"

"Yeah." She felt her eyes burn, but dammit all, she was not going to cry about this. Not now. She'd wanted sex; she got it. Love hadn't been part of any bargain, the original or the revised one.

"I mean, maybe it wasn't everything you…"

Kaki glanced at her.

"Well, I mean when Jordy and I made out, I felt like I was kissing my…best friend. Didn't do anything for me."

"That's because you were in love with Tyler."

Lauren studied her feet, crossed at the ankles. "I know. I'm just saying…maybe a lot of girls tell stories. If it wasn't great this time, maybe it will be next time. Or maybe…he just doesn't…turn you on…"

Kaki puffed her cheeks up and then released the mouthful of air slowly. She shimmied out of her slacks, lifted them with her foot and put them in the hamper, too. Pulled a pair of athletic shorts from the shelf and stepped into them.

"Except he did, Lauren." She avoided her friend's eyes. "He blew me away, and I thought…"

Lauren stood up. She moved slowly, finally stood close to Kaki.

"What?" she asked softly.

Kaki rubbed her hand over her aching throat. Shrugged.

"Dammit." She turned her head when her eyes filled.

"Kaki…"

"I'm stupid." She pressed her lips together. "I'm stupid, Lauren."

"You're in love with him." Lauren steepled her fingers and then pressed them to her mouth. "Are you? Are you in love with Jordy?"

Kaki laughed softly and rubbed her eyes. "Does it matter?"

"Of course it does!" Lauren reached for her, grabbed her by the upper arms. "Yes. It does. It matters."

"You just told me last night was all because you suggested he fuck me to see if it would make me happy—"

"I didn't say any such thing!" Lauren argued. "I didn't suggest it. I didn't say *hey, Jordy, if Kaki's not fun anymore, fuck her and give her a little charge and she'll be good to go.*"

Frustrated, Kaki sighed and tried to jerk her arms free from Lauren's grasp.

"I didn't. He was upset, Kaki. Worried."

"Yeah, that I'll get bored and leave and then this whole scam will be out in the open."

Lauren shook her head. "I don't think so. He was… bummed, Kaki. Because you weren't here. Not because you'd left. Because you weren't here. *With* him. Does that make sense?"

Kaki swallowed hard. "It doesn't matter. It's Jordy. He doesn't do love. Look at what his end goal is here. Someone who looks like she could work the corners any given Friday night."

Lauren let go of her, but she reached up to cup the back of Kaki's neck.

"Look at me. I didn't suggest it that way. I told him what

you wanted. I don't even know what happened last night, but he chose to be with you. He chose to share—"

"Yeah." Kaki turned away from her. "I know. It was great, Lauren. I can't even tell you how he made me feel." She licked her lips. "I guess I just forgot that that's what Jordy does."

"Dammit, Kaki." Lauren groaned long and loud, clearly frustrated with her. "Look, the three of us have been together for fifteen years. Remember that."

"What's that got to do with it?"

Lauren shrugged and laughed. "I don't know. I just hate this. I hate for you to be in love with him and not give him the memo. To not let him love you back."

"Not gonna love me back." Kaki tossed her hands up helplessly.

"He wasn't interested in me." Lauren's eyes roamed over Kaki's face.

"Lauren."

"No, let me finish." Lauren put a hand up to stop her. "I'm not upset. At all. I love you. I would love to see the two of you happy together—"

"Lauren—"

"Not finished." Lauren shook her head. "Trying to make a point. There was nothing. Between us. You get what I'm saying? I mean, we were all tongues and hands and…" She shrugged. "Nothing. It wasn't just me. He had nothing."

"If you took your pants off—"

"He wasn't interested. Period." Lauren smiled. "And maybe now I know why. And I'm glad. For a million reasons, I'm glad. Maybe he should have asked you to homecoming freshman year. Whatever. If he didn't want you last night, it wouldn't have happened."

"Okay. So we had mutually satisfying sex." Kaki dragged her fingers back through her hair and paced away from

Lauren. "It didn't solve anything for me, Lauren. I'm in love with Jordy Steed. Where the hell is that ever gonna get me?"

Lauren put her arm around Kaki and leaned in to kiss her head.

"You're my best friend, Kaki. But so's Jordy. It's not fair of you to hide your feelings from him."

CHAPTER THIRTY-FIVE

JORDY SAT in the Jeep for a few minutes. He shouldn't. If she were watching him, and he knew it was stupid to think she was standing in the front windows watching for him to come home, either to lay into him about what they'd done last night or to rip his clothes off him and start night two, she'd wonder why he was reluctant to come inside.

Door number one, obviously. What if she had regrets? What if he walked into the house and before she had a chance to school her features and pretend that everything was cool and happy, he saw regret or hurt in her eyes? It would kill him. If he thought for a second that she considered what they'd shared a mistake, it would kill him.

On the other hand, if she wanted to greet him at the door with that hot, silken mouth latched onto his and greedy hands sliding over his shoulders and his ass, he'd charge the door and break it down.

He was afraid. Terribly afraid she regretted what they'd done. Sure, they were adults. Lauren had reminded him that Kaki was a woman who hadn't been touched, hadn't been pleasured since well before the wedding, and sex was beautiful and natural, and they'd both enjoyed the holy fuck out of it last night. But that didn't mean it was still okay with her today. Didn't mean she wouldn't take one look at him and remember that he was the kid she'd had to help with some of his spelling when he was eleven, or that he was the same kid who'd played little league for years, and that she'd blown a fastball by him when they were fourteen. Struck him out. Sure, it was a PE game that didn't count for squat, but still. Kaki had been a kick-ass athlete, and she'd taken Jordy down a notch that day.

Just because he'd been determined to slow everything down and make love last night, just because he'd wanted more than anything to make their first time perfect for her didn't mean she wouldn't look at him and remember he'd done half the female population in Prior, and those he hadn't been with were either much too young or much too old to consider.

He didn't want her to think he'd used her for sex.

And after what Lauren had said, it had crossed his mind a time or two (though he'd shoved the thought out of his head before he could let it fester) he hoped like hell she hadn't used him for sex.

He'd texted her a couple times today. Nothing gushy with a million hearts and kissy face emojis, although he'd wanted to. His finger had hovered over the stupid little yellow face with the smooch lips, but thank God, Jason had wandered into the break room in time to catch him. Instead he'd just sent her a note to say he was thinking about her. True, no matter how you looked at it. He'd been thinking about being in love with her and what that meant for their future, but if she wasn't ready to hear that, he'd been thinking about coming home to her and stripping her clothes off her. Right down to that tiny triangular scrap of silk between her legs that women apparently called underwear. Jordy thought it looked more like a dangling carrot, a silky little arrow that pointed at her clit and said *touch here to make me crazy*.

With a deep breath, he finally climbed from the Jeep and headed across the drive to the back door. He could sit out there all night remembering the scatter of freckles low on her belly. Sort of looked like a painter had spattered them there, as he trailed the brush over her to paint. That thought made him freeze, hand on the doorknob. How many men had she been with? It didn't matter; of course it didn't matter. They were adults; they'd never been in love, and Jordy had no control over anything to do with Kaki. But he hated to think of other men touching her. He hated to think of her offering herself to anyone else. Another man's hands worshipping her.

Tate Delaney stealing her virginity. If he'd ever taken the time to make Kaki feel good. Part of him hoped so. Part of him hated the thought a jerk like that getting inside her. He'd hated that thought before they'd become lovers. Now the mental image of Kaki's breasts, bared to Tate Delaney, the guy's greedy hands on them, drove him up the frigging brick wall at the back of the house.

He huffed out a deep sigh and opened the door. He could either linger outside all night and make himself crazy with jealousy and fear, or he could wade in and test the water and see if she was up for round two. He almost crossed his fingers when he stepped inside and reached back to close the door.

Music blared from the living room. Sounded like Kenny Chesney. Okay, he could deal with that. If she were feeling low, regretting getting naked with him, she'd probably have something slower on, right? Something gut-wrenching that could make his ears bleed. He took a deep breath, realized he smelled something baking. Eyebrows arched in appreciation, he moved to stand in front of the stove and leaned over to look in the oven.

Cookies.

Kaki had baked cookies.

"Hey."

"Are those for me?" he asked when he heard her behind him in the kitchen.

"You bet they are."

"Holy shit, Kaks." He groaned and grinned his approval as he turned to find her stripped down to more of that sexy stuff women called underwear. How did she move through a whole day with that stuff on under her clothes? The lace would drive him crazy. He felt her eyes on him as he looked his fill. Well, he'd never get enough, but he needed to look at the smoking hot packaging before he peeled anything away to reveal that soft, sweet skin he'd been thinking about all day.

The lace that covered her breasts was almost skin-colored, which only accentuated the delicious pink nipples that tightened under his stare. He trailed his gaze down over her flat belly, the belly button he'd licked last night and this morning, and over that little smattering of freckles, to the tiny scrap of lace between her legs. Only a small piece of elastic covered her hips, and when he lifted his head to look, she pirouetted like a ballerina, and he found himself treated to a peek at her smooth round bottom, the scrap of material disappearing.

"Fuck. Me." He gritted his teeth, tried to adjust himself, but Kaki stepped closer to him and batted his hand away. She reached her arms around him, rested her hands on his ass. "Did you have that on when you left for work this morning?"

"Sure did."

"How do you work with something like that on?"

She cocked her head and looked at him with big eyes. They almost looked innocent, but a woman who strutted into this room wearing only a bra and a thong wasn't innocent. The woman who had locked her legs around his waist and held on tight while he'd moved inside her last night wasn't innocent.

How had he never noticed how sexy she was before?

"You don't like it?" she asked quietly.

"I love it." His voice was gruff with desire. He slid his hands down her sides and over her hips. Splayed his fingers wide on her bare skin. "I'm just trying to reconcile the girl I raced bikes with down Shenandoah Drive being the sex kitten strutting around my kitchen in a thong."

"You could always take it off me," she suggested. Lifted one hand to press against his chest. "If you don't like it."

"I missed—"

She shook her head. Reached to lay her finger over his lips.

"I want you, Jordy." She raised her eyebrows. "Now."

"What about—" he sighed as she leaned into him, pressed her breasts against his chest. "The—"

"Right here," she whispered. "I want it hard and fast and right now."

"—the oven?"

She stood on her tiptoes and flicked the tip of her tongue over his lip.

"We have at least five minutes."

"Five minutes isn't—"

"Please?" she whispered.

He didn't know if it was the whisper or her lips moving over his or the hand she'd lowered to unzip his jeans, but he moved. Turned them to press her against the counter. Impatient now, he worked blindly at his zipper, lips locked on hers. Her tongue in his mouth, she pushed his hands aside and unzipped his jeans, hooked her fingers in the waistband of his shorts, pushed everything down over his hips. He cupped her bare bottom in his hands, felt her slide her hand between them to move the scrap of lace out of the way, and drove into her, pounding her into the counter.

"Does that hurt?" he asked her.

"Feels good." She breathed over his face as he held her pressed against him.

"The counter…." he panted. "On your back?"

"Fuck me, Jordy." She drew back to look him in the eyes. "It's fine. Just do it."

Alarm bells went off in his head, but she clenched her legs around his waist and squeezed hard around him. Wasn't gonna take him two minutes. He wanted to be careful, not to bruise her back on the counter, but he wanted to move. He *had* to move. To stroke. To pump his hips.

Unaware of anything but the heat, the tight silken glove around his cock, he buried his face in her neck when he came. It was possible he'd chanted or groaned to God or Kaki or both, and then he realized she was panting and that her upper body was tense, her head thrown back in ecstasy, and he felt her hand between their bodies, and he shuddered with another small streak of pleasure.

A loud beeping noise interrupted their gasping, raggedy breathing.

"What the fuck is that?" He kissed her. Cupped the back of her head in his hand as she lowered her feet to the floor and slid down his body. He kissed her again, rested his lips on the top of her head and held her there. "Did we just break a rule by doing it in the kitchen?"

She snorted. Pushed at his shoulder gently and slipped out from between him and the counter when he moved.

"It's the cookies."

"You're killing me." He yanked his pants up, got everything situated, and zipped. "Smoking hot quickie followed by cookies."

She shot him a quick look, a knowing smile, and then grabbed an oven mitt. Pulled the oven door open and took the cookie sheet out. She set it on the stovetop.

"Want some milk?"

He lowered his gaze to her breasts, still hidden by lace.

She laughed and shook her head. Rolled her eyes when he looked up.

"Is that more like the status quo?"

"Sex and cookies?" he asked with a frown.

"Fast and hard."

He watched her wash her hands at the sink and then reach for a glass from the cabinet.

"Kaks."

She spared him a glance as she yanked the refrigerator door open.

"What?"

"I want..." He stopped talking when she turned and landed her gaze squarely on him.

"What?" She shrugged. Turned away and reached for the milk carton. "Again already?"

Disgusted by the way her words made him feel, by the quickening of his breath and the tightening in his groin, he scrubbed his face with his hands and paced the length of the room. This was a problem he wasn't accustomed to, needing to tame his cock the hell down, because the woman in the room was special, and he'd rather talk than slam her against the wall and do her again.

"What're we..." He cleared his throat. "What—dinner? Do you wanna do dinner?"

"Your mom dropped by earlier," she answered. "And delivered your dinner."

"What?" Afraid to ask, he squeezed his eyes closed and tiptoed up to it in his mind. What had his mom been doing here? Delivering dinner?

"She brought a fried chicken dinner by," Kaki answered. She didn't sound upset, so Jordy opened his eyes and found that she'd moved back to the counter. He raked his eyes over her back, over her bare bottom, and stuffed his hands in his pockets. She splashed milk in a glass for him and then turned to offer it to him.

"Why?"

"Why what?"

"Why did Mom bring dinner by?"

Kaki shrugged. "I dunno. Either she was just being nice, or she's worried that your fake wife is a bad cook."

"Did she say something? About…us?"

"No." Kaki shook her head. She took a turner from the drawer full of kitchen utensils and slipped it under a cookie. Carried it over to him in offering.

"Want one?"

"Yep." He took the cookie and took a healthy bite.

"Maybe she was just being nice." She reached up and smoothed her thumb over the corner of his lip. "Chocolate." She moved to her tiptoes and licked the same spot.

"Kaks."

"Hmm?"

"What's going on?"

"What do you mean?"

Jordy shrugged. "I…" He swallowed the cookie, chased it with a drink of cold milk, and felt like it all got stuck half way down his throat. "This isn't you."

"What?"

"This." He waved the hand with the glass at her and shook his head. "What's—?"

"You don't like coming home from work and being greeted this way?"

"You know I do," he said quietly. "But this isn't you. This isn't how it was last night. This morning."

He pressed into her space, reached around her to set the glass on the counter at her back.

"So." She touched his stomach, her hand there and gone immediately. Jordy tugged at his work shirt and studied her. Watched with interest as she fought to avoid eye contact. "You don't like it hard and fast?" She arched her eyebrows as she met his gaze. "With me?"

"I want you every way there is." His voice was gruff. He lifted his hand and held her chin in his thumb and fingers. "I want it slow and deep, and I wanna come home to you like this every night. But something feels…"

"What?" she whispered.

"Talk to me?" His voice was tight with emotion.

"If Lauren hadn't told you to fuck me, would last night have happened?"

"What?"

"Just answer me." She shrugged.

"Did you talk to her?"

"Don't ask me what she said or what I said. Just tell me." She squinted her eyes at him, and he recognized that she was fighting tears.

"How can you doubt what happened between us?"

"I've heard the stories, Jordy." She shook her head. "I know you can get it up for just about anyone."

"You think I *got it up* for you last night?" He frowned, but he nodded. "Is that what you think? That Lauren suggested I fuck you, and I decided *sure, why not*?"

She stared at him boldly, but her silence was a knife in his chest.

"I've had a hard on for you since the first time I kissed you in front of my brothers. Do you remember that kiss? Because I do."

She pressed her lips together and sniffled.

"You were wearing the dark jeans that fit you like a second skin. And we'd been hanging on each other all night. Playing cards. I could smell your perfume. It makes me crazy it smells so good. And then I kissed you. Like I thought we should do that, and I was scared that you would deck me, because nothing like that had ever…happened with us. I thought I'd just put my lips on yours, and that would be enough, but you opened your lips, and you tasted like candy. Like chocolate. I felt that down to my fucking toes, Kaki, and my dick jumped into formal salute."

"It's just kind of..." she shrugged, backed up a step. "Humiliating—"

"How did I make you feel—"

"Thinking that last night meant something. Thinking that at least when this is over, when you get Brianna back, at least I won't be just another of your girls. At least we're friends, and we like each other, and then Lauren just puts it all out there—"

"I was upset when you left the house, and I told her you were upset. With me. And she told me...she reminded me..."

"What?" Kaki whispered. "What did Lauren remind you?"

"That we aren't kids. That you're a woman. You're not the girl I used to watch go out on dates with other guys. You're a wom—"

"Lauren had to remind you that I'm a woman," she interrupted him. "Pretty much says it all."

"No." He narrowed his eyes in frustration. "I didn't need reminding of that. White string bikini. That was like a big-ass billboard reminder."

"Don't say big ass and bikini in the same sentence," she mumbled.

"Lauren reminded me that you..."

She shook her head impatiently.

"That I didn't need to treat you like a little girl. That you like sex. That maybe you *wanted* sex."

"If she hadn't reminded you of that, would last night have happened?"

"I wish last night had happened a hell of a long time ago," he answered. "Kaki, please. I don't wanna talk about Lauren. I wasn't following Lauren's orders. I wasn't...when she said that yesterday, I figured...you hated me."

"I could never hate you."

"It never occurred to me that you would want...to be with me...like this."

"This," she repeated. She nodded at the counter behind her. "Jordy style."

"This." He threw his hands up frustrated with the conversation. "I didn't think you were interested in an intimate relationship with me."

CHAPTER THIRTY-SIX

"I JUST DON'T WANT to destroy us." She licked her lips. Lowered her gaze, a little bit humiliated all over again by the whole conversation. She loved Lauren to bits and pieces, but right now, she kind of wanted to strangle her. "Too many years of friendship to lose when...you get her back."

Maybe it wasn't a great hardship, sleeping with her. Having sex with her. She'd never had any complaints from boyfriends. But that didn't mean she expected Jordy to be so wowed by her that he'd change his wild ways or wandering eyes. And hands. Couldn't forget those roaming hands.

Jordy reached for her hand and linked his fingers with hers.

"I thought about you all day," he said quietly. "Couldn't wait to come home to you."

"To this?" She glanced at him with a smirk.

"Um. This...blew me away..." He grinned. "And I do hope this happens again. But..."

"But what?"

"No. I never imagined my wife greeting me in our kitchen and seducing me like this. Making me lose control."

"What did you want to come home to?"

"Well now that you did it, my brain's gonna be conjuring up all sorts of good thoughts." He slipped his arms around her. "Are you cold?"

"Kinda." She nodded and ducked her head to his shoulder.

"But I thought...it'd be like...I'd come home and we'd have dinner. And we'd talk about our days, like always. And then..."

"Then what?" She turned her head, rested her cheek on his chest. Closed her eyes when he pulled her hard against him.

"Then I hoped we'd christen the couch. The living room floor. The kitchen, eventually."

"All tonight?"

"I'm up for it." He shrugged, but when she looked up at him, he chuckled quietly.

"Are you mad at me?" She sank her teeth into her lower lip.

"Why would I be mad at you?" He frowned. Lifted his hand to brush her hair from her face. "I don't wanna do that, Kaks. Be mad or upset. I just want us to be happy."

"For talking to Lauren."

"Before or after? We were together?'

Face flushed with heat again, she put her head on his shoulder to hide from him and shrugged against him.

"I'm not mad. About any of it." He kissed the top of her head.

"Can I ask you something?"

"Do you wanna put some clothes on?"

"Yep."

"Ask me."

"Did you really ask her to homecoming? When we were freshmen?"

He didn't have to answer her. She felt the way his body tensed against her. That hadn't hit her until after Lauren left.

The fact that the young Jordy Steed had been interested in Lauren sort of hurt. Bothered her more than knowing they'd made out the night before Lauren and Tyler got married. That meant nothing. A fourteen-year-old Jordy asking a fourteen-year-old Lauren to a high school dance was significant.

"She told you that?"

Kaki nodded once. "I don't think she meant to. I mean, I don't think she realized she'd said it."

Kind of the way Kaki hadn't exactly heard it and processed it then, while Lauren was still with her. They'd rushed on, talked about other, bigger things. Like the fact that Kaki was in love with Jordy.

"I'm sorry." He backed away from her, slid his hands down her arms to take her hands. Pulled her toward the hallway.

"What're we doing?"

"Well, I was thinking we could put some clothes on you, because you have goose bumps...or if we're going upstairs..." He shrugged.

"You don't have to—"

"Have we not established that I want to? Kaki, we made love last night. Didn't we? We had something special."

Mouth too dry to swallow, she could only nod.

"She turned me down flat," he informed her.

"What?"

"Lauren. When I asked her to the dance. Said no. Told me that there was no way she would go with me, unless I took you both."

Kaki snorted. "A little bit of foreshadowing for your future dating life, maybe."

"And she told me I was never to mention to you that I'd asked her."

"She was right," Kaki whispered. "That would have killed me to know that."

"I didn't mean anything by it," he argued quietly. "She

was cute, Kaks, but I promise you I didn't mean anything by it."

"She knows about last night."

He nodded. Watched Kaki take a step up backwards.

"Okay."

"You're okay with that?"

"Did you give her details?"

"No."

"Because I have to admit to you that I wanted to announce on the PA system at work today how incredible my new wife is in bed, but I thought it might get me fired."

She laughed quietly.

"I might have told her it was pretty incredible," she admitted, "but no. I didn't say anything else."

Except that she was in love with him. Lauren hadn't stayed long after that, after she'd reminded Kaki that Jordy was her friend, too, and he deserved to know it if she was in love with him. Kaki hadn't been able to find her voice to argue that one. She'd simply shaken her head and shrugged at Lauren. Returned her hug half-heartedly and watched her walk out.

"Do you talk to her?" Kaki asked Jordy now.

"About…"

"I know we all talk about anything, but…" She shrugged. "You said you were upset yesterday when I was gone."

Jordy sighed. "Yeah. I guess maybe we need to be careful. We can't hurt Lauren in the process of trying not to hurt each other."

She pressed her lips together, but she couldn't hold the smile down.

"What?" he asked quickly.

"Look at you, being the touchy, feely guy, worrying about hurting a friend."

"Guys care about stuff like that."

"Don't get defensive, Jordy." Still holding his hands, she tugged him closer to her. "I think it's sweet."

"I think we should put some clothes on you." He lifted her hand, used her fingers to stroke her cheek. "And have that fried chicken. And…"

"Or," she moved his hand lower, to her breast, "you could put your hands on me to warm me up."

———

HE WARMED HER UP. THEY LEFT A TRAIL OF CLOTHING UP THE stairs to their bedroom, where he slid between the cool sheets with her and then lit them and her on fire. They lingered for a long time, alternately playful and teasing and then tender and sensuous. Jordy's greed for her skin in his hands or his mouth convinced her again that he'd wanted to be with her last night, not that he'd followed through on a directive from Lauren.

The music was still pounding on the first floor of the house, and Kaki wasn't sure the doors were locked. But it didn't matter. She wouldn't care if someone came into the house and robbed them blind, as long as they were lying together in the big, rumpled, and comfortable bed.

"Have you ever been in love?" he asked her as he trailed his fingertips between her breasts. On her back, she closed her eyes and succumbed to the relaxation his fingers brought now after just stoking the fire in her thighs and her belly yet again. She'd drawn one knee up, and her leg was still resting a little on Jordy. His skin was warm; she'd been thrilled to see the curls in his hair again when he got hot and sweaty moving with her.

"Kaks?" he coaxed her. She breathed deeply and slid her foot back down the bed when she exhaled. Pointed her toes. Stretched. Maybe she was being ridiculous, maybe she was being ditzy, but at the moment, she could swear she'd never been so satiated, so well pleasured from sex, and at the moment, the man with the hands and the body that turned her on was her husband.

"I don't think so," she said quietly.

Except for you.

She wouldn't say that, though. Ever. Didn't matter how much or how hard Lauren pushed, she would never stick her heart out there and tell Jordy she loved him. It would kill him to walk away and not love her back, and it would kill her if he lied and pretended to love her.

"Do you wanna be?"

Something in his voice chased a shiver down her body. She opened her eyes and blinked at him, surprised to find him looking at her face and not her body.

"What do you mean?"

"Someday." He shrugged. "Do you want this kind of life? Do you wanna be married?"

"I am married."

His lazy grin sent a little arrow through her heart. The kind everyone drew as little kids. The puffy heart and the arrow through it with the feathers on the end to direct its flight. Probably the kind Cupid shot, she supposed. Damn Cupid for hitting her again and again and not Jordy.

"You wanna stay married to me?" He still wore the grin, but he sounded funny now, and Kaki figured he was in panic mode. Stuck in a marriage with her rather than being with Brianna. Or chasing a number of other women.

"Well, I'm not in any hurry to get out," she said softly. She lifted her hand from the bed and covered his, still drawing softly over her body. "But let me know when you are."

"You didn't love Owen?"

"Why do you ask?"

"Because these are things you never talked about with me." He looked from her eyes to their hands, now stacked on her belly. "I didn't know there was an Owen, remember?"

321

She nodded. Turned a bit toward him and slid her left leg over his.

"I liked him. I was…content." She shrugged. "Might've stayed with him, but I don't think I loved him."

"You might've stayed with him…if…what?"

Kaki shrugged. "It didn't work out, but I'm fine with that."

"Me? Did I break you guys up?"

"No."

"No?" Jordy eyed her suspiciously. "Are you sure?"

"Not really."

"Kaks."

"He didn't like the idea of me marrying you, even if it was all fake."

"Why didn't you tell me?" Jordy asked quickly. His face twisted in regret, maybe anger.

"Jordy, it's okay." She lifted their hands to his mouth and pressed his lip with her thumb. "If I hadn't wanted to do this, I would have told you no."

"But I broke you and your boyfriend up." He sighed. "I'm a jerk. What're you getting out of it?"

"I got a gorgeous diamond ring to wear for a while. I got a beach vacation, which admittedly wasn't exactly what I was hoping for." She smiled and arched an eyebrow. "I'm living in a great house. I get to see my best friend every day, and now I'm getting laid."

"Was Owen better at that part?"

"No one's been better at that part." She pulled his hand to her mouth now and kissed his knuckles. "Guess all your practice is paying off for me."

He smiled. "I kind of wish I didn't have all that practice," he mumbled. "That it was new for both of us."

"It's not new for me."

"And I'm kinda glad I sorta know what I'm doing, too. Because I love what I do to your body."

"I do, too." She nodded.

"What about Tate?"

She stared at him silently for a moment. Finally closed her eyes and rolled over to her back again.

"Really?"

"What?"

"You're gonna ask me about him? When we're lying here naked?"

"You talked to me about the other guy."

"Yeah, but you don't know him."

"So Tate was good? At this? At making you feel—"

"No." She laughed softly. "No, Jordy. Tate did nothing for me."

"Good."

She blinked her eyes at him. "Good? Oh my God, did you say *good*? Are you still competing with him? Didn't he tear his Achilles or something?"

"He did. Playing soccer." Jordy nodded. "And I don't keep tabs on him, but his dad was in the store a while back and told Dad that. But yes, it makes me feel really good that even though my lovely bride had sex with him, it wasn't good sex."

"What about you?"

"What about me?" He stared at her with wide, frightened eyes.

"Well, I'm not gonna ask you to rank me or my performance," she said with a laugh, "but if I'm not doing something you want me to, tell me."

"I think..." He closed his eyes as if deep in thought. "I think if we died right now, like if a meteor struck the house or if a tornado blew us away, I'd die the happiest guy in Prior."

Kaki smiled. "Okay, maybe it's not your bod women want, but your charm."

"And also?"

"There's more?"

323

He moved his hand. Dragged his fingers down over her breasts again to play with her nipples.

"My first time?"

"Who?"

"She was older than me, and she probably didn't get a damned thing out of it, but she rocked my world."

"You're not gonna tell me who?"

"Nope."

"I feel like I should be thanking the woman."

"And I feel like I should be thanking Brianna Fleer."

"What for?"

"She kinda set us up, didn't she? For this fake marriage."

Kaki grinned.

"Maybe when I grow up, I'll be like her."

"What does that mean?"

"I don't know but the woman's got something if she can make you marry someone else just to make her jealous."

CHAPTER THIRTY-SEVEN

HE'D THOUGHT about telling her. Just saying it. When he'd asked her if she'd ever been in love. What the hell? Had he really been hoping she'd say yes, that she was crazy in love with him? Okay, yeah. He had asked with that tiny little kernel of hope inside. Told himself no matter what she said, he was going to tell her. Just put the words out there. Let them linger in the bedroom while they made love again.

But he'd chickened out.

Every night this week, he'd chickened out. Every night this week, they'd rushed home to be together. Hands and mouths hungry and heavy and demanding and soothing. He was a little bit afraid it was just going to slip out when he was inside her. That he would whisper it to her when he was kissing her. That he would mumble it in his sleep.

If he did, if he told her he was in love with her, she might decide it was time to run. Tap out. Pack the bags. Get the hell out of dodge.

She'd asked him again this morning about Brianna. If he'd heard from her. He had. Brianna had texted him a few times. Sexted him once. A naughty picture. He'd deleted it. Considered getting a new phone number, new account. Wondered if something that extreme would get Kaki's attention and how he'd explain it if it did.

Jackson had been ribbing him a lot at work this week. Seemed a little late, all the teasing about newlywed sex. But now that he was actually getting it, now that he was head over heels in love with his bride, it got to him more. Made him antsy, anxious to get the day wrapped up so he could get home to her. Made for a hell of a long day, when Jackson started pushing his buttons at 8:05.

By now, he'd been with Kaks every which way from Sunday. He'd had his hands and his mouth all over every inch of her body. He'd taken her in the shower; he'd even joined her in the tub the other night, and though it had been crowded, he'd do it again. They'd christened every room in the house, including the spare bedroom. They'd taken one look at the new bed when it was delivered and set up, and they'd rushed to haphazardly toss bedclothes on it, and then they'd given it a shot. Not bad. Jordy thought sex with her on a bed of nails would be thrilling and dangerous, and he was ready and willing, but as far as beds went, they both decided they much preferred the one they'd been sleeping in.

He wasn't ready to let her go. Ever. He didn't care about Brianna. Any other woman who stopped to look twice at him when he was at the hardware store or working or at a movie with Kaki. He couldn't get enough of his wife. He was afraid he never would, but it was an ideal problem to have.

Unfortunately, he still worried she would get bored with him. That she might decide it was time to end the charade. That she would decide a content life with Owen was better than a pretend life with him.

Lauren called him on the way home from work. He was happy to hear from her, but Lauren sounded timid. Like she was afraid to bother him. That was new. He'd simply told her he'd call her back; no Bluetooth in the Jeep and it was illegal to drive and talk on a cell at the same time.

But he didn't go straight home. He stopped at Ricci's on the way, picked up dinner and a bottle of wine. Kaki loved their rigatoni, and he liked the chicken Parmesan, and maybe he should have asked her to *go* there. To put on a dress and go to dinner with him, and he'd love that. But he also loved that they'd spent the past week, at home, half naked, draped over each other.

Like they were on a honeymoon right there in their own house.

He beat her home, though he didn't know how. Most nights, she was there before him. Decided to take advantage of it, though. He set the Italian food on the table and rushed upstairs. No need for a shower, hadn't exerted himself yet except for the morning shower with Kaki and the run up the steps just now. He tugged his work shirt off, traded it for a soft navy Society t-shirt. Checked his jeans in the mirror in the bathroom and decided he looked okay. Back in their bedroom, he hovered in front of their dresser. Considered what he had planned.

The thought of telling her he loved her scared him. Scared the blazes out of him. His hands were cold and clammy, and his heart raced like he'd just run a relay race all the way here from Brazil.

"Jordy?"

He jumped when he heard Lauren call his name.

"Jordy?"

He stared at the dresser a moment longer and lifted his gaze when he saw Lauren appear in the bedroom doorway from the corner of his eye.

"Hey."

"Hey." He took a deep breath, relieved he hadn't taken it out of the drawer yet. Didn't want to discuss those plans with her.

"What's up?"

"Um." He sighed. "I grabbed dinner."

"At Ricci's," she finished his sentence with a small, wistful smile. "I saw the bags."

"You okay?" he asked over the sound of his heart slamming against his rib cage. Sounded like a SWAT team hitting a door with a battering ram. It was a wonder Lauren didn't hear it. Jordy couldn't remember a time in his life when he was more afraid. He'd been worried a few times about getting in trouble with his folks when he was younger. He'd been afraid at that damned haunted house he'd gone to with his friends. Yeah, even if he was fourteen, that hairless witch thing that had chased him through the maze had scared him shitless. He'd been scared the first time he'd had sex. Scared of embarrassing himself. He'd felt that same fear the first time he'd made love to Kaks, only multiplied by about a gazillion. He'd wanted nothing more than to make her feel good, and he'd been scared to death he'd come the second he was inside her and leave her hanging, wanting more.

This was so much worse. *This* was life or death. This was staring down the barrel of a gun. He'd thought that earlier, when his dad and his brother were working a sale on a couple of local hunters. He'd been walking by with football equipment in his hands, and he'd glanced at them and seen that guy with the raised and pointed gun, looking through the scope, and he'd imagined his wife's finger on the trigger, his face in the scope. If she walked away, it would be like pulling that trigger and shooting a bullet through him. And tiptoeing around—okay, they weren't tiptoeing, they were partying it up with what they both agreed was incredible, mind-blowing sex—was leaving him so tense, so worried about when she *would* leave, that he might drive her away.

He had to tell her.

Just tell her.

Say he loved her.

No, say he was *in love with her*, because he'd told her that first time that he loved her and she'd assumed he meant it the way he'd always said it. That even though he'd taken her to bed that night and *made love* for the first time in his life, nothing had changed and he loved her like a friend, same as always.

Lauren hitched her chin and finally nodded. Jordy watched her look around the room. Glance at the bed. He wasn't sure when it had last been made. They'd changed the sheets just the other day, but they never seemed to get as far as pulling the comforter tight and plumping and displaying pillows.

"I just..." Lauren cleared her throat. Looked back at him. "Haven't heard from you guys all week. Wondered what was going on."

Jordy raised his eyebrows.

"Yeah, I'm more than a little embarrassed to be standing here with you, with that bed looking like that." She ducked her face to her hands. "Knowing it's Kaki you're getting crazy with there."

Jordy grinned. Shoved his hands in his pockets and rocked back on his heels.

"So everything's okay?"

"Yep."

"Because I think she was upset with me the other day."

"It's good," he said quietly. Strange. For the first time in his life, he didn't want to rehash the details with Lauren. He didn't want to tell her that he was whipped. That he'd do anything to make Kaki happy. Whether that meant spending hours in bed with her or running the vacuum cleaner or getting groceries for her or sending her flowers. *Anything.* He didn't want to tell his best friend that his other best friend's body fit his like they were made to be together. That he loved the way she kissed him. That he was in love with her.

Not yet.

Not when he still needed to tell Kaks.

"So you guys talked, though? It's not just..." Lauren

waved her hand at the bed and arched her eyebrows in question.

"We talked," he answered quietly. Nodded. Offered her a small smile.

"Oh, thank God." Lauren's shoulders sagged with her sigh of relief. "Thank God. I thought she was mad at me. That you might be mad at me." She moved closer to him and threw her arms around him. "You guys would suck if you ended up killing all three of us in this friendship."

"Thanks for listening." He hugged her back. "But we'll be fine."

"*Be?*" She stepped back to look at him. "You'll *be* fine? You *aren't* fine? Now?"

"We are." He shrugged. "Why? What does that mean?"

Lauren eyed him wearily. "Um. Nothing." Her voice went up an octave. "Nothing. She's not home yet, is she?"

"No."

"Mm-kay. Tell her I was here. I put the crockpot on your counter."

"Lauren, did she tell you something? Something I should know?"

"Nope." Lauren turned and marched to the steps.

"Something about Owen?"

Lauren stopped on the top step and looked at him with a frown. "What about Owen?"

"I don't know. You're the one acting weird."

"I'm not acting weird," Lauren argued. "She was upset with me on Monday, and I haven't talked to her. Just… wanted to check in."

"We've been a little busy…"

Lauren chuckled softly. "I see that. Just…"

"What?"

"Just be careful, Jordy."

"I'm not gonna hurt her, Lauren."

She stared at him for a long, quiet moment. So long, that

Jordy squirmed under her gaze and wondered what the hell she was thinking. What she was hiding. She was damned sure keeping something from him, and it sure as hell had everything to do with Kaki.

"I didn't say you would." She shrugged and took off down the stairs. Jordy considered following her, but he remembered what he'd tucked away in the dresser and hesitated. When he heard Kaki come in the back door, he leaned on the railing of the stairs, tried to listen to what they were saying. Heard them laughing together, which sounded the same as always, and chalked Lauren's strange behavior up to hormones.

While they were still talking, he went back to the dresser and grabbed the envelope from the top drawer. He avoided his face in the mirror, wasn't going to be attractive frozen in fear, and he needed to believe Kaki was attracted to him and not just the sex to have the guts to tell her how he felt about her.

CHAPTER THIRTY-EIGHT

"IF YOU WERE any other woman coming downstairs in my house when I know my husband is up there, I'd be worried," Kaki said with a grin when Lauren appeared in the kitchen.

"Jealous." Lauren winked at her. "You should be jealous, Kaki Steed. I got the best man at home waiting on me."

"I'm gonna have to argue with you on that one."

Lauren grinned. "Suit yourself. Thanks for letting me use the crockpot."

"Sure." Kaki glanced at it. "Did you bring it back full? Something smells delicious."

"Your husband brought you dinner," Lauren told her and nodded her head back at the Ricci's bags on the table.

"Oh." Kaki moaned in anticipation. "Be still my heart."

"No kidding," Lauren agreed. She stepped up closer to Kaki and drilled her index finger into Kaki's chest. "Tell him."

"No."

"What's it gonna hurt?" Lauren whispered.

"Are you kidding me?" Kaki drew back in surprise. "Either he'll laugh in my face. Nobody tames him, Lauren. It's not gonna happen. Or else he'll lie to me and pretend to love me."

"Jordy doesn't lie."

"And if he knows how I feel about him?" Kaki heard Jordy on the steps. "It'll bother him that he doesn't feel that way about me. He'll be afraid to hurt me."

"Kaki—"

"Shh!" Kaki shushed her. Gave her a gentle push toward the back door.

Lauren gave her that look. That silent desperate plea to understand something when she couldn't just say it out loud. She'd lifted her gaze over Kaki's shoulder and flashed a brilliant smile at Jordy. Said goodbye and then hurried out the door.

Kaki took a moment to pull herself together. She wondered for a second what it would be like if this was real. If she and Jordy were the real deal, coming home to each other every night. Hanging out with Lauren and Tyler. With Jordy's brothers and their wives. The thought left a knot in her throat and an ache in her chest, so she swallowed them down and turned to find Jordy pulling their dinners from the Ricci's bags.

She watched him, sadness tugging at her because she was losing him. Every day they lived together was one day closer to the time he would call this whole thing quits. When he looked up and caught her watching him, he offered her a smile.

"Come sit down." He lifted his hand to her. She eyed his shirt, a little bit pleased that he'd rushed upstairs to change for her and a little bit jealous because she would like to change for him, too. Not silk or lace, but something other than the black slacks and simple gray blouse she wore. She went to him, though. Sat down and breathed in the delicious garlic smell of the Italian food he'd brought home for dinner.

"I know we don't do wine much," he said as he folded the bags and laid them on the counter. "But I thought this dinner called for wine. So I asked Jamie for a recommendation."

Kaki raised her eyebrows in appreciation as he produced a bottle of red wine from the white paper Ricci's bag she'd noticed on the counter earlier. Let her eyes move over his hands as he worked the cork out of the bottle. Thought about the way his hands moved on her body and felt a flash of heat in her face.

He took two wine glasses from the cabinet and grinned at her.

"Wedding present." He winked.

"What's the occasion?" she asked as he set the glasses on the table.

He leaned over to kiss her. A sweet, soft kiss on her lips that sort of touched her soul. She felt bruised somewhere, but if pressed, she wouldn't be able to point to the pain.

"Just wanted to do something for you." He sounded sincere. Kaki swallowed hard. Smiled. Wondered if he'd heard from Brianna lately. She'd seen the woman at the mall the other day. Kaki had been looking for a greeting card for Jordy's parents' anniversary. Brianna had strutted her stuff right by her and into Pretty and Passionate, a lingerie store Kaki had only set foot in twice. Hadn't been a point to it when she was dating Owen.

Jordy put the bottle on the counter. She noticed an envelope in this pocket when he turned his back to her. Long white envelope, nothing written on the front. She didn't ask, but she wondered what was up. Maybe he wanted to take her on another honeymoon and there were plane tickets to some exotic location in his pocket. Her blood raced at the thought. She and Jordy on a secluded beach, fruity drinks and coconut oil to slather over his hard, muscular shoulders and arms, his flat stomach. Then again, Kaki didn't need exotic. She only needed Jordy.

Dinner was delicious. Ricci's was the best Italian place in Prior, hands down. She'd gone there once with Owen, but he'd complained about the prices, and he'd been glued to his phone, following some discussion on a science site discussion board, and she'd been bored out of her mind.

"So I was thinking." Jordy shrugged. Kaki felt butterflies in her belly. What was he thinking? Did it have something to do with the envelope she'd seen? The one he hadn't mentioned?

She sipped her wine; Jordy was right. Neither of them knew anything about wine, but this wasn't bad. She almost laughed, though. Thinking about Jamie giving him a wine recommendation. After her conversation with Diana today.

"About what?"

"That one of these nights we should get dressed up and go to Ricci's for dinner."

She propped her chin in her hand and eyed him silently. When he reached for her hand, she let him take it. Nodded.

"Sounds nice."

"And then I was thinking we could go out for a drink. Maybe to that Jazz Moon place you liked."

"You would take me there?"

"I would love to take you there," he told her.

"Would you dance with me?"

"Yes."

"I'd like that, Jordy," she said quietly.

"I'm so torn." He put his fork down and rested his elbows on the table.

"About what?"

"Part of me wants to always just be here with you. Just the two of us."

Again, she bit back a smile.

"And part of me wants to take you out and show you off. Have fun. Make you smile, make you laugh."

She wanted all of the above. And more. Always.

"Me too." She nodded.

"Kaks…"

"So…Diana stopped in today."

"At the museum?"

"Mm-hmm."

"What for?"

Kaki laughed quietly. "Seems she came by Monday night…"

"We were home."

"And we were busy," she reminded him.

"Oh." His eyes grew wide. Kaki thought he blushed. She leaned toward him and reached for his hand. "Wow."

"She saw the stuff on the steps…" Kaki drew his hand to her lips and kissed his knuckles. "Are you blushing? Seriously?"

"The lace."

"Your pants." She shrugged. "And she heard us…"

"That explains it." Jordy ducked his head to his other hand.

"What?"

"Jackson's been blowing me crap all week about you and me."

"Yeah, well, Dianna came by to apologize to me for thinking we weren't seriously into each other. Seems what she overheard convinced her."

"I'm seriously into you," he told her.

"I hate…" She sighed.

"Hate what?"

"That we're gonna hurt people. When we split up. I hate that we're gonna hurt our families."

She did. It was going to crush her parents when she and Jordy divorced. Not as bad as it would crush her, but they liked Jordy, always had, and this would hurt them. They wouldn't understand; they might want to blame Jordy, and Kaki didn't want that. She didn't want her parents, her brother to believe that Jordy had hurt her, because when they divorced and she was hurt, it would be her fault for falling, not his for following their plan.

"Me too."

"And because we just brought that up, I have to ask. Have you talked to Brianna lately?"

He hesitated. Nodded and sort of shrugged. Kaki felt a little stab of sadness. Made it hard to breathe, but she sucked in a quick, sharp breath and hoped Jordy didn't see how much it hurt.

"When?"

"Um." He fidgeted with his glass now rather than look at her. "She called today...when I was in the break room."

"Mmm." She nodded. "What's she doing these days?"

"Same old thing."

"Look, Jordy, I gotta tell you something."

"What?"

Kaki scooted to the edge of her chair. Rubbed her thumb over the back of his hand.

"I like what we're doing right now." She felt the blush tingle in her face. "I like it a lot, and you know that. But if you start sleeping with her again, you have to tell me. Okay? Because I can't—we can't—"

"No, I know." He nodded. "I wouldn't do that, Kaks."

She studied his face a moment longer and finally nodded. She started to stand up, but he squeezed her hand.

"Wait."

"What?" She relaxed back in her seat.

"I...um..." He leaned forward and reached back with his free hand to pull that envelope from his pocket. A little spark of excitement exploded in her belly and warmed her from the inside out. "I wanted to give this to you. And now seems like a good time."

That sounded sort of ominous. Not like she was about to open plane tickets to paradise but a copy of a prenup or something. Even though they'd agreed on all of that stuff, the business stuff, before they got married.

"Jordy?"

"Just…" He shrugged and pushed the envelope at her. She stared at the envelope warily. Lifted her gaze to look at him. When he avoided her eyes, she felt the warmth in her belly go cold with dread.

He let go of her hand so she could take the envelope. She wondered if he noticed her hands shaking when she opened it. She pulled a single sheet of paper from it, folded in thirds. Opened it, scanned it immediately. She caught his name at the top of the paper: Jordan Jonathon Steed—all of his brothers shared the same middle name—and his date of birth.

She swallowed down a surge of nerves and sadness and wine and dinner.

"What is this?" she whispered. Rather than look at him or the damned paper—she knew exactly what it was—she closed her eyes.

"I just wanted you to see for yourself that I'm clean."

Kaki sniffled. She opened her eyes and looked from the paper in her hands to her best friend's face. Lab results. Blood tests.

"Wow." She nodded.

"Kaks. We're sitting here talking about Brianna."

"Have you been screwing her? The whole time we've been married?"

"No!"

She tossed the paper down and pushed her chair back.

"That's great. Thanks."

"Kaki, wait!"

She stopped at the doorway, but she didn't turn to look at him.

"I just—"

"Wanna know what I thought might be in that envelope?"

He climbed to his feet.

"What?"

"Plane tickets," she whispered. "To some exotic paradise. For a real honeymoon." She swiped at the tears on her face. "Well, I mean a real fake honeymoon with real sex."

"Kaki—"

"Stupid, huh?" She laughed at herself. Shrugged. "I wish it had at least just been a love note. Or a *like* note." She swallowed hard, squeezed her eyes closed wishing she could hide from him. "I forgot that this is a business kind of arrangement."

"Can I explain?" He tossed his hands up.

"What?" She propped her shoulder in the doorframe. Folded her arms over her chest.

"I haven't been with anyone but you, since we said I do."

"Did you have your fingers crossed?" she asked. "When you said that?"

"But we haven't used a condom once, and you and I both know…" He sighed and shifted on his feet, clearly uncomfortable with what he was saying. "I've been with a lot of women. I just wanted to show you that I'm careful."

She moved. Stepped forward. Reached to touch him, skimmed her fingers down his arm.

"I trust you, Jordy," she whispered. "I know you wouldn't have put me at risk of anything."

He lunged for her when she moved. Grabbed her arm and yanked her back around to look at him.

"Why are you so mad?"

She shook her head. "I'm not mad."

She started out of the room again but changed her mind. Rather than rush upstairs to hide from him, she pushed by him and grabbed her purse and her keys.

"What're—what're you doing?"

"Going for a ride."

"Kaki, please." He sighed. "Please don't run away from me again. Talk to me."

"I don't wanna talk to you!" she snapped. "I'm embarrassed, okay? I'm humiliated. I forgot. I forgot for a minute that this isn't real. That you don't want me here in this marriage. That I'm here to lure her back. I forgot that."

"Kaks."

"I'm sorry," she whispered. "Sometimes it feels so good to be with you, I forget it's all pretend."

"I didn't mean anything by this." He dropped back to sit down. "I didn't mean to hurt you. I didn't mean to...there's nothing to be embarrassed about. I would love to get on a plane with you right now and go somewhere where we can just be alone together."

Kaki swallowed hard. Now he looked like a sad puppy. What the —? What did he have to be sad about? How could he make her feel guilty? She glanced at her purse. She could drive for a while. She could go see Lauren.

The thought of crying on Lauren's shoulder made her sick. She should have known better. Than to marry him, yes, but to get caught up in the attraction and the pleasure he gave her. She should still be with Owen. She wouldn't be happy, but then Owen had never made her hurt this way, either.

"Please don't go."

She dropped her chin to her chest and tangled her fingers in her hair.

"You make me crazy," she groaned.

"Yep, I'm a dick," he agreed. "For wanting you to know for sure that I don't have any—"

"I told you—"

"Yeah, but Kaks, this is new to us. You and I never talked about this stuff before."

"Do you need proof from me? That *I'm* clean?"

"What?"

"Do you?"

When he looked up at her, she shrugged dramatically.

"No."

"So what's the difference?"

"I'm sorry." He stood. Kaki watched him blow out a deep breath. He avoided her eyes. Slipped out of the room. She waited for him to come back, but she heard the front door open and close and realized she was alone.

CHAPTER THIRTY-NINE

JORDY WALKED out of the house empty-handed. No keys. No billfold. No cell. But he couldn't go back in. Not now. God only knew what Kaki was doing right at this minute, and he was pissed at her, so pissed off at himself, so mad at the whole world right now, he didn't trust himself to speak. No idea what would come out of his mouth right this instant.

He took off at a steady pace. He'd walk. He'd just walk it off. Nevermind that he was wearing jeans, and it was hotter than the Sahara out here. No, not the Sahara. The tropics. Already, he was wet, clothes sticking to him, sweat rolling down his back.

How had that backfired? How the hell had the whole night blown up out of his control? He'd gone over this in his head. The dinner. The wine. The lab results. Okay, sure, not terribly suave, and yet he'd wanted her to know that he'd had recent tests done, and that he'd never have made love to her without protection if he hadn't been a hundred percent sure he was clean. Maybe it wasn't romantic, but it was necessary in his opinion.

He'd intended to get to the romance part of it later. The part that involved a slow dance in the living room.

Undressing her, slowly, appreciating her little bits at a time. Worshipping her and loving her. *Telling* her he loved her. That he was in love with her, and that he wanted nothing more than to stay married to her, to be really, honestly married to her. He wanted forever with her.

And it seemed like Kaki just simply wasn't interested. She was into the sex, and she was adamant that they walk away friends, but *adamant* that they walk away.

Maybe he'd be better off just going with the flow. Banging her when she wanted it, when he wanted it. And trying to get Brianna interested in him so he could save face, end this sham of a marriage, and set his best friend free.

After several blocks and what felt like a bucket of sweat, the anger had burned off and Jordy missed Kaki. He wanted to turn back. Be back home with her. Sipping the wine and playing with the buttons on her blouse. Whispering to her how hot she made him if he wasn't going to get to tell her how much he loved her.

Short of that, he just wanted to talk to *someone*.

Lauren. He wanted to talk to Lauren. Except he wasn't sure that was wise now. Who knew what the hell she and Kaki had said to each other? He didn't think they'd rip on him, talk him down, because they were all too close for that. But what if Kaki was gritting her teeth to get through every day with him, and she was telling Lauren how desperately she wanted to get away from him? How stupid would he look if he told Lauren he'd fallen in love with their best friend?

Especially considering he'd set the whole thing up, planned the whole fake wedding just to make another woman (one neither Lauren nor Kaki even liked) jealous. To make her come back, begging him to take her back. Kaki would probably say she was sorry. That she couldn't love him that way because they were friends. That they'd been friends way too long to think they could throw romantic love into the mix.

Lauren would laugh. Stick those words—*I told ya so*—in him like a knife.

God, he was an idiot. No way out of this. Except to let Kaks go. Ironic that *he'd* fooled around and fallen in love, and he had no rights to that one woman he was crazy about.

He turned around well past Twenty-Fourth and Cleveland. Headed back to the house, though he was in no hurry. First damned thing he'd have to do would be shower now that he was damp and sticky. Damned unlikely that he could sweet-talk her into the shower with him. He wouldn't manhandle her. They'd had some rough sex, and she liked it, but he wouldn't force himself on her. No way in hell he'd hurt her; that had never been his style.

When he crossed Twenty-Second, the house looked the same as it always did. His Jeep was still in the drive, but all that proved was that she hadn't driven anywhere. She could have taken off with Lauren. Or Owen. Or on foot, the same as he had. Maybe in the opposite direction.

Feeling transparent, feeling like a book every neighbor could read as he headed up the walk to the porch, he studied the door. Wondered what she was doing. Sort of hoped she was inside waiting for him to come home. Figured he'd pissed her off for good this time. Maybe he'd find her in the bedroom, packing her things.

He'd feel stupid if he tried the door and found it locked. The neighbors, if they were watching, would know immediately that they'd had a blow up. He sucked in a quick breath and reached out to try the doorknob. It turned easily, and Jordy breathed a quiet sigh of relief when he pushed the door open. No music. No TV. No noise.

Bad sign?

Well, she wasn't throwing things. She wasn't yelling. Then

again, sometimes silence was more terrifying than violent noise. Like right now.

He wasn't sure she was here. Not likely she'd stormed out and left the door unlocked, but possible.

He closed the door and stood for a moment, head bowed. Tried to decide if he should look for her. Or just go about his business. Whatever business he had in this house that didn't involve Kaki. At the moment, he didn't have a clue what that could be.

Still undecided, he wandered down the hall to the kitchen. He found her at the table, their dinner dishes cleared away. The bottle and wine glasses were still in front of her on the table. She wasn't crying, but she wasn't smiling, either.

She noticed him immediately. Sat back in her chair and lifted her legs to curl her toes around the edge of the seat. She'd changed. The stiff work clothes were gone; she wore cutoffs and a soft, clingy tee.

Eyes locked, they stared at each other silently.

"Maybe…" She finally spoke. "Maybe we're better at being married than we thought."

"What does that mean?" His voice was gruff with the emotions he'd swallowed when he was out walking.

She shifted her gaze from him to her glass. Dragged her teeth over her lip and shrugged.

"Married people fight," she whispered.

He watched her lift her glass and take a sip of wine.

"I'm sorry." He leaned into the doorframe. Hung his head. "My timing was bad, but it was important to me that you know I wouldn't put you at risk."

She nodded.

"I know." She shrugged. "It's just that I trust you. I've always trusted you, Jordy."

He stood up straight. Stepped into the kitchen and sat down.

"Okay. I'm a jerk. And I wasted a nice night." He put his

elbows on the table and scrubbed his hands up through his hair. "Let's do something."

He looked up when she laughed softly.

"Not that."

"Not that?" she repeated.

"Let's go to a movie."

"Okay."

Neither of them moved.

"Jordy?"

"What?"

"Promise?"

"Promise what?" He leaned back in the chair.

"You weren't with her?"

"What?"

"I mean, if you guys are together, that's fine. That's what we're doing this whole thing for. But. Just promise me you aren't..."

"Kaks." He pulled his chair closer to hers. "Is that what you're upset about? You really think I'd do that to you? You think I'd cheat on you?"

"She's the reason you married me," she reminded him. "You're supposed to cheat on me with her."

"But..."

"But what?" Kaki lifted her hand to touch his face. Stroked her fingers over his cheek. He wanted to argue. To tell her he didn't want to be with Brianna. That he didn't want to pretend anymore.

He turned his lips to her hand and kissed her fingers.

"I wouldn't string you along," he said quietly. "If Brianna and I get back together, I won't string you along like that."

She nodded, but she wouldn't look at him. Kept her eyes on the table.

"Kaki," he whispered. "Baby, I wouldn't do that to you. I promise."

She shook her head. Flicked her eyes up to meet his and looked away quickly.

"Don't do that."

"Don't do what?" He leaned toward her, covered her hand on his face with one hand and cupped her chin in the other. "Don't do what?"

"Don't," she closed her eyes when he kissed her, "call me baby."

"No?" He threaded his fingers back through her hair.

She shook her head against his face as he kissed her cheek and then nuzzled her neck.

"No. You can't do that, Jordy." Her voice was small and tight.

"I'm sorry." It was easier to say it when he was pressed this close to her. When her skin was soft against his face, and her perfume was heady and rich and dragged him further under her spell.

"It's okay." She nodded.

Jordy squeezed his eyes closed when she turned her head just enough to brush her lips over his cheek.

"We'll be okay," she said again. "We have to be okay."

CHAPTER FORTY

"JUST SAY IT."

Kaki glanced at Lauren, but she kept her mouth shut. Rather than talk, well, rather than spew out everything on her mind as Lauren was urging her to do, she looked around the ball field. Lauren's niece was at first base; the kid was a pretty good ball player. Kaki had played softball in high school, and though she'd given it up in college in favor of concentrating on her grades, she still loved to watch the game.

Not to mention it was something to do that didn't involve Jordy or spending time with Jordy. When Lauren had texted her and asked her to go, she'd jumped at the chance. Things had been quiet at home, a little tense since the thing with Jordy's romantic dinner and the lab results. They'd lingered in the kitchen that night for a long time. Together. Holding onto each other. Kaki wasn't sure what Jordy's deal was, but she'd hung onto him because she was drowning in emotion, and it was easier to cling to him and bury her face in his neck and hide than to run from it and make him angry.

Telling him how she felt sure wasn't an option.

"Where's he at tonight?" Lauren asked her.

Kaki watched the batter take a third strike and stalk to the dugout. She winced when the girl threw her bat, figured her coach would lecture her for that. Bad enough to take a called third strike, but never a good thing to throw the bat.

"With Jackson," she mumbled, still careful not to make eye contact with Lauren. "Jackson and Diana are talking about gutting the second floor of the house. Jordy's over there offering his two cents."

She heard Lauren snort, but she didn't look. Wouldn't take the bait. She couldn't do it. Couldn't tell Lauren. Not anymore. If she were being honest, she'd have to admit that it still stung that Jordy had asked Lauren to homecoming when they were freshmen. Still felt a little funny that Lauren had told Jordy to fuck her. Maybe it was Lauren's suggestion that had put the ball in motion, and Kaki wasn't sure she was okay with that. Maybe if she wasn't in love with him. Maybe if they were still just friends pretending to be married she'd be okay with Lauren giving Jordy that gentle push (hard shove) toward her, to the crazy good sex they'd had.

Since things had changed on her end, Lauren's help felt more like meddling, and Kaki was going to end up alone. Maybe if she could hit the brakes now, on all of it, she could salvage the two relationships most important to her in the world.

Hence Lauren's niece's softball game in the boiling evening humidity, and Jordy hanging out with Jackson. She had to put some distance between them, or she was going to lose her mind. After they'd lingered in the kitchen that night, they'd finally moved. Kaki didn't really remember the actual moving part, but they'd ended up in the living room. Jordy had turned music on, but they hadn't danced. When he'd reached for her, she'd moved without hesitation into his arms. They might have swayed once or twice, but that was it. Desperation held them together. She didn't know what had held them up.

From there, they'd gone up to bed. Still daylight. Pulled

the blinds. Made sweet, tender love. Kaki had caught herself on the brink several times. Those words had been in her mouth, on the tip of her tongue. In her throat. She refused to say them. She refused to tell a guy like Jordy that she was in love with him. Maybe he should know, maybe Lauren was right and he had the right to know how she felt, but Kaki had to protect *her* heart. She'd hoped that maybe kissing him with those words on the tip of her tongue might feel just a little different to him. That maybe he'd feel loved even if she didn't say it.

"Kaki, I hate that you're pushing me away."

Kaki turned her head to look at her friend. Lauren's voice was sad, and when she looked at her friend, she looked down. Kind of the way Jordy had looked the other night. Like Kaki was the bad guy, the one hurting people.

"I'm not..." She shrugged and shook her head. "I'm not trying to push you away."

"I never thought a fake wedding between you two would drag us down, too."

Kaki pursed her lips. She took a deep breath. Looked around again, but this time she wasn't trying to avoid Lauren's gaze. The bleachers were nearly empty, one lone guy sat up to the far left. A few parents sat together in the middle bleacher section, and some were gathered at the outfield fence in lawn chairs, Lauren's sister and her husband included.

"I don't know what to do," Kaki whispered.

She looked up to the field quickly when she heard the loud ring of the bat hitting the ball. Line drive at the pitcher. Caught for a third out. Lauren's niece grinned at them as she and her teammates jogged from the field to their dugout. Only one more inning, and the game would be over. And Kaki would have to go home to Jordy.

"What do you mean?"

Lauren knew what she meant. Kaki put her feet down and

wrapped her hands around the edge of the bleacher they sat on.

"It's gonna kill me when this is over." The words gushed out of her, as she knew they would if given a chance. Fighting to control herself, she tried not to look at her friend. She needed her right now, but it hurt to need her and not know for sure if she was on her side or Jordy's. Not to mention that she hated that there had to be sides. That Lauren had to choose.

Finally, when Lauren hadn't said anything, Kaki looked at her. She was watching her, but she looked away.

"What?" Kaki's voice was gruff.

"I just wish you would tell him."

"Would you?" Kaki asked her quietly. "If you were me?"

"Yes."

"No. If *you were me*." Kaki cocked her head to study Lauren. "Not you. He'd be into you, Lauren. If you were in love with him, you guys could work. You have the same personalities. You—"

Lauren held her hand up to stop her.

"Okay, wait." She took a deep breath. Scooted closer to Kaki on the bleachers. "Maybe not. Maybe I wouldn't tell him. Maybe I'd be scared, too."

"I just don't want him to have to lie to me. It'll break my heart when he leaves me for her or whoever it is, but I would rather that than think he stayed with me out of guilt."

"He's not into me. He is not remotely into me."

"You're sexy—"

Lauren shrugged. "Maybe. So are you."

Kaki rolled her eyes.

"And the fact remains he's not into me. He's attracted to you. He likes spending time with you. You make him laugh. You make him happy."

"Can I tell you something?"

"Please do." Lauren nodded.

Kaki took a deep breath. She shot a look out over the field. Noticed the girls had a runner on second with one out. Wondered what Jordy and Jackson were doing. Felt a pang of sadness when she remembered what Diana had said to her the other day about how wrong she'd been to think Jordy and Kaki weren't seriously in love. Kaki had laughed and gushed about how crazy she was about him, and it had to be believable because it was all so damned true, it hurt her to say it. She wondered now how little they would all think of her once she and Jordy divorced. If his family would automatically assume it was her fault. Or if they'd all assume Jordy had decided to be Jordy and cheat on her. If they'd decide Kaki couldn't keep him interested. That wasn't fair to either of them.

"The night you came by?"

"Yeah."

"He gave me an envelope. I had no idea what it was, but with the wine and the nice dinner, I...stupidly assumed...it was something romantic. Plane tickets." She laughed bitterly. "I thought maybe we were going to redo the honeymoon and do it right this time."

Lauren winced.

"It was Jordy's lab results."

"What?"

"We haven't used protection. The first time it happened, he asked me about it. Told him it was okay. I've been on the pill forever." Kaki shrugged. "I trusted him. I trusted that he wouldn't put me at risk and—"

"Are you telling me—"

"No." Kaki sniffled. "I'm telling you that I was so stupid, that I'm so in love with him, I thought maybe he felt something, too. And he took a romantic night and poured a bucket of cold water over it, and we got in a fight."

"Kaki?"

"Hmm?"

"Jordy doesn't do romance."

"Yeah, I know. But I still felt like a kid. I felt naïve. He had to make a big deal out of proving to me he was careful with all of his other women. And there I was, nowhere in that league, with more fingers on my right hand than past....flings."

Lauren groaned. She leaned into Kaki, but before she could speak, Kaki cut her off.

"It was humiliating. He didn't need proof from me that I'm safe. Because I'm just boring Kaki."

"Kaki."

"What?"

"Stop it. First of all, humiliating? Really? You shouldn't be humiliated because you don't sleep around. Second. He doesn't know how to do it."

"How to do what?" Kaki snapped. She pulled sideways and gave Lauren a sharp look. "He's done it with half—"

"Romance." Lauren shrugged. "This is new to him. From what I see, he loves it. He loves every minute you guys spend together, but it's new. Maybe he thought it was... a romantic gesture."

Kaki swallowed hard when she felt the pressure in her throat.

"He cares about you," Lauren reminded her.

And that was it. In a nutshell. Being with him day after day, night after night, Kaki was hopelessly *in love with him*. And he *cared* about her.

"I know." Kaki ducked her head and nodded. "I know. That's what makes this so hard."

"But you're still..."

"Yeah. Still married. Brianna's been texting him. She hasn't been really aggressive about trying to get him back. But, she showed up at the house one night."

"You guys used to put on a hell of a show," Lauren told

her. Kaki looked at her quickly, but Lauren kept her eyes straight ahead. Her niece was at bat.

"What do you mean?"

"I was watching you at the…open house thing for his parents…last night." Lauren shrugged. "It looks real now."

"It's just because you know how I feel about him."

"Nope." Lauren screwed her face into a look of doubt. "Looked like more than that to me. You wanna get something to eat when the game's over?"

"You can eat in this heat?"

Lauren leaned back and propped her elbows on the bleacher behind her.

"I can pretty much eat anything anytime these days," she said with a grin.

CHAPTER FORTY-ONE

STRETCHED OUT ON THE COUCH, Jordy glanced at his phone and then looked up as Kaki walked through the room. Just after five, she'd just come in from work. Her cheeks were flushed from the heat outside. She smiled when she noticed he was watching her.

"Hey."

"Hey."

She leaned over the end of the couch to drop a kiss on his lips. Moved quickly to get away from him before he could grope her and toss her over the couch to lie with him. It made him hurt inside to know that she knew his moves so well now, and he was going to lose that love, that familiarity with the woman he loved.

"Let's go get pizza," he suggested.

"Okay." She nodded. "Let me change."

"Need help?"

The sound of her giggle faded as she moved out of the room and up the stairs. Things had evened out again after the fiasco with the lab results. Jordy had been afraid it would drive her to leave, the reminder that he was a jerk. That he'd worked his way through half the women in Prior before he'd taken her to bed. Luckily, she'd stayed. Luckily, when that tension had eased, things remained mostly the same.

They still made love, still chased each other around like newlyweds should. But he'd noticed Kaki trying to draw away from him a little. Establish independence. He was all for her hanging out with Lauren or her other friends, as long as she wore her wedding ring and came home to him at night. But he missed her when she wasn't with him.

His parents' anniversary open house had been interesting. Maybe Kaki had just been playing her part, but he'd been all in. Sneaking the French kisses in the pantry. The hallway. Out on the patio. Needing to have his hand on her at all times. On her shoulder. On her knee. When she'd moved, he'd at least needed his eyes on her. She'd mirrored his actions, and by all accounts, it had been a stellar performance. Lauren had told him that night before she and Tyler left that they'd gotten better with their show.

Still.

None of it was enough.

He'd deleted Brianna's number from his phone. She still called. She'd gotten in the habit of sending the dirty pictures at least every other day. Kaki had seen one. She'd only cut her eyes to him as if to say *really?* when she'd seen the picture of a nude Brianna propped on her pillows in invitation. Didn't matter that Kaki hadn't been angry. Jordy had been a little bit mortified that she'd seen it, a little bit embarrassed about his male-slut status, and he'd wished in that moment he could take it all back. Find a different way to fall in love with his best friend, one that wouldn't hurt her.

Kaki wasn't wholesome or innocent; he got that now. But she was a confident, sexy woman. Fun and intelligent, she'd never fall for someone like him.

He continued to ignore Brianna and lie about it to Kaki. Just to keep her around one more day.

"So."

He squirmed to his side and propped himself up on his elbow when she came back downstairs.

"Where are we going for pizza?" she asked him.

"Where do you want to go?"

She sat down with him. "What're you doing?"

"My move." He held his phone in his hand still. "I'm stuck."

"Lemme see."

"We could always do delivery," he suggested. He watched her face, watched her study his phone screen. Watched her dismiss his idea with a small grin and an eye roll.

"You could play the word dandy." She leaned back on the couch, and he snuggled up closer to her so they could look at his phone together.

"Where?"

"Right there." She pointed at the spot with her other hand.

"It's a stupid word," he argued.

"But it's a word." She shrugged. Glanced at him.

"I could play the word sex, too. And the letter x has more points."

"Except that's an A, not an E. You could play sax."

"Damn." He rested his head on her arm. "I'd rather have sex."

She laughed softly. "Mm. You've gotta—"

Kaki stopped talking. Jordy watched in disbelief as a text dropped in at the top of his screen.

"Shit." He reached for the phone, but she moved her hand. Turned to look at him.

"What's—?"

"Kaks."

"Jordy?" She twisted around on the couch, pulled away from him. "Did that say—?"

"Kaks, please, let me have my phone."

He sat up slowly. Looked from her face to his phone in her hand, now in her lap. Of all times for this to happen.

"Why is she texting you?" She stood up and paced away from the couch.

Jordy groaned. Watched her face move through anger and hurt and disbelief. Back to anger.

"Why is Anna Browne texting you?"

"It was—"

She shook her head. Turned her back to him.

"My...I went to college with Anna," she mumbled. "Anna and I were friends. She was at the wedding."

He saw her look down to study his phone in her hand. Saw the moment she decided to look for herself. The way her shoulders tensed.

"Kaks." He stood up. "Don't. Please? Don't."

CHAPTER FORTY-TWO

"KAKI."

His voice sounded closer now. Like he'd moved and he was standing right behind her. Didn't matter. She knew what she was going to find. She'd seen Anna's name. Doubtful that she and Jordy both knew a girl named Anna Browne. Unless, of course it was the same Anna Browne.

She knew without a doubt the Anna Browne who'd texted her husband—she'd sent a picture, and Kaki knew exactly what sort of picture without looking too closely—was the same Anna Browne she'd known in college. The one she'd considered her friend, the one she'd invited to the wedding.

Part of her wondered now if he'd been texting with other women all along. If it wasn't just Brianna—she understood that one, didn't like it, but she got it, by God—and Anna, if maybe he'd realized he couldn't go out now, but he could still screw around with girls like this and she'd be none the wiser.

She pressed the home button on his phone so hard that the tip of her finger was bloodless and white. Didn't matter, though. Not really. Because their vows were all fake. Didn't mean a damned thing if he was out screwing other girls or sexting other girls or jacking off down here on the couch while he watched homemade videos all the girls sent him now that he was *off the market.*

Didn't mean a damned thing.

Except that she'd believed him. When he'd said he wouldn't do that.

Except that she loved him so much, and she wanted him, she wanted everything about him, all to herself.

"Kaki, lemme—"

She tapped the text icon. There was that name. *Anna Browne.* The letters on the screen blurred, but still she tapped Anna's text thread. Looked at the parts of her friend that she'd never seen, never cared to see, would rather not see in a text message to her husband.

"You fucked her."

"Kaki."

She looked at him over her shoulder. Let the tears slide. Didn't matter now. Not anymore. If he didn't love her, he didn't love her. He'd never said he would. Her fault. But he'd promised her he'd never been with any of her friends. And he'd promised to respect her and their friendship. Seemed like that was over now, too. His fault.

She shook her head. Turned to face him.

"It was before—"

She shoved the phone at him.

"I don't care, Jordy," she whispered. "I knew who you were when I married you. I knew this would happen."

"It was before we were married."

"I'm sorry." She took a step backward. "I'm sorry. But..."

She turned, hurried out of the room.

"Kaki. Kaki! Wait!" He raced after her. Snatched at her hand as she started up the steps.

"I'm..." She didn't know what she was or where she was going. But she had to move. "I can't. Can't do this."

"Kaks, I have not been with another woman since we were married. I swear to God, I didn't ask her to text me."

She stared at him silently, finally drew in a shaky breath.

"You did her the night before our wedding."

Jordy hung his head and groaned, mumbled a string of ugly words. "Yes. But that was before—"

"The wedding," she finished for him. "I know. But I asked you once…if you'd ever been with any of my friends. Do you remember that?"

He nodded.

"You lied." She swallowed hard. "You lied to me."

She whirled around and dashed up the steps.

"I didn't think she mattered," he argued. Followed her up. "I didn't think she mattered. Figured we'd never run into her around town, and it was before—"

"I don't care if it was before!" she wailed. "You made a fool of me in front of my friends, Jordy! You think they don't all know now that my husband was screwing around the night before—"

"Kaks!"

Stunned by his shout, she stared at him in silence. Hitched her chin, refused to hide her tears.

"It was before," he repeated yet again. She started to turn away from him. They'd put their luggage in the spare bedroom. She'd pack just enough for now. Come back when he was at work. "It was before…I fell in love with you."

She shook her head. "Don't—-"

"Don't tell me don't." He rushed around the top of the steps. "If we've already blown the fucking friendship out the roof, I'm gonna say what's on my mind, and you're gonna listen."

Kaki hunched her shoulders to ward off the angry words. The end of the friendship.

"I love you."

"It's not enough." She pressed her fingers to her lips and shook her head. "I'm sorry."

"I didn't even know it. Hell, I was in love with you when

your stupid ex-boyfriend put the brakes on the honeymoon activities."

"Jordy."

"I told you I loved you." His voice dropped to a mumble. "I told you I loved you the first night I made love to you. You didn't hear—"

"I heard you. We've said it to each other—"

"You didn't hear me," he repeated. He thumped his chest with his knuckles. "I didn't say it right. I didn't say something deep and perfect, but I said I love you, and I meant it. I love every fucking thing about you, even the way you're so pissed off at me right now you're trembling. I love your laugh. Your smile. I love the way you say my name in your sleep."

Kaki was trembling, but not from anger. Not now. She eyed him suspiciously. She wanted to go to him, throw her arms around him. But the thought of the picture on his phone made her hesitate.

"Did Lauren…" She cleared her throat. Dropped her gaze to the hardwood floor between them. "Did Lauren tell you to say that? To me?"

"What?"

"Did Lauren–"

"I heard you!" he shouted. "Are you kidding me? I've been carrying that around for weeks, desperate to tell you. Scared that you would walk out. That you would laugh in my face. That you would run from me. What the hell do you mean, did Lauren tell me to say that?"

He threw his hands up in frustration. Kaki watched in disbelief as he rushed back down the steps.

"Where are you going?" She meant to yell, but her throat was so tight with emotion, she could barely speak. He disappeared down the hall. "Jordy."

She couldn't see him now. Didn't hear him. She wasn't

sure if he was in the kitchen. Or if he was leaving, if he was heading out the back door.

She closed her eyes. Let the tears slide off her cheeks. Clutched his phone in her hand.

"Jordy," she said softly. "I love you, too."

CHAPTER FORTY-THREE

JORDY WOULD HAVE DESTROYED the phone if he could have, but Kaki was still holding it when he rushed back downstairs and stormed out the back door. Unsure where he was going, he'd marched to the garage, his stomach twisted in knots. He was impotent with rage. He couldn't just pound the hell out of everything anytime he was upset, and even in the thrall of that anger, he knew it wouldn't help a damned thing.

The only thing that would help was Kaki.

Being with Kaki.

Well. Not just being with her, but putting this whole ridiculous charade to bed, and having something real between them. How the hell had he believed he could do this? True, he'd lived over half his life around her and never been struck in the heart or the ass or whatever Cupid usually aimed for. But he'd been stupid to think he could live with her like this and not be so in love with her, it made his whole body ache.

She loved him. Sure, she loved him. Not just any friend would have agreed to his hare-brained scheme. Marrying him just to make his ex jealous. Girls like Brianna were a dime a dozen, and he'd married the gem, and he'd known it. Somewhere amidst the wedding plans and the wedding day, when he'd seen her dad walking down the aisle with her, when they'd exchanged rings and vows, something had changed. No wonder he hadn't been able to troll the beach for a playmate; he'd had the perfect woman all along. Part of him must have known even then that something was different. Something had changed.

For him.

He supposed it was exactly what he deserved, but that didn't make it any easier to swallow. Any minute now, his bride was going to walk out of the house, bags in tow, and throw them in her car. If he was lucky, she might look at him and tell him off, but that was about all he should expect. She'd get in her car, and she'd be gone. Just like that. The best times in his life would be over.

He could be a dick about it. He could move his Jeep up and kiss the bumper of her car with it. Make it impossible for her to get out. But Kaki had a streak of stubborn as wide as a city block, and he wouldn't put it past her to walk. Maybe to Lauren's. Maybe to her parents' house.

The thought made him sick. Please let her go to Lauren. If she went to Lauren, maybe he had a chance of bringing her back. Talking her into staying. Even if they were just roommates. Friends. With or without benefits.

He stood in the open garage door and stared back at the house. He loved it. The brick bungalow was the perfect starter house for a newly married couple. Might be a great bachelor pad, but he wouldn't live here alone. He had no interest in living in a house haunted with Kaki's voice, with her laughter. With the memories of the love they'd made.

No interest in Brianna.

Anna.

No interest in anything but Kaki.

He took a deep breath. Realized suddenly that she hadn't

come outside. She hadn't stormed the garage, intent on the getaway car, and demanded that he move his Jeep so she could leave. In fact, the house pretty much looked the way it looked every night. Still daylight outside, he couldn't even tell if there were lights on inside. He'd banged the back door closed, but it hadn't latched, and he saw now that it had bounced back open. He and Kaki were currently air-conditioning the whole backyard.

Unfortunately, he was still burning up with anger. Wanted to direct it at Anna, but he knew it wasn't her fault he'd found someone to love. Maybe she shouldn't be texting nude pictures to a married man, but then said married man shouldn't have been boning her in the coatroom of the restaurant where they'd had the rehearsal dinner the night before the wedding. Couldn't direct his anger at Brianna, either, because at the moment, she had nothing to do with anything. His desire to get revenge, to make her jealous had led him to concoct this crazy-ass plan to marry Kaki. But that wasn't anything to be angry about. If anything, he should thank her. That was the *only* thing he'd done right in ages. Well, that and finally taking Kaki to bed.

He sighed. Flexed his hands, still wishing he had something to take a swing at. There had been times he and his brothers had blown off some anger and steam with punches thrown. Some connected, some missed. Didn't matter. He didn't have time for that. If Kaki hadn't run yet, if she was taking her time packing her things that meant he had one more shot at winning her over.

His heart hammered in his throat as he shoved his fingers back through his hair. Wet with sweat—because it was hot or because he was so nervous, he thought he could puke—he rubbed them over his shorts, took a deep breath, and headed back over the yard to the back door. He was jittery like he was stepping onto the court for the first game of the season.

He didn't find her in the kitchen, but he breathed a small

sigh of relief when he spotted her purse on the counter. Her keys where she'd tossed them when she'd come in. He'd watched her evening rituals often enough that he knew every move she made when she walked inside the house.

At the hallway, he paused. Stood for a moment and listened. Didn't hear a thing. Not even a clock ticking, because the only damned clocks they owned were digital. He took a few cautious steps and stopped again. Still nothing. At the foot of the stairs, he looked up. Now he could see that their bedroom light was on, but Kaki wasn't in sight.

He hesitated at the bottom of the stairs. Decided he'd leave. If this was it, if she was done with him, he'd go. Let her stay in the house. They'd talked about all of this, of course, since they'd planned the divorce as well as the wedding, and they'd agreed she would stay. Jordy had assumed his dad would buy the house, and Kaki could pay him rent. He didn't want to uproot her. She needed a place to live.

Besides, the house meant nothing to him without her.

He trudged up the steps a few at a time, paused to listen a few times. She wasn't throwing things. No loud crashing and banging noises anywhere in the house. No music. She wasn't yelling and screaming. She hadn't called Lauren.

What the hell had that been about, anyway? Asking him if Lauren had told him to profess his love to her?

The floor at the top of the stairs creaked under his feet. Jordy hesitated again. Waited to see if she threw something, the lamp, for instance, out the doorway hoping to tag him. When there was nothing, he moved slowly to the bedroom doorway. Found her in a heap in front of the open closet door.

Arms wrapped around her knees drawn to her chest, she heard him and lifted her head to look at him. Her tears had wrecked her makeup, and her hair was tousled and messy, like she'd shoved it back from her face impatiently time and time again. Jordy thought she'd never been so beautiful.

"Hey." He cleared his throat.

He saw her swallow, saw that she was struggling to control herself. Their eyes held for a long moment, but she turned her face away without responding.

The open suitcases around her feet scared him. The piles of clothing on the floor, the blouses draped over them made his stomach ache.

"I'm sorry." He approached her timidly, afraid to spook her and make her run. She wouldn't look at him, but she didn't scramble backwards to get away from him or ask him to leave. Emboldened by a tiny jolt of hope—maybe they could at least salvage their friendship—he lowered himself to sit by her. Uncomfortable, he shifted and reached to pull a pair of strappy black sandals out from under his butt.

She breathed, then. A loud, wet breath, and he knew she was still crying. But she shook her head as if to dismiss him. Swiped at her eyes.

"About Anna."

"You lied to me." She tucked her hair behind her ear. Refused to meet his eyes. "I don't want to look like a fool."

"I'm sorry that I was with her," he interrupted her. "I shouldn't have lied, but I'm sorry that I was with her."

She gave him a quick glance, looked at her suitcase, and shrugged her eyebrows.

"You are who you are."

"I had no idea I was marrying the woman of my dreams, and it was stupid, and I'm sorry. I'm sorry I hurt you."

"Don't, okay?" She finally looked at him. Head on. Full eye contact. "Don't do that."

"Don't do what?"

"Don't joke about this. You're only going to make it worse."

"I'm not joking," he said simply. "I get it." He made a point of looking at her suitcases, the clothing she'd undoubtedly yanked from hangers and tossed to the floor in a fit of rage. He wondered if doing so had made her feel any better than his march to the garage had done for him. "You're leaving. You're done. You've had enough of me."

She swallowed hard and rubbed her hand over her lips.

"You have to let me go, because it hurts to be so angry with you. I don't want to lose you, Jordy. I don't want to end up hating each other."

"Hating each other?"

Her words were a blow to his gut, and he gasped to breathe.

"We should've known this wasn't going to work. I hope you get her back—"

"I don't want her back," he said quietly.

"What?"

He watched her reach for a pair of jeans, one leg tossed over the edge of the suitcase closest to her and the other wrinkled under a red Converse tennis shoe.

"I don't want anyone," he waited for her to look up before he continued, "but you."

"Jordy." She squeezed her eyes closed. Dropped her face to her hands and sobbed out loud. "You can't do this to me–"

"I mean it, Kaks." He scooted closer to her. Draped his arm over her shoulders and kissed her hair. "I'll let you go, but you're gonna rip my heart out when you do."

She didn't answer him, but he felt her shoulders tense under his arm.

"I love you." He kissed her again.

She turned her face toward him, but the silence between them was heavy and intense. He blinked when his own eyes burned. Kissed the top of her head again and reached for a pile of clothes. Would she want his help? Or would it be easier if he just left her alone?

She sat motionless, watched him refold a couple of t-shirts. He'd had to learn to do it the right way at the store, lest his dad ride his ass about it all the time. Sloppy merchandise did not appeal to customers.

Kaki's merchandise appealed to him. He pushed the pile of t-shirts away. And reached for a crème-colored silk nightie. He was drawn to her, heart and soul and body, in a way he'd never been attracted to any other woman. It killed him to touch her belongings, the intimate things like the nightie, and know that someone else would be pawing at her one day.

He groaned out loud, squeezed his hand into a fist around the silk. His eyes burned again, so he ducked his head to hide. It was enough that he'd bared his soul to her, that he'd told her he loved her. He wouldn't make her feel guilty, wouldn't embarrass himself and let her see him cry over losing her.

She reached for him slowly. Closed her hand over his.

"That's...it," she whispered.

He nodded. Cleared his throat a few times and huffed out a harsh breath.

"Okay." He sighed. Turned his hand over to hold hers for a second and then started to stand.

"That's what the girls gave me for my bachelorette," she told him. She looked up at him then, and her eyes were wide with fear.

He swallowed hard. Nodded.

"I wish you would have worn it for me." His voice was gruff. "Just once."

"Jordy."

He started to climb to his feet again, but she scooted closer to him. Shook her head.

"You should stay," he told her. "I'll go."

"Jordy, I love you, too," she whispered. "I don't wanna end this."

Mouth hanging open in shock, he stared at her silently. She drew his hand to her mouth and kissed his knuckles.

"You don't?" He managed to squeeze the words out, but they were small, hard with pent up emotion.

"No." She shook her head. Pressed their hands to her face and met his eyes. "No. I just want it to be real."

"You want what to be real?"

His chest hurt again his heart pounded so hard. He wanted to think she meant she wanted *them* to be real, but he was afraid to believe it was possible.

"You and me." She kissed his hand again. "This marriage. I love you. I need this to be real."

"Me too." He nodded.

She laughed and sobbed and used their hands to swipe at her eyes.

"You wanna stay my wife? You want to be married to me?" He arched his eyebrows.

"Yes."

He tugged her closer, drew her into his lap. She curled into him as he wound his arms around her. Dropped a kiss on her upturned face.

"Forever? Just you and me?"

"You and me," she agreed. "Forever."

He smelled her perfume again and felt his blood go hot and thick. She watched him as he lowered his face to hers. Settled his lips against hers and kissed her. She slid her hand up over his shoulder and into his hair as he stroked her lips apart with his tongue.

"Did we just get married again?"

Her lips curved under his.

"Because I want you to take your clothes off and put that little silk thing on and slide all over me."

He drew back from her. Kissed her again when she tugged his face back to hers. She moved to straddle him. Broke the kiss so she could yank her t-shirt off over her head.

"So when we celebrate our anniversary will it be the day of the shenanigans or the day we fell in love?"

She leaned into him, arched her back when he reached behind her to unhook her bra.

"I told you I might have loved you the day of the shenani-gans," he reminded her.

"Just as long as we get a do over for the honeymoon." She planted her hands on his shoulders and gently pushed him back to the floor.

"I think that can be arranged, Kaki Steed."

"That's Mrs. Steed to you," she whispered as she flicked the tip of her tongue over the center of his lip.

PLAYLIST

Wedding Day Shenanigans
   Playlist
   She Likes Rock 'N Roll ~ AC/DC
   Little Bitty ~ Alan Jackson
   Cheat On You ~ Big & Rich
   I Can't Live Without You ~ Bad Company
   Only The Good Die Young ~ Billy Joel
   The Stroke ~ Billy Squier
   Sangria ~ Blake Shelton
   Love her Like She's Leavin' ~ Brad Paisley Feat. Don Henley
   Lover Come Back ~ City and Colour
   Once You've Loved Somebody ~ Dixie Chicks
   Baby Hold On ~ Eddie Money
   The Red Strokes ~ Garth Brooks
   Parachute Heart ~ Grace Potter & The Nocturnals
   Let It Go ~ James Bay
   Heaven In Your Eyes ~ Loverboy
   Girlfriend ~ Pat Monahan
   I'll Give You Something To Miss ~ Reba McEntire
   Rude Boy ~ Rihanna

EVERY LITTLE THING

Turn the page to read Chapter 1 of Every Little Thing, Lorelei Bluffs, Book 1

EVERY LITTLE THING, CHAPTER 1

CODY DRAGGED his hands down over his face and swallowed hard. Jorie watched his struggle to not look at her or Russ. He kept his bloodshot eyes trained to the left, but the pinched expression on his face gave him away. No daydreaming. No pretending. He was owning up or trying to, anyway, and for just a second Jorie almost felt sorry for him.

Until she remembered.

What he'd just said.

"You wanna say that again?" Russ asked quietly.

"She's pregnant," Cody repeated.

"Amy's pregnant?" Jorie whispered. She'd caught *that* word the first time around. *Pregnant*.

"Not Amy," Cody answered.

Jorie flinched. She closed her eyes, maybe thinking that Cody and Russ would both be gone when she opened them. It was barely three-thirty; she'd barely been home five minutes when Russ had knocked at the door and then Cody had bounded down the steps and said he was glad Russ was there because he had to talk to them and now *this*. Now someone was pregnant, only it wasn't Amy, and Cody had just turned eighteen—

"You cheated on Amy?" Jorie asked the first question that popped into her mind, though she had more questions and maybe more *pertinent* questions, the first of which might have been *why weren't you careful?* And maybe a follow-up might have been *what the hell do you mean she's pregnant* and *what were you thinking* and *what the hell are you going to do now?*

"I didn't cheat." Cody's voice was all sharp edges. Jorie opened her eyes to find Cody pacing the floor by the bay window. She saw him take a quick glance at his father. When Cody looked back at the window—there was fresh snow on the ground and still ice in the trees and Jorie thought again that she hated winter—she glanced at Russ.

"Oh, I know," he said with a nod. "I know. Cheating means I taught him that. Got it, Jorie. Loud and clear."

"Russ—"

"Look." Cody cleared his throat and drew their attention back to him. "This isn't about you. It's about me and that I got someone pregnant, and I don't think it's—she isn't going to —" He took a deep breath and shook his head. "She doesn't want to keep it, and so it's not like I'm gonna hand you a kid and ask you to raise it. It's just...it's just been bugging me."

Cody raised his eyebrows and shrugged. "It's been on my mind, and I thought you should know."

"It's been—but—" Jorie rubbed her forehead with her fingertips. She still had her heels on. Granted, they weren't the same kind of sexy, fuck-me heels she'd worn when she was younger, but they were heels and her feet hurt and her back hurt, and she could still hear phones ringing and her head hurt. "Cody..."

"Mom, can I go to the lake? Hockey game."

Jorie glanced up when Ethan flashed through the room, grabbed an apple, and disappeared to the front hall.

"No," she answered too slowly. "No, Ethan, you can not go to the lake. You're grounded, and you know it."

"I finished my homework in study hall," Ethan called.

Jorie glanced at Russ again. He wore that infuriatingly calm mask that had driven Jorie crazy when they'd been married. He was pissed but trying to hold it back.

A baby. Cody had gotten someone other than Amy pregnant. But don't worry, because she—whoever she was—*didn't want to keep it, so hey, no baby. Not like anything would really change.*

"Ethan Michael, I said no!" she yelled as the front door slammed.

He didn't listen. Ethan never listened. Ethan did whatever the hell pleased Ethan. Always had.

But not Cody. Cody was her good kid. *Well*. Bryce wasn't a bad kid, but he was a handful.

But *Cody*? *Cody* was going to give her something to worry about?

Okay, so really she worried about all four of her boys pretty much all the time. Probably just one of the things that had driven Russ away. But she'd never really had *cause* to worry about Cody.

"Cody, you can't just—" Jorie shook her head. She looked over her shoulder, as if she could see through the kitchen wall and the front door and watch Ethan rush across the yard to meet up with his friends. "You can't just say that...and then think it's all okay...and I mean...who—"

"Your mother's right, Cody." Russ sighed. "This isn't like flunking a test or something. This is a big deal. This is a problem."

Jorie nodded in agreement. "It is. It's a problem, and we need to talk about it. We need to know what's...who...we need to talk about it."

"I'm just telling you she's made up her mind, and um." Cody had stopped pacing. He stood with his back to them, his forehead resting on the window. Jorie thought about washing that same window just a couple of weeks ago.

The front door opened. Jorie turned around, surprised that Ethan would come back. Not like it was because of anything she said. Apparently wires had been crossed, and there was no hockey game, so he was back home to play the PS4 or something.

"Hey."

Jorie glanced at Russ with only her eyes. Valerie Fannon studied Jorie's face and then looked over her shoulder to Cody and finally she turned to look at Russ.

"It's not a good time," Jorie whispered.

"Mm-hmm." Val nodded. She set a quilted paisley print bag on the counter and offered Jorie a small smile. "I know."

Jorie felt Russ' eyes on her as she watched Val disappear the same way she'd just come in. From the corner of her eye, she saw Russ reach out and open the bag.

"Val still cooks for you?" he mumbled.

Jorie pressed her lips together and folded her arms over her chest. "I think you need to go."

"I think we need to talk." He dropped stubbornly onto a barstool and pulled the familiar old Tupperware container from Val's bag. "And I think you can share the wealth."

"So you can make snide comments about Val bringing food over here, but you're not above eating that food."

"I'm just saying we need to talk, and there's...what is this?" Russ peeled the corner of the lid back and nodded his approval. "There's homemade ham and bean soup here, and so, while we talk, I'll eat some of this."

"Yeah," Jorie examined her thumbnail and picked at a hangnail, "well, I don't think Val brought it over here with you in mind. So, no."

"No?" Russ frowned at Jorie. "No? Seriously, Jorie? Jesus, it's a bowl of soup."

"It's a lot more than a bowl of soup, Russ, and you know it. Just go."

Jorie watched him climb to his feet, circle the island and open the utensil drawer. She noticed Cody slumped on the couch again.

"Please? Russ? Just go."

"Our son just announced that his girlfriend is pregnant, and we need—"

"She's not my girlfriend," Cody mumbled.

"Maybe this is your area of expertise. Maybe you should handle it."

Russ paused in the act of getting a bowl from the cabinet above the sink. He shook his head and smiled. "Point, Jorie," he said quietly. "This bowl has a crack in it. You and Finneas should have registered for new bowls when you got married."

"Russ, you're being a dick."

"How am I being a dick?" Russ asked with an innocent shrug of his shoulders. "You should have asked for new stuff. I mean, who wants reminders of me and our marriage left around here, huh? Seriously? You have a new life."

"Please, just go."

"Finn's at work, right? Works at that website design place, right? And we've got a pretty big damned problem, not to mention what I came over here for in the first place, and good ole Val brought soup, and so let's talk. I mean, why not?"

"What you came over here for—What? Why are you here?" Jorie sighed. The waistline of her slacks was cutting into her gut, and her feet hurt. And she was going to have a grandbaby and apparently never see it.

Was that a good thing? Or was it bad?

Hell if she knew, because maybe Cody was going to roll right down her and Russ' past and was that a good past? Or bad? Hell if she knew. Life with Russ and life post Russ was something different every day, and she didn't know up from down. What she did know was she was tired.

"Please? Russ, please go? I'm tired. You followed me in from work. Cody's...and I...Ethan—"

"Go." Russ put his bowl in the microwave and turned and waved her away, spoon in hand. "Go. Go get comfortable.

Kiss your baby, and check on Bryce and then come back down. I'll warm your soup."

"I don't want you to warm my soup," she answered. "It's not even four o'clock. And I don't want to eat dinner with you. And I can't just check on Bryce. It's time for homework. I have to sit down with him, and we have to do his homework."

"'Kay." Russ shrugged and yanked the door of the microwave open. "Shit. Where's your 409? Got soup on the tray."

Jorie sighed and tucked her hair behind her ears. "Seriously, Russ? You know where the 409 is."

"I do," he agreed. "I'll get it. Go change."

"Where are you going?" Jorie asked as Cody walked through the kitchen on the way to the front door.

"Supposed to meet Amy."

"I...but. Cody, you can't—"

"I didn't cheat on her, Mom," Cody said softly, again with a glance at Russ.

"I don't really think we need to discuss—"

"We broke up," Cody told them. "A month ago."

"You broke up with Amy? A month ago? Honey, what happened? Why didn't you tell me?"

"Because I didn't want you to freak out." Cody shook his head. He yanked his denim jacket off the back of the end barstool and pulled it on. "Like you're doing right now."

"Yeah, well, I'm freaking out now because I didn't know Amy was gone, and you have a baby on the way, and I'm never gonna know that baby. It's cold out, Cody. Wear your winter coat."

"Don't have one."

"What? Yes, you do! You have that Under Armor thing...that navy thing. It's warmer."

"It's also four years old and doesn't fit," Cody answered. She heard him open the front door.

"What? No, it isn't. Put it on." The door shut. Jorie ran her fingers through her hair. "I just...I really just want you to leave." She didn't look at Russ.

"I'm ready to do my homework, Mom." "Okay," she agreed and turned to Bryce.

"Let Mom change her clothes first, Bry," Russ said as Bryce sat down at the table in the corner of the kitchen.

"No." Bryce unzipped his backpack and started to remove his books and folders. "It's three fifty. That means it's time to do my homework. I have a math worksheet and social studies questions."

"Okay," Jorie said quietly. "Okay."

"Bryce."

"Russ." Jorie turned to him.

She saw the life of their marriage flash over Russ' face, the way his playfulness vanished and the way the frustration dragged his lips down into that permanent look of discontent. Something she was all too familiar with.

"I'll go." He nodded. "I'm going. I do need to talk to you."

Jorie licked her lips. "Why? What's going on?"

"Some of your medical paperwork turned up with my insurance company. I just wanted to tell you—"

"What? How is that possible?"

"Are you kidding me? It's a black hole bureaucracy. How doesn't it happen more often?"

"But it's been almost two years." She licked her thumb and scrubbed at an invisible spot on the counter. Truth be told, she wasn't comfortable with any of her medical information anywhere near Russ' hands.

"Yeah, well, they probably—"

"Mom."

"What are we gonna do about Cody?" Jorie blinked as tears burned her eyes. "I mean, this is huge. Even if...I mean...if she doesn't...if they aren't...but...It's huge, Russ."

"I wish—"

"No." She shook her head and stepped away from him. "You don't get to wish anything. No."

"Mom, it's time to do my homework."

"Look, I have to go. We'll talk some other time."

Russ nodded. She looked away as his eyes searched her face. She wondered if he was thinking about the baby. If he was thinking about Cody's baby. Or Cody *as a baby*. As their first baby.

"Of course you do." His words bit into her, but it was the tone that burned like venom in her blood. She glanced at him in time to see the discontent tugging at his mouth again.

"Don't be an ass, Russ. He's your son, too."

Russ shook his head as he walked away from her. "Haven't we done this at least a million times? Don't you get tired of it? I get tired of it. I get—"

"Yeah, I know." Jorie followed him to the door. "I know what you get."

"Say hi to Finneas for me."

"Goddammit, Russ, his name is Finn, and you're being an ass. Just get out."

"Mom!" Bryce yelled. "It's three fifty. It's time for my homework."

Jorie saw Russ's gaze flick over her shoulder before it landed on her again. She watched his lips, because she knew he wanted to say something. Something that would cut her again.

Instead he turned and carefully followed the sidewalk that Finn had shoveled last night to his car.

"Mom!"

"Bryce, not so loud!" She answered as she stepped back inside and closed the door. "You'll wake Noah."

"He is awake," Bryce snapped. "How can you help me with my homework if you have to deal with him?"

A grandbaby. She could have a grandbaby. A grandbaby that wouldn't be much younger than her youngest son.

She pressed her hand against her heart, wishing to ease the hurt there. She was balanced on the flat of a double-edged blade. Cody couldn't just watch some girl give up his child, could he?

But he couldn't raise a baby. Could he? Would she even want that? For Cody to give up his life for a baby?

The thought brought a jolt of guilt. She kicked her shoes off as she hurried to the living room to tend to Noah before the noise set Bryce off.

"Mom."

"Right here, buddy." She pulled out the chair across the table from Bryce and sat down, Noah in her arms. At least he'd stopped fussing when she'd picked him up.

"He has snot on his face," Bryce told her.

She glanced at Noah and saw that he did indeed have a candlestick over his now grinning, toothless mouth.

"Let's do your math, Bryce."

"Why was he here?"

"Huh?"

Bryce concentrated on writing his name on the top of his math paper.

"Why was Dad here?" Jorie raised her eyebrows, surprised by the question. Bryce rarely acknowledged Russ's presence.

"We...um—" Jorie reached for Bryce's paper and looked at his first multiplication problem. "We just had to talk about something."

"You never talk."

"What?"

Bryce glanced up from the paper and met her eyes for a moment. A ripple of shock slid down her spine. First bringing up Russ being here and now making eye contact. She knew better than to get excited, but this tiny change in Bryce's behavior was the highlight of her day.

"You don't talk," Bryce repeated as he looked back down at his paper. "You fight."

"Yeah." Jorie blinked as tears filled her eyes again. "Yeah, we do."

"I thought you were divorced, anyway. Isn't that what you said? You guys got a divorce so you wouldn't have to fight anymore."

Jorie didn't answer right away, and Bryce shot her an impatient look.

"Yeah, we did, Bryce," she mumbled.

"Then he shouldn't ever be here again. Why does he come over here? You have a new husband, and he shouldn't ever be here anymore."

"Bryce, he's your dad. He comes here for you. And Ethan and Cody."

"Whatever. Is this right?"

Jorie pulled the paper toward her with trembling fingers. She tried to read the numbers Bryce had written, but her eyes had filled again.

"Yeah. It's right, Bryce," she said softly. "You're right."

HOLIDAY FLING

Turn the page to read chapter 1
of Holiday Fling

HOLIDAY FLING, CHAPTER 1

MONICA MCHENRY WATCHED yet another Rudolph fly by in the oncoming lane of traffic. From the corner of her eye, she watched her friend Tipper to see if she'd noticed. Then again, Monica wasn't sure she wanted Tipper to notice. Her friend was a Christmas nut; in fact, it wouldn't have surprised Monica to find a red nose and antlers on Tipper's white Passport when she'd come by to pick her up this morning.

The dull ache in her lower back finally too much to bear, Monica put her hand on the seat to scoot around just enough to ease the pain. She squeezed her eyes closed at the quick stab of pain in her wrist. Held her breath and counted to three before shifting slightly to take her weight on her right side.

"You okay?"

Of course Tipper had noticed. She noticed everything.

"Mm-hmm." Monica turned away from Tipper to look out her window. Easier than looking at her friend, although the sunshine on the snow turned up the dull ache behind her eyes. Despite the snow on the ground, the highway itself was bone dry. Still, Monica had to fight to keep from sneaking a peek at the speedometer. Kind of felt like Tipper was driving eighty.

She wasn't. She might push the needle up to seventy in a sixty-five mile per hour zone, but who didn't?

Monica heard the Christmas music playing, but she was doing her best to ignore it. Concentrating so hard on not hearing it (wasn't blaring, but it was most definitely audible) had probably added to her headache. She'd have been fine listening to the hum of the tires on the pavement, but Tipper was a fidgety driver, and music seemed to calm her. Monica had considered asking her to play something other than Christmas music, but she'd simply closed her mouth and gritted her teeth. Taking away Tipper's Christmas music was like taking candy from a little kid.

When her vision started to tunnel a bit, Monica drew in a deep, cleansing breath through her nose and exhaled slowly. She'd already stripped down from her sweatshirt to a t-shirt, and now she was sweaty again.

"Monnie?"

"I'm fine." Unfortunately, her voice cracked as she spoke. She glanced at Tipper, grateful for her sunglasses. Then again, it didn't matter. Tipper McAllister knew her so well; Monica couldn't hide anything from her. "Just warm."

She lifted her hands and pulled the elastic from her right wrist.

"You're gonna catch a cold," Tipper scolded her as she pulled her long, dark hair up in a ponytail.

"You don't catch colds from being cold," Monica mumbled as she fanned the back of her neck.

"Well, it's twenty-six degrees out, and you're sitting here in short sleeves—"

"In your car. Tip, I'm sweating."

Monica sighed when she felt Tipper ease off the gas.

"Are you okay?" Tipper reached over the console and brushed her fingers over the back of Monica's left wrist. Monica stared at her friend's hand; the perfect manicure made her eyes burn with tears. "Need me to pull over?"

Monica considered it. It might do her some good to get out and stretch her legs. But her throat and stomach felt a little thick and unsettled, and odds were, if she got out to stretch her legs, she would probably vomit, too. And then she'd have to listen to Tipper lecture her about taking care of herself for the rest of the drive.

"I'm fine," she repeated.

"I can stop up here. In Marshall. Get a bottle of water—"

"I'm fine."

Monica squeezed her hands into fists. Tipper pulled her hand away from her and set it back on the steering wheel. Chris Isaak was still singing "Pretty Paper" but somehow, Monica's heavy tone had sucked the air out of the SUV. She swallowed a mouthful of guilt. Tipper was tough, but Monica had chased everyone else in her life away. She licked her lips and struggled to find the words to apologize. She'd tried before, but Tipper had always read her mind and brushed her off. Told her there was no need to apologize. Still, Monica feared the day she pushed too hard, and Tipper walked away for good.

She rolled her head on her neck and huffed out a sigh. Leaned against the headrest and found herself staring at Tipper's left hand, also curled around the steering wheel. At her ridiculously simple, gorgeous wedding ring. The whole wedding had been simple and gorgeous. Kind of summed Tipper and Alec up, though. Ridiculously simple and gorgeous and happy.

"Have you heard from him?"

Monica blinked, surprised by the question. She watched Tipper's knuckles go white, realized her friend was nervous to ask about Billy.

"No."

She moved only her eyes to see Tipper flinch.

"So." Tipper cleared her throat. "The cabin. It's pretty

modern. I mean, you'll have electric heat and the gas fire-place. And you'll have electricity and modern appliances—"

"I'll be fine," Monica promised her.

"And you'll have neighbors. Not like, people in your backyard, but the nearest houses aren't that far away. All within walking distance."

Monica closed her eyes and turned her head away from Tipper. She nodded.

"I'll be fine."

"I could stay—"

"Alec would kill me if I asked you to stay with me!" Monica tried for a laugh, but the joke fell flat.

"Why?" Tipper cleared her throat. "Why do you have to do this again?"

They'd been through this at least a hundred times. Monica was tired of the argument. That familiar pain was back, nagging in her right side this time. She squeezed her eyes closed before she could think, before she remembered too much. Put her hands down on her seat and lifted her butt to twist around to something more comfortable. The pain in her wrist this time was dull. She rubbed the fingers of her right hand down over her left wrist and the palm of her hand. Linked her fingers together and dropped her hands to her lap when she felt Tipper watching her.

"I just need some space, Tip," she whispered.